STARTING OVER

FAR AWAY

By Linda B. Myers

"**We came to Alaska** to escape our pasts. All Outsiders did. Leona was no different. She arrived broken in 1921, but the stark magic of the glacial mountains and fjords, the native people and wildlife, the autonomy of living there soothed her. It soothed, but did it cure? The past stalked the person Leona became. I have my opinion on whether Alaska saved her. You may well have a different one."

- Ivy Bolton

ABOUT THIS BOOK

Starting Over Far Away is a work of historical fiction, set among actual locations and events in the early twentieth century. Characters, names, and happenings are from the author's imagination. Any resemblance to actual persons, living or dead, is entirely coincidental.

ISBN: 978-1-7352477-1-7
Library of Congress Control Number: 2022910991
MyComm Enterprises
Distributed by OlyPen Books, PO BOX 312,
Carlsborg, WA 98324
Cover design by Roslyn McFarland, Far Lands Publishing
Interior design by Heidi Hansen

For updates and chatter,
Visit with the author at myerslindab@gmail.com or Facebook.com/authorlindabmyers

DEDICATION

To my sister, Donna,
and my critique group, Heidi, Melee, Jill, and Jon
who all kept me on this journey to Alaska
when the days seemed darkest.

Table of Contents

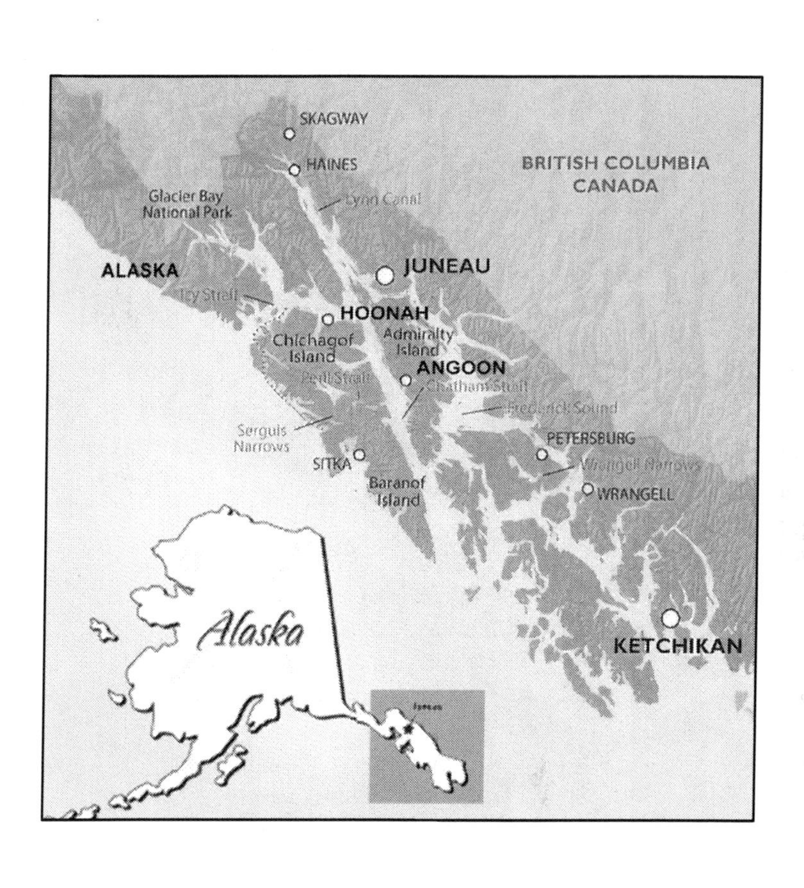

SKAGWAY
HAINES
BRITISH COLUMBIA
CANADA
Glacier Bay
National Park
Lynn Canal
ALASKA
JUNEAU
HOONAH
Chichagof
Island
Admiralty
Island
ANGOON
Chatham Strait
Serguis
Narrows
PETERSBURG
SITKA
Baranof
Island
WRANGELL
Alaska
KETCHIKAN

CHAPTER ONE

August 2, 1946
Rome Coleridge

Rome felt the porch steps sag under his weight as he reached for the handrail with an arm that wasn't there. He couldn't get used to it, this empty sleeve on his left. Tucked into the crook of his right elbow, he carried *The Heart is a Lonely Hunter* and *A Tree Grows in Brooklyn.*

"You're new."

Rome heard the voice as his eyes adjusted from full sun to shade. Its source was a woman whose age no longer numbered in years but in decades. Her porch swing was of a similar vintage.

"I'm new, Ma'am, but the route's the same. Most of the Olympic Peninsula, Port Townsend to Forks." Rome raised his voice the appropriate decibels for aging ears. "Here are your books, all signed out and ready to read. Good ones."

"Thank you. I need something to stir up the gray matter. Come sit with me a while. This wicker chair here. It's butt-sprung but comfy. Supported a lot of behinds in its day. And there's no need to yell at me."

Rome lowered his volume. "Just thought I should speak up, Ma'am."

"My knees and teeth aren't worth a crap, so I don't chase or bite anymore. But my ears are fine. Have some of this lemonade." She pointed her chin at the end table where an iced pitcher sweated on an ormolu tray.

"I'd like to, Ma'am, I surely would. But I need to get the bookmobile open for patrons." He'd parked the 1937 DeSoto panel van on the grassy verge of the street. "I have other stops to make as well."

"Fiddlesticks. Henny Lightmen – she had the route before you – used to sit here while folks chose their books. They know the drill. They'll come right up to sign them out. Besides, nobody on the Peninsula reads more books than me, making me your Number One Patron. And you don't want to rub your Number One Patron wrong on your first day. Simple business sense. Take a load off while word spreads you're here."

Rome knew when a battle was lost. He sank into the concave seat of the wicker chair, setting the novels on the end table next to the tray. "Well. Lemonade does sound good."

"Fine. Then pour away."

He'd hoped she'd do the honors because he feared he'd spill the pulpy liquid, since he could no longer hold both a pitcher and a glass. He wondered if she always sat here with an extra glass, hoping to attract a passerby like a hummer to a feeder.

Meanwhile, she rattled on, seeming to ignore his plight. "A person needs to talk as well as read, you know. Consider it part of your community service. Did you know where short arms could reach. Today he had *The Little Prince*, *Johnny Tremain*, and a handful of the *Bobbsey Twins*.

Rome greeted his patrons, took back books, and signed out new, including two Tom Mix comics for Ed Duncan who tried to hide them from sight, rolling them up inside his newspaper. But Ivy Bolton must have seen it all from the porch. Rome pictured an eagle in her aerie, awaiting rabbits in a field.

"Morning, Ed," she bellowed. "Looks like you got some colorful reading there. I don't much care for comic books myself."

The old man stomped down the street, waving an arm as if her words were hornets.

A smile crept across Rome's face. Ivy had that effect on him.

"Morning, Rome," she yelled again. "Hold down a chair with me."

"I should finish here, Mrs. Bolton."

"Poppycock. Folks around here won't thieve from a bookmobile. They love to come up here to sign books out. Gives them a chance to howdy with me."

"Mrs. Bolton, I really…"

"I've made a nice blackberry buckle. Still warm. Heavy cream to cool it."

"I'll be right there. I have your glass to return." Rome pocketed a pencil and his book stamp, then climbed her steps. He could watch for customers from up there. "Are you trying to get to my heart through my stomach?" he asked as he set the glass on her end table.

"Yes."

Her unadorned reply caused him to snort. "Nobody's sweet-talked me since before the war, Mrs. Bolton."

"The name's not Mrs. Bolton. It's Ivy. I thought I told you that. And I'm not making goo-goo eyes, Rome Coleridge. But you will benefit from my conversation. Who wouldn't?"

The warm buckle, fresh stewed berries with a crisp streusel top, was home cooking unlike any Rome ever experienced. His mother had been nobody's idea of a good cook, although not even his miserable father had said such a thing out loud. And the army, well, there was a reason their hash was known as dog food. Rome thought he might tear up as the buckle's tart sweetness burst in his mouth.

Ivy launched into gossip he hadn't known. "The library board was pleased when Henny Lightmen finally married Rusty Murdoch, an Alfalfa-looking pipsqueak who pursued her all through high school. She wanted nothing to do with him back then. But now, the war has culled the herd of available beaus. Anyhow, she gave up the bookmobile job because married women shouldn't take jobs away from vets, or so she was told. And that's how you became the new bookmobile driver."

"You mean I took the job away from someone else?" Rome didn't want guilt to tarnish what pleasure he had in the job.

"Well, maybe not entirely. She'd have been let go anyway. She couldn't always find the brakes when she needed them. Ran over a couple of farm cats. Even hit a cow. Nobody mourned the cats, knowing they have extra lives and all, but the cow was too much. The animal population is glad Henny's off the road."

"Maybe the farmers around here need armored cows … you know, the kind that give canned milk."

"That's a very bad joke, Rome." She set aside her empty buckle bowl.

"It's one of the few clean ones I learned in the army, Ivy."

"I'd prefer the dirty ones."

He snorted again. "I'll try to oblige."

She pushed her glasses up her nose closer to her eyes and picked up her knitting. Today's yarn was spring green. "You were a soldier in Italy, then."

After a moment, and another mouthful, Rome confirmed. "Yes, Ivy. I was."

"Battle fatigue as well as an amputation, I imagine."

Rome's apprehension about recalling the war caused him to take offense. "Battle fatigue is one diagnosis I dodged. Nobody accused me of shell shock or shirking, either. The hole where my arm used to be is proof enough I had brass."

He scowled. Ivy knitted calmly. His pique drained and, for reasons he could not explain, he found himself admitting his truth to this nosy old woman. She didn't seem afraid of it. No pity, just curiosity.

"Maybe battle fatigue isn't so far off the mark, Ivy. Recovery was bad. Still is. Months of headaches, insomnia, dreams. I don't think that's all about losing an arm. I'm pretty sure I lost part of my marbles, too."

"Was the hospital in Italy?"

Rome nodded. "First one was an open battlefield. They couldn't find my arm amidst all the others." His breath shortened and his heart raced. This was enough. More than he'd shared with any other civilian.

He watched a plump housewife down at the bookmobile pull a volume from a shelf, read the back cover, smile to herself, then look around for him.

"We're up here, Cora," Ivy sang out as a whoosh of breeze picked up, rustling the chestnut leaves. Sunlight was turning to pale gray.

Cora placed the book in her apron pocket and hurried up the steps. A row of curls, still flat in their bobby pins, peeked from under her headscarf. "Gonna rain, Ivy. How's the arthritis?"

"Telling me it's gonna rain, same as you, Cora."

Cora turned her freckle-spattered face to Rome, handing him her book. "Rain's sure to spot up your bookmobile. If Henny'd kept it that clean, the cow mighta seen her coming. I'm Cora Brennen."

"Nice to meet you, Mrs. Brennen," he said as he stamped her book, and added her name to his list of borrowers. "I'm Rome Coleridge."

The two women chatted a moment then Cora patted her pin curls. "I just stepped out long enough to get my book. Should get back and gussy up before Harlan comes home." She went on her way.

Rome could smell the rain coming. Trees spoke in the wind, the heat of the day released its clutches, birdsong faded. A neighbor dragged screeching metal patio chairs back under her eaves, and another called to a child or dog named Charlie. On the porch, Rome finally spoke. "We're not supposed to be talking about me, Ivy. You promised to tell me a story about my aunt."

"I believe they call this quid pro quo."

"Well, my quid has been quo-ed for today. It's your turn."

"I'll start, but not with your war. With the Great War. American Red Cross nurses going overseas. Thousands of them, right on the front lines. Leona Herkimer was too young for such a thing. But she'd been born to nurse, curing her dollies and ministering to fallen birds. She even cared for her parents when they tippled too much. Which was most of the time. Anyway, during the war, she went to nursing school. By the eleventh hour on the eleventh day of the eleventh month of 1918, when the War to End all Wars ended, Leona was a floor nurse in an Everett hospital."

"Huh. That's long before I was born. Ma never mentioned she had a sister."

"No, well, she wouldn't I guess, considering what happened."

"Why? What did happen? Is she dead?"

"You're getting ahead of the story. Patience, Rome."

"Another bit of this buckle would be a good cure for unbridled curiosity."

"It's known for its curative powers. Help yourself. Leona worked at the hospital for a couple years, fighting the godawful battle against Spanish Flu. After that blight ran its course, she was done with hospital wards. She craved nursing in the bush, in hard luck conditions where she'd be toe-to-toe with disease."

"Like those World War One nurses, I suppose."

Ivy nodded, in rhythm with the needles. "That's who she grew up admiring. She passed a Civil Service exam, then signed up with the government to be what they called a Traveling Field Nurse in the island possessions. She didn't know what an island possession even was. She thought maybe one of the islands off the Washington coast."

"But that's not where she ended up?"

Ivy shrugged at him. "When does life ever take you where you started out for?"

"True enough."

"Leona was offered Hawaii or Alaska. Alaska was closer. Besides it won her coin toss. In 1921, she was shipped to Hoonah, a Tlingit village on Chichagof Island, a million miles from Anywhere, Alaska."

CHAPTER TWO

September 4, 1921
Leona Herkimer

Leona's new life began when she boarded the ferry. The Alaska Steamship Company whisked her from Seattle to the Alaska territory. She was giddy as they steamed away from the other ferries docked at Pier One to lace through Washington's San Juan Islands, then between Vancouver Island and mainland Canada, and on up Georgia Strait to Ketchikan.

The sixty passengers on the ferry were primarily miners and sales representatives. The afternoon they were underway, a pianist entertained in the saloon while the only other woman traveling alone, one who introduced herself as Danielle Lester, taught Leona how to play pinochle and poker.

"You'll need to know how to pass the time on long winter evenings. They start around three in the afternoon," Danielle explained. "Cards are a must. I'll teach you canasta, too. And learn to knit if you don't already know how."

Leona said she was to be a nurse in Hoonah, and Danielle confessed, "I'm what they call a lady of the line."

"Oh, yes? You have your own trapline for, what, fox and maybe marten?"

Danielle guffawed, then explained the line she worked would be with other dance hall dollies in Juneau. "I guess it's a trapline of sorts," she said with a wink to Leona's delight.

Oh, what an adventure lies ahead of me! How exotic the wilderness life is already, Leona enthused to herself. The promise was for even greater things ahead, with all rumors about her left behind. How glad she was that the past was past. She would only be known as Leona Herkimer, a nurse stationed at the Hoonah frontier clinic. She envisioned herself as an Angel in White, saving innocent native children from smallpox, cholera, and tetanus. She would stop consumption in its tracks for all the adoring parents.

After the first spectacular day, the steamer entered the Pacific Ocean at Queen Charlotte Sound. The open ocean thrashed the ferry as it chugged its way up the wild coast. Leona discovered how sick an Angel in White could get. As the boat battled heavy seas, her stomach did, too. She felt too awful to be afraid of the thunderous waves, hoping death would take her soon.

Not until the steamer scooted into Clarence Strait, many hours later, did Leona stop vomiting and begin to believe she might live. The strait entered the inland passage, and land masses on both sides of them soon smoothed the violent waters of open ocean. Leona walked the deck around and around, filling her nose and lungs with the sting of cold sea air. Her stomach returned to nothing worse than hunger pangs.

That evening she shared a dinner table with a middle-aged couple, Harold and Judith Binder. She learned they were all heading to Hoonah. Reverend Binder was the new missionary for the Presbyterian Church and orphanage, and his wife, Judith, would join a teacher named Ivy Bolton who had established a school.

"She better not think to treat you all la-de-da," Reverend Binder boomed to his wife while passing a bowl of creamed corn.

"I doubt there is much la-de-da-ing to be had in Hoonah," Judith murmured. They were nearly the first words Leona heard the tiny woman say, since Judith ebbed while her boisterous husband flooded the room with his opinions.

They'd been told that the government station in Hoonah held both the school and the clinic, at opposite ends of the building. The clinic, as Leona understood it, was a large examining room with a six-bed patient facility. The school needed rehabilitation to accommodate two classes instead of one; Reverend Binder had volunteered to spearhead that project. "A helpful overlapping between Church and State is good for all," he announced during the dessert course on the ferry.

Between the clinic and the school was an open vestibule large enough for waiting patients, what passed for the post office, and the ham radio station. Behind this area was the kitchen and dining facility for the staff. Leona wondered aloud if the new building would have indoor plumbing.

"You'll have your answer soon enough," the reverend replied with a frown. "We're not really used to discussing such delicate subjects at the dinner table."

I'm not really used to such a picklepuss, Leona thought.

When the large ferry arrived in Ketchikan, all passengers debarked. Salesmen headed off to call on trading posts at the southern tip of the Panhandle, offering essential staples from bags of flour to kegs of nails. The rest of the passengers, including Danielle Lester, the Binders, and Leona, transferred to a much smaller ferry that was bound for Juneau.

Juneau was the end of the line for the ferry. Now, only the reverend, the teacher, and Leona awaited transport to Hoonah where all three would minister to the needs of the people, each a healer in his or her own way. The prospectors left them behind, returning to gold claims that never quite paid out. *Nothing is so enticing as hope,* Leona supposed. *Heaven knows I'm feeling hopeful myself.*

Her new friend left as well. "Come see me when you can," Danielle said as she hugged Leona. "Taverns outnumber anything but churches, but I shouldn't be hard to locate."

Leona had a scandalous thought about fur and live traps and women. She should be ashamed but instead smothered a giggle.

The trio awaited their next ride on a pier as old and gnarled as an arthritic finger poking into Gastineau Channel. It was the rickety landing for small boats in Juneau. They observed an ore carrier load at a larger facility farther up the bay. As they watched, locals scuttled around the docks, whippet-thin men dressed in a hodge-podge of old doughboy britches, cowboy scarves, miner boots, and immigrant caps of all sorts. Most had facial hair dense as thickets, and many appeared to have broken their noses at one time or other. She thought of the phrase Danielle used when she accused Leona of going to Alaska to find a husband. *The odds are good, but the goods are odd.*

"Odd, indeed," Leona muttered, looking the rough prospectors, loggers, and fishermen up and down while they, far less surreptitiously, looked at her. No women other than Judith and she were in sight once Danielle had hip-switched into town.

Outsiders. A miner on the first ferry had told her that's what Alaskans called people from the United States. Outsiders. It made sense now that she gaped with awe at this alien landscape of dilapidated structures, rugged men, freezing channels, and arresting mountains. She felt very much an Outsider and wondered if she'd ever fit in.

"I'd heard of the Tlingits, of course. But Chichagof Island was new to me when I was told that's where I was going." Leona spoke to make conversation.

"You probably think the island was named for a Ruskie trapper, but you'd be wrong," Reverend Harold Binder announced. "Chichagof was an Arctic explorer who never laid eyes on Alaska. His namesake island has the highest population of bears anywhere in the world." The reverend's every statement sounded like he was orating from a pulpit.

Leona found him tiring, and she'd known him less than a week. "Yes. I looked it up before I left, um, Outside."

Of course, I looked it up, she thought. *Why would he think I'd aimlessly wander onto a ferry, destination unknown?* At the age of twenty-two, she was aware that most men thought most women were nincompoops.

The rubberized interior of her bombazine raincoat kept her dry, but she pulled her scarf tighter around her neck and ears. Maybe it would block the reverend's blather along with the cold air. But wind blew through the loose wool weave. She hoped to purchase a fur hat before winter set in.

Watching for their next boat, Leona squinted down the channel, a sapphire fjord between towering cliffs of spruce and cedar. Low-flying tendrils of mist spread across the deep passage. She turned back toward the stamp-sized town. Eagles and seagulls bickered as a fishing boat disgorged its catch at a cannery across the way.

When at last their boat arrived, they gawked. The little steamer was not much bigger than a pleasure craft, a speck of flotsam on the huge channel. After the captain got a look at them, he frowned and grumbled, "I'm Captain Aleck. And you're cheechakos, all of you." He demanded they walk into town to purchase knee-high rubber boots.

That in itself should have told them about the rain. But in case they needed to know more, Reverend Harold blustered, "Hoonah receives sixty-eight inches of rain annually. Twice the average of the United States."

By the time they returned from a general merchandise store in downtown Juneau, each in a pair of no-nonsense footwear, their luggage had been loaded. There was hardly room for them to sit behind a tiny pilothouse, with suitcases and duffels piled all around them.

"Sorry about that, folks," the wiry captain said, having removed a sliver of wood he'd been poking between his teeth. He was maybe fifty with a face as craggy as a relief map. "Cargo area is full to the gills with goods for the government station. Anyone going that way carries goods. Flour, schoolbooks, medicines, whatever. And mail. Most valuable staple there is."

Mail. Not a valuable staple to everybody. Leona was sure nobody would write to her, not after her last days in Washington. Not when she'd skulked away with the fumes of alcohol still circling her like an evil mist.

The steamer pulled away from the dock with its catch of three Outsiders squashed between their possessions. "At least the togetherness will help us stay warm," Leona observed to Judith.

Captain Aleck yelled over the chug of the engine. "Hoonah is thirty, thirty-five miles as the crow flies, but more like sixty by water. You'll see why." He handed them each a blanket, and they soon wrapped themselves into three cocoons.

The ferry, aptly named *Small Fry,* steamed north from Gastineau Channel into Lynn Canal, then jackknifed to the southwest around the tip of an island, and entered another channel before hooking into Icy Strait. Leona had no idea where they were after the constant zigzagging, but ice-capped peaks twirled around them as they serpentined along.

Guess I'll get a compass when I get that fur hat.

Maybe Reverend Harold heard her thoughts. "They call all this country the Alaska Panhandle. Dozens of inlets and islands."

I wonder if he has an off switch, Leona thought. I wonder if Judith Binder is deaf.

The solitude and high drama all around astounded her. On the entire journey, Leona saw nothing human. Narrow beaches overshadowed by high walls of spruce, fluking whales, rafts of otters clinging to kelp, hints of the glacier field to the north, but nothing human.

Icy Strait ran along the wild east coast of Chichagof Island. *Small Fry* veered into a waterway that wedged into the island, and at last, Leona spotted the Hoonah Packing Cannery with the village of Hoonah not far to the south of it. She'd known the town would be small, but not miniscule. As she stared at the few buildings clinging to the back of beyond, she muttered, "Guess I won't be doing much hat shopping here."

The reverend took to the pulpit again. "No, Juneau is the closest thing for that. Did you know it was named capital of the Alaska Territory in 1906 after the Gold Rush made it much more significant than Sitka?" He looked from his wife to Leona, making sure they were listening.

"Interesting, dear," Judith muttered.

Shut yer yap, dear, Leona thought.

"A large vessel would be met by small ones to offload the cargo in a place like this. They call it lightering in the shipping trade," said Reverend Harold.

The captain stared at him. "Afraid we won't be lightering today," he said as *Small Fry* nestled against a ragtag pier amidst a variety of smaller crafts. Canoes lined the pebbled shore. Leona wondered if he was thinking "Shut yer yap, mate," but her attention was drawn to the first Tlingit tribesmen she had ever seen. She beamed at the several who came forward to grapple with the luggage and the cargo, some glancing shyly and others calling a hearty "Hello" with an alien accent. *I suppose I'm the one with the alien accent,* she corrected herself.

To Leona's surprise, none was dressed in cedar bark, deerskin, or a loin cloth as she'd seen in the library's old picture books. Several women had beautiful shell headbands, and some chose moccasins instead of boots. But in general, they dressed as everyone in Alaska dressed. The women were encased to the ankle in patched skirts, and the men wore trousers and jackets that were old a decade before.

Leona nodded happily to them all. These were to be her people, her lives to save. Reverend Binder tried to establish some order, but everyone ignored him. The natives, laden with the luggage, headed toward the biggest building on the shore, while the captain and his crewman peeled off to a hovel unmistakable as a tavern.

Prohibition doesn't appear to have reached Alaska. Perhaps Alaska doesn't go by United States rules, Leona mused. She didn't want an oration, so she didn't ask the reverend.

The Binders and Leona shuffled along in their new rubber boots, following the natives to what must be the government station. On a wide covered porch at the front, stood the only white woman in sight.

She was tall and straight-backed as a statue. Leona couldn't help but notice she was broad in those body parts that always attract a man's attention yet maintained a girlish waist. As they neared, Leona was surprised to see that she was old, possibly even late-forties. Yet she was beautiful, with hair the color of dark honey blowing in the wind. Leona imagined this woman had broken a few hearts in her day. Maybe she still was breaking them (not that Leona had yet seen a heart in Alaska she'd consider worth breaking).

The reverend introduced himself and his wife to this vision. Leona came next. "I'm Leona Herkimer, here to nurse with you."

"You mean with Jessica. I'm Ivy Bolton, the teacher. I'm pleased to have so many new companions." A smooth and rich voice matched the honey of her hair. "There is so much for us to do here among these remarkable people."

Leona wondered if she'd just met a real angel, whether she wore white or not.

September 4, 1921
Ivy Bolton

"We must all agree to go by first name or job title," Ivy said as they gathered around the crude-hewn table for a meal together, before the Binders were escorted to their church. "It's easier for the natives to learn one word per person. Easier for us, too, for that matter. Don't be surprised if the Tlingits just call you nurse, reverend, and teacher."

"Do you always serve such lovely meals?" Leona asked.

The young nurse's enthusiasm tickled Ivy. The girl was maybe early-twenties and would need that zest in the bleak days ahead. And yes, the table, in fact the whole kitchen, looked rugged by Outside standards, but today, the food was worthy of a top-notch restaurant.

"Well, sometimes it's seal liver and pickled kelp, but you're in luck," said Jessica Chambers, the weathered nurse who Leona would work alongside.

"Hambone alerted us you were on your way," Ivy said, passing a jar of gooseberry jelly and a mustard pot. "He's the radio operator in Juneau. So we had the venison steaks ready to grill."

"Quite delicious," said Judith Binder. "And such interesting potatoes."

Reverend Harold corrected his wife. "Not potatoes, dear. I believe these are mashed camas bulbs. A native favorite because they are sweet."

Ivy couldn't refrain from saying, "You might avoid picking them yourselves because the death camas, also local, looks much the same."

"Make a note of that, Harold," said Judith.

Was there a hint of sass there? So far, Ivy found Judith's voice nothing but subservient, maybe because she so rarely got to use it. Her husband could certainly bray like an ass; only once during the meal did anyone ask a question he didn't attempt to answer.

"You called us cheechakos, Captain. What did you mean?" Leona caught the boatman with a large chew of venison in his mouth.

Ivy filled the empty space with a chuckle. "That's what sourdoughs like Captain Aleck call newcomers. And that's why he's known behind his back as a Smart Aleck."

The captain swallowed a great gulp. "Now Ivy, I meant no harm."

"And how long do we remain cheechakos, Captain?" Reverend Harold asked, removing a small notebook and pen from a shirt pocket. "I write down all that I learn for self-improvement."

"Well ... well ... I reckon forever," the captain answered with a shrug. "Never gave it a thought before."

"I've been here twenty years, and I'm still called New Nurse," said Jessica with a smile. "Now that you're here, Leona, maybe I'll be Nurse Sourdough."

"Oh dear, I do hope I'm not thought of as Nurse Know-Nothing in the meantime."

"You're skilled, or you wouldn't be here," Jessica responded with a light pat to Leona's hand. "We'll teach you the Alaska peculiarities in no time."

"I'll take it as a challenge to learn as quickly as I can."

While the others chatted, Ivy considered the perky Leona Herkimer. Her wholehearted eagerness was a good thing, of course, if it gave her resilience. Leona was not a beauty, exactly, but possessed a round, open face that demanded you smile at it. No visible deformities or wounds. Seemed bright and personable. Looked no more than twenty-five but must have passed as thirty. Any younger and the government wouldn't have hired her. Although when you need nurses, Ivy doubted anybody checked too closely.

So why is she here? In Ivy's experience, attractive single women from Outside were a troubled breed. Traumatic backgrounds flushed them into the open and sent them to the north country to escape whatever their particular prisons happened to be. *What has gone on with this one?*

After their meal, Jessica took Leona to tour the clinic at the far end of the building, and Ivy escorted the Binders to the school at the opposite end.

"Private quarters are upstairs," she said on her way, pointing upward as if they could see through the ceiling. "There is a room for the nurses and one for me. We have cleared the spare room for the two of you in case you would prefer to spend a night here before moving to the rectory. I warn you it can become quite noisy here in the night if an emergency comes into the clinic."

"Judith and I will proceed to the rectory," the reverend said. "No time to lose when helping the heathens. I understand they suffer many diseases. Is being so close to the clinic really safe for you and the school?"

Ivy tried not to bristle at the comment. Hoonah was small, and she would be working with Harold and Judith for months to come. It would be better to find a way to coexist. With some difficulty, she curbed her tongue and calmly answered, "Yes, they do have diseases. Of course, much of it did not originate with them. We had the devil's own time wiping out Spanish Flu in these last few years. And consumption plagues us all. But the clinic is well-sanitized at all times as is the school."

The school was one large room with an ample storage closet. Small high windows along a back wall allowed scant daylight to force its way in.

"Dark in here," Harold said. "I've read that Juneau has at most eleven hours of daylight this time of year."

"And not much more than eight in December. Get used to working in the dark." Ivy answered.

"If the windows were bigger, more light could get in."

Ivy felt her sass-level rising. "If the windows were bigger, bears could get in."

"Bears! Well, I'll be. They really do exist around here." The reverend beamed at her. He appeared delighted by another lesson learned. Out came the notebook again. "I thought maybe it was just a tale told to...ah...cheechakos!"

"Indeed. Both black bears and browns. You'll learn a great deal about living with wildlife. Especially the denizens who'd like to eat you."

Ivy saw Judith looking wide-eyed, as if a hungry bear might be lurking in the shadows of a teacher's desk. Ivy felt churlish. Frightening this woman was not the best of all welcomes. She softened with a smile. "For light, we use seal oil lamps to save on power. But when the kids come back, we have electricity for lights and wood stoves for heat. We'll be warm and safe."

The dusky room was stacked with boxes and crates. Most had government labels, but others came from Russian Orthodox, Presbyterian, and Catholic charities. "These are school supplies shipped to us from the government. And toys, books, and clothing from the churches for the children. Our first order of business tomorrow will be to open the crates and begin to organize. Separate things for the orphanage from things for the school. Teachers here are our own disciplinarians, janitors, builders, office personnel. There is no school superintendent on the island."

Ivy became aware that both members of her tour had gone silent. *Have I been too ill-natured? Too scary? Why the hell did I mention bears?* She turned to see if the Binders had actually left. But in the gloaming of the day, both pairs of Binder eyes sparkled as the couple surveyed the room and its chaos.

"Oh, Harold," whispered Judith. Tears beaded in her lashes.

He put a hand on his wife's shoulder. "Yes. It is perfect. Just what we hoped for."

Hmmm, Ivy thought. And because she was a woman who loved good stories, she couldn't wait to hear theirs. But not now. Daylight was waning. "You must be tired. And eager to unpack. Your bags have been taken to the rectory for you, the lamps are lit, and you'll find food in the larder to get you started. Captain Aleck has offered to escort you there before he returns to his boat." She didn't see the need to add that it would give him one more shot at the tavern before he sailed back to Juneau.

After the Binders said their goodbyes, Ivy went to the kitchen and brewed a cup of wildflower tea. She'd harvested and dried the blossoms and leaves the spring before, and the tea's aroma tickled her nose throughout the summer. Here on the brink of a new school year, at the start of winter's dark days and bleak weather, spring seemed very far away.

"Oh, bother," she muttered to herself, realizing she'd forgotten to tell the trio of Outsiders about the outdoor facility. Some wag, before Ivy's time in Hoonah, had posted a sign that called the pit toilets The Bog. Smiling to herself, Ivy presumed the newcomers would ask someone about it sooner or later.

She decided on an early evening in her room with her knitting and letter writing. Jessica would appreciate time alone to begin training Leona. Ivy went to the storeroom next to a pantry and picked her chamber pot from the row of them that were emptied and washed each morning by their owners. Hers was porcelain, with a pattern of wildflowers, of course. Even the baser things of life didn't have to be ugly.

Chamber pot in one hand and teacup in the other, Ivy climbed the wooden stairs to her room. It was small and largely unadorned. On her floor was a thick warm bearskin, given to her by a grateful Tlingit parent. She stood there now, in the dark, changing from day clothes to a long flannel nightgown. Only then did she turn up the oil lamp next to her bed. Ivy always changed in the dark, alone or otherwise. She wanted nobody to see the scars, least of all herself.

She continued a letter she was writing to her daughter, Poppy.

Outsiders arrived today. The Reverend Harold Binder is full of himself, a walking encyclopedia. But I guess a know-it-all beats a know-nothing. His wife Judith and I will get together tomorrow to see how we propose to handle the school year. For so many years, it's only been me. Time will tell how much more we can accomplish with two teachers. The reverend is too boisterous but appears harmless enough, but I wonder if Judith is possibly too fragile for Alaska. Her diminutive size and her quietude may work against her.

The new nurse appears a bright addition, instantly charming and fun. I'll get a moment alone with Nurse Jessica tomorrow to see what she thinks of Leona so far.

I saw Captain Aleck pat Jessica's bottom again tonight. The two of them have sparred for years. I wonder which would be more disappointed if the other ever gave in.

CHAPTER THREE

August 16, 1946
Rome Coleridge

Wednesday morning, Rome dropped the bookmobile at Central Motors Parts on First Street for an overall service. The husky mechanic popped the hood, poked inside, and whistled "Mule Skinner Blues." After his examination, he assured Rome that when he was done, the bookmobile would be, "Fine as wine, fit as a fiddle, and ready to roll." The library would be billed, and Rome could pick up the vehicle that afternoon to head on down the road.

Rome walked away, wondering if people so happy in their jobs had to be a little dotty. He thought about the last time he'd felt a smile and guessed it was when Ivy Bolton promised to tell him his Aunt Leona's story. He was intrigued. This unknown Leona had been a nurse in Alaska way back when she was about the same age he was now. Why would a young, single woman choose such a remote place to live in the 1920s?

The unveiling of a family secret must have made him feel fine as wine, fit as a fiddle, and ready to roll. At least it caused him to hum "Mule Skinner Blues" until he noticed he'd walked all the way uphill to Ivy Bolton's front porch.

What the hell? Had he intended to end up here? He turned back toward the Port Angeles business district, a stretch of four downtown blocks.

"You gonna leave without so much as a word? How like a man of you." The voice blared like a foghorn over the morning quiet of the neighborhood.

Rome felt heat creep up the back of his neck and flood his cheeks. He turned back once again, completing a full circle on the sidewalk. "Oh...ah...didn't see you there, Mrs. Bol...Ivy. Of course, I'd say hello. If I'd have seen you."

"Well, all right then. It's not polite to make an old lady cry, you know."

"And I'm nothing if not polite."

"Then come explain what's happened to your bookmobile. Don't tell me you're a worse driver than Henny."

As he climbed the steps and took his seat in the old wicker chair, he assured Ivy that the bookmobile was having an annual checkup. "The library uses a different shop each year to spread the work around. Support the community, you know."

She harrumphed. "I've known people who did that to spread bad debts around."

Rome didn't just smile. He laughed. "I don't think the library system is based on the long con, Ivy."

She had a large pot of coffee and several cups on the end table next to the swing. "You never know who'll stop by, so you must have coffee at the ready in the mornings. Grab yourself a cup, and one of those muffins. My neighbor Gladys made them for me. Not as good as mine, but they're free."

Rome did as he was told. The muffin was good, but Ivy was right. She was the better baker. Or maybe she had more sugar which was still under rationing following the war.

"You got a girlfriend who bakes for you?" Ivy asked.

Rome was getting used to the fact that if a thought crossed her mind, it tumbled out of her mouth. She had informed him that at her age, there was no time for questions left unasked.

"No, Ivy. I don't need one as long as you bake for me."

"Now don't go being a chucklehead. Everybody needs a baker. I'll see if I can find you one. I know a lotta girls on the Peninsula."

The idea of Ivy tracking down a girl for him crashed over Rome like a tidal wave. "Oh, no, Ivy. I can find my own..."

"I have several candidates in mind already."

The tidal wave smacked him again with its backwash. "You mean, you..." He stopped when he heard her chuckle upgrade to a full cackle.

She slapped her knee. "Of course, you need to find your own girl, Rome. Why would you want a fossil like me to do it for you? I just wondered if you have somebody because, if so, I want to know about her."

He sipped his coffee.

"A girl who waited loyally for the war to end perhaps?"

He sipped his coffee.

"Or maybe you met an I-tal signorina who nursed you back to health and will be arriving by warship as soon as the paperwork clears."

Rome sipped his coffee.

"Really, Rome. If you don't want to talk about it, why'd you bring it up?"

"Golly, I just don't know, Ivy. I was pretty sure I was thinking more about my aunt's story than my own." But he wasn't, not now, at least. He was half lost in that night before he left for war.

The breasts of the girl astride me swayed like ripe fruit as she pumped slow, bending low toward my chest.

"If you go to war, I won't forgive you," Barbara whispered through her heavy breaths. Her hair hung like a curtain over her lowered face, hiding her eyes from my view. "I don't want a dead man to grieve. Or a broken one. Not like my mom had."

As my emotion rose, she pumped harder. When I finished, she collapsed on top of me. "Hell, I don't know if I want a man at all."

I wound my arms around her. "Barbara, I have to go. A man has to answer the call. You know that."

"Men are asses. That's what I know." She untangled herself, got up, dressed, and left. Without a good-bye.

I doubted I'd ever see her again. I'd miss those lovely breasts, those strong legs. What had she meant by not wanting a man at all?

"Rome?" Ivy poked his knee with a knitting needle.

"Ivy! Sorry! Guess I was daydreaming."

"Must have been a humdinger."

Christ, did I say anything out loud?

"Your aunt's story is ready and waiting. You want to hear more?"

"Yes, Ivy, please." For crying out loud, please!

Ivy stared at him for a moment. He saw concern in her pale eyes. But whether it was sorrow, understanding, mystery, or a hint at upsetting things to come, he couldn't guess. All he knew for sure was that her voice soothed his nerves in a way he hadn't felt since the war.

"Your Aunt Leona was an exceptional woman," Ivy began. "From the moment she arrived in Hoonah, she worked hard, laughed harder. Everybody there delighted in her, Tlingits and white folks alike. She was welcomed as a fresh spirit from Outside. But if you looked close, you could tell from the tremble of a hand or a haunted look that flashed through her eyes, that Leona Herkimer kept dark secrets to herself."

CHAPTER FOUR

September 11, 1921
Leona Herkimer

Leona was alone in her room, muscles aching, eyes scratchy from too little sleep. She had to get up, had to put her warm toes on that cold floor. She heard pans clanking in the kitchen below so Cook was already at work over breakfast. Squinting, she focused on the other bed in the room; Jessica was asleep, softly snoring.

Leona groaned as she pulled her last clean nurse's apron from the wardrobe that held her clothing. She'd soak and wash her others today, in soap and bleach. They were short on Lysol until Captain Aleck brought the next load of supplies. Leona was not sure how much longer this particular uniform would suit her image of an Angel in White.

Angel in off-white? Angel in stained-with-blood-and-baby-poop? Attending to her appearance would be a good use of her first afternoon off, especially if it was still raining.

She had never worked so hard in her life as this week, but it suited her, and she flourished. On her first day, Jessica and she had washed down the entire clinic, all health equipment, and the patient room with disinfectant, and organized the medical cabinets with new supplies that had come in *Small Fry's* hull. Leona made her own mental inventory, poking in drawers and cabinets, to know what they had and what they didn't. Jessica showed her how to add needs to a government order form which was as arcane as the local language to Leona. She hoped to learn both Tlingit and government-ese in the weeks to come.

On her second day, with school soon to begin, children lined up at the clinic for inoculations. The only vaccines the nurses had in stock were for smallpox and tetanus. A new diphtheria vaccine was supposed to arrive soon. Leona and Jessica gave shot after shot, taking turns boiling syringes and other equipment.

"Why so many children in such a small village?" Leona asked.

"Orphans. Lots in all the villages up and down the territory. Their parents died by the dozens of Spanish flu. Next week, we'll travel to other villages to inoculate," Jessica said over a wailing boy. "Consider today a lot easier than that will be."

In the afternoon, an assistant showed up to aid the nurses. She was a plump girl, with long braids swinging gaily. She instantly kept the children as quiet as children stuck with needles could be kept. As she filled in their names on the medical records, she told Leona her own name was K'eikaxwéin. She must have seen the panic in Leona's eyes because she chuckled before saying, "Call me Flower. That is close enough to what it means."

Coming down the stairs for breakfast, Leona thought about the exhausting night of labor before this day even began. She'd assisted Jessica in the delivery of a baby boy at 3 a.m., exchanging fatigued smiles with his mother, Jissika. This first-time mother had also been delivered sixteen years earlier by Jessica and was named for her.

At breakfast, Leona told Ivy about it.

Ivy nodded. "Since Harold isn't here yet to explain everything to us, I'll explain that Tlingit people often name children after a person they admire, so that person will live on after death."

"That's lovely," Leona said, then yawned over a bowl of oatmeal. She wondered if a baby would one day be named Leona. And had Ivy really said that about the Reverend and his explanations? Might she have an edge that was pretty sharp? Leona certainly hoped so.

Few Tlingits stayed overnight at the clinic, although a child with pneumonia had been recovering in the patient area for the week that Leona had been there. It had rained non-stop as well. Leona began to wonder if she would drown before she ever had the chance to tour her new hometown. At least she had the boots for it!

Fortunately, evenings, other than babies and emergencies, were usually quiet. Jessica and she often played pinochle. "A woman on the ferry taught me how," Leona said, thinking about Danielle and wishing her well. "I'm sure I'll get better at it."

"I do hope. You're pretty bad at it now."

"Only to lure you in. It's all a front."

As the game went on, Leona asked about the doctor in Juneau who was their closest contact. "He comes when we need him, right?" asked Leona.

"Yes. No." Jessica, capturing a trick, frowned. "He should. But you'll find, he chooses to have us transfer a patient to him."

"But … "

"Ivy calls Hambone on the radio. He calls the hospital in Juneau, and they locate the doctor. Then he says he isn't coming."

"But … "

"Next, Hambone and Ivy radio for any boats in the area that can help us. If Captain Aleck is near, he always comes. But it might be a halibut fisherman or the forest ranger boat or a dory from a passing ferry. Whatever it is, we load your patient aboard, and off you go with her to Juneau. It can take hours. Maybe she'll get there alive. Maybe not."

"Wouldn't it be easier on the patient if … "

"If the doctor came here? Of course. But he won't. Not unless the trip was planned well in advance."

Leona sighed. It had been much the same at the hospital in Washington. Doctors ruled like czars. Patients came after that. Nurses were third-rate citizens. She'd hoped it would be different here. She vowed she wouldn't lose a patient because a doctor couldn't be bothered to show up. While she was making that mental declaration, Jessica took the last trick.

The week, overloaded with labor and startling lessons, nonetheless steamed on by. Jessica showed Leona more about dentistry than either had learned in school. "Bad teeth can't be blamed on the arrival of white folk. Malnutrition, broken bones, drowning, knife fights, mothers and babies dead in childbirth. There are plenty of problems that predate us. And will continue after we are gone." While Jessica spoke, she used a tooth cutter on a young man's jaw. Then Leona pedaled the foot-powered drill while Jessica filled two more teeth. Even from a distance, Leona was aware her face mask worked hard to dispel the aroma of decay and the rotgut hooch the man had used to medicate himself.

"Hooch got its name from a village near here," Jessica said. "Lots of stills around."

One night in the following week, Reverend Harold and Judith were invited to dinner. Cook made a cake for Jessica. Flour and sugar were not often used for such silliness. But, oh how delicious it looked to Leona whose sweet tooth had gone unattended since leaving Seattle.

"Is it your birthday, Jessica? Why didn't you tell me? We should all sing." It took her a moment to realize that Ivy, Harold, and Judith had gone quiet. She looked from one to the next.

"No, it's not my birthday." Jessica tightly twisted the small towel that served as a napkin. "Not my birthday. But a goodbye, my girl. I am leaving Alaska in two days' time. Tomorrow early, a forest service boat will come for you and Flower to go inoculate folks down in Tanakee, a long day south of here. I'll be gone before you get back so I thought we should share this goodbye tonight."

Leona felt protest in the pit of her stomach. Emotion rose through her body and stuck in her throat. Her teeth clenched as though she had lockjaw. What was this poison squeezing her? Anger she had not been warned before this? Concern that something was wrong with Jessica? No.

Absolute certainty she would fail on her own. Leona desperately needed a drink.

Her distress must have been obvious to everyone at the table. "You are the best young nurse I have seen in Alaska in many years. You are smart and flexible and clever in finding solutions. The natives here like you …" Jessica babbled.

Ivy, always the calmest among them, stepped in. "Leona, you have been blessed to have such a fine mentor even for a week. Most aren't so lucky. Judith and I are here to help you when we can and hold down the fort when you are gone. It's not merely because we are Gertie Goodbodies. It's part of what teachers here are expected to do. Just as we'll enlist your help for our projects. Jessica is a loss to us all."

Leona heard the "stop sniveling" loud and clear.

Reverend Harold appeared to be on the verge of opening his mouth when Judith said, "I can help midwife and teach sanitation. I've done it before."

The blockage in Leona's throat began to open. She found her voice although it was a little one. "You are well, Jessica? You're not leaving for Outside because you're sick?"

Jessica reached across the wide table and patted her trembling hand. "No, my dear. After twenty years in this territory, it's time for me to return to my family and see the sun again." She ended with a grin. "It appears I am soon to be a grandmother, and I have a yen to be there."

Leona breathed deep. Then she worked on a grin of her own. "Jessica, you've taught me so much in so little time. I desired a wilderness post, and now I have one.

You're leaving me a fine assistant in Flower. You've done far more than enough. I will miss you dearly, but I'll be fine. I can manage my duties with the help of all my new friends."

What a load of horseshit that is, Leona thought as the others enjoyed the cake. She'd felt safe with Jessica in charge. On her own, she was the only soldier on the front line. *What if I make another mistake? What if I cause another lonely death?*

That memory struck like a knife when she least expected it, and she could not protect herself from how it pierced her. *The old woman ... alone ... my fault, my fault.*

She turned her mind to the bootlegged brandy hidden in her luggage. Sweeter than whiskey, less burn, but the same smoky taste of the barrel. She fantasized a fruity sip of it soothing her mouth, her mind, the sharp edge of that never-healing wound.

The Alaska Territory was dry, as was the U.S. under Prohibition. But that hadn't prohibited Leona from bringing a bottle aboard the Alaska Steamship Company as she traveled to her Hoonah home. Using the excuse that she needed to pack for her early morning departure with the forest ranger, she stood.

"... so soon?"

"... the fun's just getting started!"

"... do some dancing if the captain shows up."

Expressing her regrets, she went up the stairs to her room. Leona needed solitude.

As laughter from Jessica's party floated up to her, Leona dragged her suitcase from under her bed. Carefully, she unwrapped the precious bottle from the medical gauze that protected it. She stroked the curve of its neck down to its base, then placed its coolness against her hot cheek. Next, she got off the floor and sat on the side of her narrow bed, cuddling the bottle.

Alcohol, for Leona, was as addictive as an unfaithful lover and every bit as bad for her. A drink warmed her with whispered promises, embraced her body with loving release. It calmed her fears, gave her strength, helped her forget, removed her shame about herself. And it could destroy her if she ever gave in to it again.

She kept a bottle close at hand at all times, an icon to scare away the evil spirits. As long as it was always there, unopened, she could convince herself she did not suffer alcoholism. She could believe she just liked a bit of fun now and then. Every young woman did ... even one who had taken the Florence Nightingale pledge to pass her life in purity. Enjoying a tipple did not make her a woman with a drinking problem, a position near society's lowest rung. If the bottle stayed corked, the genie was caught inside.

I do not have the disease of alcohol addiction. She could deny it to herself. But she knew better. Her training told her the truth of that ugly phrase. Her body and soul shivered.

Long into the evening, Leona battled against drinking away her demons. She won one more time. Each of these hard-fought wins exhausted her but proved she was strong. Gently, she kissed the bottle and returned it to hide once more in its lair. She sighed, stood, and made ready for bed. The journey tomorrow would be hard. She must sleep to be ready for a trek through a long Alaska day. The image of the old woman's face faded into her gray matter once more.

CHAPTER FIVE

September 18, 1921
Ivy Bolton

Ivy was up in the wee hours grinding coffee before the other residents would roll out of bed unless an emergency appeared for the nurses. Cook wouldn't arrive for an hour at least. Ivy's hair was loose and wild, a sprinkling of gray swirling through the honey gold. In her nightgown, her breasts and hips felt wonderfully free of daytime constraints. *At least corsets don't stick you with whale bones anymore,* she mused. *Why the hell do women agree to such contraptions?*

She wrapped a wool plaid blanket around her shoulders and opened the kitchen's heavy back door when she heard the ranger arrive. The low light of a seal oil lamp outlined the shape of Fredrik Makinen. It revealed how one shoulder was lower than the other in the rolling gait created by a trick knee and how the angular planes of his body were comprised of long ropy muscle. A mop of blond hair and high cheekbones marked his face as one whose ancestors sailed the Scandinavian fjords.

Ivy ushered him inside. Neither spoke. Instead, they embraced. Then Ivy led her ranger by the hand through the kitchen into the storeroom where she'd spread her bearskin on the floor. They wasted no time. Her nightgown was easily dispensed with, then Ivy watched with pleasure as her lover peeled off all his own layers. The low light was gentle on the hard life lived by two middle-aged bodies as they melded together. It hid his ill-advised tattoos and the burn scars on her back and arms. He'd stroked her tortured skin many times before, once whispering the welts were part of his admiration for her. "You should have been honored. He deserved annihilation."

It was as close to love language as they got although they had been sexual companions for many years, whenever his job brought him to Hoonah. Their lovemaking was intense but quiet so as not to awaken occupants on the floor above. The storeroom was much safer than Ivy's bedroom for that.

The time soon came for Ivy to confine her body once again and prepare for the day. At dawn, when Leona and Flower yawned at the kitchen table, Ivy was dressed and pouring Maki a cup of coffee that she followed with a plate of fried mush. It was still too early for Cook to arrive, but Ivy knew all three travelers must eat for a long, demanding day or two. Ivy served the women, nobody questioning the presence of a Tlingit girl at her table. It was Ivy's nature to ignore absurd customs.

"Leona, this is Fredrik Makinen. Forest ranger in the Tongass. Most folks here call him Maki."

"Nurse," he said. "I'd doff a hat if I was wearing one at the moment."

Ivy stared closely at the nurse. "Are you feeling well, Leona? You look pale."

"Yes, I'm fine, just slept a bit poorly. Your coffee will perk me up."

"Eat your food, too. All of it. It will be a long day."

Flower said, "The supplies are ready to load, Maki. I will go with you today, as assistant to Leona."

Ivy, pouring herself a cup of coffee, said, "Flower is studying with the Itinerant Nurse Program."

Maki's cheeks raised when he smiled, forcing his eyes to squint. "That's great, Flower. You got a fine student here, Nurse."

"Yes I do. And it's Leona, not Nurse. Ivy told me I only get one word."

His laugh was more of a chuckle. "Ivy's a tough one. But I have a hunch some of these Tlingits will allow you up to two." He soon rose, stretched, and picked up a load of supplies. "Thanks for the breakfast, Ivy. I'll start packing the boat. You ladies hurry along."

Flower grabbed more gear, including the chest of vaccines, and followed him out.

When they'd both gone, Leona turned to Ivy, who swore the nurse looked even paler than she had before. "Please tell Jessica goodbye for me. Tell her I left this morning full of courage and enthusiasm."

Ivy gave her a nod, wishing she could transfer a measure of her own confidence to the young woman. "Jessica knows you're ready for this, Leona. If not, she wouldn't go. And she's waited so long to feel that she's leaving her tribe in safe hands. Now you just need to be as sure of it as she is."

"Thank you, Ivy." Leona muscled up the last of the supplies along with her suitcase, then went out the door.

The kitchen was suddenly quiet. Ivy put her elbows on the table, then locked her fingers and rested her chin on them. She nearly dozed until the sound of mice alerted her that she was no longer alone. No, not mice. Rabbit fur slippers shuffling on the hardwood floor.

"You ever gonna make an honest man out of Maki?" Jessica asked.

Ivy squinted at the nurse who'd been her friend for a decade. Ivy would miss the old nurse more than Leona could imagine. Jessica alone knew of her arrangement with Maki.

"When it comes to a man, Jess, honesty is no longer one of my priorities. Besides, I figure Maki has a wife somewhere Outside, one not squawking as long as he sends her his pay now and then. He'll go back to her one day. Leave the wilderness when the cold gets too much for his knee."

"That's all well and good for him. But are you sure you want to end up alone? You're no spring ptarmigan. Maybe you should be waving your tail feathers in another direction."

"I've been in a twosome, and I've been alone. I'm telling you, alone is better." Ivy raised her voice. "And who are you to talk? I suspect Captain Aleck hates to see you go."

"If a man is too slow making his move, a woman needs to make one of her own. Even if he came with me, which I don't want, he'd hate it Outside. He'll live and die running *Small Fry* up and down glacial waters."

September 18, 1921
Leona Herkimer

The early morning wasn't sure what it wanted to do. It was more misty than rainy, more gray than cloudy. *Like my mood,* Leona thought. *It could break either way.* She was aware the days were getting shorter and that a chill caused her to shut her window at night. But she had not been an Alaskan long enough to read clouds and sea water. The first lessons learned were to have a slicker at hand always, and it was okay to wear long johns peeking out from under your skirt and nurse's apron. Bare legs were ridiculous, if not from chill then from the voracious mosquitoes that hadn't all packed up along with the summer.

The ranger boat had docked its sturdy self among the smaller craft at the shabby pier. "How do you do, *Ranger One*?" she asked it, reading the boat's name on the side of its bow. "See that you stay on the topside of the water today."

Maki overheard and answered, "She's stayed on the top for well over a decade. I suspect she'll mind her manners today. You'll like her, I reckon. She's got electric lights, a galley, a head, bunks, and a bookcase. Plus a desk for me. She's my office and my house, a lot of the time. Yours, too, for the next couple days."

Flower said, "This is a good boat, Nurse. We call it *Yashee* which means sing. It has a happy whistle."

Leona met the skipper and crewmen, then they loaded the women's gear into the small cabin. The skipper, his face a dour frown, pointed out their bunks. "You ladies pull this curtain tonight, and we gents will stay at our end. See that you stay at yours."

"I don't know, Skipper. I've heard Flower is a wild woman," Maki teased. The boatman huffed and withdrew to his pilothouse.

Flower let loose a burst of Tlingit and squinted miniature arrows at the forest ranger.

Leona was lost, but Maki belly laughed. "She gave me an evil eye and called me a name so nasty that I can't even translate it into English."

"As well she should," Leona said. "I wonder what the people here call me."

Flower thought for a moment then said, "They call you *Koonénaa.* This means, um, messenger, but a good one. An angel. You bring them comfort from pain."

Leona nearly burst into joyful tears. Of course, maybe it wasn't true that they called her Angel. Maybe they really called her Bossy Witch Woman, and Flower was being kind. If so, she didn't want to know it.

Ready to leave, *Yashee* whistled, and Leona had to agree it was a friendlier toot than the bigger fishing boats and freighters. She took a bench near a window, and Flower sat across from her. They soon turned into Icy Strait, onto the Chatham, and chugged steadily along the Southeast coast of the island. *Yashee* might sing but she certainly crawled along at the speed of a dirge.

"Why so slow?" Leona called to the skipper.

"She's built for strength, not speed, young woman," he growled over the sound of the gasoline engine.

Fearing she had offended him, Leona said no more. And the skies began to brighten. After days of rain, it was a minor miracle. She saw fall color that hadn't existed a week ago. Along the beaches and below the trees, squash berry shrubs and devil's club were turning orange, high bush cranberries a deep red, and millions of ferns coppery brown. The trees themselves, primarily cedar, spruce, and hemlock, maintained their somber dark greens. Maki pointed out a brown bear on the shore, and sea otters resting in the kelp, their tails wrapped around the stalks to hold them in place. Leona was no birder, but anyone could identify a bald eagle, and Flower taught her to pick out puffins, guillemots, and kingfishers.

As they pushed up the Tenakee Inlet which nearly split the island apart, Maki said, "You'll like Tenakee Springs if you enjoy sitting in stifling wet minerals."

"The springs are hot springs?"

"Yep. Not my cup of whiskey, but folks have used them for decades for restorative soaks. The Klondikers discovered it was the only place they could get warm, so they'd come over from Juneau. They sort of shoved the natives aside."

"The springs were not cement when I was a child," Flower said.

"Yep. Cemented and covered with a bath house now. They've posted times for ladies when men aren't allowed."

Yashee docked in front of a handful of ragtag buildings. Leona read signs for a barber shop, restaurant, two taverns, and Snyder Mercantile. *Maybe they sell fur hats,* she thought. Winter was close now. She wondered what the two taverns sold during Prohibition. Or whether anybody this far from Outside gave a damn what the locals drank.

As Leona watched, a pasty-skinned woman exited the mercantile. She appeared so tightly bound beneath her somber dress that she walked as stiff as a wind-up nutcracker. Apparently the official greeter of Tenakee Springs, she halted at the land end of the dock, in front of a long line of Tlingit children and mothers.

"Looks like they're waiting for you," Maki observed.

"How did they know when we would arrive?" Leona asked.

Flower smiled broadly. "Tlingit people know everything."

Leona figured that was as likely as any other answer. Maki helped them unload their medical supplies, carrying the cases to a rough-hewn table at the head of the line of children. The official greeter introduced herself as Edna McCormick, employee of the mercantile and wife of the saltern's manager.

"The saltern?" Leona asked.

"Across the inlet. They evaporate salt from the water. The salmon canneries use it," Maki explained. "Your cook asked me to pick up a bagful before we head home. If you're set, I'll go load my backpack, then be on my way."

Mrs. McCormick took back the conversation. "The table and chair are for you, Nurse. Nurse Jessica always wanted them so I assumed you would, too."

"Thank you. Could we have another chair for my assistant?" Leona asked.

Mrs. McCormick straightened her spine another notch. She scowled at Flower, then back at Leona. "If your girl needs a chair, she can come get her own." Leona felt slapped into speechlessness, but Mrs. McCormick continued unaware. "You can see the eight white children at the head of this line, then seventeen Indians. More will appear through the day. We round them up for you, even though only whites go to school here."

The children were wide-eyed and flighty in the presence of the newest Woman With Needles To Poke You. Mothers in the line smiled and nodded shyly.

"I'll get back to work now and recommend you do the same," Mrs. McCormack said.

So much for chitchat, Leona thought, watching the old crow stomp back to the store, even her skirt twitching in agitation. *I alienated her in less than a minute. I'm doing very well, Jessica.*

"Follow her and get a chair," Leona said to Flower.

Flower, expressionless, said, "I prefer to stand."

Together, they unloaded supplies, piled the government paperwork on the table, and set up a kerosene primus stove to boil water for sterilizing syringes as they inoculated. Meanwhile, Leona built to a slow boil herself.

Maki, with backpack in place, stopped by once more. "Getting along with the locals already, are you?"

Leona blew out a long breath. She wasn't totally naive. She was aware white and red did not always mix. They didn't in Washington where she'd come from either. But still. "Is Mrs. McCormack's nose so far in the air as to reject giving a Tlingit a chair?"

"Yes," said Flower.

"Maybe," Maki agreed. "Or she's mainly in a lather because a young single nurse is of too much interest to the married men in her community."

"Oh, horse feathers!" Leona was astounded at Maki's statement. "If so, she's a Dumb Dora on two counts."

"Yes," said Flower.

Maki shrugged. "Either way, ladies, I'll be going. Official Forest Service inspection tour of a couple of fur farms and logging camps, see that they're staying within their boundaries. It's a hike, so it'll take a few hours. I suggest we eat at the restaurant tonight. You want to avoid the crew cooking on *Ranger One* if you possibly can."

Leona resolved to stay away from Mrs. McCormack. There was work to do with children who had already been waiting too long. *Funny how the white children are all at the head of the line.* She thought of claiming loudly, "Okay, I'll practice on the first eight little ones since I'm new at this." But she bit her tongue and went about her business, not wanting to cause more mayhem in the medical community even before Jessica left the Territory.

Clouds threatened but rain held off the whole afternoon. After a rocky start, the day passed joyfully for Leona. She was in the wilderness doing the job she loved. The children of Tenakee Springs were vaccinated against smallpox and tetanus, and Leona was forgiven for the syringe when she gave each boy and girl a piece of Black Jack gum. She also treated two ear infections, dosed three coughs, and examined a pregnant woman in the privacy behind the pulled curtain on *Yashee.*

From her table at the dock, Leona watched the skipper and crewmen load fresh supplies mid-day, then disappear from sight to hunt, fish, sleep, visit the hot springs, or drink. Oh how she'd like a drink to celebrate her success this day, but that was not to be.

When they had seen all the patients and were packing up their medical supplies, Leona said to Flower, "Let's take Maki up on the offer to meet at the restaurant later on."

"You go. I'll stay," Flower said.

"But you'll be hungry. It'll be fun."

"There is food here on the boat."

Leona said, "You heard Maki's warning about crew cooking."

Flower said a phrase in Tlingit in the same tone of exasperation she'd used before, then switched to English. "Nurse! Leona! They will not allow me in. You must learn this. White women do not befriend Tlingit women. Learn this for your own good, and for mine when we are outside the clinic." Tears formed in her dark eyes before she turned away.

Leona was furious with herself. Speaking of Dumb Doras. How could she have embarrassed Flower with her ignorance? "I'm so sorry, Flower. That attitude is such malarkey to me that I don't think about it."

Flower relented. "You are different. Ivy, too."

"You are part of the clinic family. I refuse to think of you as any less than me. But I begin to see what it looks like through your eyes."

Flower said nothing, so Leona added, "Give me time. I'll get better at this." An idea hit her. "I tell you what. Let's make dinner here on the boat for the crew and Maki. It'll be better than any darn old restaurant." She touched Flower's hand. "I'll rummage in the galley. Can you see if anyone is selling fish?"

Flower did more than that. She found a Tlingit fisherman who, glad of the nurse's care for his children, gave them fish and shellfish. Then he sent two young daughters with Flower to harvest berries.

"This will be such a treat," Leona enthused as she stared at the abundance. The two women, friends regardless of the prevailing winds, began to peel, slice, and chop.

And it was a treat. As the men returned to *Yashee*, they were each surprised by a spicy stew of salmon and clams with potatoes, onions, canned tomatoes, and evaporated milk. It was followed by cobbler made from blueberries and crowberries gathered by the children.

"How is it you two are still single gals?" Maki asked Flower and Leona, after making happy, slurpy noises.

"And which of you will stay with my vessel as her chef?" asked Skipper who, for the very first time, managed a slight smile for the women.

In the evening, Leona intended to relax in the hot springs. She imagined the mineral water bubbling into a tub at over one hundred degrees and rushing over her body, cleaning every nook and cranny, loosening each muscle. But now she thought better of it. She intuited that Flower could not go with her, and she didn't want to leave her behind.

The fear of failure that she'd felt that morning was long gone. She'd done well today. Leona's brandy was hidden in her suitcase, always near at hand to prove to herself she could overcome her ghosts. For a moment, she wondered if there was a private place on the boat for a tipple. But the brandy was not a strong enough pull to take that first dangerous sip. Not this time. Another victory. Another celebration.

Her bunk was small, and she felt protected by it, tucked in on her side against the bulkhead. She had no fear of the men aboard. The boat, tied to the dock, rocked amiably, and everything soon grew quiet, other than masculine snoring and farting from the other end.

Leona drifted off thinking about this first day of nursing on her own in the Alaska Territory. She'd made a false step, but what she'd told Flower was right; she would learn. In the meantime, twenty-eight children would live on, without two of the many diseases that could kill them.

Angel, indeed.

In the early gray of dawn, crew activity awakened her. *Yashee* had left dock en route for Angoon, further south and on the other side of Chatham Strait. While she dressed, she felt that massive waterway become rougher as they cut across its current.

Fewer children awaited them in little Angoon on the sunny side of the strait, and none of them was white. Mid-morning, a Tlingit messenger approached Leona, requesting she come see a sick man. She ducked inside the small doorway of a large wooden structure. As her eyes adjusted to the low light, Leona observed that a family, at least three generations, appeared to live together. None spoke to her.

Leona and Flower approached the firepit in the center of the room. They crouched next to a male who Leona judged to be around twenty. He lay in a stupor, flat on soiled blankets.

"What's his name?" Leona asked, and Flower translated her question.

"Edensaw," one of the women said. She pointed at herself then looked at Leona. "Ma." Leona figured it might be her only English word. But her eyes spoke loudly of her fear.

Edensaw was gaunt, sweating profusely, mumbling, and surrounded with plant bundles that burned like smudge pots.

"What are these?" Leona asked, recoiling from the acrid odor of the smoke.

"They are to fight the evil causing his sickness," Flower explained.

"We must get him away from those things. He needs to be washed thoroughly and all the blankets changed."

Flower hesitated. Leona looked up from the ailing man to her assistant. On that round face, she saw concern. "What?" Leona asked.

"We will be blamed if he becomes dead. We must be right to win their trust. We both need it."

Leona nodded. "I realize that. If we do what I ask, he may die. If we don't, he almost certainly will die."

Flower hesitated no longer. "Then tell me what to do."

"First, he needs fresh air. Let's get him outside into the sun. Ask his mother for hot water."

Flower translated. Three female elders and the mother chatted swiftly, one obviously angry. But then the mother nodded. At that, two tribesmen carried the man to a blanket that one of the women spread outdoors. Leona washed Edensaw with Fels-Naptha and gave some to his mother to wash his clothes in what remained of the hot water. "Tell them we will treat him at the clinic. They can come check on him in a week's time."

Before *Yashee* left Angoon, Tlingit men and a worried mother carried Edensaw aboard and placed him on deck with a large fur over him.

"Not crazy about consumption on my boat, young woman," Skipper said to Leona.

"He must get to the clinic for constant care, or he will die."

"Still ... "

"He is clean, not hacking blood, and the air will move infection away on the breeze. You and your crew might drown at sea, but you won't catch tuberculosis from this fellow."

The Skipper's face darkened with incoming storm. But then he guffawed. "Aye, aye, Miss Captain." He was still laughing as he took himself off to his pilothouse.

September 19, 1921
Ivy Bolton

Captain Aleck carried Jessica away on *Small Fry* the morning after Leona left Hoonah on *Yashee*. It was a day earlier than expected, but by going then, Jessica could catch a ferry bound for Seattle in Juneau.

Ivy was in a mood that could only be described as sour. She'd lost the last day to spend with her old friend, and she already missed Jessica mightily.

Old is right. Forty-eight! Now I'm the oldest one here. Older than Cook even. Guess I can mope if I want to. I think I will. She'd always suspected that being a battle-axe was more fun than a sweetie. It might be a good time to give it a whirl.

To make matters worse, she'd received a radio call from Hambone in Juneau that morning shortly after Jessica left. His Highness, the doctor, planned to pay a visit next Monday to perform physicals on the children before school began on Thursday. Another government regulation. Now Leona would come home to that ordeal without Jessica as a buffer.

We'll see what the girl's made of. Piss and vinegar would be in order. Maybe a hatchet, too.

Ivy's doldrums made her cantankerous through planning sessions with Judith Binder, who had arrived in Hoonah full of fresh ideas. Judith appeared quite startled by the newly moody Ivy.

Good to put her in her proper place. I am the senior teacher here. Ivy was ashamed that she was enjoying her case of the morbs.

"We can paint all the walls white again," tried Judith.

"No. Colors are better for the children."

"We can have one open area so the grades can intermix," suggested Judith.

"No. Now that there are two of us, we can separate them for better efficiency."

"Harold could build desks in two sizes to fit..."

"No. The little ones should have benches at a table to get used to working together, don't you think? Then the older ones will feel rewarded by desks of their own."

Fortunately, the two teachers came together on who would teach what. They decided Judith would educate the youngest children and Ivy the seventh grade and above.

Reverend Harold, along with two Tlingit fathers, began building half-walls in the schoolroom to separate the two age groups; the teachers would still be able to see each other over the walls in order to eyeball the whole room. As the men finished in each area, Ivy and Judith scrubbed it and added fresh paint. Ivy had to give in here, since all the paint the government sent was white or a bleak military green.

Outdoors, Harold's work crew constructed the low benches and tables for the little students. Ivy could hear the reverend rattling on in English about the efficacy of various woods for building. Ivy considered telling him the Tlingits neither understand nor paid much attention. But they were diligent workers, and the schoolroom was being revitalized, so why interrupt progress? Ivy felt herself mellowing out. She was not one to maintain a slump for long. She even praised the flowery "Welcome Students" that Judith drew in colored chalk on the school's only blackboard. Ivy was beginning to like the reverend's tiny wife and even tolerate the reverend.

It was dark when *Yashee* docked. Ivy opened the door to Maki and a crewman, who carried a Tlingit into the patient room. Leona and Flower followed them immediately, while another crewman unloaded their luggage.

In time, Maki dropped off a bag of salt for Cook. Ivy was writing lesson plans at the kitchen table. Maki reported, "Leona said to tell you that she and Flower are settling their patient, then she'd be along for a chin wag."

Cook, who was about to leave for the night, turned back to the counter. She was a noiseless Tlingit woman who used to cook on fishing vessels until she knifed a man who pushed his luck once too often. Because she was a good cook, the fishing fleet hated to let her go, but even at sea, a good meal wasn't worth a fillet knife to the neck. Ivy felt fortunate that the weathered sea witch liked working with women, even to the point of helping out with cleaning now and then. And Cook put up with men as long as she didn't have to speak to them very often.

Cook served Maki and Ivy the fresh frybread that she must have meant for breakfast.

Maki stared at it. "Frybread? Did a Navajo pass by this way?"

Cook, who almost liked the ranger, admitted to some English. "No. My secret. Navajo know nothing."

The bread was crisp, greasy, and sweetened with honey.

"Go on home, Cook. I'll clean up," Ivy said.

After Cook left, Maki asked, "What do you suppose her frybread secret might be?"

Ivy answered, "Bear grease instead of pig lard, I suppose. Don't guess I want to know."

They heard Leona bustle out of the clinic and enter the kitchen. "Do I smell something hot and sweet?"

"You mean other than me?" Maki asked.

The women exchanged an exaggerated roll of their eyes. Then Ivy said, "Have a big piece of this. Keep me from eating it all. And tell me about your trip."

"Okay," Leona said. She nattered on like a tour guide, covering her journey south with all the autumn color, and her first sighting of a bear thanks to Maki, and the hurt she felt for Flower, and had Ivy ever heard such a goose as that honking Mrs. McCormack, and the rescue of Edensaw, regardless of the skipper's opinion about that. "There are no sanatoriums anywhere around, so I had to bring him here. Jessica warned me it would happen sometimes."

When Leona finally wound down, Ivy asked, "So I take it, it went well?"

"Oh, Ivy. It was wonderful. I love being here, feeling useful," Leona said. "But now, to bed I think." She picked up her frybread and headed toward the stairs. "Thank you, Maki, for helping Flower and me."

The room seemed quiet. Ivy said, "Guess I'll wait until morning to tell her the doctor's coming next week. Where you on your way to, Maki?"

"Glacier Bay, in the morning. A slide knocked down some timber, so we'll check it out, make sure it's stable. There are some trapping cabins up in that area. Probably our last run of the season into those waters." Maki pulled a metal flask from a vest pocket and added a swig to Ivy's coffee as well as his own. "But we don't leave 'til morning. If you'd like company tonight." He leered in her direction, twirling an invisible mustache.

"Maki. I'm the oldest lady in the territory. Closer to fifty than forty, if you must know. You should find yourself a fresher face to kiss, don't you think?"

"You mean like that young nurse?"

"Well, maybe."

"She's a child, Ivy. I prefer a little age to my whiskey. Smooth. Nothing harsh, not so raw."

Ivy smiled, thinking Reverend Harold and Judith might not agree after her behavior this week. "Yes, well, I can be plenty harsh apparently. And don't be taking your hiking boots off."

"Not even to visit the storeroom?"

"Not even. Flower's here for the night. Plus Leona. Neither has picked up their chamber pot yet, so it would be one interruption after another."

Maki laughed, slipped off his chair and onto the knee that didn't bother him. "For the hundredth time, will you marry me, Ivy?"

"For the hundredth time, no."

He sighed and stood. "So. Until next time I come this way?"

She stood and hugged him. "I will hold that thought."

When Maki was gone, a blushing Leona returned to the kitchen. "I ... I forgot my chamber pot and came back for it. I'm sorry, Ivy. I'm not a snoop. But I couldn't help overhearing. Maki wants to marry you?"

"No."

"But ..."

"If I said yes, he'd bolt like Man o' War. We've played this game for a decade, have Maki and I."

"He seems such a good man."

"Which doesn't make me a good woman." Ivy felt old hurts threaten. "It's a long story which I will tell you one winter evening when we are snowed in. Everyone up here has secrets, Leona. Including you, I imagine."

They cleared the table, washed the few dishes, and went to their rooms.

CHAPTER SIX

August 16, 1946
Rome Coleridge

So his fabled Aunt Leona had dark secrets. Rome smiled to himself as he walked to Central Motors Parts to pick up the bookmobile. The jolly mechanic announced the DeSoto was now right as rain. Rome wondered how many idioms for "it works" the man knew, but he drove away before getting another one stuck in his brain.

Rome had never really thought about women having independent lives before. The women he knew liked to have babies, make clothes, cook three squares each day, and prepare potluck casseroles for the church. At least that's what he'd always believed. His mother had taught his sisters all that stuff.

But were women really happy to wash men's dirty underwear? These two, his aunt and Ivy, lived independent lives two decades ago, without men to tell them what to do. Maybe a lot of women were like that. Maybe Barbara was that way.

He stopped to let three arguing geese cross the road in front of him. "Huh!" he suddenly burst out. *Were Leona and Ivy and Barbara, what was the word, Sapphists?*

Maybe that's why his family never talked about Aunt Leona. But no. He honked at the honking geese to move them along, then he put the bookmobile in gear again. His people wouldn't have heard of such a thing as a homosexual woman. He'd only discovered it himself after he joined the army. That grunt from New York had those pictures he passed around in the trenches.

The shell blasted the guy's head clean off, leaving the rest of him frozen in the mud, his arms still clutching the M1 Garand. I swallowed hysterical laughter, thinking the body should get up and run in circles, like a headless chicken. Then the guy's buddy dug the dog-eared deck of erotic cards out of the dead man's pocket. When he saw me watching, he yelled over the din, "These shouldn't be sent home with the rest of his belongings to his mother."

No, not the type of thing the mother of a dead boy wanted to see. But now Rome wondered if that view of a woman wasn't quite right, the idea that a man could shield her from grief. His unknown aunt and Ivy seemed to be changing his view of women in general. Rome decided they were damned complex. And tough.

He thought about the nurses at the field hospitals in Salerno, covered in blood and fighting to save enough of a life to evacuate. Those women knew the truth of war. They had a more accurate vision of what could happen than the propaganda that green young men carried onto the battlefield.

Rome could see the truth of that now. Mothers didn't believe that war bonds or war posters would close the open wounds of their sons. Women fought against war not because they were weak, but because they could foresee the results, the gaping holes in their hearts where their boys had been. It was a new thought for Rome.

His own mother died in the fire before Rome came home from war. But he had no doubt she would have changed his bandages, grappled with his physical therapy, and taught Rome how to function after he'd left a limb behind in Italy.

His father would have done no such thing. Maybe laughed at Rome fumbling around. Rome felt a cringe as he drove home to his rented space above a garage tucked behind a farmhouse. Well, he was doing okay on his own. A home nurse kept the wound clean till he could manage it on his own. He was getting along.

The owners of the garage let him keep the bookmobile inside. He reloaded it for another run tomorrow. Going through his stacks, he tried to find adventures involving women that his aunt or Ivy might have read as young girls. But he only came up with things like *Kidnapped* and *Captains Courageous* and *The Mark of Zorro*. Why didn't the library send him adventures about women? Hadn't women liked to write back then? He decided to ask his supervisor why he had no stories involving daredevil heroines.

Rome wasn't a bookworm or anything. He had this job because he only had one arm, not because he was a mobile library himself. True, he had started enjoying books more than before the war. It helped the evenings go by faster.

He climbed the staircase up the outside of the garage to his quarters. It was a small kitchen, a living area with his bed, plus a bathroom with a tub and a toilet. It was the first place with indoor facilities that Rome ever had. He thought an indoor toilet was an eighth marvel of the world.

When he opened his icebox, he saw that his landlady had left a plate of fried chicken for him. The only positive thing about being an amputee was how many women felt the need to feed him.

August 22, 1946
Rome Coleridge

It was so hot the ice melted in their limeade as soon as Rome added more chips from the block in Ivy's icebox. Even on the porch the breeze was dead. Rome noticed that Ivy was not knitting. Maybe the weight of the blankets she made was finally too much heat for her. But still, her blouse's long sleeves were buttoned to the cuff.

"Aren't you hot, Ivy? I'd help you roll your sleeves, but it isn't a skill for a one-armed man."

She pulled back, spine as straight as a church lady. "No, thank you. You aren't the only one with wounds, you know."

He looked at her closely, maybe for the first time, what with all old ladies looking pretty much alike to him. He realized she didn't really look so fragile as others. What did she mean by wounds? As tight-lipped as she now appeared, twitching the swing ever so slowly with a toe while she sipped her limeade, he certainly wasn't going to ask.

Maybe it was the squareness of her shoulders that made her so regal. He'd never seen her settle in the way so many seniors did, as if they melted after sitting too long. She did not have that old lady smell, in fact if anything she smelled like Lilies of the Valley, a scent so delicate he found it incongruous on this tough, opinionated woman. She should smell more like deep forest than flowery meadow. Or maybe Eau de Wrought Iron.

Ivy's cheekbones were more pronounced than they would have been in her youth. The skin of her cheeks had begun the inevitable downward slide. Still, her smile had a touch of magic that warmed him like the sun, even though her eyes could penetrate like darts. She had a presence that some people never achieved, himself included. Maybe his aunt, young as she was when she met Ivy, had marveled, too. Ivy Bolton was a woman strong enough to carry another person's secrets. He felt the pull to divulge all to her.

"No man has stared at me with such concentration since I danced at the Moose Turd Tavern in Juneau," Ivy said, interrupting his reverie.

Moose Turd? She must be kidding. "Well," said Rome. "I was probably having less lecherous thoughts than those boys back then. But you're still a fine-looking woman, Ivy."

"That kind of talk will get you a second slice of peach pie."

He never said no to such a treat. "Being an attractive woman on your own in 1920s Alaska must have been damn dangerous."

"Yes, it could be. But not so much as you think. It was assumed that a single woman wasn't up in that country unless she had a sad story down here to escape. Some men avoided us for no other reason. Damaged goods, you know. Others were very protective. Reverend Harold, bless him, felt a need to be sure Judith, Leona, and I were all safe and sound, even though I could outshoot him any day of the week. Sure, some men were trouble. And some women were bound to find them. Your aunt struggled with that."

"I've been thinking lately about women, because of your story about Aunt Leona. Before the war, I never gave it any thought but what marriage was a woman's only goal. Kids. You know. But you and Leona tell a different story. I guess that's true for Barbara, too."

"Did you talk with her again? Give her a chance? Have you been in touch?"

"No, no, and no. Saw no reason to. After I went to war, I had little time to give it much thought. I wrote once. Okay, twice. But letters weren't coming and going from Italy as regular as the tides. And since I came back a cripple, I guess she was right to get out when the gettin' was good."

"Are you aware how thick-headed you are?" Ivy asked.

Rome snorted. "Good thing I'm not thin-skinned, or I wouldn't be on this porch with you."

"Did your parents die in the fire before your brother Paris was killed?"

He was getting used to her rampant curiosity. Rome nodded. "Parry got his at Omaha Beach. That was after my baptism by fire in Italy."

The battle raged. Confusion terrified me, everyone. Explosions so close. I couldn't use my rifle. Soldiers ran us over, ragged Italian boys, some with no shoes and eyes already dead. Must stop them! But I couldn't use my rifle. What the fuck?

I looked at the gun. My left hand wouldn't support the barrel. Then I saw I had no left hand. I fainted from blood loss, shock, fatigue.

Rome made a noise, half cry, half grunt as he left the battlefield behind, but carried the memory of it to Ivy's porch. He sucked in a deep breath.

Ivy put a hand on his knee. "Tell me."

For the first time since it happened, he poured his story into the willing ears of a woman nearly three times his age.

"I was found by the body snatchers. They carried me on their stretcher, dodging rounds of fire to get me behind the lines to the casualty collection point. They put my stretcher on a jeep with five others, then drove miles through insufferable noise, a village of broken walls, children begging for help. I don't remember it all, mostly the pain and the odor of my own waste. They dumped me at the tent hospital, gave me massive doses of morphine and whatever. I can still smell the other filthy men stacked around me. Hear their shrieks. Some of that crying must have been me."

In the pause that followed, Ivy sighed. "Oh Rome. Who wouldn't yell his head off?"

"A sawbones cut away everything left dangling below my left elbow. He wrapped that joint tight. Told me I was lucky to have it. I'd have some use of it after rehab."

"But you don't have it now," Ivy observed.

Rome shrugged the shoulder with no arm. "I was shuffled aside to await transport with the others who would never fight again. Men without legs, without eyes, shattered spines, faces wrapped in gauze. Non-priority soldiers. "

"Non-priority?"

"We knew who we were. We were the g.d.s.o.b amputees that Patton had in mind when he said to let us go to hell since we were 'no g.d. use to us anymore.'"

The two silenced themselves and listened to the balm of summer birds, sandlot baseball, childhood laughter.

When he could control his voice, Rome continued. "So there I was, an inconvenience to shove aside until those who could be patched together were returned to fight. Finally, I got space on an air transport to an army hospital in French Morocco. By the time I arrived, my wound was infected, and they had no penicillin. I had two more amputations, just ahead of disease galloping up my arm. When it was over, the entire arm was gone."

He tried for a bite of peach pie, but his hand trembled, and the sweet morsel dropped to the porch floor. "'No g.d. use to us anymore.' That's what the General said, Ivy."

August 18, 1946
Ivy Bolton

Ivy knew it was impossible to talk someone out of a dark place until he was good and ready to be gently led. Rome wasn't ready.

After he left, she cleaned the crumbs from her porch floor. She'd seen a lot in her years, but this wounded young man battered her heart. He wasn't ready to hear that what made Patton a good general did not necessarily make Patton a good human being. Rome wouldn't hear her if she told him he was too young to know there was always hope. He wouldn't believe that the time would come when his missing arm would not make him feel second rate. Rome wasn't ready.

But he'd taken the first step. He'd talked about it. He'd said aloud so much of the pain he shoved deep inside. Grievances needed the light of day before they could shrivel away.

The evening was still too hot. That, and the sorrow of the conversation, drained her. Ivy went inside and closed the door. She found the Lux Radio Theatre on her dial, removed her blouse and skirt, and sat down in her slip in front of her Emerson oscillating fan. She lifted her letterbox from the three-tiered table beside her, and when the drama went to commercials, she continued a letter to Poppy.

Rome is in trouble. I think it's my duty to help the boy if I can. I owe at least that. Nothing wrong with doing a little investigation on his behalf. I have other things to tell him one of these days when he's ready to hear them.

Meanwhile, I know ladies who know ladies. Somebody will have been Nancy Coleridge's friend in a church group or a sewing circle or the Junior League or the Extension. That somebody might know who this Barbara person is.

Rome may not be ready. But he will be. And if Barbara is still interested, what's the hurt in helping paths to cross?

CHAPTER SEVEN

September 20, 1921
Leona Herkimer

Every day of Leona's first weeks in Hoonah, angry waves of rain slapped the little village in its face and left rivers of mud at its feet. Leona had not really seen the town before her trip to Tanakee Springs. Even if the deluge had let up, it wouldn't have mattered much to her. She'd spent every daylight hour shadowing Jessica, learning as much about running a clinic as she could.

The morning after her return to Hoonah on the *Yashee,* she awoke to bright sun. After checking her consumptive patient and turning him over to Flower for a couple of hours, she announced to Ivy at breakfast, "I brought sun back from Angoon. I believe I'll tour Hoonah before I open the clinic this morning."

"May I come with you? Be your guide for such an exhaustive tour?" asked Ivy. "Nobody stays indoors here when the sun decides to shine."

"I was hoping you'd come along." Leona ate her egg. Only if Cook was not baking did they have such luxuries for breakfast. Local chickens were a fierce and independent brood who did not give up their eggs gladly.

"After meeting Mrs. McCormack, I need to spend time with a kinder colleague."

"Perhaps relations between Tlingits and whites in Tanakee Springs are rawer than here," Ivy observed. "Tlingit people here have lived with the effrontery of white folks since the first Russians paid them a visit twelve decades ago. They've become fairly used to being informed their beliefs make no sense. Expect them to be openly polite to us, friendly even. But I wonder how deep that goes. I couldn't stand us if I were in their place."

They set out after the kitchen was cleared. Leona opted to leave her boots behind, in favor of shoes and a full-skirted dress that came to mid-calf. She wore her nursing apron and cap to give the locals a visual purpose for her presence. The Hoonah population was primarily Tlingit with a smattering of white trappers, failed prospectors, retired fishermen, and workers from the cannery. There were several Chinese families, experts at canning salmon all along the Pacific Northwest coast. "Without my long johns, I feel quite scandalously unclad!" Leona said to Ivy, taking a spin out the doorway onto the boardwalk.

"Good thing I'm coming along. You may need a chaperone."

"A chaperone?"

"You'll see."

The government building was at one end of the village. The row of structures along the shore was raised on stilts, requiring several steps up to the boardwalk. Each structure looked nearly identical to its plain neighbor, and they all had steeply pitched roofs.

"Stilts protect us from high tides and the roof peaks from the weight of winter snow," Ivy explained as they began their stroll. Now low tide, a wide pebbly beach sloped down to the water's edge. Enormous canoes rested there, in close quarters to the dock where *Yashee, Small Fry,* or fishing boats rested when they were in town.

The buildings formed a row like dominoes following the curve of the shore. The Presbyterian Mission was at the far end from the government building. A second row of structures hugged close behind the first and offered a trading post, a general store, a restaurant and hotel combination, as well as a tavern.

As the two women walked, a few native children ran on ahead of them, apparently announcing them in all the stores and houses along the way. Leona soon noticed people leaving the buildings to stand along the boardwalk and stare or smile at her. She said to Ivy, "What are they doing? Do they expect a parade?"

"Leona, you are the parade. The women who haven't met you yet are very eager to. They know you're here to help their children, and that Jessica vouches for you. A nurse means less pain for many of them. You are a godsend in a life that has few enough pleasures."

A large group of men emerged from the trading post and tavern. They lined up one after another, orderly and civil. Some nodded, some doffed hats and bowed, others sucked rounded bellies back inside their dungarees to improve their profiles. Suspenders over grimy long john tops was the favorite look of the day although Leona saw several wool plaid or deerskin shirts. Most of the men appeared too shy to make eye contact. And two or three very handsome young ones, tall and muscular, made the rest of them look quite like a different species.

"Why are these men staring at us?" Leona's cheeks felt warm.

"Not at us . . . they know the hands-off situation with me. They've tried; they've failed. But each is hoping you might marry him."

"What? How preposterous!" Leona huffed under the gaze of so many eyes.

Ivy laughed. "Leona, you are about the only single white woman within miles who is neither hooker nor nun. That makes you marriageable material. And you even happen to be attractive. This is the biggest news in the tavern and cannery for months. Like I said, you may need a chaperone just to walk the street."

"They're drinking too much giggle juice in that tavern if they think I'm interested." Leona remembered the taverns in Tenakee Springs and wondered again about their trade. "If they can't serve alcohol, what do they do?"

"They serve alcohol. In whatever dose cures whatever ails you. They call themselves pharmacies, and that makes it legal. Legal-ish. But only to whites."

Leona laughed, but it was cold comfort. Now she knew where to come if she needed to. As soon as the thought formed, she chastised herself. She wouldn't need alcohol if she didn't drink her brandy, and she wasn't going to do that.

Ignoring the mostly polite men, Leona and Ivy walked on. The nurse looked up at the great sweep of forest rising to high cliffs behind them. "Looks like two rows is as wide as Hoonah can ever be."

Ahead of them, far up the shore, was the cannery. Most of the newer homes in town were for the management and their wives. The rest of the buildings were primarily Tlingit family dwellings. "Several generations might reside in one. Kind of a carry-over from the way their ancients lived," Ivy said.

"I saw that in Angoon. It looked less settled than here."

"Probably so. Angoon was burned to the ground not that many years ago. Here the tribe exists fairly well with the cannery up the way. Tlingit fishermen can sell big catches to it. Even some of the women work there. The town has less poverty than many of the other villages."

Leona was astounded by the artwork painted on external walls or carved into totem poles. She'd seen the weird, devilish looking animals in Juneau, as well. "They worship animals?"

"No, I don't think so. But they believe every living thing shares a bond with every other. The Russians and now the Presbyterians in the form of Harold try to convince them there's only one God. At least the half of them who outlived smallpox."

"You sound bitter, Ivy."

"Do I? Mmm, maybe more of a realist. I know education and medicine are improving their lives, so I do not feel like a blight. And they seem to agree. They accept that you take care of them when their own medicine can't, and that I educate them to get along with us. But they've paid a helluva price to receive what little we give back."

As Ivy predicted, everyone not staring at them was outdoors washing windows, sweeping the boardwalk, lifting their faces to the sun. A group of weavers made room for the two to sit with them on logs and kegs in the warm daylight. Their hands flew as they wove patterned baskets and hats from spruce root. "They've tried to teach me before," Ivy admitted and gave it another go. Soon she had created a useless pile of small knots. The ladies laughed heartily at her failed craftsmanship.

"Next time, you try it," Ivy said when Leona joined the laughter.

At the mission, Judith was out in front of the rectory, hanging laundry that billowed in the sun. The church next to it was a tidy rectangle, four windows down each side in precise order, with an actual bell tower. As one of the few buildings that had ever been painted, its bright white was a beacon amidst all the other drab walls. Three young orphans played around Judith, two with a ball and the other with a mongrel willing to chase sticks.

"Good morning, Judith," Ivy greeted. "I have a message for you, and Leona, too. Figured I'd tell you both at the same time."

Any news was met with great curiosity in a town so far from the places where news occurred. "What is it?" Leona asked, eager for any gossip. Judith set her bag of clothespins into a laundry basket.

"Dr. Edward Reardon will grace us with his presence next Monday. He is now required to give the school children physicals. I didn't tell you last night, Leona, because you looked like you could use a good night's sleep, and I knew you would worry about this."

"Worry? Of course not. I'm not a worrier. It's time I met the good doctor." The worry churned in her stomach.

"Um, I must get back to the clinic and start the cleaning before more patients arrive."

"I'll be prepared to bring the orphans when I see the boat get to the dock. I assume it will be *Small Fry*," said Judith.

Ivy nodded. "I'll round up the other school kids for the afternoon. We'll keep Dr. Reardon busy."

"How exciting to have a new person to meet." Judith beamed, obviously enjoying a few words with other women.

"Why don't you and Reverend Harold come for supper that evening?" Ivy asked. "I can invite the cannery's manager, too."

Leona felt ready to bolt. She had to get back to work! The doctor was coming in, what, just four days, and here she was lollygagging. When they finally headed back toward the government building she asked Ivy, "Tell me about this doctor. Why does it seem you dislike him? Is he incompetent? An evil troll who drools and eats worms?"

"Oh, no, nothing like that. In fact, he is a rather handsome man. And I've never heard him called incompetent."

"Then what?"

"Well, he's such a … such a *doctor*. High above others, especially you nurses. He treated Jessica like his personal slave, and I resent that. As did she. I believe she told you that he rarely comes this way, requiring instead that you go to him. I can't imagine that this new requirement of physicals for school children has pleased him."

"So I get this ill-tempered fellow even iller-tempered than usual," said Leona as they climbed the steps to the government building. "I'm glad you're easy to get along with, Ivy."

"Ha! Wait till you hear me the first day of class. Such a monster I am with geography."

Three patients awaited Leona. Two brothers had fallen from rocks onto more rocks. A beleaguered mother sat between them, keeping them from kicking each other. "Bad boys," seemed to be the extent of her English.

"Yes. They are." Leona launched a stern glare in their direction. They directed puppy dog eyes at her. It made her laugh. *So much for severity.*

The third patient was an ancient named Farley with a clear case of alcohol disease. He shuffled to the clinic now and then, mostly to dry out in a bed more comfortable than the wet pebbles under the dock. Jessica had warned Leona about him and others like him. "Let him sleep, dry him out if you can, then see if he'll eat anything. He'll be gone after that until the next time."

At the moment he was passed out, snoring in a clinic chair. Leona believed he could wait while she took on the children. Flower helped them remove their anorak shirts, pulling the thin hides over their heads. One did indeed have a broken arm, but the other appeared to be more bruised than broken.

Leona patched the boys, then she and Flower wrestled the drunken Farley into a tub. He smelled fetid enough to make their eyes water. The nurse knew his teeth must be bad, but he was far too gone to let her look. They washed him down, found him a donated shirt and pants, then struggled him into a patient bed.

"Now then," Leona said. "If Edensaw feels up to it, let's take him to a chair outside. Fresh air will do him good. And while he's out there, we can disinfect this whole area. Then we should air out the extra bedroom. Dr. Reardon will be here next week, and he may need the room."

The days passed quickly. With elbow grease from all involved, not only the clinic but the entire government building sparkled. The night before the doctor's arrival, Leona scrubbed herself from head to toe. In the morning, she put on her last new apron. "I am ready to meet this terror of a doctor. He will not find fault with me."

That's when all hell broke loose.

First, the family from Angoon arrived. They crowded into the antiseptic patient room, a family of eight or ten, the youngest several jumping on the beds. In the confusion, Leona did not get them counted. They over-spilled with joy on seeing how improved Edensaw looked. Hugging commenced all around, and gifts were piled for Leona, including a large basket of clams.

While this was going on, a man rushed in with a youngster in his arms, a girl who was sobbing. Leona hustled the exuberant Tlingit family out of the patient room as fast as she could, accepting their thanks as they took Edensaw back home to convalesce. Flower gave them a stern warning about fresh air, while Leona turned her attention to the little girl. She asked the father to place the child on the examination table.

"Her name's Wren," he said. He was white under the hat, mustache, and beard, or so she thought. Maybe one of the trappers who ran lines in the woods. From the look of the girl, her mother would be a native. *Where is she?* It was rare for men to bring in children.

Leona gently undressed the girl and tried to keep her still, but Wren writhed from pain around her belly button and toward the lower right side.

"Started a couple days back. Thought it was collywobbles. Now it's worse." The father removed his hat once he lay the child down.

"Her fever is high. Too high."

Wren vomited, targeting Leona's new apron.

"When she started heaving up her boot heels like that, I picked her up, and we came here."

"Her belly is so swollen."

Leona knew it was a ruptured appendix or one that was about to go. What she didn't know was what to do. As she wiped down her new apron, her mind raced. This was not a nurse's province; to cut a patient open required a doctor. And one was on his way that day.

But could the girl wait? She might die if Leona didn't act.

Leona had seen the surgery done several times in the hospital in Washington. She had even assisted. She was pretty sure she could open the abdomen and remove the appendix or clean out the infection before peritonitis killed the girl.

Pretty sure.

It was no choice, not really. She couldn't let a child die. Leona prepared for surgery. "Flower! Please get what surgical equipment we have ready. Sir, you must go to the waiting room now. We have your daughter in good hands."

Silently, the man bent to kiss Wren's forehead and left the room.

"Now then, Wren, we will put a mask over your face. It might look scary, but very soon, you'll feel no pain. You'll go to sleep and wake up good as new."

"NURSE!!!"

Leona leaped. Flower leaped.

"MOVE AWAY FROM THAT CHILD."

Leona and Flower backed away.

The doctor had arrived. He took one look at the child, touching her belly ever so lightly. "BRING ME HOT WATER."

Flower was already on her way with a bucket of it. He removed his coat, rolled up his sleeves, and washed. "Now I begin." He frowned at Leona, but at least he stopped yelling. "Scalpel, nurse. We will talk about discipline later."

Well, thought Leona. *So far, so good.* She ceased to care if she smelled of a child's vomit, this close to the doctor's stuck-up nose.

The surgery went well. Wren's appendix had not yet ruptured, so a deadly infection could be avoided.

That's what's important, Leona thought, trying to soothe herself as the operation progressed. Nonetheless, as she assisted the doctor, she seethed at his suggestion of discipline. *My hands in stocks for the villagers to mock? An extended time under a dunce cap? Enclosure in an iron maiden?*

She had never been good at keeping her emotions to herself, so she decided to utter as few words as possible. She grabbed a few glances when he wasn't looking. He wasn't unattractive for a pinheaded grumbletonian. Dark eyes, aquiline nose. She watched his slender hands as they flew through the surgery, precise, with no wasted motion.

At one point, he appeared to eye his surroundings enough to notice the area where Edensaw had been. "Is that an unmade bed over there at this time of day?"

"Yes, it is."

"Is that a bucket of clams on the floor?"

"Yes, it is."

Today, of all days, Farley the boozer staggered into the room, chose a patient bed, and crawled into it. Seconds later, a rattling snore serenaded the surgery.

"Did a sozzled old man just put himself to bed?"

"Yes, he did."

Leona began to think the disciplinary hearing might go on for a week or more once it began. A firing squad maybe. But when the surgery was complete, there was no time to talk. They were rushed to begin the physical exams now that their timetable was shot. They could all hear Judith and Ivy trying to calm the orphans and other children in the waiting room. "Sounds like a loony bin out there," Dr. Reardon said.

"Actually, just excited children." Leona noticed Flower make a shhh! gesture in her direction, finger to her lips.

The goal of the government-required physical assessment was to establish a baseline, a medical history that would grow with the child and increase the paperwork on file. After a time, the doctor, the nurse, and the assistant settled into an efficient rhythm. Flower measured height and weight while Leona checked pulse and blood pressure, and together they filled in the forms as the physical progressed. The doctor evaluated eyes, ears, nose, and throat plus lymph nodes, heart, joints, and spine.

Adding the clinic's completed inoculations to the paperwork, Leona asked, "Do you have the new diphtheria vaccine?"

"How do you know of such a thing?" He looked at her steadily, as if seeing her for the first time.

She couldn't take much more of holding her tongue. "I can read, Dr. Reardon."

There was a pause before he answered, "Logical, nurse ... Leona, isn't it? Of course, it is also logical that if I had it, I would be using it."

"Yes, that would be logical. I can see that now."

"Why would you think Alaska would be at the forefront of receiving such a miracle?"

"I thought a person of your stature might find performing a miracle to be rather a cakewalk."

He snorted, maybe in good humor but probably not. Leona knew she must sweeten up. As hard as it was for Alaska to get nurses, it was nearly impossible to attract doctors. One word in the wrong government ear, and Dr. Reardon could have Leona shipped out of the territory faster than a canned salmon, back Outside where she never again wanted to be.

That thought surprised her. She never again wanted to see the land of Outside. Alaska was her true home.

September 20, 1921
Ivy Bolton

By the time the medical crew was finished, it was evening. While Flower and Leona set the clinic to rights, Ivy showed Dr. Reardon to the room they had prepared for him. "It is too late for you to return to Juneau this evening, and the local hotel is rather an adventure. I'm told someone once shot from the restaurant below through a bed above. I believe it was unoccupied at the time."

Dr. Reardon laughed. "I'm sure I'll be fine, Mrs. Bolton."

"There are towels and hot water in your room. The necessary is out back."

"Yes, I've heard it called The Bog. Thank you for your hospitality."

She sought criticism in his dark eyes but saw none. His smile seemed genuine enough. He appeared to know how to behave in polite society when outside his own medical domain. "You're most welcome, Dr. Reardon. Jessica left behind her regards to you."

"A good nurse, Jessica. Sorry to lose her."

Ivy felt her jaw start to drop so she quickly clenched it. Through her teeth, she said, "Jessica would have liked to know you thought so."

"Really?" He looked surprised. "I would have thought she knew it. Otherwise, why would I have worked with her? She trained this new one, did she?"

"For a few days, yes, but not long enough to impart all the lessons you might wish." Ivy gave him a squint that she hoped approximated a warning. "We are all quite pleased with Leona. A hard worker, devoted to her charges. We would miss her if she were to leave so soon after Jessica departed."

She could not tell if the "hmm" noise he made was one of surprise or contemplation. "Please join us for dinner when you have refreshed from your day, Doctor. There are others who will enjoy you, and any news of the world you might have to share."

Before dinner was served, Flower told Ivy that the doctor and the nurse were not exactly happy with each other. She was not sure who'd taken the first skirmish. "Leona is not in awe of the doctor. She gives him more trouble than Tlingit women give a chief."

Oh dear. Ivy prepared herself for a fractious evening.

The cannery manager arrived with his wife and a pre-Prohibition bottle of Old Grand-Dad. With delight, the men shared the recognizable whiskey brand straight, and some of the women tamed it as Old Fashioned cocktails. They had the bitters and sugar, but without the required lemon peel, they improvised with a drop of sour gooseberry juice.

Reverend Harold volubly enjoyed his glass. "Ahhh! Imagine a quaff of such quality. Most around here is homemade. Did you know, ladies, that cocktails are now raging in popularity as a means to hide bad alcohol with their honey or sugar?"

Ivy, Judith, and the cannery manager's wife sipped while Leona and Flower abstained. Ivy understood about Flower. Whiskey was illegal for everyone but most especially for natives. Ivy had not realized Leona was a teetotaler.

Dr. Reardon noticed as well. "You will not give it a try, nurse? A small amount can be quite medicinal."

"Do I appear in need of medicine?" Leona placed a hand to her cheek. "Am I flushed?"

Ivy wanted to warn Leona to tone it down. The doctor was being civil, and her sass with such a powerful personage could hurt her.

But he seemed to accept it in good spirits. "No, not at all. You appear quite agreeable. But it was a long and difficult day."

The reverend proclaimed, "Quite a few whiskey bottles now proclaim 'For Medicinal Use Only.' Makes it legal for pharmacies to sell."

Dr. Reardon continued to speak to Leona. "You do not imbibe, nurse?"

Reverend Harold had not finished his lecture. "Pharmacists carry pint-size bottles in small boxes to look more like cough syrup and less like firewater."

Leona spoke. "No, I don't, Dr. Reardon. But I will enjoy my cup of wildflower tea and honey." She toasted him with her teacup and a smile.

Ivy could tell how forced it was. Could His Highness tell, too?

When the meal finally began, the cannery manager and the reverend launched an extended discussion of the relative merits of coho, sockeye, humpback, chinook, and chum salmon.

Ivy was aware that both Judith and the manager's wife could roll their eyes without their husbands' notice. *Kindred spirits,* she thought, then endeavored to put an end to the fish tales. "Tell us about your background, Dr.

Reardon. How did you find your way to Alaska?" She felt it would be a safe subject. But it soon devolved to a variation of the recruitment poster, "Daddy, what did YOU do in the Great War?"

"I was a military doctor. Mucked about with the doughboys in France, saving them from the Kaiser, then the Spanish Flu. When I returned, I could not face settling again in San Francisco. I needed elbow room after so much proximity in the trenches. And freedom to manage my own time for a while. Alaska seemed perfect when I arrived."

Ivy wondered if he still felt that way. Or did I hear a bit of wistfulness? Does Alaska no longer seem perfect?

Reverend Harold served as a chaplain, but the government considered the cannery manager too valuable to the food chain to send him overseas. Canned food was as vital to soldiers as their helmets, so he served by keeping production in step with the fishing boats.

During the war, Leona was in school, Ivy taught in Hoonah, and Judith gave up giving piano lessons to drive an ambulance. Like all stalwart American women, they rolled bandages, knitted socks, cultivated their own food in victory gardens so they didn't take it from the mouths of fighting men.

Flower, who was still a schoolgirl taught by Ivy during the war, gathered treats for packages that went to the Tlingit boys who signed up. Natives bought war bonds, and the women joined the Red Cross. The war left its scar on Hoonah but wreaked far less devastation than Spanish Flu. Not since smallpox had so many in the tribe perished.

Ivy silently blessed Reverend Harold when he pulled the conversation back from the war years to the explosion of decadent behavior afoot on the land. "I mean, jazz? No sense to it at all. No rules. Bah!"

Ivy laughed. "Women bobbing their hair and shortening their skirts."

Leona joined in. "Smoking cigarettes! A total breakdown of moral fiber."

"Personally, I like a lady with pizzazz," said the cannery manager. He lifted the last of his whiskey and toasted, "To the gal with a little sway in her sashay!"

Everyone else at the table appeared to be too low on liquids to "here, here" such a toast. They dabbed napkins to their lips, mumbled compliments on the food, commented on the pleasantness of a few days with sun.

Mr. and Mrs. Cannery Manager were not speaking to each other at the end of the evening. Other than that, Ivy thought things had gone better than they might have. Leona hadn't set the doctor on fire, and he hadn't called her a disappointment. Maybe there was hope for the Hoonah medical team.

September 20, 1921
Leona Herkimer

Leona would not dream of creating a scene at Ivy's dinner party. But, oh! she wished to get Dr. Reardon alone afterwards to discover what sort of penalty she would pay for attempting a surgery without him.

It didn't happen. Maybe he meant to discuss it in the morning before his journey back to Juneau.

In the night she lay awake, worrying. Why did that pesky cannery manager bring whiskey on the very night she could have used the entire bottle? Not that she would have tippled anyway. She'd always found false courage loosened her jaw ... its mere proximity made it that much harder to keep it shut. As it was, the doctor needed no more ammunition about her to be critical.

Tossing in total wakefulness, she heard someone at the building's back door. She donned her robe and went down the stairs. A Tlingit boy said, "Baby."

Leona swiftly dressed, gathered her birthing kit, and followed the boy to a home halfway down the row. At least it wasn't far. The mother-to-be was young, healthy. She had come to the clinic for instruction and vitamins in the last weeks. Her own mother and sister planned to assist.

Leona spread out her materials and placed a rubber blanket on the bed. She sterilized her implements as the girl bellowed in labor pains.

It was over in three hours. The new mother had a beautiful little boy who was already unruly. The force of his opinions tickled all the women, and while they did not share the same language, they shared the language of new life. Leona felt very much at home.

It was near 3:00 a.m. when she walked through the quiet of a village at rest. She moved slowly from her own weariness, enjoying the soothing sound of gentle waves lapping the shore.

"You've had a busy night."

She did not see the speaker until she zeroed in on the glow of his cigarette. He was on the boardwalk in front of the government building.

"Is that you, Dr. Reardon?"

"It is."

She climbed the stairs and stood next to him. "Hoonah had a population explosion of one in the wee hours."

"Did you need me? You could have called me. I sleep very little."

"It is early for you to be up. And midwifery is one of the procedures we nurses are allowed to perform without supervision."

"Ah," he said, inhaling. "You are peeved with me."

"You read clues as wisely as Sherlock Holmes."

"I remember now using the word 'discipline.' In retrospect, I see that as harsh."

Is he attempting an apology? Leona saw little of him in the cold light of the moon. She was aware of his height and the size of him next to her, but she couldn't work out a single facial feature other than the silhouette of his cheekbones.

Dr. Reardon continued. "But you must know that no surgery is within your purview."

No. Not an apology then.

Leona's pleasure in the evening dissipated. Anger stirred. "That little girl might have died if I had waited."

"But she didn't."

"How was I to know that?" She could hear the frustration in the way her voice rose toward a whine.

"You weren't. But I was. Which is rather the point. You must not allow emotion to cloud your judgment, nurse. You'll find yourself in similar predicaments again and again out here in the wilderness. You are far too valuable to allow all your good decisions to be overwhelmed by one bad one."

Leona was afraid she would cry with the frustration of not fighting back. *Please, no! Predators revel in the weakness of underlings.* She breathed deep twice, then with as much control as she could muster, said, "I understand. But I fear I could not let someone die without trying."

He sighed. "If you take it on yourself to do what you have not been trained for, and have now been warned against, then it would be my duty to have you recalled. I do not want to do such a thing. You clearly have admirable abilities, although the clinic was in a bit of a pickle when I arrived. We will let that pass. I am sure you will become a great asset to the people you serve. And wiser as you become more seasoned."

She said nothing. Could he feel the heat from her burning desire to strike him?

He threw the cigarette butt to the ground and stepped on it. "And a great asset to me, Leona. I hope I may call you Leona. Shall we go in now?"

She turned on her heel, stomped up the stairs to her room, and went back to bed. She slept so soundly she did not hear Dr. Reardon depart later in the morning.

CHAPTER EIGHT

September 21, 1921
Leona Herkimer

Leona and Flower straightened the clinic, removed the bucket of clams, and awakened Farley the boozer, sending him on his way. Then they washed the bedding, disinfecting for lice. As they worked, they giggled together at the doctor's expense.

"Is that a bucket of clams?" said Leona in a deepened voice.

"We will serve them for dinner this evening, Doctor," said Flower. Then she borrowed the deep voice. "Is that an unmade bed?"

"I'm just up from my nap," answered Leona. Then, "Are those lice from that sozzled man?"

"What's that crawling about in your hair, Doctor?" With that, they both collapsed on empty patient beds in fits of laughter.

As she wound down, Leona wiped tears from her eyes and noticed the material folded on the foot of the bed. She picked up the gift that Edensaw's family had left for her, a gift she'd overlooked when the doctor arrived. She unfolded it and was astounded by the beauty of the

Chilkat woven tunic with long fringe along the sleeves and hem.

She was speechless, a state quite rare for her.

"It is a type of anorak," explained Flower. "The yarn is made of mountain goat fur and dog hair. Cedar, too, in the weaving."

As the two admired it, Ivy came into the room. "Such tittering I heard all the way from the schoolroom. Making fun of the doctor loud enough for all to hear, for heaven's sake."

"Look, Ivy!" Leona held the exquisite piece in front of herself. "From Edensaw's family."

"Goodness, Leona. How beautiful. Look at these animal patterns. It's quite mysterious how weavers manage such curves on a loom. It's a gift of honor for you."

Leona thought the bold animals of yellow and black were similar to the art she'd admired in the totem poles. She ran her fingers across the tunic lovingly, recognizing the stylized eagles and whales, wondering about the bear . . . or was it a wolverine?

"This is a crest of the Angoon tribe." Flower pointed to the complex design in the center of the bodice. "And all the animals around it are there for your protection."

"It's the finest thing I've ever been given. I will keep it always," Leona said, folding it. A nasty gremlin within her sniped, *Look at this, Dr. Reardon. People trust me just as I am. What gifts have you been given?*

"Yes, keep it. But you must wear it," Flower scolded. She picked it up, shook it loose, and pulled it over Leona's head. "It cannot protect you kept in a drawer."

The fringe hung as low as Leona's knees. "It's so warm," she said, twirling the fringe.

Ivy pointed to the strip of fur around its hood. "That's wolverine, amazing fur. It doesn't freeze even in the greatest cold. Your breath won't cause your face to ice. Doesn't often get that cold here. But if you inoculate villagers to the north this winter, you'll want this under your parka."

Inoculate villagers to the north in the winter? Leona thought Ivy was joking.

On a day soon after school began, Wren and her father stopped by the clinic. Neither looked quite so rough as their last visit. Wren wore a fresh dress, a little oversized with growing room. Leona gave the smiling child a bill of approval, a piece of Black Jack for later, and told her to join Judith's classroom.

When the child looked at her quizzically, Leona amended. “I don’t mean Judith. I mean Mrs. Binder.”

“Oh! Okay.” And off she skipped.

Wren's father had washed his black hair and clipped his beard. Leona could see by the hints of sable brown in it that he had non-native blood. His oval face was Tlingit, but maybe he'd received his sizable nose and gray eyes from long-gone Russian ancestors. He told her his name was Mikhail. "Last name is Elim or Neviarcaurluq if you prefer the Tlingit."

"I fear my Tlingit is not up to Nevi ... Nevi ... well, Mr. Elim it will be."

"I prefer Mikhail." He smiled, then told her he ran traplines on the island. The forest ranger Maki was a friend of his. "I tell you that by way of a credential on my behalf."

Leona chuckled, then said, "I believe Maki would be amused to be someone's good reference. But it certainly works here."

Mikhail gave her a pair of mittens, the rabbit fur to the inside and its supple leather to the out. "They are not strong like fox mitts for heavy outdoor work. But okay for a nurse's delicate hands, going about the village. Your care saved my Wren's life."

"Oh, Mikhail, thank you. They are lovely. But it was the doctor who saved her life."

He looked at her a moment. She read stubborn in that gaze. He said, "I know what I know. Besides, the doctor would look silly in these mittens."

It made her laugh. He might be stubborn, but he was also wise. And funny. And, okay, quite a specimen of male handsomeness. A blush of pleasure started up her neck, not just for Mikhail Elim but for his praise. It made her really think about what she had done. Imagine saving the lives of two young people, both Edensaw and Wren.

Might it be possible to make up for past mistakes?

Leona spent the afternoon humming "You Made Me Love You" until Flower begged her to stop.

September 27, 1921
Ivy Bolton

School was in full swing. For years Ivy had taught all grades, and she'd worried she'd be jealous of turning over one of the reins. That sort of envy could ruin the job for her, not to mention what it would do to Judith.

The opposite happened. Ivy loved the separation into two classes. The partition the reverend built (known to Judith and Ivy as Harold's Wall) was a perfect division between the kindergarten-through-sixth grade and the seventh-through-twelfth. Even when the youngsters were singing, reciting, or otherwise raucous, it did not bother Ivy and her older kids. She found that she could impart more in a day, engage the Tlingit and white children both with their shared needs, but still explore their different histories. She always had projects in mind to intrigue, entertain, educate. Ivy found new joy in teaching.

She grew fond of Judith who, earlier on, struck her as a little too milquetoast. But Ivy soon learned that "reserved" by no means meant "fragile" as Judith nurtured the youngest in the brood, urged them on, and steadfastly kept their tiny noses to a gentle grindstone.

"You have the patience of a saint," Ivy said to her one morning. They often shared tea in the classroom before the children began to arrive. "You're a natural with the tots."

Judith quietly answered, "I just wasn't a natural at having them."

Oh my goodness! I've stepped in a cowpie! Ivy was rarely flustered, but she was now. She exclaimed, "I'm so sorry, Judith. I didn't mean to get too personal."

"Two miscarriages then a hysterectomy." Judith took a tiny sip and shrugged. "I wanted to die, but it was not the Lord's way."

"I am so glad of that. You are invaluable here with the children."

Judith brightened somewhat. "Do you mean that? Thank you for saying so, Ivy. I've worried I'm merely in your way."

"Not at all. The little ones have never had it so good, here or at the orphanage."

"That's why we are here, you see. Harold has been so good to me. He would like to be a father himself, of course. He found us this place, where we would have all the children a person could need. I knew it was perfection from our very first day here."

Harold? Bombastic, know-it-all Harold? The truth of people amazed Ivy.

Judith patted Ivy's hand. "He is not a bad man, Ivy. He has his faults, but another man would have left me for failing in my duty. He has stood by me."

Ivy was distressed that Judith felt a failure. But she also felt chastened regarding Harold's worth. *For damn sure, it's time to nip my opinions in the bud.*

Judith had surprised Leona and Flower, too, Ivy happened to know. When Flower was not available to assist the nurse with a childbirth, Judith often filled in. The reverend's little wife had quickly become indispensable in the school, the clinic, the orphanage, the church.

For the first time in twenty years, Ivy began to wonder if her village could get along just fine without her. Maybe it was time for her to consider returning Outside.

There were people she missed. She'd like current news for a change; the Sacco and Vanzetti murder trial was long over before Hoonah knew it had begun. She'd like to hear a baseball game on those new-fangled radios people had in their houses. She craved walking into a library. Ivy thumbed the frayed collar of her frock and thought how nice it might be to have one of the slinky new dresses with the lowered waistline and raised hem. And dainty slippers instead of work boots on her feet. But the real reason for her thoughts of Outside came in the last batch of mail delivered by *Small Fry*. The letter was written two months earlier by her daughter. Poppy reported that Ivy's husband had died.

It's about time.

CHAPTER NINE

August 28, 1946
Rome Coleridge

Ivy's prodding had sent Rome back to the battlefield the last time he had joined her on the porch. She'd released memories he'd packed away to rot in the attic of his brain. But once started, those memories kept tumbling out. They bit at him like fire ants as they industriously broke down walls he'd constructed months ago. The resulting rubble felt like untrustworthy, dangerous footing.

Clearer memories did not hurt any less. Far from it. But facing his ghosts diminished their power to haunt him. Rome began to wonder if one day he might even feel something like hope again.

This activity in his brain was so new, he wasn't ready to let Ivy poke all the raw spots. Nonetheless, he craved her proximity. "You've bewitched me," he said alone in his bookmobile as he went to pick her up. "You nosy, cantankerous, wonderful old woman."

He'd been so isolated before she pushed herself into his life. She'd never known him whole of body, so he was not a thing of pity to her. She accepted what he was and made him accept it, too. It didn't matter to her that he couldn't shift the vehicle without using his knee on the wheel. That he couldn't lift what another man could lift. That he was clumsy. It was all okay with Ivy. "So it certainly should be okay with you," she had said to him during one of his visits, as though her opinion on his wellbeing was far more important than his own.

She challenged him with her pointed questions and sense of entitlement. Well, turnabout was fair play. He'd ask her a thing or two. One hot morning, he picked her up, and they headed out of town. Wind whistled through the open windows of the bookmobile, swirling wisps of her hair around her head. He saw the gray but also the remains of a honey blond. She'd given up on her hat and now held it in her lap.

Ivy was making his rounds with him today before they had a picnic. What the library didn't know, the library couldn't criticize. Besides, Ivy proved rather helpful filling out the order forms while he distributed books.

"You're smiling at me. Why?" she asked.

"I was just thinking that you're not quite as useful as a left arm, but you're close."

"I was just thinking you got me off that porch in the nick of time. I was taking root. Needed to get out."

Rome laughed as he downshifted to turn from the main road onto a track that disappeared in the woods.

"This probably was a timber road," Ivy observed. Grass grew in its center, but enough vehicles kept its tire paths open. "Maybe a Klallam trail before that."

"Half a dozen families live up this way with double that many littluns. I'm loaded with extra children's books today." Rome slowed the DeSoto, and as it growled its way upward, the cyclone in Ivy's hair lost its violence.

"How far is it?" she asked.

"A fair way. Kinda meanders through the foothills then back to the main road."

"Good. Time for you to tell me more about that French Morocco hospital run by the Allies. Never heard of such a thing."

He was ready for her. "Nope. Not today. It's your turn to spill the beans. Tell me what lured you to Alaska in the first place. And what brought you back."

She went quiet. And stayed that way for an uncomfortably long pause.

"You okay, Ivy? Did I say something wrong?" If he'd upset her, he'd have to bang his head against a tree.

"No, dear boy. But I had to think about it a bit, get things in order. To tell you that story, I must start before the turn of the century. And admit to a crime. All before you were born. This better be a long drive, young man, 'cause you'll be an old man by the time I'm done."

"I'll prepare to go bald and develop a beer belly."

Ivy started with a history lesson. "At the end of the 1890s, a hundred thousand prospectors stampeded to Alaska. Called it the Klondike Gold Rush. It was a gold mine for Port Townsend, too. Considering the town's location, it was one of the last ports of call for many ferries bound to Alaska.

"My husband, Cyrus, owned the Bolton Store, a little mercantile in the lower town. He saw the potential in that golden stampede. Every one of those prospectors needed heavy clothes, lanterns, canned food, gold pans, picks, shovels, tents, and ammunition. Cy took on a money partner named Samuel Daltry to expand the store and stock up the shelves. The quiet Bolton Store became the bustling Daltry & Bolton Provisions."

Ivy looked at Rome and asked, "You sure this is interesting? You losing hair yet? Old people know they bore young people with their stories."

He ran his hand over his head. "Nope, hair still intact. Keep going. How old were you then?"

"Mid-twenties, as I remember. About your age. And content, by and large. I taught school each day, then picked up our daughter from the other teacher's classroom. Poppy was, um, eight at the time."

"Poppy? So another flower in your family."

She looked surprised. "That's right. You've got a good memory for an aging man."

"You've never mentioned having a daughter."

"I haven't always just lived on that porch, you know. I've been around. I have a life."

Rome knew better than to interrupt, and her snit soon ended. "Anyway," she said, "Poppy and I walked to the Bolton Store where I ran the place in the afternoons."

"Mother, wife, teacher, and store keep?" Rome didn't disbelieve it, but he struggled again with the concept that motherhood wasn't enough of a challenge for some women. Women were weird.

"Well, I couldn't draw a salary at the store because it was frowned upon for teachers to make a second income in a family. I clerked and stocked every afternoon and some evenings."

"What about your husband?"

"Oh, he had his skills, but they ran toward bookkeeping and purchasing. Cy used to say I was the sparkplug that made the store a success with the locals. He was amazed how many hair ribbons and lengths of linen the ladies of Port Townsend would buy.

"Little Poppy was my biggest joy. We shared the same sense of humor, love of reading, curiosity. She did her homework in the storeroom, atop a barrel-cum-desk, while I waited on customers. When she was done, I gave her a chore like sweeping the floors or dusting the shelves. We could talk to each other then."

"Where's Poppy now? Does she live around here?"

"Now, Rome. I'm telling my story in my own way. So that's how you'll hear it."

"Yes, Ma'am. But shall I look for a spot to stop for our picnic?" Ivy had packed a basket, and he was keenly aware of the intense aromas of baked goods and fried chicken.

"Yes. A spot next to running water that gurgles and under shade trees with dapples of sun coming through. Maybe a field across the road with a breeze perfumed by wildflowers and summer grasses. And some elk to watch along with cows."

Just around the next bend, he found the exact spot. Yes, she was a witch. "You sure you haven't seen this place before?"

"All the best picnic spots have these things. And no ants."

Rome stopped by the creek and spread out blankets. It took extra time, what with only one arm. Meanwhile, Ivy carried the picnic basket from the car, then lowered herself to the soft nest he created. "You'll have to hoist me up when we leave," she muttered. "You lost your arm to the war, and my knees are giving in to old age."

"I might leave you behind if you don't continue the story." Then he sank, legs akimbo, across from her.

"Now where was I? Yes. In the late afternoons, Cyrus came out of his office to handle the last hours of business and count the day's receipts. Meanwhile, Poppy and I went home to prepare dinner. I learned to cook quick meals of venison steak or salmon while Poppy set the table. Only on the weekends did I have time for the slower things like stews and casseroles. Or bread like this."

As she sliced the loaf open, Rome's stomach gurgled.

"Life worked well for me, but Cyrus wasn't happy. He wanted me to quit teaching. 'A man's wife shouldn't work,' he would grump. I'd remind him we needed the money to keep the store up to date with new merchandise." Ivy smiled slyly. "I'd puff up his ego. 'You are so good at procuring what the locals want!'"

She opened a Thermos and poured them each cold tea with fresh mint. "But money wasn't my real reason. Rome, I loved to teach. Loved it more than I loved Cy, I guess. If I had my druthers, I would have given up my duties in the store and taken correspondence courses in almost anything. But my higher education was a low priority to Cy."

Rome heard steel enter her voice, and it unsettled him. "Did he turn on you? You can stop if you want. Here, have another piece of chicken. I'll tell you what new books the library has ordered."

"Well, I'm coming to a tough bit. But you asked."

"That I did."

"So sit still and listen. We maintained a precarious balance until Samuel Daltry entered our life with big ideas. We expanded for the Klondikers, and Sam demanded that I work full time for Daltry & Bolton Provisions. 'You attract business to the store,' he said, staring directly at my bosom. 'A good-looking woman is the best sales tool there is. Cy and I know money ... but neither of us is a pretty face.'"

She shook her head and picked at a chicken leg. "I told Cy I would not leave the school, and we fought about it. More than once. He'd never raised a hand to me before, but I could feel it coming. I was an embarrassment to his manhood."

"Ivy, you're crying." Rome dug around for a napkin to give her.

"No I'm not. My eyes are watering. Must be the fresh air. Anyhow, I received a letter from the school releasing me from my contract. Cyrus had told them I must leave. My income would be from the store now, and it wasn't fair for me to keep a job if someone else needed it."

Rome felt gut-punched on Ivy's behalf. "What a self-absorbed cad."

"Well . . . yes, although I might use different words these days. I will make no excuses for him about stress and financial worry and drinking too much. For the first time, I let myself think he was not the man I wanted him to be. I spent all my days, along with Poppy, minding the store, never receiving any wages for myself. I watched Cy fall deeper under Samuel's spell. He even began to dress like a dandy, spend recklessly. And he turned mean, like it was his right.

"The first time he paddled Poppy was in the storeroom. He spanked her hard for sassing him. The second time, she'd spilled ink on his ledger. He was furious and he used his fist. I rushed into the room when I heard her cry, slammed the door on the customers in the shop, and demanded he stop. He did. But he gave me a look that terrified me. I've seen that look in the eyes of dogs cornering a cat. He would have hit me then if the shop wasn't so public. I knew I could never leave Poppy alone with him again.

"He apologized that evening at home, of course. But Poppy was no longer sure of her father's love. And neither was I."

"Oh, Ivy." Rome could think of nothing else to add so he remained silent, listening.

"Sunday nights, Cy prepared the receipts for the week. He and Samuel had started going to Seattle on Mondays to deposit the money in a bank there. They didn't want the locals to know how much they were raking in. And they didn't want me along to infringe on their good time.

"The next Sunday, Cy was off somewhere with Samuel after the store closed. In the evening, I unlocked it, went to the office, and withdrew the week's receipts from the safe. I stuffed it all into a carpetbag. I don't know where I was heading, but I was leaving.

"This next part of the story happened in slow motion, but I'll tell it as fast as I can. I don't like to dwell on it. Cy caught me in the act, of course. He was enraged when he saw what I was doing there on my knees in front of the safe. He jerked a buggy whip from its display and slashed me across the back. The laceration broke my skin, and I felt the blood. It was agony. I fell forward to all fours. Then he lashed four times more, harder, leaving deeper lesions. Samuel came in then, and Cy stopped.

"Samuel was not there at my rescue. 'About time you trained the little woman,' he sneered. While they laughed and turned away, I struggled up, grabbed a prospector's pick, and swung with all my might. I hit Cy as hard as I could. The pick stuck in his back, and he dropped like a sack of bones. I picked up my carpetbag, but Samuel tried to grab it. We struggled, knocking over a tall rack of the store's cleaning supplies. A bucket of bleach poured on us both. His face, my mutilated back. He shrieked, let me go, and raced to the sink for water. I was in anguish, bleach on those open wounds, but I could not stop. I fled while Samuel washed his eyes.

"I ran home. I should have removed that tattered and bloody blouse, but I didn't think. It made the bleach burns worse, of course, the material flapping into the wounds on my arms and back. At home I woke up Poppy, grabbed her coat while she dressed, and shoved a few things into the carpetbag on top of the money. We were gone in minutes. Outside, away from the house, I finally removed the blouse and splashed water on my back from the livery's hand pump. Poppy was crying but she found a cup, and she helped. It was the best we could do. I put on another blouse, and we ran.

"Both men were hurt when I left. Maybe I'd even killed Cy. But Samuel could have gotten the police on us pretty quickly. They must have thought I would hide with a neighbor or at the school. Why they didn't look under

Union Wharf I don't know, unless the idea that a woman would run from her hometown never dawned on them. Poppy and I huddled dockside until I could buy tickets on the first ferry in the wee hours. I had no idea where it was going, but I had plenty of money for a private cabin. I probably was in shock, whatever, but I don't remember much of anything else. Just the need to keep going."

She smiled sadly up at Rome. "And that's how Poppy and I left for Alaska."

August 28, 1946
Ivy Bolton

She'd rarely told anybody the whole story except Jessica, her oldest friend from Alaska. And, of course, Maki. She might not have revealed it to him either, but he alone had seen her back. Her sorrow overflowed one tearful night while he held her, listened, said he marveled at her grit. And, of course, Poppy grew up knowing what her mother and father were capable of doing.

Now Rome knew. As they finished his route, Ivy explained how Poppy had located the ship's medical man. The old Swede, a ferry to Alaska no doubt his last handhold on the slide down the medical hierarchy, acked and tutted and oohed as he examined Ivy's back. He gently cleaned and wrapped her torn skin in gauze, asking no embarrassing questions of her. But for all that, the wounds festered on the long haul to Juneau.

Poppy stayed close to her mama, holding her trembling hand as Ivy lay on her stomach, crying out at the lightest touch to her back. Only once along the way had the child asked her, "Daddy did this, didn't he? Why does he hate us?"

Ivy tried for an honest answer but could not defend his side. "He doesn't hate us. I don't think. I don't know. I don't think he knows. Nobody could hate you, Poppy."

"Well, I hate him."

Had Ivy not been in such pain, with a brain numbed by whatever the doctor was giving her, she might have found something more comforting to say. But decades later, she still didn't have a better answer. And even as a young woman, Poppy never asked again.

Ivy was offloaded in Juneau. Prospectors who'd been onboard carried her on a door from the ship to the St. Ann's Hospital, while Poppy was taken to the Sisters' orphanage. For two weeks, Ivy thrashed and cried in oblivion. Death danced through that bleak hospital room more than once during her stay, but in the end, did not choose Ivy as its partner. Her determined mind and body – not to mention the determined will of two tough nuns – fought through sepsis and even outran pneumonia.

When she left the hospital, after a final week of recovery, Ivy was weak, to be sure, but employed almost immediately. Teachers were rare, and even one who mysteriously appeared from nowhere was quite a catch. Ivy was not thrilled by the all-white school in Juneau. She was interested in the locals. Hoonah put in their bid and captured her in order to upgrade their education program. A youngish Captain Aleck on a newish *Small Fry* carried Ivy and Poppy to their new home. It was many years before she left Alaska again.

But she changed. If she'd ever been naive, she no longer was. She knew now that men choose times to go to war with each other, but women were at war with men all the time. She struggled against bitterness as she learned how to stand straight again, to lift weight, to reclaim physical flexibility.

Ivy could not look at what was once the downy skin of her back, which was now broken, angry red, ridged with thick scar tissue and burned flesh. So were the backs of her arms which had not escaped the whip and the bleach. What had happened to her was not rape but could hardly have been more personal. The scars did not destroy her because they made her body ugly ... they destroyed her pride in herself as a strong, independent person. To her, those welts were a mark of subjugation.

For the first eight years in Hoonah, Poppy was Ivy's student along with the Tlingit children. In time, other white families moved to the area. The kids all played together, learning each other's languages far quicker than adults managed such a feat. As they grew and learned, they eventually restored Ivy's pleasure in herself, but that took years. Her will to make her own way became as tough as the leather of her back.

After the first year in Hoonah, she gave up worrying whether Cy or Samuel would try to claim the money she stole. It was surely not enough to be worth a trip to the North Country to recover it. And if one of them did try, she was a lot harder to find in Hoonah than in Juneau.

Besides, Cy might even be dead, and she did not much care if she were a murderess. She'd murder him again if he tried to take Poppy away.

When Poppy was seventeen, Ivy knew the young woman had to return Outside for the higher education that Ivy had never received. Poppy went south to Seattle, then on by train for school in Portland. It broke Ivy's heart to say goodbye. But like all the best mothers, it thrilled her, too. Poppy was a woman who was never told she had no options.

That evening at home, after her picnic day with Rome, Ivy became engrossed with the copy of *Animal Farm* that he left for her. For a lighter read, at bedtime she snuggled with *The Thurber Carnival.* It was full dark before she realized she hadn't completed a letter to Jessica.

She picked up her pen and wrote:

I've always hated my wound as a mark of subjugation. Rome's is a mark of sacrifice. But we both see them as diminishing to us. We are ashamed. Is that why I find myself so free to talk with him about his wound? Is that why he responds to me? Rome must learn to look at his loss with pride, not a sense of humiliation. He is grappling with it now. It is too late for me to change my attitude toward my wound, but it would be such a relief if I could help him change his. This is something I could do for Leona, not that he knows a thing about all that.

A teacher never stops teaching. Maybe it's time for me to start learning.

Ivy got up and turned on the overhead lights. She removed her nightgown. For the first time in decades, she stood naked in brightness, open to her own judgment. She picked up a hand mirror and turned in front of the dresser mirror until she could see her back. The wounds were there, now cuddled within the loosened flesh of a septuagenarian. The wounds on her back and her arms were no uglier than the skin of old age. Neither was a mark of shame so much as a mark of life. Tomorrow she would wear her jumper without a sweater under it. What showed would show.

CHAPTER TEN

October 10, 1921
Leona Herkimer

The eyebrows on Flower's round face lifted like little question marks. "Why do you ask me so much about Mikhail Elim? How old … where he lives … what he does … who he … "

"Oh, well, no reason," Leona answered, continuing to stitch the thigh wound on the toddler as he squirmed in his mother's arms. She hoped this mom did not understand enough English to follow the thread of the conversation. She didn't want the whole village knowing a man had been on her mind.

"You find Wren's father attractive, and you wonder if he is your man?" Flower pushed against Leona's discomfort.

"Flower! No, not at all." Leona couldn't admit her bluff had been called. Even though the clinic was chilly now that autumn was long in the tooth, she felt heat in her cheeks. "How could you think that?" She took her next stitch. The toddler yelped and flailed as Leona dodged his tiny fists. "Kid has as many arms as an octopus."

Flower spoke louder, over the fray. "Because you are a normal woman, and he is a handsome man, and you speak of him more than you are aware."

"Even if such tommyrot were true, people shouldn't reveal such things."

Of course it's true. I think about him an unseemly amount of the time, and it must stop.

"Why not reveal such things?"

"Well . . . well . . . one just doesn't."

Flower muttered, "White people," and shook her head.

Leona finished her mending and smiled at the young mother. "Keep him away from sharp sticks if you can." Flower had to translate, so Leona felt her secret was safe from the village grapevine.

Mother and child left, but Flower was not done with Leona. As she cleaned the exam table, Flower said, "Mikhail has no woman now. Wren's mama is dead. And he is a good man. Many women look his way. But he is not for you."

Just like that, Leona flipped from embarrassed to petulant. "Well, why not? Is he too good for me? Is that what you're saying?"

Flower's forehead wrinkled as she huffed. "Leona! Indian women are taken by white men, but not the other way around."

Not this again. It was a constant, the distance demanded between the races. But Leona spent her days looking after native families. She felt close to them.

"Flower, I am flabbergasted." Leona put her fists on her hips until she realized what a caricature she was, then she crossed her arms instead. "You know I would have absolutely no trouble taking a Tlingit for a husband. I mean I would have no trouble if I were looking for a husband. Oh, go tell the woman in the waiting room we can see her now."

On the next crisp afternoon, when they'd finished with their patients, Leona discovered two things about Flower: first, she may not know the English word for matchmaker, but she certainly knew the meaning of it, and second, she could outfox Leona.

"It is a lovely afternoon," Flower said, a bright smile on her round face. "Put on your new anorak and come with me to a hidden beach. I show you where to gather mussels and clams, maybe sea urchins if otters haven't found them." She handed Leona a beautiful but worn basket and carried one herself.

They walked in silent friendship, a breeze rattling the firs and the earthy aroma of dried leaves circling them from the bushes. A Steller's Jay lectured them about trespassing. As they hiked higher, Leona was glad of the Chilkat tunic she wore. It blunted the damp chill of the woods. Thinking about that made her question where they were. "You know, Flower, this trail seems to lead up, not down toward a beach."

Just about then, a clearing before them revealed a tidy cabin. Wren burst out the door as they approached. "Nurse! Flower! You've come for a visit!"

Leona narrowed her eyes at Flower. "You conniver!" But she quickly smiled at the child. "Well, we were out to gather clams, Wren, and ..."

"You thought clams grew up here on bushes?" Mikhail's voice was directly behind her. Soft English spoken with a trace of Tlingit. Like Flower, he had been schooled in English somewhere along the way.

Leona whirled toward Mikhail and then back to Flower who managed a grin before grabbing Wren's hand and saying, "We came to see the toy horse I have heard about from the other children at the school." Together the two skipped toward the cabin.

"I am glad to see you," Mikhail said. "Flower can be cunning."

Ye gods what a smile! "We can't stay. We ..."

He took the empty basket from her grasp. She felt something like sparks as his work-roughened fingertips brushed the soft skin on the back of her hand. "Stay for a while. I will show you my work. And Wren will bend your ear. Since going to the school, she chatters all the time."

Leona relented. The truth was, she wanted to stay. She turned to a rack of drying pelts. "They're lovely."

"I trap hare, ermine, muskrat, prepare the skins, and sell them to whatever fur trader is buying. Some wolverine, but not so much as trappers north of here. I don't hunt larger animals like wolves, bear, or lynx."

"Why not?"

"I rarely use a gun."

Leona wasn't sure whether natives were allowed guns. Or maybe Mikhail didn't qualify as a native. His reason to avoid guns was simpler than she was making it.

"Ammunition is very dear out here." He reached out to untangle some of the fringe on her tunic. "Your anorak. It is striking. Rare to see such a thing on a white lady."

"A gift from an Angoon family."

"An honor. The natives in the area value you."

"You've been talking about me?"

He laughed. "Everyone's been talking about you. New faces, especially pretty ones, are always big news on the island."

He thinks I'm pretty! Oh, for heaven's sake, quit acting like a schoolgirl. And quit staring at him.

Mikhail told her he crewed fishing boats or worked in the cannery when it was not hunting season. But it was by trapping and fur preparation that he and Wren survived. "It's the skill of my ancestors, Russian and Tlingit alike. I am good at it, with snares and dead falls that produce all winter."

"So that's what you are doing now?"

"Not a lot until November. Fur is better when critters have their winter coats. Now I mostly create clothing from skins I've already dried and stretched."

Leona wasn't crazy about the idea of killing wildlife. But in Alaska, if it weren't for pelts, whites would never have come in the first place. The fur rush began many decades before the gold rush.

"My Russian ancestors crossed the Bering Sea for fur to sell to the Orient. After America bought Alaska, only natives were allowed to trap. But then the Klondikers came, and prospectors wanted to trap in the winter months. So now, natives and whites compete."

Leona was tickled with this fresh piece of information. "Fascinating!" *Like your gray eyes.* "Um, now I will have something to tell Harold about local culture. Usually, it's the other way around."

Mikhail frowned. "This Harold. He is your ... fella?"

"Oh no! He's the missionary, the husband of Wren's teacher, Judith Binder."

"That doctor, then. He is your fella?"

She frowned. "Hardly. We're barely civil to each other. He makes me angry. But I must be agreeable since he is the big cheese in my world."

"He is cheese?"

"I mean he is very important."

"I suspected the day of Wren's surgery that you have a temper."

"It is no match to his."

"You are agreeable in my estimation."

And you are what the girls Outside call a dish. Leona wanted to touch his hair, to determine whether it would be silky fur or coarse mane. She wanted to feel his hand on hers once more, by way of experimentation with those sparks. She'd read about a sensual switch merely from touch, admittedly in a questionable novel that had passed from girl to girl at her nursing school. But she didn't know till this instant it was real. A nurse should not believe in a thing so improbable. But the non-nurse parts were quite delighted.

In the cabin, Wren made herbal tea and entertained them with the multiplication tables, as far as she had managed them.

"Sevens are very hard," Leona agreed when the child faltered. "But you will soon have them all. I'm impressed." Due to her nurse-ness, she was pleased the cabin was tidy and clean, although sparsely furnished. Part of it was masked off by a hanging curtain woven from cedar. Next to the right wall, close enough to feel the heat from the wood stove, a rocking horse sat beside a cot. It must be Wren's nest, judging by the large woven doll dressed in fur.

It gave Leona an idea. "Mikhail, could I commission you to make me a fur hat? I've wanted one since I arrived. And winter is so close."

"What kind of fur?"

"Whatever is warm. Um, maybe rabbit? Like my mittens?"

"Yes. And no. I will make you a hat. But not rabbit. Something stronger for winter."

Stop staring at him! Leona stood. "Flower, we must go. Work at the clinic calls."

"It does?"

"It does."

And, as it happened, it did. Two Tlingit oarsmen in a canoe had paddled a third person to the clinic. He had a hook buried in the cavity of his eye. The trio was on the beach when Leona and Flower arrived back at Hoonah.

All thoughts of Mikhail flew from Leona's head as she went into Nurse Battle Mode. She sent Flower to the government building for her medical bag and to ask Ivy to alert Juneau. In moments, Flower galloped back to the beach with the bag, and Ivy called through the door, "I've already radioed Hambone to find a boat to get the patient to Juneau."

Leona made the man lie flat in the body of the canoe. Flower tucked blankets around him, while Leona gave him morphine and a tetanus shot, then flushed the eye and cleaned the area around it. She covered it loosely with gauze. While close to him, she noticed he felt far too hot, feverish. His lips were swollen, and she ordered him to open his mouth. His tongue was too red. He groaned when she opened his trousers and observed reddish spots on his abdomen.

"Hambone can't raise Captain Aleck or a passing steamer," Ivy called to her. "He'll keep trying."

Using Flower as her translator, Leona told the two oarsmen what they must do. They ran to the village to find two extra men to help them row. Meanwhile, Leona rushed inside to throw supplies along with a few personal possessions into her carpetbag.

Flower had made the fisherman, now groggy with drugs, as comfortable as possible in the bottom of the canoe. Leona climbed in and let him rest his head on her lap so she could stop any bleeding and protect the wound. She yelled, "Ivy, tell the hospital to have typhoid vaccine at the ready."

"Typhoid? Here?"

"It's what I think. If they don't have it, tell them to send for it. For this man, the oarsmen, and me. More if they can get it."

Flower placed an eel-skin wrap over the man and another around Leona to fend off rain or splashing seawater. When the oarsmen returned with two others, they launched the canoe. It swiftly cut through the water, disrupting a raft of sea otters sunning themselves in a kelp bed. Leona wished for *Yashee* or *Small Fry* to appear around the point in Icy Strait. A boat bigger than a twenty-foot canoe would be much more secure. Eye-level to an otter felt damn risky.

What if a whale ...

The injured fisherman, jarred by the rocking of the canoe, began to fuss. Leona bent over him and said in his ear, "I cannot save your eye, but Dr. Reardon can. We are getting you to the hospital as quick as possible. It will all be well. You'll see." She blanched at her faux pas, hoping the man had no idea what she was prattling about. "I mean, you'll be fine in no time at all."

Entering Chatham Strait was always a thrill. Glaciered peaks to the north frowned down on the miniscule canoe across hills covered with endless forest. The Strait could be as rough as the ocean to the west, but at this moment it was benign. Still, the light was dying. It was not late, but the sun set so early in the Alaskan autumn. Leona was sure these oarsmen did not want to be out here in the dark, nonetheless camping was out of the question if they were to deliver the fisherman in time for anything to be done for his eye. She could see the strength and pull of their efforts in the muscles of their backs and arms; she smelled their sweat even in the dropping temperature. Rock outcroppings could snag them, unseen, anywhere along these waters. And on the shore in the dark? This was bear country.

Maybe she should stop them. Leona remembered the words the doctor had said to her after their argument over Wren. "You will find yourself in similar predicaments again and again out here in the wilderness. You are far too valuable to allow all your good decisions to be overwhelmed by one bad one."

Was this one of those bad decisions? To continue when wisdom said to stop? To pit the lives of four oarsmen and herself against that of a man who might lose an eye? Who could die of typhoid disease even if the eye was saved?

Leona wanted to cry in frustration, knowing it would do nothing to help the situation. She wanted to question any Spirit she could grab by the ear, be it Tlingit or Christian. She was about to scream "Stop!" to the oarsmen, when she saw the light, literally. *Small Fry* was coming toward them like a squat, smoky St. Bernard to the rescue. It rose and fell over the swells, chugging at a speed that could best be called majestic.

As Captain Aleck smiled from the deck and lowered his hand to lift her up, Leona was pretty sure one of those Spirits had answered her back. Together, the oarsmen, crewman, and a sling made of rope lifted the injured fisherman to the deck. Leona had learned the words for please and thank you, so she called the appropriate, "*Gunalchéeshtlein.*" The oarsmen answered in words she didn't know but with emotion that was surely happiness, relief, or pride. Then *Small Fry* turned and noisily grumbled on toward Juneau. The canoe silently slipped away toward home.

It was not yet six o'clock but full dark in Juneau when they arrived. The biggest city in the Alaska territory had a population of three thousand white souls, almost all of whom had come for gold, either to mine it or prey on those who did. By 1921, there was an actual downtown in a bowl between Gastineau Channel and the huge sweep of mountains all around. The buildings were no longer tents and shacks; permanent structures included banks, fashionable shops, hotels, and saloon after dancehall after brothel after church.

Little of this was important to Leona, other than the lights pouring from windows and along streets. Captain Aleck and she stopped a wagon that was willing to haul the injured fisherman along Franklin Street then up the steep climb of Sixth at the foot of Starr Hill. They arrived at St. Ann's Hospital, which had a capacity of fifty-five beds and the only surgical unit for hundreds of miles. The three-story unit's stern but handsome edifice had two full length porches. A chapel was tucked on the hill beside it.

Leona noticed little of this as she galloped up the front stairs, calling for help to come with a stretcher. Dr. Reardon was not on premise when she arrived, but the hospital nurses efficiently moved the fisherman to a bed that attendants had prepared for him. As they took charge, Leona was shown to a place to clean away her travels and given a room for the night in staff quarters. She felt wilted, after the fear and tension of the rush from Hoonah. When prepared in a fresh dress, she went back to check on the fisherman. He was clean, warm, and drugged enough to sleep with fresh gauze over his eye.

"The doctor will be here at eight," another nurse told her. "That's almost two hours from now. We'll look after your patient if you are hungry, Nurse Leona. There is a tearoom two blocks from here where a woman can feel safe having a meal on her own."

"You don't mind?"

The woman smiled at her. "In the hospital, he is actually our patient, not your patient. You'll have him back soon enough. Now go take care of yourself."

Food!

Leona soon found the Tongass Tearoom. A chalkboard advertised venison pie as the special, and she ordered it along with bread and butter. She'd wedged her mouth full when she heard, "Hello, stranger."

She looked up and had no idea who was speaking to her. But the woman slipped into the cane-backed chair across the table from her. She was a gift-wrapped package of glitter and bows over a green velveteen skirt so short it revealed her stockinged knees. Her hair, screaming red, sparkled in the tearoom's low light. Soft breasts overstuffed her bodice as though two loaves of bread had risen too far.

"We met on the ferry. I was Danielle Lester there. Here I'm Danielle LeDanz. Nice to see you again, Leona."

As quickly as she could without choking, Leona swallowed her bite. "Danielle! How wonderful! You look ... well, very different. Exotic."

Danielle's laugh was low and raspy. "Those were my travel clothes. These are my work clothes. I dance at the Golden Garter. Hope that career choice doesn't offend you, dear nurse."

Leona laughed. "Of course not. Heaven knows I couldn't choose to do the same, what with my two left feet. It is a good thing you do what you do, and I do what I do."

"Dear girl, it is not your feet that interest the men here. With your looks, you'd do just fine. Now then, I appear to have joined you for dinner, so I hope that is okey-dokey with you. I stop by here often before my nights begin." Danielle ordered the same meal as Leona but added a ginger beer. She leaned closer. "It actually *is* beer, but revenuers don't visit places like this where just us ladies congregate. If you like wine, order the grape juice."

Dinner was fun. It had been a long time since Leona had gossiped and giggled with a woman her own age. They exchanged tales about their Alaska life, talked about raised hemlines and higher heeled shoes, even the men they had met.

"So the brooding doctor or the muscled woodsman? Which do you choose?" Danielle asked as they paid the bill of fare.

"Neither, Danielle! Such a question. But I must hurry now and meet the brooding doctor to discuss my patient."

They parted, maybe not best friends but good ones. One was on her way to the Golden Garter and the other to St. Ann's Hospital. They exchanged addresses and promised to be in touch if not over the winter, then in the spring.

Leona was humming "Oh, Dem Golden Slippers" as she bounced up the front steps of the hospital and into the lobby.

Dr. Reardon was not seeing patients or looking at charts. He was in the darkened waiting room, head down and very still.

Leona stopped. "Dr. Reardon? Are you well?"

He sat back and squared his shoulders. "Nurse! I'm well. You're finally back."

"Excuse me?" *Finally back?* She'd just had a meal. Gracious, how this man could irritate her.

"Come with me."

Leona followed him as he strolled down the hall. His stride was so long, she nearly skipped to keep up. They entered the fisherman's room. A rivulet of blood had dried from the gauze of his eye down the side of his face.

"He's dead," Dr. Reardon proclaimed. "He died before I got here. The eye socket must have hemorrhaged. Or the reaction to drugs was severe."

Somewhere, in whatever part of the anatomy holds our deepest secrets and shames, a dark notion erupted within Leona. *I am a nurse who endangers patients. Did I do this?* "But ... what could have happened? Did I miss anything?"

"No one here noticed when it happened."

"But ... I only went to eat. The nurse said ..."

"Do not cast blame on the other nurses." His words were quiet, but their impact was worse than a slap across her face. He shrugged then, softening. "No one is to blame. People die."

The fisherman was her patient, and he died alone. Leona knew exactly who was to blame.

"As to your theory about typhoid, Nurse, I have taken it seriously. I sent away fluid samples. In case you were right about that. If so, that is the greater concern."

Leona put her hand on the dead man's head then touched his hand. Maybe the doctor saw the pain she was in. He moved closer to her. "There is nothing you could have done, Leona. Not really. I am frustrated. And I blame myself for being late arriving. The handoff between doctors and nurses is so difficult in the wilderness. We have discussed that before, you and I." He touched her shoulder with a gentle pat.

She furiously battled tears, gulping great breaths of air.

"May I offer you a drink? I have an edifying brew in my office," Dr. Reardon said. "It will help you sleep. Things will look better in the morning."

Kindness from him was harder than his criticism. She knew there was nothing more she could have done for the fisherman. Her head knew it. But her heart was breaking. She shook her head and walked away, back down the steps and to the Tongass Tearoom.

Leona purchased a bottle of "grape juice." She took it back to the hospital. Dr. Reardon was nowhere in sight. She went to her room in the staff quarters, shut her door, and opened the bottle.

October 11, 1921
Ivy Bolton

A fishing boat from Juneau dropped off mail before breakfast. Over coffee, Ivy sorted it and laid piles on the counter in the foyer next to the ham radio. There were stacks for the school, clinic, church, businesses, tribal chiefs, and residents of the town. They would all stop by during the day, looking for their letters each time a boat arrived.

The nurses and teachers farther north had it worse when the land and sea froze them into the winter for months on end. The only mail they got came by dogsled, which was infrequent and undependable. Drivers and dogs both were at the mercy of heavy gales and impenetrable snows. It made Ivy shiver to think about it.

Hoonah, on the Panhandle coast, did not freeze so completely and bleakly. Mail bags arrived on whatever boat was coming their way from Juneau or Ketchikan, rarely more than two months old on arrival. Ivy had heard rumors that one day mail from Outside would come by aircraft, but what hogwash.

"How could a two-cent stamp pay for such a thing?" she scoffed aloud to nobody as she opened her letter from Poppy. In Ivy's estimation, a letter ranked with rich chocolate or a warm perfumed bath. Each should be savored slowly, and all were equally rare. Poppy talked about a college class she attended in Portland where the professor made her an assistant. She also mentioned a classmate, the third letter in which his name cropped up. Most important, Poppy enclosed a clipping from the *PT Leader* about Cy Bolton's death and the memorial service in Port Townsend. It appeared he had remarried because a widow was named, but there was no mention of an earlier wife or daughter.

Father's death was something of a mystery. He was walking the top of a coastal ridge. A loosening of the ground tipped his feet over the ledge and into the Strait below. It is as well I was in Portland at the time, else I might have been blamed!!

Ivy reread Poppy's letter in the afternoon, as her class tromped around the woods studying fungus. Her feet were cold, so she folded Poppy's words into her pocket and clapped her hands to move the kids along. "Don't eat anything," she reminded them once again then quoted the local adage. "There are old mushroom hunters and bold mushroom hunters but no old, bold mushroom hunters." They uncovered remains of decaying morels hidden in the leaves, angel wings in rotting logs, and a poisonous growth aptly known by the locals as the Sickener. When Ivy discussed the importance of fungi and their reproductive spores, the older kids tittered as they always had and always would at anything verging on sex.

Ivy was happy leaving the little ones in the care of Judith and marching around with her older learners. It hadn't been possible when she taught alone all the years before. The two teachers worked well together, and the forty-some youngsters liked them well enough. Ivy was tougher than Judith, so a better match for the older ones. They often were sullen, not wanting to be in school to learn a white version of the world. They didn't have the long view of their parents, to understand the purpose of it.

Ivy's thoughts turned to Leona. If all had gone well in Juneau, the nurse should be back in the evening. By that time of day, Cook, Flower, and Judith had usually left for their own homes, so Leona and Ivy were often alone in the government building, unless Farley the boozer had checked himself into a clinic bed. Dinner on those nights was a ladle of the soup that simmered on the stove nearly non-stop, replenished daily by leftover meats and root vegetables. "Whatcha Got" soup, they called it. Cook always left a loaf of bread or biscuits, as well. Ivy enjoyed these evenings; Leona was good company.

Small Fry arrived at sundown, and Ivy went to the waterfront to meet it. "Is Leona aboard?" she called to the captain as she wrapped a shawl around her shoulders.

Captain Aleck did not respond until he was close enough to lower his voice. "She is aboard, indeed. But young Leona is in need of some nursing herself."

When Leona left the boat for the dock, she was colorless, trembling, and smelled of vomit. Ivy was shocked by her condition. "Leona. What is it? Have you influenza? Are you seasick?" She moved to put her hand on the nurse's forehead.

"I'll be fine," the nurse snapped, pulling away. "I merely need a cup of tea." She stumbled off toward the government building.

Ivy looked at the captain, raising her eyebrows at Leona's unexpected conduct.

He shrugged. "I'd never say such a thing of a lady like Leona, but if I had to guess, I'd say it's a case of the bottle-aches."

"Bottle-aches?" Was this a new form of illness?

"Our nurse is hung over, Ivy. This is a subject I know something about, having experienced it a time or two myself."

"Heavenly days, Aleck! Say nothing of that to anyone else."

"Nothing of what?" he answered with a doff of his cap, then he returned to *Small Fry* to help his crewman unload a barrel of butter and bags of potatoes and onions. Ivy grabbed two of the bags and headed toward the kitchen. By the time she arrived, Leona was not in sight. Ivy set the bags on the counter, and the crew dropped the barrel and other bags on the floor near the sink. Cook would deal with them in the morning. After they left, Ivy checked the storeroom and noticed Leona's chamber pot was missing. The nurse must have grabbed it and gone immediately to her room.

"Golly Moses," Ivy muttered to herself. "What happened to the girl in Juneau?" She made tea, climbed the stairs, knocked lightly on Leona's door, and set the cup on the wooden floor along with a small green apple and a plate of Uneeda Biscuits. Whether flu or motion sickness or alcohol, Leona would appear when she was good and ready. Ivy must put her curiosity on hold until then. She loved a good story, but this one might not qualify as good. She began to fret.

It was four hours later, around ten o'clock at night, when Leona appeared in the kitchen and sat across the table from Ivy who was grading a stack of arithmetic quizzes. Ivy looked at the pale nurse, got up, and served her a bowl of soup and hunk of bread.

"I owe you an explanation," Leona said.

"Eat first."

Leona picked up a spoon then set it down. Tears slid down her face. Ivy graded another quiz. And another.

"I will tell you everything. You can see to it that I am returned Outside."

Ivy graded. And waited.

"The fisherman died, Ivy. I wasn't there. I could not have saved him, but I wasn't there. He died alone in that hospital." Leona told Ivy the story in spurts, stopping for tears and gulping cries along the way.

Ivy listened then pronounced, "But Leona, according to your story, even Dr. Reardon said you should not blame yourself. You were off duty. Sad, but these things happen."

"That's not all, Ivy. It's far from all. I ... I purchased a bottle of wine last night. And made a pretty good dent in the brandy I always carry with me." She cupped her hands over her face and sobbed.

"You carry brandy with you?" Ivy put down her pen. To hide her surprise, she went to the kitchen sink, found a clean rag, and doused it with cold water. "Here. Use this."

Leona wiped her eyes and caught her breath. Once the nurse ran dry of tears and snot, Ivy said, "Now see here. Women of the north country must be tougher than this. Sometimes we all need a little false courage. You are not the first woman to overindulge."

"But I'm a nurse. And it's not the first time I overindulged. Or the first time I abandoned a patient to die alone."

Her misery was profound. Ivy reached across the table for Leona's hand and said, "Tell me."

October 11, 1921
Leona Herkimer

Leona felt like a rag, wrung nearly dry. Her throat ached, and her head throbbed. But she didn't think she would vomit again. Maybe. Dry heaves? Maybe. Her voice grew stronger as it stopped hurting to talk. "Oh, Ivy. I didn't just overindulge. I suffer the curse of the alcohol disease. I must not drink, I swore I wouldn't, and yet I did. I even downed the last of my brandy just now in order to come down here and confess to you."

"It's not just a bit of fun? You really can't stop?"

Ivy's concern mortified Leona. "No more than I can stop feeling this shame of myself. One seems to feed on the other. I thought I was over it, in control. I was wrong. I'm useless."

"I didn't know it was so hard, Leona. It is not a subject I understand very well. Although I see how some people fight Prohibition. I myself miss wine with my meals."

"This is something altogether different. It's an addiction, Ivy."

"How did it happen?"

Leona shrugged her sagging shoulders. "Maybe I was born with it, maybe not. That is unknown. My parents both suffered it. They tried it hide it, just like I do. I didn't understand then, but I do now. Alcohol is why Pa hit Ma, and why she'd forget to feed me, and why they yelled if I made too much noise."

"Is there no cure?"

"Not then, not now. Research doctors in New York tried a belladonna elixir, but it created another addiction for their patients and didn't cure alcoholism."

"Your parents couldn't conquer it?"

"No more than I can now. I thought they were sick, and that if I took good enough care of them, they would get well. But I couldn't make them better no matter what I did. Sometimes they'd get by for a while when Pa found work. But the illness always came back. No matter how quiet I was, or how much housework I did, or how well I behaved, I could not make them stay well. I believed if I were a better person, they would love me enough to stop drinking. I was more ashamed of me than I was of them."

Leona began to wretch and wobbled up, muttering, "Damnation." Ivy hustled to unlock the back door. Leona didn't make it to The Bog before her stomach emptied of the nothing that was in it.

When she came back in, Ivy met her with another clean rag and placed an empty bowl on the table. "Just in case," she said. "Now eat the bread at least, Leona. You must have something inside."

"You're a better nurse than me, Ivy."

"That's a right old load of codswallop, that is."

Leona smiled sadly. She sat down and picked at the loaf, eating some bits and forming the rest into little balls of dough. "Nursing was the only thing I ever wanted to do. I worshipped the women who mended fallen warriors during the war. How romantic it seemed. White Angels, I thought of them.

"When I graduated from high school, I went to nursing school in Everett, a long way from home. I was glad to leave. I lived with three other girls. We studied hard at night, often exhausted from long rounds at the teaching hospital during the day. I loved every bit of it, even the grumpy professors. Then one evening, one of the girls came home with a bottle of vodka. She mixed it with the syrup from preserved peaches her mother had sent. She said it would help us all study. Well, it hardly did that! We all got giggly and were done with books for the night."

She stopped long enough to pinch another dough ball from the bread. With a sigh, she continued. "It was so much fun, Ivy. Such a release of tension. But I now know that our little hen fest awakened something very dark in me. I wanted more. I wanted that euphoria to continue. I'd had little enough hilarity in life up until then.

"So, despite what I knew of my parents, I bought my own vodka the very next day at a pharmacy. I drank it at night, mixed with anything, even honey if that's all I could find. I went pharmacy to pharmacy so no one would suspect how much I was drinking. My favorite breakfast became broth spiked with vodka and Tabasco. Sounds dreadful, doesn't it?"

"Well ... well, yes," Ivy agreed.

"Ah, but the days went by so much quicker. And everybody enjoyed my company. 'You're such a cheery girl,' a patient would say. Or 'I love sharing shifts with you' from another nursing student. After graduation, I worked in the hospital in Everett. I stayed there for five years gaining a reputation for dependability. But the truth, Ivy? I got worse with each year. Only when tippling did I feel good. The rest of my days were haunted, waiting for nights when I could drink openly with the gang instead of hiding a flask in my purse or my apron.

"Just before Prohibition, alcohol flowed free at men's service organizations and lots of clubs where single women were welcomed. A group of us nurses would go out together on nights off, looking for a bit of fun. And, of course, it was easy to find."

Leona inhaled one great sob, then went quiet. The next words stuck in her mouth. She couldn't speak them to Ivy, but the scene replayed before her eyes like a movie on a nickelodeon.

"Give me another drink, and I'll show you something new," I purred.

He did, and so did I. He cried, "God Almighty!" as I straddled his lap, my skirt shoved up to my waist. The alcohol beast raged inside me … look at this Ma and Pa … poor lost little Leona.

Leona vaguely heard Ivy calling to her, but the vision played on.

"Nurse by day, naughty by night," I whispered into his ear as he climaxed. I'd chosen him simply because he had money enough to buy booze without question.

"Nurse Naughty," he panted. "You can check my chart anytime you wish."

"Chart. Chart! What time is it?" Fear swept my brain. I needed to know. Was I late? I ran from the storeroom back to the main parlor. I was on the midnight shift at the hospital. "What time is it?" I yelled to the crowded room at large.

"Time to haul my ashes next!" Another man grabbed at me.

I pushed him away, straightened my skirt. "I have to go! I HAVE TO GO!"

Leona returned from the memory when Ivy shook her gently. "Where, Leona? You have to go where? You're right here, safe with me."

"Go?" Leona looked around, lost for a moment. A kitchen … Ivy. She took another deep gulp of air, relieved to see that lovely face looking so concerned for her. But ye gods, had she said all her thoughts aloud, or only that last "I have to go"?

Ivy's face puckered as though she, too, was nearly in tears. "I thought I'd lost you there for a moment."

Leona could never share all those disgraceful details with anyone, not even Ivy. She said, "I was at a party at one of the clubs. Drunk. I realized I was late for my midnight shift. A clock on the wall told me the frightening truth. It was 1:00 a.m. I had to fly. The night was cold. My brain began to clear, and I ran. Intoxicants had never truly impaired my work before." She shook her head and wrapped her arms tightly over her chest. "I knew I'd be in trouble with Maggie, the nurse with the shift before mine. I ran into our ward, saying 'I'm sorry, I'm sorry!' but Maggie wasn't there. At first, I was thrilled. She must have left, knowing I wouldn't be long. After all, I was never late. I was the perfect nurse. Everyone loved me."

Ivy cut in. "Leona it's true. We do love you. And I've never known you to be late or shirk a duty in any way."

Leona snorted. "I checked charts and checked rooms. All was quiet other than Mr. Pierce's raucous snoring. I began to breathe easy. But then, oh Ivy, then I realized one room was too quiet. I went back to that door. I could smell the body odors of death. Mrs. Nord had finally given in to her bronchitis. Maybe I can't be blamed for this fisherman's demise, but that old lady died all alone, in pain, suffocating with nobody to even hold her hand. No nurse to offer her comfort. And there's nobody to blame but me."

It was an ugly tale. Ivy would hate her now.

But Ivy didn't flinch. All she asked was, "What did the hospital do?"

"Nothing. They never knew the truth. Maggie didn't confess that she left early, and I didn't confess I arrived late. As far as the hospital knew, sweet Mrs. Nord passed with attendants by her side. But I knew.

"I vowed never to drink again. And I didn't. I was miserable without it. The beast never quit eating my insides. But even that wasn't punishment enough. I needed to extract more from myself."

"Leona, punishment? You made a mistake, yes. It was bad, yes. But you resolve it won't happen again. And you go on."

"I had to change, to get away from those clubs. I left the hospital and the parties behind, joined the Traveling Field Nurses who transported me into a totally different world. I came to Alaska to get away from that good-time girl, to start again sober as a church bell. I make myself carry a bottle of brandy so I can fight the beast away every single night. There's some pride in that. It feels sort of like winning. And I love it here. But now I've lost again."

Ivy struck. "Stop right there. No, you have not lost. And don't you dare think about leaving here or leaving nursing. You are haunted by dereliction of duty. That happened. You are letting the loss of a patient yesterday cause you pain you don't merit. You've controlled the beast before. You will again, starting in the morning. Booze will not rob you of everything, and strip Hoonah of a dedicated nurse or me of a friend I admire."

Leona came around the table and collapsed into Ivy's arms.

"Come, now," said Ivy after a long moment. "It's time for bed. In the morning, I have students to teach, and you have patients to mend."

CHAPTER ELEVEN

October 4, 1946
Rome Coleridge

Rome had never climbed Ivy's steps in the near-dark before. At this time of year the sun set around five, so it wasn't even that late. He frowned to himself. The risers were slick in this rain. It was so cold it could sleet tonight, but it was early in the year for that. Maybe he ought to lay some of those new safety strips, the abrasive ones said to keep you from slipping. He wouldn't want Ivy to fall.

Could a one-armed man do a job like that? A few months ago he wouldn't even consider it. But now he thought it was worth a try. Maybe Ivy's can-do spirit was rubbing off on him.

She'd invited him out to dinner at Harrington's Cafe. She said she had a yen for a breaded pork chop, and theirs couldn't be beat. She was wrapped in a fringed shawl when he met her at the door.

"Wow. That's right snappy, Ivy."

"It's a Chilkat shawl given to me years ago by my friend Maki. You might meet him one day."

Him? There was a man in her life? It was not the sort of question he felt comfortable to ask. She had no qualms about what she asked him, but he maintained a certain decorum in proper behavior to a lady.

Rome was about to escort Ivy toward the bookmobile when she said, "Not this time. We'll use the back door." She took him through the kitchen, then across her little backyard to a garage that housed her 1940 Studebaker Champion straight-six sedan. "A young man needs a car to squire a girl around, even an old girl like me." She handed him the keys. "You drive."

"Goodness, Ivy," he said as he stared at the gleaming red shine. "I didn't know you had a car."

"Did you think I get around by shank's mare? By broom? That I'm too feeble to trust behind the wheel?"

As he backed the Studebaker out of the garage, he muttered, "Ivy, I'd believe you could fly if you said you could."

They cruised downhill toward town. "In fact, Rome, I have a proposition for you. I don't really drive it enough to own it anymore, but I can't get myself to give it up. If you were to take care of it for me, I'd let you use it whenever you want."

An automobile! Old and red as an apple, but just look at the size of it! And the cushy seats.

His world expanded by leaps and bounds. "Holy mackerel, Ivy! That's a sweet deal for me. I really shouldn't drive the bookmobile as much as I do."

"Don't be too grateful. I might be a worse slave driver than the library."

Rome parked then hurried around to open her door. He took her arm and escorted her into Harrington's, on the corner of Laurel and Front. The place wasn't fancy, but it emanated warmth and coziness.

They took a table for two since the rest were for four or more. Booths along the wall were already filled, dishes clattered at the counter, and fans high overhead added a constant whir to the atmosphere. A waitress dropped off menus without stopping as she hurried on to the kitchen. "Be right back!" she called over her shoulder as she flashed past with a tray of dirty dishes.

"Now let's see," Ivy said, peering at the menu as if she hadn't already made up her mind about the pork chop. "Maybe we should split a carafe of red wine?"

Rome's eyes followed the waitress as she passed, up the seamed stockings on her muscular legs, over a swaying of hips in a full-skirted dress as she cut through the crowd, to her long dark hair caught up in a net that bounced behind her back.

Ivy looked up from her menu. "What do you think Rome? I'm told everything's good. Order whatever you want. It's on me tonight. I'm celebrating Poppy's birthday even though she's not along to share."

Rome stared at the waitress as she called an order through a pass-way to the cooks. She turned and came back their way.

Ivy picked up the card displayed on the table. "The special is hamburger steak and grilled onions."

He tore his eyes from the waitress and zeroed in on the old woman across from him. He made every effort to be sure his voice was more whisper than growl. "Ivy. What have you done?"

The waitress arrived, flipping open her order book. She looked up and smiled. "What'll you folks have this evening?"

As Ivy ordered, Rome concentrated on the face of the waitress. It was round with ivory skin and pink cheeks. Dark waves around her face had freed themselves from the net. Crooked front teeth kept her from looking too doll-faced for belief. When Ivy finished, the waitress turned to Rome. "And you sir?"

"Hello, Barbara."

She looked at him. Her pencil froze over her order pad, and her dark eyes flashed a spark of surprise. "Rome," she said, drawing out the syllable. "It's nice to see you. I heard you were back in town."

"Yes. I'm back. War's been over some time, you know."

"Um, I guess it has. What would you like, Rome?"

He stared at her. A blush reddened her pink cheeks.

"I mean, from the menu," she added.

"Most of me's back, Barbara. Left an arm behind on the battlefield. So I guess you were right to send me packing. Wouldn't want half a man."

She heaved a large sigh. He watched those wonderful breasts stretch the thin fabric of her work dress. She said, "I'll bring you the special. It's good." And she bolted away.

Rome felt chained to his seat. He wanted to bolt, too, but he couldn't just leave Ivy there no matter how angry he was.

"Don't look at me like I'm one of those Huns you fought. Just listen for a moment will you? Please?" Ivy pleaded. "Take a deep breath. I know you're angry with me."

"You planned this," he seethed.

"And I'm truthful enough not to deny it. Yes, I did bamboozle you. It took a fair amount of doing what with not knowing her last name. DeMarco. Barbara DeMarco. Beautiful. Maybe that's why the ladies at the Guild remembered she was a friend of Nancy Coleridge's boy."

"Ivy. Get to the point." He spit out the words as staccato as gun shots.

"Good, Rome, good! Five words in a row and not one of them a curse word."

Someone other than Barbara brought them their carafe of wine, pouring their first glasses. Rome instantly drained his, then poured a second. "You're lucky I'm not the sort of man to scream at a miserable old woman in public."

It made her giggle. Then chuckle. Then laugh as tears tumbled to her cheeks. Ice between them began to crack.

Soon, even Rome was coming around. What the hell was he going to do with her? Finally, he snorted a burst of air. "The fact that I'm laughing does not mean I am happy with you."

She sipped her wine. "Do you remember telling me that women are different than you thought? Most of us have been taught to look pretty and do what we're told. It's never been the strong suit for some of us. But there's a downside to independence. Sometimes, you make people uncomfortable with what you say. You poke them in their sensitivities. If you think about it, Rome, you haven't minded my input."

It was true enough. Rome enjoyed Ivy for how she was different, not how she was the same.

She continued. "You might not have really understood Barbara. You have unanswered questions. And I figure that you won't be comfortable in your skin until you have some answers."

That was true enough, too.

"But you have yourself so wrapped up in male pride over a missing limb that I knew you'd never confront her."

Damn her old hide, anyway.

"Besides, maybe you've both changed. Maybe she wouldn't have made that decision today, what with being older and wiser. A war makes us all that way. In fact, she could be very glad to see you. Or maybe not." Ivy looked around the cafe. "She seems to have run for the hills." There was a long pause before Ivy asked, "Are you not speaking to me?"

"I'm letting my blood pressure settle. And my head quit aching. I'm drinking enough to get tipsy. And, yes, I'm considering never speaking to you again."

"Meanwhile, I'm going to eat my pork chop."

An unknown waitress served them their orders. Before she left, she pulled a folded piece of paper from her apron pocket. "Is your name Rome?" she asked him.

"Yes?"

"Barbara asked me to give you this."

Nonplused, Rome took the note. He unfolded it and read it. Read it again, then folded the paper and put it in his jacket pocket. He did his very best to keep his face free of emotion.

"Well? What did she say?" Ivy yelped like an excited pup.

"I think I'm just going to eat my meal before it gets cold." He cut into the hamburger steak.

"YOU MEAN YOU'RE NOT GOING TO TELL ME?"

Other diners stared at the raucous old woman. But Rome merely gave her a cheek-busting smile and said, "How's that pork chop, Ivy?"

October 4, 1946
Ivy Bolton

Ivy didn't tell him how irritated she was. They chatted politely, agreed dinner was yummy, and said "no thanks" to dessert. She paid the bill, and he drove her home without saying another word regarding Barbara. Rome parked the Studebaker at the entrance to the garage.

"Aren't you going to put it away?" Ivy asked.

"Yep. But I thought I might take it for a little spin first."

Rome walked her to her back door and waited for her to turn on the kitchen lights. Then he kissed her on the cheek, thanking her for the meal and for allowing him to use her car.

"But not one damn word about that note!" She fumed aloud in the house with no one to address but a hissing radiator and the ticking clock. She threw her shawl on a chair, switched on the hall light, and went into her dark bedroom.

Ivy kicked off her wedged shoes and rolled down her stockings. The slip, girdle, underpants, and brassiere came next, before she pulled a nightie over her head. Only then did she snap on the reading lamp on the nightstand. She applied night cream in the bathroom and brushed her teeth until her gums began to hurt. Finally, she brushed her hair with such vigor, it snapped with static.

Damn, damn, damn.

Crawling into bed, she knew he had every right to shut her out. In fact, he had behaved altogether better than she was acting now. Sleep would certainly elude her, so she set up a bed tray and slapped out a hand of solitaire. Then another.

Her curiosity was always harder for her to control than anger. Still. How in hell's bells could Rome go quiet on her? Ivy rarely needed company, being comfortable with her own. But tonight, she wanted something else to do, someone else to think about. She wished Maki was there beside her, where he belonged. He'd be home for the winter soon.

Her evening with Rome had brought back another mystery, as well. Curiosity was like that, leaping from place to place. Rome had once asked her if his aunt was alive, and Ivy had – by a narrow definition of the truth – told him she didn't know. But what was the news of Leona? *Is she okay? Will Wren write again?*

October 4, 1946
Rome Coleridge

The note said: I get off at 9 o'clock.

Rome sat outside Harrington's Cafe thinking, *What am I doing here?* He'd nearly not come. He'd meant to drive Ivy's red Studebaker into the garage and go home. But somehow, it reversed itself, pointing back to the restaurant and to Barbara.

The cafe was dark with a CLOSED sign in the large front window. He waited. When she appeared, he was free to stare. Her herringbone trench coat sported large square shoulders, padded in a military fashion. The belt nipped in her narrow waist. She stood looking up the street then down. He watched her through the hazy mist. She smoked a cigarette. Finally, she ground it out, shoved her hands in her pockets, and began to move. She walked like a woman now, not a girl.

Ivy was right. The war made us all older.

He nearly let her go. At the last moment, Rome opened the car door and called, "Barbara. I'm here."

She stopped, turned, then strolled to his car window. "The Rec Tavern is still open. If you'd like a drink."

He nodded. She circled the car and got in. Now she would see how clumsy a one-armed man was. He maneuvered the steering wheel with a knee to shift with his hand before grabbing the wheel again. He didn't try to hide his awkwardness from her.

She didn't react to it or speak of it. Maybe she didn't care. But she said, "I've thought about you often, Rome. I missed you."

"It was your choice." He needed to hurt her with his words.

"Yes. It was."

Instead of going to the tavern, he drove to the waterfront and parked in the dark by the marina where fishing boats were moored for the night. "Let's walk," he said.

"Let's not. My dogs are pooped after a day waiting tables."

He hadn't thought of that. What else might he not have thought of? What, after all, did he know about Barbara anymore? "Are you married?"

"No. I still live with my mother. How about you?"

"Folks are dead. And who'd marry a cripple like me?"

She was silent for a moment. He felt guilt at trying to shame her but was not up to an apology. Not yet. He felt like an ass which magnified his need to act like one.

In time she asked, "Was that your grandma at the restaurant?"

"Ivy? No. She's my friend. And a conniver who set up our paths to cross."

"She did? Why?"

She turned her body toward him on the spacious bench seat. Her eyes were huge, glistening as she stared at him in the dark. The longest lashes ... he remembered her butterfly kisses.

He said, "She thinks I have unresolved issues involving you."

Barbara opened her purse and pulled out a pack of Old Golds with a lady's lighter. She lit up and inhaled. She took another puff. "I didn't want to hurt you, Rome. I didn’t know what I wanted."

"Barbara, it was a long time ago. I'm not that guy. You're probably not that gal."

"No. Still, I should have known that you weren't like my dad. He was hurt, sure. But he turned mean. Mom could have lived with his injured body, but not his injured brain. He was vile to her, as if she personally caused his pain. He accused her of … things." She turned back to roll down the window and tap the ash outside. A distant foghorn moaned. "She turned against all things involving war. Raised me to believe it destroyed people and to stay away from anybody who had anything to do with it. Sounds naive now, but that's how I felt."

Rome considered it. "I understand. I guess."

"Well, there's something else you didn't understand back then. I didn't either. But I prefer women to men."

"You mean?"

"Yes, I mean. Of course, I enjoy some men, too."

She moved closer. He heard her underwear rustle and slide on the seat. The scent of smoke wrapping itself around her perfume in the darkened car made him crazy with desire. But he couldn't abide the idea of being less than he once was in her eyes. What if that stump repelled her as much as it did him? "I'm not a good choice anyway. I'll never be worth much. I can't do all I'd like to do. I still fight battles that make me cry in the night, and that doesn't appear to be ending."

"It's just tonight, Rome." She opened the passenger door and stepped out. Surprised, Rome wondered where she was going. He watched as she crushed the cigarette with her heel. She turned toward him, lifted her skirt, and shimmied out of her underpants, leaving garters and nylons that hid very little. Then Barbara closed her front door and opened the back. She climbed inside and stretched one leg the length of the seat. Slowly, she lifted her other leg up toward the back window well. "I think you are just the man I need right now."

Rome agreed. In the next hour, they proved what a one-armed man in the big back seat of a Studebaker Champion could do with a woman whose imagination was boundless.

CHAPTER TWELVE

October 12, 1921
Leona Herkimer

"There's no fool like a young fool," Leona said to herself the next morning, clinging to the side of her narrow mattress until the bed spins in her head slowed down. Finally, she could stand without wobbling too badly. Soon after that, her head stopped pounding.

At the breakfast table, coffee was ambrosia. But the aroma of smoked salmon nearly started the war with her stomach all over again. If she'd learned nothing else from her escapade, she knew that keeping a bottle of brandy to test her pluck had been a colossal failure.

"Bollocks!" she muttered to herself, breathing in the hot coffee steam and hoping nobody would speak to her with too much cheerfulness.

Hooch. Firewater. Rot gut. When circumstances caused her to despair, she'd guzzle whatever low spirit she could get her hands on. And circumstances weren't likely to change. Patients died. She couldn't stop that from happening.

She was a disgrace. She must not have alcohol, never ever again. Fortunately, she had no place to purchase it in

Hoonah anyway, other than to waltz into the tavern cum pharmacy. Even driven by the greatest need, she was unlikely to do something quite that public.

Leona trudged through the first day of hang over agony. Crabby and temperamental she was, but she made it. Flower took the brunt of her snappish mood. As they cleaned the clinic, that faithful assistant finally stopped mopping, and asked in exasperation, "Leona, you are unreasonable. Are you pregnant?"

Leona began to chuckle. Then she laughed, bent over, holding her belly, still sore from dry heaves. "No, Flower. I'm not with child. I'm hung over."

Flower's dark brown eyes blinked like an owl. "I thought you might be turning mean like white ladies often do."

"Not at all. I was swizzled. Pie-eyed. Lushy. You don't think that natives are the only ones who can't handle booze, do you?"

Flower retained a deadpan. "I appear to handle it better than you."

Leona's guffaws turned to tears. Flower set the mop aside, wiped her hands on her apron in an age-old feminine gesture, and wrapped her arms around Leona until the storm passed.

"I'm so sorry, Flower. I'm such a harpy. You don't deserve it."

Sniff, gasp, snort.

Leona finally pulled back and breathed deep. "This must remain a secret. Nobody will accept me as a nurse if they know the truth. I'll be sent away."

"You do this often?"

"No. Especially with you and Ivy to keep me on the path of sobriety from now on."

"That is a very difficult path. But we can handle it."

The three women had a quiet dinner together. Leona was ready for the thin venison soup and a whacking great hunk of dense bread to sop it up. She was also ready to talk and told them about the Tongass Tearoom and startling Danielle LeDanz.

"On a dull night, we could all three go join the chorus line," Ivy observed. She pantomimed whirling a feather boa over her shoulder.

For Flower's benefit, Leona repeated the story she told Ivy the night before. "This desire to drink is with me always, but I can fend it off most of the time. When it overtakes me, it feels as though my muscles and organs are on fire for just a small taste. You two must watch me like guard dogs."

Ivy and Flower looked at each other and almost in unison yapped and growled like hounds of hell.

"Don't make me laugh!" said Leona, grabbing her sore sides. "And Flower, I know you have a home to go to, with your parents and siblings. But would you consider moving into the nurses' room with me? Without Jessica, I could use the company."

"Live here, like a real nurse?" For the second time that day, Flower's eyes opened wide, reminding Leona of an adorable owlet.

"You'll soon be a real nurse, you are so good at it now. You just need the book learning," Leona said. "You already help with births or whatever takes one of us away from the clinic. And I don't know how I'd manage without a translator as good as you."

One night of drinking had not been enough to put Leona through the many stages of the alcohol disease. No yellow bile, no shakes, no convulsions. She was far more controlled than her parents had been. Her anxiety dissipated as days passed without her becoming gossip for the whole town. But she was restless as that obsession deep within her hungered for more.

Walking helped. When Ivy or Flower could, one of them trekked with Leona, along the waterfront or into the forest. Otherwise, Leona went alone. She medicated herself with the cold, crystalline air, and the physical effort of ascending and descending trails through knobby hills and dripping forests. Tiring her body had the residual effect of easing the shame she felt. And it afforded the privacy to lecture herself.

I can quit if I want to badly enough. It must be a matter of willpower.

The problem was that she loved the way she felt while the drinking was fresh. She was full of humor, affection, wisdom. So very sure of herself. Tension and shame disappeared into the wilderness.

All I have to do is refuse the pull of that elixir warming my throat, soothing my brain. That's all.

She wished she knew more about alcoholism, but her medical books had little to say that she did not already know firsthand.

Sometimes, when the clinic was slow, Leona walked Wren home from school. The child chattered as endlessly as the downy woodpeckers drummed hemlock trees.

"Don't you just love Dr. Dolittle?" Wren asked while riding a gnarled stick as though it were a pony. "Teacher is reading it to us. That doctor talks to animals. Do you?"

"No. I'm a nurse for humans. I think it is even rare for animal doctors to talk to them."

"Well, that's what I want to do." Wren next employed the stick for a duel with an invisible foe. "Did you know woodpeckers bang their beaks on trees to get bugs? That's what they eat. Bugs and worms."

"What makes you so smart, Wren? Does your father read to you?"

"My mother did. He likes numbers more. He says math is pure. You can count on it."

"What do you suppose he means?"

"He means books end and numbers don't. Mom was a book, and he is a number. He said she's gone, but he will always be here."

Leona could have choked on the sadness. "What happened to your mother, Wren?"

"She died. There's a lot of ways to do that." Her stick poked the ground from side to side as though she were blind.

Mikhail often heard them coming and put a kettle on the stove before they arrived. He served Leona herbal tea. She brought tarts if Cook had baked that day. The threesome talked, and as the days passed and the visits continued, Leona French-braided Wren's hair, and had her read aloud to them from ragged copies of *Sun Bonnet Babies* and *Old Mother West Wind* that she found in the cabin. One day, she brought cups and saucers, sugar, spoons, jam, and pound cake to show Wren how to serve a fancy tea, just like the ladies Outside. She told Wren about the 'invisible creepy-crawlies' on her hands and why she had to wash away germs after each trip to the outhouse here or The Bog at school.

Mikhail often appeared quizzical about their chatter. "What is becoming of my little tomboy?" he asked and received an "Even boys should wash their hands," from Leona, and an outraged "I was never a boy," from Wren.

Many days he walked Leona part way home, leaving his daughter in the cabin to do her schoolwork. Before he finally touched her, Leona was beside herself with an itch nearly as bothersome as the lack of alcohol. It happened on a day the sun was still offering a bit of warmth before setting in the afternoon. As they meandered side by side on the trail, Mikhail ran his hand down the sleeve of her tunic, parting the fringe, and cupping her hand with his. "My girl is no longer a tomboy around you," he said. "And I wish to be less of a gentleman."

Leona had begun to think he wasn't interested. She wasn't used to gentlemen. She explored the roughness of his skin with her fingertips, then pressing harder against his palm. "Being a lady is not all it's cracked up to be."

"There is much to discuss. About Wren and my wife ..."

"About a bad habit of mine ..."

"About the problems for a white woman with a man who has native blood. About ..."

"Yes, there is a great deal to discuss. But first I think we set our worries aside. Is it a Russian custom to kiss? A Tlingit custom to kiss? If not, I have an American custom to teach you."

"Please begin the lesson now."

And she did.

After that first kiss, Leona found it harder to stay apart from Mikhail. He discovered reasons to come to town more often. Leona often invited Mikhail and Wren to join her for a mid-day meal with Ivy and Flower at the government building.

"Cook appears glad of the company," Ivy observed to Mikhail. "She doesn't like men usually. But she seems to bake better on the days you are here."

On many walks in the woods, Leona was with Flower, Ivy, or Wren. Their chatter kept them from startling a lynx or bear or wolverine. Ravens, hearing the noise, often added their ca-caws to the conversation to alert all creatures great and small. When by herself hiking to the cabin, Leona often sang to make her presence known.

One day she chose a song popular during the war gone by. "There's a long, long trail a-winding," she belted. During the following pause for breath, she heard a huff. "Into the land of my dreams," she continued with far less gusto. The huff was still there, like a steam train but much softer. She rounded a bend in the trail and froze in place. Carrion in the path was not totally unusual, because animals fed on animals, and the Tongass was full of animals. Leona wasn't naïve about that. "Where the nightingales are singing and a white moon beams," she sang in a near whisper.

Ferns shook and glistened with the freshness of the blood on their fronds. She could smell death. She registered the corpse of a deer, its legs moving in a grotesque parody of dance under the massive paw of the giant now chewing on a haunch.

Leona's innards turned to jelly. The rainforest bear, aware of her presence, lifted his head from his feast. He huffed louder, then huffed again. He claimed this kill as his own and wasn't leaving it because of a song.

"...until my dreams all come true," she whimpered brainlessly, staring at the bear who stared at her.

Beneath the teddy bear ears, the monster's eyes looked tiny within his massive head. She knew that if she met a bear, she should speak quietly so as not to alarm it. She was to walk away. And she was never, ever to disturb one that was eating.

She broke all these rules. As the bear lifted his weight slowly and lumbered in her direction, building up speed, she did all she could do. She threw the tray of cinnamon rolls she'd made for Mikhail directly toward the bear. Then she backed away fast. Almost in shock, she saw the giant stop, sniff the air, and lower his head. Awestruck, Leona realized he was eating the cinnamon treats.

She turned and fled, sing/screaming, "down that long long trail with you-oo-ooo." She sprinted at a speed that would do a blacktail proud.

Flower told her that night that she was lucky.

"Lucky? Lucky to be terrorized by a bear?" Leona squeaked.

"It was probably a brown bear. A black bear is smaller but also meaner. It would not have been quite so put off by your plenty bad singing."

Flower's eyes twinkled. Leona was sure of it. As far as she was concerned, the moral of the story was if you didn't have a gun, carry baked goods.

As the calendar moved into November, Mikhail presented Leona with the fur hat she had requested. "It is a Russian design with the fox fur within," he said. He also made rabbit mittens for Ivy, Flower, Judith, and Cook as thank-you gifts for their meals and friendship. When school was in session, Judith and Ivy tried not to treat Wren as family or even as a favorite, but she was becoming such.

All four of the women made it clear to Leona how disappointed they would be if she didn't accept this man.

The problem was night. A night together was difficult to arrange. It was too cold outside to roll around in a meadow or on a beach. Any plan for the cabin depended on whether Wren could stay with a friend overnight. Flower had moved into Leona's room, so that avenue was closed to romance. With a grin, Ivy told Leona, "You can always use the storeroom if Maki and I aren't there. Just watch out for the chamber pots." Mikhail and Leona found it funny at first, until their lust forced all wit out of the situation.

In mid-month it finally happened, a full night together in Mikhail's cabin. Flower's family invited Wren to gather clams and mussels and to dry seaweed for the winter. The child spent the night with them. On a second outing, Wren, along with Flower's sisters, flew kites made of seal intestine which were light and strong enough to flutter in the coastal breeze. The third occasion, Wren stayed with Flower in the clinic as a sleepover while Nurse Leona was off "nursing" somewhere.

Nobody, least of all Wren, was fooled by the guise. "My father likes you," Wren told Leona one day. "He can be a lucky number for you, too."

The first time Mikhail unlaced her bodice in front of the wood fire in the cabin, Leona turned shy as a bride. She'd already confessed to her demons with alcohol; he had ridded the cabin of his whiskey. She'd explained she was no virgin; he'd said neither was he. Now it was time for bodies to talk.

Will he notice my left breast is a smidgeon larger than my right? Will he mind that I can't keep from touching the tattoos on his arms? Will he wait for my body to catch up with his?

As he slowly unlaced and unbuttoned her clothes, stopping to touch or kiss whatever was revealed next, she realized he controlled time better than she. Leona pulled him down onto a pile of furs and rushed their first union. After a rest to catch her breath, she was far more proficient at drawing out their second.

Between innings, she snuggled and kissed his shoulder. "I have a birthmark there," he said.

"I know," she answered. "They're little clusters of extra blood vessels. Close to the skin's surface. Nothing to worry about."

"I need a nurse to keep me from worry."

"Meant to be together."

As their trust grew, Mikhail told her his wife had died in a fall from an icy outcropping in the wilderness. By the time he found her, she was gone. His need to raise Wren kept him sane; maybe all her chattering these days would make him crazy anyway. His native blood meant he would never amount to much in a white man's world; Leona told him she was becoming more comfortable in the Tlingit world, anyway. Over the weeks, they hacked their way through all this underbrush, and found nothing to fear underneath.

They couldn't live together, not yet. Mikhail needed to be out in the woods to tend to his trapline now as the temperatures dipped to freezing, and Leona had duties at the clinic. Early winter gifted them with seven hours of icy daylight, and the workload for the nurses intensified. Flower took temperatures, pulse and respiration, bathed patients, and made beds. Leona kept a typhoid victim clinging to life for a month; a burn victim's wounds seeped and smelled in the clinic through many days of recovery; an accident with a blade at the canning factory led to an arm so infected it hardly looked like a limb at all. Broken ribs, conjunctivitis, tooth extractions, rheumatism, strep, and staph. Head lice spread through the schoolchildren to Judith and Ivy as well as the nurses. After that episode, Leona and Flower wore bathing caps while treating others with pediculosis. Judith cut her hair into one of the bobs that had been the rage not so many years ago.

Leona and Mikhail decided they'd figure a way to live together in the spring when the obstacles weren't so great. That was a long way off. Now they grabbed privacy when they could and let worries take care of themselves.

November 16, 1921
Leona Herkimer

Leona received word via Hambone in Juneau that Dr. Reardon ordered her to come at once, bringing her warmest clothes. They must travel up the Chilkat River with the new diphtheria medication.

Leona was thrilled with the opportunity to see fresh territory and meet new tribes. She would even bring the vaccine back with her to Hoonah. The last medical treatise she'd read blamed the bacteria for killing twenty percent of the children who died under five years of age. Nursing couldn't get better than helping babies live.

Imagine an end to this scourge!

Nonetheless, she was once again petulant about the unpleasant Dr. Reardon. "Ordered!" she protested as she threw clothes into her case. "Not requested but ordered! Not a "could you" or a "please." The Kaiser has spoken! Dr. Reardon is such a stinker." She cocked her head at the contents of her bag.

"Any brandy in there?" Ivy asked.

Leona stared darts at her. "Brave woman to ask me that when I'm in the midst of a temper tantrum."

"Just doing my job, sister. The one you assigned. Guard dog Ivy, on patrol. Woof, woof."

Leona grinned at her friend. "And a very good dog you are." She wrinkled her forehead as she considered what to pack. "Do you suppose it will be frozen? The river? Won't the antitoxin freeze? Will we use dog teams on the ice?"

"I don't think so. It will be cold, but not cold enough to freeze the river or lake all the way across. Mushing is for farther north. I imagine mushers will take the antitoxin up to the tundra. No other way. But I'm guessing you'll canoe past Haines. Or maybe ride mules."

Leona stared down at her suitcase. "I have a parka, my tunic, my new hat from Mikhail. I'll wear a dress with my nurse apron on the boat."

"Here are mittens, the scarf, and socks I knitted you. Merry early Christmas. Dog hair repels water better than wool." As Leona "oohed" and held the softness against her cheek, Ivy added, "I traded tutoring lessons for the blue dye that the Tlingits make. Not even Flower will tell me how they do it."

"Ivy, they're wonderful. I'll sweeten up now or you might not want me back."

"Yes, you have been rather a pest, nurse. Do you have leggings?"

"Only my overalls."

"Then take these, too. Jessica made these bib and braces for me long ago. They'll fit over everything you own for a second layer." The dark brown pants were heavy corduroy with leather pockets and straps at the shoulders. "If it's really wintry, you'll need them."

Leona laughed at the heavy trousers. "I'll be a vision on the ice fields."

"Be sure you don't take any floral tea or soap that smells sweet. In fact, don't wash too often."

"I believe the doctor already finds me repugnant enough."

"No, silly. So the bears won't bother you."

"WHAT?"

"Chilkat is bear country. As much as here. And you know what sweet scents can do to them."

The next morning, the ranger boat *Yashee* stopped to pick up Leona. Maki was on his way to a meeting of regional rangers in Juneau. The skipper even favored Leona with a smile.

"You've made a conquest there," Maki murmured to her. "He doesn't smile at anyone else I know." He looked at Leona's medical bag but frowned at her suitcase. "That won't do the trick," he said, returning to the boat.

Leona looked at Ivy who shrugged. Maki reappeared with a contraption of straps, hide, and wooden frame. "Take this. It'll keep your hands free in case you have to carry your own gear."

"What is it?" Leona asked.

"The Inuits north of here make these packs out of sticks and seal skin. This frame stabilizes against your back after you put your whatnots in the pouch."

Leona had never carried such a contraption before. She transferred her possessions into it from the suitcase.

Maki lifted the pack onto her shoulders and reconfigured the straps to her small size. She tried it out, stomping around the boardwalk, then up and down the beach. Tribe women gathered to chuckle at her progress. "I believe I will fall over backwards on the slightest of hills," she observed to Maki who walked beside her. "It's like a heavy beast is hitching a ride on my back."

"Here's hoping Dr. Reardon will have mules to do the lifting for you," Maki said.

Leona removed the pack so it could be loaded onto the boat.

Just before they left, Ivy gave them both one more order. "Leona, you won't make it back for Thanksgiving, but you simply must be here by Christmas. You, too, Maki."

Leona was surprised. "You mean this won't merely take a week or two? She thought it would be a short-ish trip. *What about Mikhail? How can I go days without him? Will he forget me? Figure out he's better off without my faults?* Her self-confidence crumbled when alcohol no longer shored her up.

"Leona, we'll all be here waiting for you," Ivy said sternly, with substantial emphasis on the word all.

Not for the first time Leona wondered if her friend was clairvoyant.

"Even if it goes on much longer, you walk home if you have to," Ivy added. "This is Harold's first Christmas as the minister and Judith's as the new teacher. Their Christmas program for the village is far more important than wandering around in the wilderness. It's the event of the year. Unless, of course, Nordstrom chooses to open in Hoonah."

Leona laughed aloud. "I'll let the doctor know. I'm sure he'll understand that I cannot miss such a momentous event. If I have to, I'll invite him."

Mikhail, I won't be gone any longer than I must be.

Leona removed her pack and boarded the *Yashee* for the ride to Juneau. She was familiar with each island they skirted and the passages the ranger boat took. But she never grew used to the magnificence of the place. A turbulent sky changed by the moment, exposing and closing around ice peaks that marched on forever like a frozen gray army. Milky glacial water poured down waterfalls into the sea, swollen now with so much rain. Orcas cavorted near the boat to take a look at them.

Maki sat at what passed for a table, reading a bundle of papers he'd pulled from a flat leather pouch. She supposed he was preparing for his meeting, as he occasionally scratched a note with a fountain pen.

Leona left him to go to the pilothouse. "Skipper?" she asked.

He harrumphed at the interruption. "What is it, Missy?"

"Do you know a place in Juneau called the Golden Garter?" If Maki was familiar with it, she hadn't wanted to know.

He frowned. "Now see here ... why would I ... are you suggesting ... well, possibly I could find such a place."

She pulled a note from her pocket and handed it to him. "If you happen to find it, could you give this note to my friend Danielle LeDanz?"

"I make no promises, Missy, but I'll see what I can do. Although I'm astounded that a young lady like you would have a friend in a place like that."

Leona's temper nearly flared before she saw the wink in his otherwise sour countenance. She smiled at him sweetly. "If that is your best poker face, Skipper, you might stay away from the tables while you are there."

He placed her note into his jacket pocket. "I will take your advice under advisement."

Leona went back to the room where Maki still concentrated on his papers. It gave her time to study the man whom Ivy had chosen. Leona hoped he was worthy of her friend. It certainly seemed their relationship had gone on forever.

She knew he had a trick knee which might explain why he hitched one foot up on the chair crosspiece. He had no uniform other than a bronze US Forest Service badge hanging from one of his suspenders. Since he was so slender, he might actually need those braces to keep his britches up. His shirt was ancient cotton, and he sported those pants called Levis, like cowboys wore. But his hat was more rain gear than Stetson, and his boots were logger, not westerner.

When he stretched and looked up from the paper, he said, "You're staring at me like I'm an exotic beast."

She laughed, caught in the act. "I'd say you're a rare bird, Maki. I'm trying to decide if you're a crossbreed between a cowboy and a logger."

"A ranger's gotta be prepared for what comes along. Kinda like a nurse," he answered. He leaned back until the chair balanced on its back legs. Meanwhile he dug around in his pockets.

"But what do rangers really do, other than boat nurses from place to place?"

Maki went through the prolonged process of lighting a pipe. Tamp, light, puff, light. "What do rangers really do? Depends on where we're assigned. I worked down on the Columbia, so I can ride a horse, pack a mule, cook a meal over a campfire, herd cattle or sheep. I'm a good shot with a pistol or Winchester. Those are good cowboy skills for Outside. But here, as you can see, I wear caulk boots with spikes to keep me from falling off logs. I'm pretty good at surveying, estimating timber value, lumbering, minding the fur trade. I wield a mighty fine ax."

Light, puff, puff.

"I'm the policeman, fireman, fish and game warden, rescue party for thousands of square miles of forest. I should be stopping the moonshiners, but I figure the people making it need it to fight off the cold. Still, trappers and timber bosses tend to think of me as a buttinski. Which I am."

"Sounds like a lot of job security, doing all those tasks."

"Least till airplanes take over patrolling woods faster than I can." He patted the leather pouch. "Or the paperwork kills me. I surely do hate meetings."

"Mikhail says, apart from your very bad jokes, you are a good man."

His grin forced his cheeks upward until his eyes squinted. "If you don't mind me saying, you could do worse than Mikhail, Nurse."

"And Ivy could do worse than you."

"I've tried to tell her that. But I fear she could do better."

Leona thought for a while how to phrase what she wanted to say next. "You know, Maki, there was a time other people had rooms at the clinic. Now there's only Flower and me sharing a room."

"Glad you've taken the girl under your wing. She's smart and makes the tribe proud."

"Yes, I am happy about that, but it is not my subject or my meaning at the moment. I'm trying to say that Flower and I don't care what Ivy does in her room. It is far less congested than the storeroom these days."

Leona blushed at her boldness. But Maki roared with laughter.

CHAPTER THIRTEEN

Leona Herkimer
November 17

Leona clambered up the hill to St. Ann's, puffing from the steep climb. The pack on her back nearly toppled her. She narrowly avoided smacking into a prospector who was wobbling down the street in the opposite direction, so she veered to a streetlight and rested against the pole. After catching her breath, she moved on, grasping her medical bag in one hand as she used the other arm for balance, like a seagull's stiffened wing.

The hospital receptionist was aware that Dr. Reardon had arranged for Leona to spend the night in the staff quarters. The moon-faced young woman said, "He instructed he would meet you at the dock in the morning at first light."

Instructed!

"But first, he wanted you to receive a typhoid inoculation." She held up a small vial and syringe for Leona. "The vaccine just came in, he said and you could have a nurse here do it."

Leona was surprised he remembered as she went to the staff room and gave herself the medication. She had nearly forgotten that, amidst all she'd done wrong, she'd been right in her diagnosis of the fisherman's disease.

Maybe he wasn't as unreceptive to her as he seemed. On the other hand, he hadn't planned a meal with her. It was merely the polite thing to do with guests from afar. By not asking, he hadn't allowed her the pleasure of refusing him. She'd made her own plan, and now he wouldn't know she had better things to do than spend her free time with him.

Just before six, she walked to the Tongass Tearoom. Danielle LaDanz waved at her through the window. Her friend wore a nicely tailored suit which was far less revealing than her get up last time they met. Danielle looked more like a woman with style and less like a woman with a reputation. The most provocative part of her outfit was the confection of aqua feathers on her wide-brimmed felt hat.

"You received my message!" Leona burst with joy. The two women hugged.

"Yes! I was so happy to hear from you, I gave the skipper a free kiss and hug."

Leona snickered, picturing the reaction of the old sourpuss. "It must have well pleased him."

"Surprised him at least. He needed to sit down to recover. At least he stayed through several of the girls' dances before he managed an exit."

Leona removed her anorak and took one of the ice cream parlor chairs. A heart was woven into its ironwork back, and the wooden seat was hard as granite. Clearly, the Tongass Tearoom was for women; men would never put up with such beastly seats no matter how cute they were.

"I've taken the evening off, so I dressed accordingly. For the town, not for the stage," Danielle bubbled.

"And I've worn all I have to leave for the wilderness tomorrow." Leona indicated her trousers and flannel.

"I thought you would like to stroll about town after our meal. Meanwhile, I've ordered you a glass of grape juice to join me." Danielle lifted her own glass, gesturing a toast.

"A delighted yes to a stroll, but no thank you to the other. Let me tell you what happened to me the last time I was here. I'm warning my friends so they can help me with my resolve."

Leona spun her story while Danielle's mouth slowly gaped in surprise. The nurse bemoaned her lost patient and the drunken night that followed. Danielle, for her part, asked the waitress to remove the wine.

"Please leave it," Leona countermanded to the waitress. To Danielle, she said, "Please tipple away. I must learn to be with people who can enjoy what I can't. Otherwise, I'll have to sit at home like a frump."

In agreement, Danielle drank both glasses as they each enjoyed the special of the day: thin-sliced venison steak with rhubarb gooseberry chutney.

They batted subjects back and forth like a shuttlecock. Danielle told Leona about a new dressmaker in town who had a line of gorgeous unmentionables. And about one particular gentleman whom she'd never charged for sex. Leona overflowed about Mikhail and their possible plans for spring.

"So the good doctor is out of contention?" Danielle asked.

"The good doctor was never in contention," Leona corrected. "Although he is a knowledgeable man and quite a comely one as well. I'm fascinated by this trip to inoculate against such a dreadful disease. He has made that possible for me."

Danielle described the apartment where she lived on nights that she wasn't detained at the Golden Garter. "I consider myself a nurse of sorts, too, you know," she said with a wink. "And I earn far more than you."

"Perhaps. But I can nurse anyone, not just old horn toads with over-eager twiddle-diddles."

Danielle squealed. "Touché! But where did a woman like you learn a phrase like that?"

"Probably the last time I was sauced," Leona admitted.

Danielle patted her hand. "I'll keep your secret, Leona. And we don't need liquor to have fun."

"The disgrace of my past is mine forever, but it means a great deal to have support for the future."

"Let's go for that stroll, shall we?" Danielle stood and tossed a wrap around her shoulders. The slight breeze of the act released an aromatic cloud of flowers and spice. "What would you like to see?"

"Is that dressmaker still open, do you suppose?"

She was. And the underthings were lovely, silky, and naughty. Leona bought her Christmas present for Ivy. One she thought Maki might appreciate, too.

Back at St. Ann's that evening, she tucked her new purchases into the bottom of her pack. She was glad she'd bought a pretty for herself, too. Heaven knew this dark, gray winter could use a bit of color. As she slipped into bed, she admitted that Danielle was right. She'd had fun without a drop of alcohol. And for the next few days, plowing around in the outdoors, there would be no opportunity. Cutting off supply was key to handling her demand.

She wished she didn't have to bear this gnawing hunger for a sip, just one sip. It festered within her all the time.

The next morning, Leona was at the dock by daylight. The walk took half the time as the afternoon before, as she nearly galloped downhill pushed by the pack.

"I'm here, Nurse. You need not rush."

She heard his deep voice. When she located him in the dim light, she said, "I would not want to hold you up, Doctor. But I have many questions once we are underway."

He looked different, no longer in the funereal suit of a doctor, but the rugged clothing of an explorer. The leather jacket, Levis, and boots suited him, made him seem more at home with his environment.

He even smiled. "Many questions! I can count on you to be eager to learn, Nurse Leona. It is an admirable quality." He pointed to the northeast where the waterway disappeared into a wall of mountain. "We boat to Haines and spend at least two days there vaccinating. Then we pick up mules to go north. The beasts will carry your burdens for you. In the meantime, let me take that pack which appears to overwhelm you."

"No, sir. I don't expect you to be one of the mules, Dr. Reardon. I'll deal with it until we get on board."

"Fine then. It is a beautiful ride toward Haines. That should give us ample time to converse."

November 18, 1921
Ivy Bolton

With Leona off to the wilderness, Ivy spent her first couple evenings knitting mufflers and socks as Christmas gifts for all the orphans. They'd want toys, but they'd need warmth. She worked in the kitchen because the lamplight was best there, and the room stayed warm from the stove and oven that overheated it during the day.

Flower worked on her own project across the table from Ivy. The Tlingit men of Hoonah had carved toy canoes, one for each orphan, and Flower volunteered to paint them. A half dozen little cedar crafts were on the table in front of her, as she decorated each with a traditional animal design.

"Your fleet is beautiful," Ivy said, breaking a companionable silence at the end of the evening.

"There will be eighteen when I'm done. Squinting at these tiny designs makes my eyes tired." Flower stretched her back. "Is Cook making her chocolate creams this year?"

"She says she will. But she believes sugar is affected by weather and will be easier to handle on a clear day without rain." Ivy smiled at the very idea of a clear day.

"Maybe the orphans will be waiting till spring for their Christmas candy."

Ivy stretched in a mirror action of Flower. "It's time to quit. My bed is calling my name."

Flower left the canoes to dry but gathered together her paint supplies. "What will the party be like, do you suppose?"

"It's Judith's affair really. I know she'll have Christmas dinner at the church for all the orphans and anyone else who wants to come. She wants to do a nativity play with the school kids, and I say more power to her. I've offered to decorate the church with the help of my older students." She replaced her skeins and needles into a battered sewing bag. "Other than that, I'll pressure-cook jars of soup and jam for Captain Aleck and for Maki." Then she gave Flower a grin. "I also plan to give Maki his own chamber pot."

Flower smiled back. "He is a fine man, Ivy."

"Yes, he is."

There was an awkward pause while Flower didn't ask more, and Ivy didn't answer more. They honored what was private. Flower was first to leave the kitchen. "K'idénnatà Ivy."

"Good night, Flower." As she turned down the seal oil lamps, Ivy heard a soft knock on the door. Somebody needing Leona, no doubt. Whoever it was would have to wait or let Flower take a look. The only other option was a boat to Juneau tomorrow. Ivy opened the door. "I'm sorry, but ... Maki!"

He came in and threw his arms around her, his coat full of the night chill.

"Brrr!" she said.

"Some greeting," he muttered into her ear as he pulled his coat open and wrapped her up inside with him. Her head fit just under his chin.

"Better," she purred. "It's good to see you. Leona is on her way with the doctor?"

"When last seen, she was heading up the hill to St. Ann's Hospital to spend the night. Wobbling a bit with the backpack, but she'll get the hang of it. That was, let's see, two nights ago. I assume they are well underway by now."

"And your meetings?"

"Done, thank God. Why be with a bunch of men in Juneau when I can be here with my woman?"

"Can you spend the night?"

"That's my plan. And in your bed, not on your floor."

She pulled back and stared up at him. "Oh? Who changed that rule?"

"Leona gave me permission."

"She did, did she?"

"Well, in so many words. I believe she feels we're less in the way in your room than in the storeroom."

"I wouldn't want to disobey the nurse."

"That's good because under her rather close scrutiny, I have passed her inspection as far as you're concerned."

Ivy made a noise like a giggle, although she would deny such a silly, girly sound. She came out from the warmth of his coat, took his hand, and led him into the part of her world that he'd never seen before.

A bed, even a narrow bed, was better than a wood floor. They were well acquainted with each other's bodies and likes. Ivy hated anything involving her ears; Maki willingly explored trails through the wilderness but usually returned to his favorites.

"You know this is called the missionary position, don't you? Because it is so basic?" he asked.

"I know, but I hate the term. I don't want to imagine Harold in bed."

"Ivy, I hope you imagine no other man in your bed."

After making love, they made conversation. Ivy needed to share something with him. She'd prefer to wait a little longer, but she was never sure when she would have private time with him. "Maki, do not go to sleep just yet."

"But it's a bed, and we have the night."

"We must talk."

"Now?"

"Heaven knows when I'll see you next."

"All right." He rolled on his side to face her. "Spill the beans." He delivered gentle kisses to the ridge of her cheek bone.

"Stop that. How can I talk when you're doing that?" She pulled back so she could stare at him. "I have been thinking about returning Outside."

Pause.

"Oh?" he asked after a lightyear.

She leaned back into his chest when she felt his muscles stiffen slightly. Ivy wrapped her leg over his. "I told you that Poppy's last letter said my husband is dead. I came here to escape him. But I don't have anything to fear from a dead man."

Maki said nothing so she carried on. "Poppy is a grown woman, and I would like to see her, to be closer to my daughter again. I think it's time for a home of my own, someplace more permanent than Hoonah."

He finally spoke, low, close to her ear. "I thought Hoonah was your home."

"Yes, in so many ways it is. I've been here for two decades. You had every reason to think it was permanent. I might have, too. But I'm missing things."

"Things?"

Was he mad? Happy? Did he not care? Ivy couldn't tell from his whisper in her ear.

She stumbled on. "I'd like to learn to drive a car and go to a library. I'd enjoy going to a motion picture theatre and maybe traveling by train to Portland. How fun it would be to cook whatever I want again, not just what comes by freighter or mail boat."

When he said nothing, she added, "Maki, I've known you for ten of the twenty years I've been here. I've always thought maybe you had a wife Outside, a family you support but don't see. It's true for many men living up here."

He gave her a little squeeze, then untangled himself and sat on the edge of the narrow bed. "Ivy. There's nobody else. There was, but she died years ago. Long before I came up here. Marriage doesn't really mesh with the life of a forest ranger. Not the way most women want it to be."

She ran her fingertips over his back, a butterfly touch. This was insanely hard, this saying of goodbye if that's what it must be. She didn't dare hope for any more from him. "Maki, you are the only person who knows how I look, what I've suffered. I've trusted you like I will trust no other man."

At last, she could hear an emotion from him. It sounded like exasperation. "I love how you look, Ivy. You know that. But you've always rejected me. Did you think my proposals weren't real? That hurt, you know."

This surprised her. "I didn't know. I didn't have that kind of faith, I guess. I had to move slowly. I don't want to presume love on your part just because I feel it. I was so taken in before."

He nodded. "I knew that. I've been willing to wait. But now you're leaving."

"Maki, turn back to me. Look at me."

He did. She placed her arms around him and held tight. "Would you love how I look Outside?"

"Are you asking me to come with you?"

"I rather hoped you would ask if you could."

November 18, 1921
Leona Herkimer

When their boat arrived at the dock in Juneau, Leona was delighted to see it was *Small Fry* commissioned to taxi them to Haines. Captain Aleck and his crewman greeted them, then hauled their provisions on board. Two large crates were marked FRAGILE.

"The vaccine?" Leona asked.

"Part of it. We get more at Fort Seward," Dr. Reardon answered.

"So we make a stop before Haines?"

"Same stop," Captain Aleck said. "The fort is on the water, in front of the town. Brand new."

Leona was not aware that Alaska had an army and said as much.

"Cheechako!" Captain Aleck sneered at her.

"Sourdough!" She sneered back.

"Are you two fighting?" the doctor asked, sounding perplexed.

"No," Leona laughed. "I learned those terms on my first day here. But I'm no newcomer anymore."

"And Fort Seward is no Alaska installation. It's a genuine U.S. of A. government project to keep the miners of Haines from killing each other." The last crate was loaded, and the captain left for the pilothouse.

Once underway, the little steamer made enough noise that Captain Aleck couldn't be heard. Leona and the doctor sat on opposite benches surrounded by medical supplies and luggage. No matter how she maneuvered, her knees knocked into his. They did a seated shuffle until he crossed his long legs to aim them in one way, and she claimed the other. This resulted in a twisted body position. Now connected to the bench with only one buttock, Leona wondered if Dr. Reardon was as uncomfortable as she was.

She also wondered why he looked better than she'd noticed before. His face had lost its icy coldness and relaxed into calm instead. His smile seemed genuine, even eager. Maybe getting away from the hospital and out into the field was a pleasure for him. Maybe his tension level plummeted. She could only guess.

"Fort Seward has a purpose other than policing the miners," the doctor said. "The boundary between Canada and Alaska is not agreed upon. With all this land, you'd think it wouldn't matter, but mining rights are on the line. Brits, Canucks, and Yanks are working it out."

"So a military presence by the United States keeps them close to the claim and visible for anyone who asks."

"Exactly. At least that's how it appears to me. Very perceptive of you, Nurse Leona."

I'm perceptive because I can think as well as a man can. She nearly snapped it at him. Just in time, she reconsidered and held her tongue. They would have many days ahead to battle or befriend. Might as well start out on an even keel. Besides, had some ghost of sociability inhabited the doctor? If so, this trip could cement their working relationship into a good one. She hoped so. She didn't like the confrontational role she had with him in the clinic. The outdoors might be a cure-all for them both.

"You're smiling. Is something funny?"

"No, oh no. I was merely admiring this breathtaking view." Leona opened her pack and took out the long blue scarf knitted by Ivy, winding it around her neck.

They steamed northeast up Lynn Canal, a long deep fjord with water the milky teal color of glacial run-off. As they chugged closer to Chilkat Peninsula, the snow grew heavy in the forest. Behind the first row of mountains, endless formations covered with glaciers stretched as far as she could see.

If there is anything in Alaska that's ugly, it must be manmade.

But then she saw she was mistaken. An enormous elk, on the bank near the water, was deformed in all possible ways. Overgrown head, legs out of all proportion to the rest of its body, shaggy fur sparse in many areas. "Look at that poor elk!" she gasped.

"There aren't any elk in Alaska, although there's talk of importing some from Washington. Oh wait ... do you mean that moose?" The doctor pointed at the deformed elk.

"Moose! I've heard of them, but had no idea they were so big and ..."

"Ugly?" He laughed. "They are at that. God's mistake in the looks department. But they can run like the wind, they handle these winters, and they're usually shy of us. One kill feeds and houses many Chilkat Tlingits for a long time. They use every bit of it."

"Then I guess moose are not mistakes after all. Thank you for clearing up what was sure to be a disturbing nightmare."

"May I call you cheechako?"

"No, you may not. Nurse Leona will do quite nicely." She raised her nose in a haughty gesture, flinging the end of the blue scarf over her shoulder.

"Yes, Ma'am." He touched the brim of his hat.

For the rest of the journey, they rode in companionable silence interspersed with information on what lay ahead.

"Imagine the opportunity to stop the spread of diphtheria, Doctor. I've battled that treacherous gray substance closing over a child's tonsils and larynx, not always successfully."

"The pseudomembrane. Waste product caused by the toxin secreted from the bacteria. We've all lost patients to it, or to the damage the toxin does to the heart, kidneys, or liver. But this new antitoxin seems a cure to such woes."

Thank heavens for men to explain things to women. Leona thought he sounded like Harold, giving a lecture on what she already knew. A smile crossed her lips again, and she worked hard to make it more grateful than scornful. "Pseudomembrane. Such a difficult word! Now then, what will our schedule be?"

"We'll spend two or three days at the fort, inoculating soldiers first, but word has been sent to the natives in the Haines area to come to the fort, as well. When we've finished there, we'll pick up more supplies, then rent mules to pack back to Chilkat Lake. It's about thirty miles. Tlingits live all around that area. We'll catch as many settlements as we can."

"Do we go alone?" Leona, for the first time, gave thought to the propriety of such a situation. And not for the first time, she gave thought to more bears.

"Well, there's the mule skinner, of course. I don't imagine either of us is expert at packing the beasts and maintaining their good humor."

"If one doesn't respond to 'Good boy, Jack,' then I am out of my depth."

Dr. Reardon laughed heartily. "How many mules named Jack do you suppose there are in the world?"

"I can't imagine, and don't particularly care to find out."

"We'll have a guide who knows the Chilkat dialect. I've worked with Coy before. You'll find him ... interesting. Where we stop to inoculate, he'll get help from the local women, to boil equipment and manage the line-ups."

During the silences, Leona's eyes filled with the scenery, but her mind drifted to Mikhail. She had never felt like this before and assumed it might be love. Either that or dyspepsia caused by the alcohol disease greeting another uncontrollable predicament. The jittery feeling was disconcerting. Mikhail and she had shared few days together and even fewer nights. Was it only four? She accepted that things moved fast in the Alaska back country, where there was limited opportunity for courtship. Hoonah was no Seattle in the niceties of civilized behavior.

Mikhail was the only man she had ever made love to when alcohol was not in the picture. She was quite pleased to be fully there for the event, enjoying herself without the hazy veil. If the doctor's knee was Mikhail's knee pressing into her thigh, she'd be reacting very differently than flattening even more against *Small Fry's* side.

She vaguely remembered doing unspeakable things on a man's lap while drunk. Would she have desires like that without booze? Was it demented behavior? How astounded would Mikhail be if she gave it a try with him? She could always claim that Danielle told her about such things.

Captain Aleck came out of the pilothouse and stared at her. "You have a rosy glow, Nurse."

"It's all this fresh air, Captain." She smiled, feeling affection for this man who'd seen her at her worst but appeared to like her anyway. Did he wonder whether she had control of her addiction? She spread her arms wide and pronounced, "Who needs anything else when you have all this majesty to soothe your soul?" She winked at him. "Do you know what I mean, Captain?"

"Indeed, I do. That's good then." He reached into a bin and came out with a wrapped packet of sandwiches on thick bread, as well as coffee in a newfangled Thermos vacuum flask. "Eat. We'll be there in a couple more hours."

The doctor had been listening since he was only a kneecap away. "You two seem to know each other well. You speak in code."

"I travel on *Small Fry* a fair amount. Yes, Captain Aleck is a friend."

"That is all it is? Friendship?"

"Well, yes! Of course. What are you implying?" She squawked like a bantam with a fox in the henhouse. "I could be his daughter!" If he hadn't irritated her so, she might have told him that the Captain's interest had been with the other nurse in Hoonah. She chose not to share that bit of gossip with him. *So there.*

"It might be easy to misconstrue as a questionable interest. That's all I meant."

Is he frowning at me? "Not by anyone with an ounce of common sense." She would have stormed away in a huff, but she couldn't, pinned to *Small Fry* as she was. *Seriously. Is he thinking I need a chaperone?*

As they chugged up the passage, she had a second thought. *I suppose a chaperone wouldn't have hurt me a time or two.* The subject was dropped by both.

Lynn Canal narrowed to Chilkat Passage and soon buildings came into view.

"That's the fort," Captain Aleck yelled from the pilothouse.

Far to the north and west, the foreboding peaks of the Yukon spread to the end of the earth. Fort Seward clung to the waterway as though the channel was its only path to safety. The installation did not have the upright log walls that Leona imagined from history books. Instead, it was a grouping of white buildings, the paint glistening in what chilly sun there was. The headquarters, barracks, and what appeared to be officer housing were constructed on a timbered and manicured stretch of parkland. It looked more like Fort Worden in Washington than the western outposts of earlier years.

"It's quite handsome," Leona observed. "I believe a white paint salesman has made great inroads with the military of the Northwest."

The doctor stared at her, raising an eyebrow. "You are a witty companion, Nurse Leona. Humor is missing in most of my days. It is refreshing."

Careful, Doc, she thought. *You're handing out a compliment*. She considered with some sadness how he seemed so much more at ease here in the wild than within the medical community.

When they came to shore, *Small Fry* was met by a lanky teenage boy with a face ravaged by acne and a grin that made it acceptable. "I'm Charlie, Doc Boc's assistant. I mean Dr. Boccaccio. The soldiers here shortened his name for him. Please come with me."

As he led them toward the headquarters, some soldiers across the frostbitten green took surreptitious looks while others smiled broadly. Leona found it rather jolly to be admired. But she was startled when the doctor took her arm.

Protective or possessive?

She had no more time to think about it as the boy directed them up the stairs to the headquarters, into a spacious room that had been set with worktables and a burner for heating water. She was pleased. It was an excellent set-up for an inoculating operation.

Charlie said, "Doc Boc asked to see you as soon as you arrived, Dr. Reardon. He's in surgery and could use your help. I'll take you to him, and be right back to assist you, Nurse."

"Good, Charlie. We'll open the crates." She would have preferred Flower to help, but she was willing to give this gawky boy a try.

Dr. Reardon said, "You'll start with soldiers first and begin natives tomorrow."

"Yes, sir. The men are on alert to come alphabetical-like," Charlie said eagerly. "Soon as you're ready, Nurse."

Dr. Reardon turned to her with a trace of wit creasing his cheeks. "And, Nurse Leona, it is good you have a sense of humor."

She cocked her head, not understanding. "Why do you say that?"

"Because it is preferable to administer the diphtheria vaccine to an adult's gluteal muscles, making an effort to avoid the sciatic nerve. You will be seeing the naked backsides of 186 men."

CHAPTER FOURTEEN

Rome Coleridge
October 7, 1946

Rome's neck was stiff from the athletic night in the back seat of Ivy's car. His emotions were mixed. He knew he should marry Barbara after such an episode, and he'd dutifully proposed. But she turned him down flat.

She snorted at his offer, as they untangled themselves to sit upright. Then she lit up an Old Gold, inhaled deeply, and expelled smoke through her nose. "Honestly, soldier boy," she said, "this has been ducky, and you are a lovely specimen of manhood. All the best bits of you certainly made it back from the war." She patted the zipper on his trousers.

"But a man is not what you want?"

"While the men were away at war, some of us gals played. I learned marriage is not for me. But until the right woman comes along, I'll meet you on the playground anytime. No reason not to enjoy whatever's on display."

He'd heard of queer women among the WACs, but he'd thought it was just so much malarky, nothing he'd seen proven. But a woman who liked men and her own kind? Well, even smut in the trenches hadn't alerted him to such a thing. Barbara had more guts than he did, at least in that way. "I'll never understand the fairer sex," he muttered to her and the world at large.

"There's nothing very fair about it," she answered as she climbed out of the car. She reached back and gave him a peck on the cheek. "See ya' kid."

He wasn't hurt any deeper than his pride. He wasn't in love. Barbara was not the same angel he'd left behind (although he was quite pleased her angelic breasts were the same). Still, he hoped she'd provide him friendship until she was gone for good. She'd told him that she longed for adventures in cities across the world from Port Angeles, Washington.

"You haven't seen what I've seen," he'd replied. "I want to forget foreign hellholes." Rome didn't want his horizons broadened any more than they'd been by the tortures of war. The Olympic Peninsula felt like home, and home felt like safety.

He wasn't ready to share his fears with her, and Barbara wasn't ready to listen. He could only talk about all that emotional stuff with Ivy. Maybe old women were just a lot wiser than young ones. God knows Ivy was wiser than young men.

Ivy Bolton
October 15, 1946

Ivy talked Rome into helping her put up autumn bounty. She tied an apron around him, an apron that was pre-stained from years of hard use.

"I've always looked good in cabbage roses," he said, eyeing the faded print as she finished with the apron strings.

"Yes, and the butterfly sleeves add a fetching touch." She flicked the empty one to make it flutter. "Now then, much for you to do."

It was a long day.

"You make me do this stuff to prove a one-armed man isn't useless," Rome accused her after several hours of washing, boiling, and stirring.

"I'm making you do it because my feet hurt," she answered, now sitting at the table, adding brown sugar and cinnamon to the windfall Jonathans she'd sliced.

It was true, though, what he said. Through the summer, she'd been teaching him how to prosper. "You like to eat, you better learn to cook," she'd said one afternoon. She taught him to crack eggs, peel bananas one-handed, and wring out a rag by pushing it against the side of the sink then squeezing. She was tickled when he arrived one day with a small wooden frame he'd made to hold a bowl in place so he could stir the contents.

Now, in the season of abundance, Rome worked with his disability, not against it. He appeared to take pleasure in figuring out his own puzzles. "My mouth or knee or stomach can be a pretty good second hand."

He learned to roll out a crust, eventually replaced his wooden frame when he discovered a wet cloth under a bowl worked nearly as well, and by holding a potato or onion against his body he could peel it with a sharp knife in his only hand. Ivy couldn't watch this trick, but Rome excelled at it after enough practice.

Ivy watched him this morning carry in crates of vegetables and apples with the help of a hip bone. "Moms learn that maneuver when their babies get bigger than watermelons," Ivy said with approval. But she didn't enthuse. She'd irritated him before with too much of that.

In fact, early in their friendship, she'd properly pissed him off, thinking she was being oh so subtle. "You know about Pavlov's dogs, don't you?"

"Is this a new topic or a dirty joke?"

"Maybe both."

Rome frowned in thought. "Well, let's see. Pavlov experimented with conditioned response by making dogs salivate. We bookmobile drivers have quite the education."

"That's only part of the story. Pavlov's cohorts played dirty tricks on those mutts. They ran current through the bottoms of the cages. The dogs would yelp and leap. Once they learned there was no escape, they would lie still, silently accepting the inevitable. The psychologists called it learned helplessness."

"Learned helplessness," he'd repeated.

"Don't let that arm or the lack of it get the best of you."

"I'm not a dog learning tricks," he'd snapped. "You don't have to say I'm a good boy."

But Ivy knew he feared living with a second-rate body, and Rome knew she could improve his abilities. They learned to give each other room. She quit rushing to help when he fumbled; he allowed her to see him struggle. Their friendship accommodated each other.

Now, at the kitchen table, Ivy set down her wooden spoon and leaned back. "Nobody ever made Apple Brown Betty better than me. It won't ever happen unless I bequeath the recipe in my will. Not sure I know anyone worthy of it."

"Thanks for the consideration."

"You're welcome. While I finish this for dessert tonight, you sterilize those jars, then run the rest of the apples through the corer. And stir more sugar into the carrots."

"How much sugar?"

"Until it feels right."

"Ivy, even if I had two hands, I don't think it would ever feel right."

They worked in silent comfort until Ivy got up to make tea, causing Rome to dance around her in the snug kitchen. "Glad I don't have to do all this alone, Rome. I'm not as agile as I was. Now tell me about Barbara."

"Barbara?" he asked, his eyebrows reaching for the sky.

"You've mentioned nothing about her since our dinner weeks ago," she said.

"You mean one week ago."

"Don't quibble. What happened after that?"

"After what?"

"For all that's holy, Rome, after *dinner*. I'm old but not demented. I heard my car. Your car. Our car. I doubt you had a late-night desire to go shine deer."

He laughed. "Oh. No. I was with Barbara." Then he stopped again.

"Are you teasing me? Is it love?"

Rome sighed. Leaning against the counter, he picked up his cup of tea. "No, Ivy, it isn't love. I liked her before the war, and I like her now. I'm glad you engineered a meeting. We'll be friends. But we're very different people than we were. She prefers wom ..."

The kitchen door burst open.

Ivy beamed as a wiry old man, wind-wrinkled and sun-browned, strolled in with a nearly invisible limp. She gasped in delight. "Welcome back, my love! It's been a long while."

He grabbed her and hugged her tight, a hug she gladly returned. As they embraced, he peered at Rome, then said to Ivy, "You been dating younger men while I'm gone? Is that your dress he's wearing? What's going on here, Ivy?"

She laughed and pulled back. "Rome, this is my friend. Maki."

CHAPTER FIFTEEN

November 18, 1921
Ivy Bolton

They slept awhile, then Maki woke her up, whispering close to her ear. "You would really want me to? Move to the Outside? With you?"

Ivy had been dozing. "If you want to. Yes, I think I would. Even though you just woke me up."

"Is that against the rules for living with you?"

"Waking me up? Yes, it is."

"Already with the rules." He sighed. "Women."

"How many women do you know all that well, Maki?"

"Why, none other than you, Ivy."

She pulled herself out of the spoon they'd created on the narrow bed and turned toward him. "Maki, now listen to me. Yes, I have rules, same as you. But they aren't the same as other people. After all these years, you know that. I don't intend to make many changes. And I don't think I'd like it much if you did."

"I don't see that in the cards."

"I know you love it here, Maki. You are such a part of the forest that you'll stop growing hair and start growing twigs any day now."

"Olympic National Forest is nearly as big as Tongass," he said. "And still wild. Might need another ranger. It surrounds towns called Port Angeles and Forks and Sequim, out on the Olympic Peninsula. I've seen it on forest service maps. Kinda interests me."

She smiled in the dark, her lips skimming the stubbled skin below his chin. She murmured, "Farther west than when I taught in Port Townsend, but a growing area. There's a new Carnegie Library in Port Angeles. Read about that in a month-old Seattle paper. Imagine all those books at your beck and call."

"When would this be? A move Outside?" Maki asked.

"This spring or summer, I think. After the school year and before the next. I could go then."

He hmphed.

"You hmphed?" she asked.

"I couldn't go that early, Ivy. Spring, summer? Too busy here to leave, I'm thinking. But I could train a new ranger then. Leave toward winter. Follow you then."

Ivy felt a flutter as stomach butterflies rose in excitement. "I'll start applying now for a teacher position. Not many to be had."

For a while, they both lay quiet, each in a headspace of wonderment.

We're seriously considering this thing! Ivy felt quite flummoxed.

"You think we could stand living together full time?" Maki asked.

"I don't know."

"I like the idea of a bed more than a storeroom floor." He put a rough-skinned hand around her soft-skinned breast.

She cupped her hand over his. "I like the idea of sex on a more regular basis."

"*Sex*? What a way for a lady to talk."

"You would prefer amorous congress? Pully hawly?"

"Blanket hornpipe, I think," he said. "I'll show you how."

Leona Herkimer
November 20, 1921

Leona tried very hard not to react to Dr. Reardon's comment about 186 naked backsides. Charlie blushed to the tips of his ears, but she wouldn't let the doctor shock her, by golly. She said, "Charlie, after you see Dr. Reardon to the surgery, bring back a privacy screen or two if Doc Boc has any extras. Some of the lads will be shy regarding their sit upons."

The doctor smirked as he and Charlie left the room.

Leona smirked, too, once they were gone to wherever the fort doctor was performing an operation. It must be a doozy if one doctor requested another. Her curiosity rivaled the best of cats, but she turned her attention to her own operation. After a bit of planning, Leona shoved two sturdy tables perpendicular to each other, creating space near the wood stove for the equipment to dry after Charlie boiled it. She missed Flower to keep records, but she could do that and inoculate. She stoked the flames in the stove then stopped a young officer in the hallway, asking where she might obtain water. Leona knew the value of her own smile. He whisked away her bucket and kettle, then returned in next to no time. By then, Charlie was preparing the Montgomery Ward kerosene burner they carried with them, to help the stove in the constant sterilization of syringes, trays, and rubber gloves.

Together, they put up frames for three cloth dividers to separate the pants-down area from the rest of the room. Charlie ushered in six soldiers at a time. Each bent, behinds in a row toward Leona, and she shot them quickly and efficiently. As she caught up on records, Charlie placed the used syringes in boiling water, then ushered in the next six. Leona also handed out creams for the occasional rash, and in one case, told Charlie, "Have Doc Boc see to this fellow. He seems malnourished to me." With so little fat and muscle to his buttocks, Leona knew something was wrong, something worse than malnutrition, but she didn't want to scare the man.

Charlie and Leona worked steadily for hours to finish their mission. And then they were done. As they stretched their backs, Charlie said, "We set up out on the green tomorrow, for the injuns. That many at a time's not allowed in the fort buildings."

Leona sighed. "I'm sure they are a danger," she said, but her sarcasm flew over Charlie's head.

"First thing I was told when I got here. Don't trust an injun. He can't help but tell taradiddles even when he ain't drunk."

"Charlie. I prefer we call them natives. Or Tlingits," Leona chided. "Not injuns. And not liars. And not drunks."

"Right you are, Nurse," he answered with a bow and a tip of an imaginary hat. "No offense meant to you nor the redskins."

Leona gave up. She hated the way the tribes were viewed by nearly every white miner, adventurer, and soldier from Outside. She missed Flower all the more, but Charlie was who she had. Best let the issue alone, so she moved on. "We'll need two privacy areas, one for women and one for men."

"Right, Nurse."

"And you must stay away from the women's area. According to Dr. Reardon, a woman will be provided to sterilize equipment so you'll have some help. The doctor should be available to us tomorrow, too. You oversee the patients and records. We'll start at first light and go as long as we have lines."

They were packing cases for the evening by the time Dr. Reardon returned to check on their progress. He looked haggard to Leona, his earlier good spirits gone. She had no opportunity to ask him about the surgery, or to gloat about how she and Charlie had managed, before they were hustled off to the officers' table for a dinner of some kind of potted meat and preserved orange vegetable. Now Leona missed Cook as well as Flower. She chatted with the men to the left and right, but the doctor, across the table, primarily stared at his plate in some dark mood of his own.

A married officer provided housing for Leona for the night, but the doctor went immediately to the officers' quarters. His attitude during dinner upset her, and she wondered what had happened. She even questioned herself, whether she had done something wrong, overstepped an unseen boundary. The need for a drink, just one, rolled over her like an armored car, insistent and unstoppable. She was very glad of the household's children who kept her busy with an evening of dominoes. While their parents had brandies, Leona wolfed sugar cookies with the kids.

By the time she tucked herself away into the small bed at her disposal, Leona's belly fire for alcohol was overcome by the exhaustion of the day. She felt like she could sleep. A warm feeling poured through her. Maybe she'd add sugar cookies to her nightly routine. How could it hurt?

The next day began without the doctor. Charlie explained, "He's with the surgery patient. He and Doc Boc. But he says he'll be along."

The day was largely free of troubles. The fort had set up two tents, one for each sex. The translator had not appeared with the promised woman to help, but Charlie was a whirlwind, sterilizing instruments and getting the men in line for Leona to whisk into their tent and jab. Charlie began calling her Six-Shooter.

The natives, living close to Haines, had received vaccines before. They might not understand why the nurse woman wanted to see them half-clothed, but they were resigned to the oddities of white people. The women and children took longer than the men. In this chill, getting through all the layers of clothes to naked skin was time-consuming. Leona insisted on giving the youngest children the shots in their thighs. Her experience was that it caused less pain at the injection site, although she didn't know why. So much of her job was experience with no data to back it up other than her own observations.

One little toughie gave her a good kick in the ribs after she jabbed his thigh. "This is supposed to hurt you more than me," she said with a grimace while he wiggled.

Dr. Reardon appeared mid-morning and took over in the men's tent. Leona felt relief for his help. Charlie had time to find a Tlingit woman in the line who could speak a bit of English. He put her to work with the cleaning, promising her heaven knows what. Leona decided not to ask.

They worked until their backs ached, then they stopped for the night. The rest of the willing Chilkat Tlingits in the area would be done in the morning.

"Would you care for a nightcap before going to your lodgings, Nurse?" Dr. Reardon asked after another mediocre meal in the officers' mess. "I'm sure we can find an appropriate spot to discuss the day."

She wanted to respond, "Would I ever! Set 'em up!" But she took a deep if shaky breath and announced, "I am so tired, I believe I will have tea for my nightcap. But please, help yourself to something stronger."

They sat in easy chairs in the fort's main entrance, no doubt placed there to look appealing to visitors. They could hear clean-up going on in the kitchen, which had provided a pot of tea with its service. Otherwise, they were alone. The doctor produced a flask that he poured liberally into his cup. "Ah, whiskey. My favorite kind of doctoring," he said with a smile.

"Dr. Reardon. You are exhausted, but you managed a joke," Leona observed. Meanwhile, the aroma of the alcohol nearly pulled her from her chair to his.

He stared at her long enough that she felt a blush warm her face. "You are right, Nurse. I have been a muttonhead. I will try to be less ill-tempered."

"I didn't mean ill-tempered, exactly. More sullen. Troubled. You have had a hard time with the fort doctor's patient?" How quickly she'd moved the chat to the source of her curiosity.

"More with the fort doctor than with his patient."

"Explain, please. Is he a poor surgeon? What kind of surgery? Have you disagreed over procedure? Is the patient recovering?"

His laugh was spontaneous and seemed heartfelt. He was appealing when he relaxed and exposed those even white teeth. "How many of your nine lives have you lived?"

Her blush was nearly a sizzle now. "You are right, sir. Shame on me. I apologize for my curiosity."

"Quite the contrary. You are a playful cat, taking me out of my mope." He sighed and returned to the subject at hand. "You are right. It has been ... difficult."

"What is the nature of the ailment?"

"Ah. A young soldier was missing. A small patrol went in search of him. He was in quite a state when they arrived."

Somehow, Leona shut her yap while he sipped his whiskey.

Dr. Reardon continued. "His skin was inflamed with spines from devil's club. He appears to have fallen into a patch of it. But far worse, he had stepped into a bear trap. The metal jaws nearly removed his foot. I believe he was chained for two days, long enough for pain to knock him off his chump. He's been hallucinating about a bear waiting to eat him."

Leona trembled at the memory of her own recent introduction to a bear.

The doctor shrugged. "Maybe it's true. Anyway, Doctor Boccaccio was about to amputate when I arrived yesterday. And I admit, the ankle bones were a mess of breaks and infection. But with skill and ether, I thought we might save the boy his foot. Doctor Boccaccio relented, and we slowly rebuilt the area. But this morning, when he saw that the infection had not abated, he sawed off the limb before I arrived at the surgery."

Leona was astounded. "Good grief. And you believe you might still have saved it?"

"That I do. Newer techniques than Boccaccio knows. His military training impedes him from lengthy recoveries. Saw off the problem and send the lad home a cripple. Doesn't have to be like that."

Leona held her tongue and let him work it out.

"You should see the equipment he has. Not old, exactly, but sparse. He doesn't even have ether, only chloroform. The surgical table is a slab of wood. The patient area has three beds, but they're not even hospital beds. I came here, to Alaska, to get away from war and carnage for a while. But now I am missing the advanced work I would find in San Francisco. More research, new techniques, less backwoods wisdom." Another deep sip. "Have you considered leaving here, Leona?"

Yikes! Is he a bit too interested? "Oh, I love it here. The tribe is like family to me."

"I see." He nodded. "Well, you're still new to it."

The emotion of the moment, and the aroma of whiskey, nearly overcame her. She wanted to drink, to help him be cheerful again. To help herself be cheerful again. She stood to go. "I promised the children of the house where I stay a game of checkers before I retire."

He stood as well, his eyes catching hers. "You are sure you can't stay a while?"

What are you asking me? She lowered her gaze. "Duty calls. Like a good soldier, I have a job to do."

"Then I will walk you home. In case there are any bad soldiers or bear traps out there." After that, conversation died until Leona bid him a good night, not lingering in the dark. Whatever might be growing between them needed to go no further than affection. She hoped he was thinking the same thing. A good working relationship between doctor and nurse depended on it. Her relationship with Mikhail depended on it.

Sleep was a long time coming. "Too much tea with too little alcohol," she pouted as she turned the last page in the book she had packed for the trip. She'd leave it behind and pick it up on their return trip this way.

The next day, in the late morning, they finished the inoculations of the Tlingits at the fort. The bilingual guide named Coy, as well as the mule skinner met them with six beasts to load with medical supplies and equipment. Coy's beard and hair obliterated most of his head. He whistled through his teeth, but Leona could not zero in on his mouth through all the facial hair. His odor of unwashed skin was so much worse than a mule, in the days that followed, she let him lead the group along the trail with the doctor between them.

CHAPTER SIXTEEN

November 27, 1921
Ivy Bolton

The evenings passed quietly in the warmth of the kitchen where two women prepared for Christmas as diligently as Santa's elves, although not without complaint.

Ivy exploded. "Ye gods! I'm damn tired of knittin' mittens. Couldn't one of the orphans wear *gloves*?"

Flower, whose fleet of canoes could now invade a sizable village, set down her brush. "Wouldn't one of them prefer to play with a toy horse?"

Thanksgiving had come and gone without Leona. Ivy missed her, eager to gossip about the possible move with Maki. "Where's a nurse when you need one?"

Flower went on point like a German shorthair. "Are you well, Ivy? Do you hurt? Can I help?"

Ivy laughed. "No, Flower. I'm fine. I just miss Leona for a good chin wag. You've already heard what there is to say about Maki and me."

Flower nodded. "I am glad the two of you have moved from the storeroom floor to the bed. But I do not want you to move Outside."

"Who knows if it will ever happen?" Ivy answered. Who plans a life together after ten years of doing just fine the way they were? Won't living together ruin everything? "Let's thaw a couple of moose steaks for breakfast."

Moose had been the meal for Thanksgiving. The holiday itself hadn't been quite as entertaining as the preparation. Ivy was visiting the parish when the manager of the cannery came by to provide the orphanage with a fifty-pound hunk of rump. "Stalked the bull myself, but a coupla boys helped me pack him home on a sled. And here's the real prize." With a showman's pride he unwrapped a skin to reveal the enormous moose tongue. "Quite a delicacy, that," he said.

Harold, Judith, and Ivy stared at the dismembered glossal muscle, as alien to them as a celestial wonder. Harold immediately turned the whole shebang over to the women and wandered away with the manager. Judith and Ivy looked at each other, bursting into laughter.

Judith said, "I have little idea what to do with the mound of meat, much less the yapper."

"Cook," Ivy said.

"Cook," Judith agreed.

Cook came to the rescue after Ivy sent word via orphan for her to take a look. "Tongue? You pickle it in Mason jars." She rolled her eyes, no doubt at the ignorance of white people from Outside. "Then eat it with bread-and-butter pickles."

Whether this was good advice or not, Ivy and Judith turned the rest of the moose project over to Cook. First, the tall stern woman frowned at the hunk of deep red rump meat, circling it like a sculptor seeking the secret within a piece of marble. Finally she snapped, "Butcher knife. Bowls. Salt. Honey. Judith's cranberry wine."

Judith and Ivy scrambled to assemble the requirements from the parsonage or the government building. As Ivy later wrote to her daughter, Poppy:

That's how a taciturn native woman became the provider of the Thanksgiving feast in Hoonah, Alaska. Once again, a tribe and the immigrants on their land celebrated the union.

Nobody knew Cook's complete background. Her willowy height and long ropey muscles placed her somewhere on the American plains where food year 'round would have been far harder to procure than in Hoonah. For the feast, Cook braised the meat marinated in honey, red wine, and garlic. With the remains of the monster, she butchered steaks, created meatloaves and stews to freeze for the winter days ahead, and by adding pork lard from a barrel to the lean moose meat, she made sausage.

On Thanksgiving Day, tables for the villagers and orphans were set up outside the parsonage under tarps. Everyone contributed something, although the wolverine stew from Mikhail was nobody's first choice. As she left the government building to walk to the church that morning, Ivy realized for the first time that there was no lock on the front door. Someone had always been there, due to the clinic and ham radio more than the school. Now Leona, Flower, Cook, and she were all out. But who would break in? Everyone was on their way to the parsonage.

While Captain Aleck waited to help carry her two large trays of pecan caramel tarts and pumpkin pies, she scratched out a quick note and hung it on the doorknob.

We're at the church for feasting. Come join us.

November 27, 1921
Leona Herkimer

Leona loved the hike to Chilkat Lake, and the days that followed. They trekked along the river, stopping now and then to watch the bears fish or the eagles swoop. It was cold, but the wind was muffled by the trees the farther they walked from the Chilkat fjord into the woodland. The snowy trail was easily tromped by the mules into the duff under their feet. Their pace was a swift walk that stretched Leona's abilities along rough terrain, but the muscle aches at night only seemed to enhance her sleep in the tiny tent allotted to her. "Maybe it's all this oxygen," she said to the doctor before inhaling a great breath of crystal-pure air. Letting go slowly, she added, "I never sleep so deeply at home."

They camped in native villages around as much of the lake as they could reach with the mules. From the remote foothill locations, many natives appeared to them. These leathery souls were compliant and friendly, even more so than the natives closer to the fort and Haines.

"White people are still a novelty to them," Dr. Reardon observed. "We're here to cure a disease our people brought to them in the first place."

"How do they know we're here?" Leona asked.

"It's in the wind," he answered. "We'll save hundreds of lives. That much they understand."

There had only been one awkward event so far. The translator Coy, in a drunken stupor, entered Leona's tent in the middle of their fourth night. Later, she explained to the doctor, "I may have heard him, but I'm inclined to believe I smelled him first." Whichever, she employed volume and language she rarely used in order to eject him. It scared the mules who brayed and awoke the doctor, the mule skinner, and the village.

Dr. Reardon assured Leona that the translator would be sent packing back to Haines at first light. "How dare he enter my nurse's quarters!" he fumed.

Leona realized by his tremble of outrage that the doctor was more upset than she herself. She couldn't be sure whether it was because she was a she or "his nurse." Whatever the truth, it proved unnecessary to boot the offender out. When they emerged from their tents in the chill dawn, Coy and one of the mules were gone.

"I hope he sobered up enough to find his way home," Leona said.

"Hope the scurrilous bugger gets Jeremiah back to me," the mule skinner huffed, employing one of the phrases Leona had used the night before.

"Hope he doesn't expect to work as a translator again," the doctor snarled.

Leona had to smile. She was glad that her virtue, while less important to the mule skinner than the whereabouts of a good beast, was taken seriously by the doctor. She didn't wish Coy any harm, having dealt with more than one drunk, including herself. The threat had not been very great. Still, it was nice to feel protected.

By now, they could do well enough without a translator. One of the Tlingit women stayed with them as they traveled camp to camp. She taught other local women how to set up the inoculation station and sanitize the equipment.

Their trip ended when they used the last of their vaccine. "We will start again in the spring," said the doctor. "Maybe make one winter trip back to Haines if you are willing, Nurse. The fjord is not likely to freeze."

"If you get more vaccine, I will be happy to help, although I worry about Hoonah in my absence. Even though my assistant is doing very well."

"You mean the Tlingit girl?"

"Yes, Flower."

"You think of her as an assistant? Beware giving too much freedom to someone still learning," he lectured.

How does he manage to attract and repel simultaneously?

They packed up possessions and equipment, then headed toward home.

Within a morning's walk of the fort, they came across a large chunk of raw red meat. The surefooted mules snorted and rolled their eyes, then gracefully stepped around it. But Leona froze, stunned by what she saw. There was enough bone left amidst the strings of gore to identify it as a piece of rib cage. As the doctor came alongside her, he said, "It's human."

"Yes," she whispered. "Coy?"

"Maybe. Probably."

They walked further, stepping gingerly around patches of blood, bits of entrails, and tatters of clothes that had belonged to the translator.

"Did a bear do this?" Dr. Reardon asked the mule skinner, who was comforting the distressed mules.

"Whoa, settle," the man cooed over the braying. "Maybe knocked down by a moose to begin. Or a bear mighta started it, maybe. Mules hate their stink. But could be wolverines pestered the bear away. If so, Bruin's still around here close, waiting to get back to whatever he mighta buried. Looks to me like lots of things helped themselves. Even birds, if they found bits of the kill soon enough." Remains were scattered as though dragged to different feasting sites in the open or under the trees. Leona, who had seen much as a nurse, had never seen a decapitated head bereft of meat and eyes, or a pelvis with its privates shredded. She gasped, then went behind trees to empty herself of what mush was still in her stomach from breakfast. She huddled between two massive cedars, glad of their surrounding support.

The doctor came with a blanket to tuck around her. "We'll cremate him, Leona, what we can find of him. I want you to take this. To settle your stomach and calm your nerves." He removed the tight cork from a dark vial and handed it to her. She took a deep swig while he watched. He suggested she keep it for the hike still ahead of them.

He didn't know her secret. She didn't know the composition of the medication. But after that first slug, she realized it was largely alcohol, probably with an opiate. Before they continued the journey, she swallowed the entire vial. Her own caged beast had been released. And Leona needed more.

At the fort, Leona went to the house where she had stayed before. The wife was in a tizzy over what to wear to an officers' party that evening.

"If you have a brandy to warm me up, I'll help you choose," Leona said. The wife gladly filled her glass once, and Leona filled it again. A message arrived from the doctor saying Leona and he had been invited to the party. It was politic that they attend. He would see her there. And the boat would arrive in the morning to take them back to Juneau.

"Well, let's see then," said the wife, cocking her head at Leona. "I'm far larger than you now, but I used to wear this. You could borrow it." She rummaged through a trunk and unfolded a dress far fancier than anything Leona owned, lace accents over rose-toned crepe georgette. Its swingy skirt was built for dancing. As Leona was inches taller than her hostess, the length would likely expose a long expanse of leg.

That ought to capture the admiration of a few military men. Leona giggled then went to bathe and fix her hair. Maybe I'll wear that new underwear I bought in Juneau with Danielle. Leona was in the arms of an alcohol embrace, ready to forget the remains of Coy and dance the night away. Wish Danielle was here. We'd have such fun.

She walked to the officer's headquarters with the married couple. Charlie, outside the building, was first to see her. The color rose to his cheeks as he gawked at how she looked, without a nurse's apron and her hair pinned back.

"You ... you are ..."

Taking pity on the awestruck boy, Leona said, "Will you be coming, Charlie?"

"Far from an officer, Nurse. Far from it."

"A pity or we'd share a dance." She kissed him lightly on the cheek, and the crimson of his face clashed with the orange of his hair.

She'd grown fond of the boy. Of course, at the moment, she was fond of everybody.

An officer whisked her away to provide the wine she requested. A second asked for a dance. She needed another drink then, and next found herself in the arms of Dr. Reardon. She stiffened. She could not forget this man was as good as her boss. He could ruin her if he chose. She must be careful. But they had become such friends in the days before! He'd protected her from Coy, both dead and alive. The thought caused her to laugh, and that caused her to forget caution. Besides, surprise of surprises, the doctor was a fine dancer.

"I'll trade you one spritely foxtrot for one traditional waltz," he whispered on the dance floor.

She joyfully matched him step for step to tunes from a piano, a horn, and a badly tuned violin. A breather for more drink, then another waltz. When he whispered "Kitten" into her ear, she was lost to the forbidden thrill of him.

They left together. She heard him tell the hosting officer that they needed to check on a patient in the infirmary. Either that, or it was her doing the talking and leading the doctor to the empty patient beds. They undressed each other, Leona careful of the borrowed dress as he pulled it over her head. His eager hands could so easily destroy the buttons. She took delight in his demeanor, as serious as though he were performing delicate surgery. Nothing moved fast as they resisted their urgency and observed each other naked in the light of the infirmary. Whatever he wanted from her body, she gave; whatever she touched of him was fair game. She was the far better player at this sport: sex while drunk. Fucking. It was the only word that applied to this night that never should be.

He'd been drinking too, of course, so he was first to collapse in sleep. She drifted off in a stupor. It was warm and reassuring, until it wasn't. When enough alcohol wore off that she could assess her situation, she was appalled. Her humiliation was complete. She'd exposed herself as a common guttersnipe, out of control on alcohol. She could only hope he'd be none too proud of his own conduct. Maybe he'd keep this adventure to himself. She prayed he wouldn't remember, but she knew he would. She always remembered, each time she ran out of control.

She was a failure. She had not left her sordid addiction behind; it had followed her to Alaska and found a way to flourish at every opportunity. She was used goods in a borrowed dress.

Leona stood. She silently left the room, then the building, and like a thief she entered the quiet home of her host and hostess, creeping to her room. Hopefully they slept too deeply to know the time. She wanted nothing as much as to never see the doctor again. She rummaged through her pack for her sewing scissors and sliced the beautiful new underwear to shreds. Pretties that only Mikhail was meant to see.

He'd want nothing more from a drunken whore like her. Not anymore. He deserved so much better. Nevertheless, as she destroyed the delicate fabric in crippling misery, as she lost whatever respect she'd finally gathered for herself, all she really wanted to do was tiptoe downstairs to find the rest of the brandy.

In the early morning, before the family stirred, Leona packed. She wrote a note to thank them for their courtesy, leaving it on the kitchen table along with money for the brandy she took. She left a second message for the doctor. It said he was to take the boat back to Juneau without her. She was staying behind.

Quietly, she left the warm house, shuffling through the fluff of new snow on her chilly walk into Haines. Her footprints would soon be lost in the heavy traffic around the fort. Leona had to be gone before the doctor or Captain Aleck could find her, even if either chose to look.

Why would either bother? Why would anyone bother to look for me? Dulled with exhaustion, humiliation, and desolation, her mind could only form one plan. She would find a room where they asked no questions of a woman alone. Then she'd get money and a message to Charlie, telling him to bring her two bottles of alcohol, any kind would do.

CHAPTER SEVENTEEN

December 2, 1921
Ivy Bolton

The captain steamed into Hoonah on the second day of December. It was still dark at 8:30 in the morning when he came through the back door of the government building into the kitchen, looking for a warming cup of tea and maybe one of Cook's biscuits.

Ivy smiled at him as he sat at the table, feeling the chill in the air he brought in. They talked of winter for a bit, then she asked him about Leona. "Is she back in Juneau? Coming home soon? I told her she *had* to be here before Christmas."

"Leona? Isn't she back yet?" the captain asked, looking confused.

Flower, fixing a patient tray in the kitchen, stopped to listen.

Cook, whipping something on the stove, turned to stare with a frown.

"Don't you *know*?" Ivy felt a shiver of dread run down her spine like fingers on a flute.

Captain Aleck shook his head. "I know the doctor came back, but I didn't have that charter. I assumed she was with him."

"If the doctor is back, then where is Leona?" Ivy marched out of the kitchen straight to the radio where she got through to the fort communications officer via Hambone. No, the nurse wasn't there. After a confusion of conversations, it was determined that the people at the fort didn't know she was missing; they assumed she'd left with the doctor. The family she stayed with thought the same, having a goodbye note from her. She'd been so much fun for the missus to have around. And Doc Boc thought she was dandy. She was welcome anytime.

Hambone radioed the hospital in Juneau. Dr. Reardon knew, it turned out, but apparently he wasn't concerned. All he would say was that Leona planned on staying at the fort, so from his point of view, she wasn't missing. No other explanation was given. In fact, the doctor seemed grumpier than usual in Hambone's opinion, not that he liked to speak ill of anyone.

"If anyone at that fort knows and doesn't tell, I'll ... " Ivy growled herself into a corner. *What the hell will I do?*

"I'll go for her, Ivy," Captain Aleck said. They exchanged a worried look, one edged with fear. Many bad things could befall a woman alone in Alaska. And they both knew of Leona's battle for control over alcohol.

"You might need help convincing her to come." Ivy wrung her hands in agitation. "I can't leave the school, and Flower can't leave the clinic."

Flower donned her anorak. "I'll go for Mikhail. He will travel with you. Wren can stay with us."

Captain Aleck agreed. "I'll get my crewman back before he spends overlong in the tavern. *Small Fry* will be ready when Mikhail arrives."

When the captain and Flower were gone, Ivy sat with her cup of cold tea. She was furious at, well, just furious. "Leona disappears five days ago, and I'm just hearing about it?" She slapped a kitchen towel onto the table. Even Cook shrank a wee bit in the presence of Ivy the she-bear.

Ivy stood and paced around the table. "She could be lost in the wilds. She could be dead. And if she isn't, she'll be in serious danger from me." Ivy stomped to her room and came back with stationery plus her Parker Lady Duofold fountain pen. All she knew for sure was that this was no time to mollycoddle if Leona was on the bender that Ivy suspected. While Ivy's heart wanted to say, "There, there," her pen talked tough.

Leona:

A shipment of diphtheria vaccine arrived at the government building for our nurse to inoculate her people. But we don't have a nurse. Get back here to your own tribe. Old man Keijín needs a tooth pulled. He is in pain. The Henya lass is due soon. She is only a schoolgirl and is terrified. You are needed. These are commitments you have made. Flower can't do this without you.

If alcohol has trapped you again, I know you are alone somewhere, heart sick and mortified. But your self-pity is not as important as the lives of your patients. Half of Alaska drinks too much, but many are still productive. When you sober, you will realize that. Put a bag over your head if you must, but get off the booze and get on the boat. The village needs you. Hell, I need you.

Ivy

Next, Ivy put together a basket of provisions Leona might need, first and foremost, a canvas pouch of ground coffee. In the medical cabinets, she found a bottle of Emerson's Bromo-Seltzer which promised, among other things, to remedy "depression following alcoholic and other excesses." Ivy had heard that rubbing vinegar on your temples could end a hangover quickly, but she'd never tried it herself. Still, a bit of vinegar went into the basket. For foods, she stuck with bland ... Uneeda biscuits and two jars of pears in juice because the nurse would be dehydrated. A jar of Cook's chicken soup, too, when Leona could keep it down. While Ivy fussed, Cook packed another basket of heartier foodstuffs for the captain, his crewman, and Mikhail. She filled her warm crispy biscuits with thick slices of ham.

Finally, Ivy sat at the table to await Mikhail. She fretted. What does he know of Leona's drinking? Will he refuse to go? Can anybody refuse Flower when she puts her mind to something? Will Leona talk to him?

Ivy was not one to cry, but tears ran down her cheeks and off her chin. It wasn't anger; it was frustration. "There's nothing more I can do," she said when Cook quietly placed a hot cup of tea in front of her.

"You are helpless."

"That's it. Yes." Ivy thought the taciturn cook had summed it up exactly.

It was 3:30 in the afternoon, and the sun was setting when Mikhail finally arrived. He'd been out on a trapline, so Wren and Flower had to track him down. Ivy, Flower, and Wren stood side by side to watch *Small Fry* chug out of the inlet with Mikhail aboard. They continued the vigil until the boat was a speck rounding the headland into Icy Strait. The women knew that the rescue party planned to sleep on the boat in Juneau that night and go on to Haines the next day.

Mikhail made Ivy a promise before he boarded. "Ivy. If she is there, I'll find her. If she isn't there, I'll find her. Leona belongs with us."

Ivy believed him. But still, dammit, the waiting would be hell.

December 4, 1921
Leona Herkimer

A week? A lifetime? What day? Who cares?

Leona lay on a mattress that was not much thicker than the dirty quilt over her. The slats beneath squeaked with every move so she lay as still as she could. She kept her eyes shut tight. If she opened them, the beast came for her again. And she was out of the hooch that held it at bay. She needed another trip to the tavern's back door where she, and the rest of the rummies, acquired a grim homemade firewater.

Charlie hadn't been dependable after all. He brought her food. But the little shit refused her any more drink. She told him not to come back. She couldn't count on anybody. She felt her face go wet again.

Goddamn tears. What's the use? Kill myself. First, I need a drink.

Slowly, she sat up, carefully balancing so she wouldn't tip over again. *Like a lady on a tightrope. How pretty. Oh, see her plummet! Down, down she falls.* Leona's head began to spin. She grabbed for her chamber pot and vomited again. Surely there was nothing left to come up other than her organs.

How much time passed, she didn't know. When her system settled enough, she went to the outhouse, emptied her pot, and cupped cold water onto her face at the hand pump in the alley. The room she rented at the back of a boarding house, a room no better than she deserved, did not have its own water supply, not even cold. Leona tried to straighten the dress she'd been sleeping in.

Maybe I'll put on my nurse's apron. It's all I have left of a clean life. She chortled at her joke, but it ended in tears again. I need a drink. That would be jolly. Where's money? Did the little shit take it? Some other lowlife?

Leona clambered up the backstairs. The door to her room was open. *Shit. I'll have to get the landlord out of there again. I won't pay my rent that way. Not the way he wants.* She went inside and faced the man standing in the middle of the floor.

"Get out!" Leona screeched. "Stay away from me. I may be a loose woman, but I'm not your harlot."

Wait. Not the landlord.

She stared. "I ... I know you," she whispered in her whiskey voice. Wisps of hope fluttered in her brain.

Mikhail put his arms around her. She sunk into him, as needy as a whipped dog. Her knees began to buckle, but with a gasp, she recoiled. "No. I'm filthy. I'm filth."

"Stop, Leona. You're sick. We will see you well." Again, he tucked her close to his chest.

She was aware Charlie had come into the room and was packing her clutter on top of the kit already in her bag.

She began to blubber. Over her slurry of sorries and love yous and hate mes, she could hear Mikhail order, "Take her things to the boat, Charlie. Tell the captain that she is safe. I'll get her aboard. We can soon leave."

"What should he tell them at the fort?"

"I'm sure the captain will come up with something suitable. Now go."

Charlie sprinted away.

With Mikhail supporting Leona, the two made it out the front door and down the steps. Leona's head spun but her stomach held fast. A tall pallid man, his hair slicked back with Brilliantine, scurried out of the house to bluster at Mikhail. "Who the hell are you? What's your right to that woman?"

"Are you the landlord here?" Mikhail asked.

The landlord put his fists on his hips. "I am. And if she's to grind any man's corn, it'll be mine."

His aggressive stance left his nose wide open for Mikhail's fist to shatter its cartilage.

Leona cried out. "Mikhail! He's done nothing."

"Maybe. But I had to do something, and his beak was handy." They stepped over the landlord's crumpled frame and walked downhill toward *Small Fry*.

Leona would have preferred death to the next few hours on a boat. The fjord was calm, but the little craft still rocked. She hung over the side most of the way. "Can't you keep the boat from rolling?" she pleaded with Captain Aleck.

"Ain't the boat rolling. It's you."

"Can't you shoot me?"

"Might be Ivy will when we get you home, if Mikhail doesn't first. As for me, I guess it serves ya right, lass," Captain Aleck said. "Not that I haven't been in shaky boots very much like yours a time or two myself."

She was aware he loved a good thumper. She half-listened to him tell Mikhail that the fort now thought she'd been called out by a Tlingit family in the middle of the night, was beset by thieves on the way, and the family who found her unconscious took her in. They looked after her till she was right as rain. Even Leona, in her present state, could see the holes in this story. "Swiss cheese," she managed to say.

"I believe the nurse may be hallucinating," the captain stage-whispered to Mikhail.

Mikhail was disturbingly quiet. He sat watching the scenery instead of her. With Juneau in sight, Leona took a great gulp of the crystalline air, turned away from the water, and squared her shoulders. She had to face the Mikhail music. Sitting down beside him, she blurted, "We must talk. I have things to tell you."

"Not now. Hambone got a message to your friend, Danielle. You can spend the night with her, rest and recover. I'll help the captain load an order for the cannery office. We can leave for Hoonah in the morning."

"But about Haines ..."

"Leona, I'm not ready to hear it. Nor you to tell it."

"But I need to explain!" Fear grabbed her. *Won't he listen? Can't he hear me?*

He touched his finger to her lips. "Leona, I love you. But I can't reassure you at the moment. We must be very clear with each other. Get yourself together. We'll talk then."

Danielle awaited them at the dock in Juneau. Captain Aleck stared at her. "Ye gods! An exotic bird has dropped amidst the dowdy gray gulls."

Leona managed to respond. "You're not the first boat captain interested in my friend."

"We captains are a very smart breed."

Mikhail handed Leona over to Danielle; a smile passing between her lover and her friend took the place of a formal introduction. Danielle grasped Leona firmly by the arm and pulled her away. "You'll be wobbling all over the street if you don't hold tight to my arm. I'll strut for the both of us. Just two good friends out for a stroll."

"Oh, Danielle…" Leona gasped.

Danielle had a hanky at the ready. "Use this nose rag. Then no more snot till we get home. So that was your mountain man? I must say, I do see the attraction. He's the prime article in Juneau today."

"Danielle, I was not faithful to him." Leona squeaked out the words between two monumental blows into the hanky.

"Hush. Here we are. Into this alley and up the stairs. Good girl." The wooden steps led to the third level at the back of a storefront building. They creaked and complained with every step the women took. Leona thought they were in worse shape than she was.

Once Danielle unlocked the door, she ushered Leona to a straight back chair. Leona slumped and confessed. "It was the doctor who did the deed with me."

"Well, well. You have had a bit of an adventure. Take off that dress and your underthings. You smell awful." While she lectured, she set a large kettle of water on her stove to heat to a boil.

"I was so drunk. The doctor was so willing." Leona managed the many buttons on the dress then stopped. She felt too shamed to strip.

"All of it."

"Am I not allowed the dignity of my chemise and bloomers?"

"Your dignity smells of rotgut," Danielle said as she untied Leona's boots. "Now step out of these shit kickers while I fetch you a robe." Danielle kicked the dirty clothes into a pile, filled two buckets with hot water, then gathered her own toiletries and towels into her arms, and ordered, "Up, up. We march down to the bathroom now. You carry both buckets. It'll keep you balanced."

Leona propped herself against a wall while Danielle filled the tub from a cold-water tap, then added the scalding hot to it. Leona dropped the chenille robe to sink into a heaven of soapy warmth. "Oh, my stars. My first bath in a week. You are an angel."

"Here. Let me scrub your head."

"I don't deserve you."

"No, you don't. Now then, tell me true. Did that blackguard attack you?"

"I believe it might have been the other way around."

"Well then, I will not march to the hospital with a horsewhip."

While Leona soaked, Danielle went back to her room. When she returned with a nightgown, it was the first time

Leona laughed in a week. The garment was a very thick, long sleeved, full length, gunny sack styled by a tentmaker.

"I wouldn't have thought you owned anything so grandmotherly." Leona snickered.

"You never know what kind of fantasies a gentleman caller might have."

The healing effect of a friend and laughter began its magic, and Leona felt as though she might live, even if she wasn't sure she wanted to.

"I must go now, Leona. I have a shift at the Golden Garter. I'll see if one of the other girls can take the evening just this once. In the meantime, you sleep." Danielle gestured at the only bed in the room. "We'll talk when I return. And we'll eat a real meal because you'll want one by then." Just before she slipped out the door, she hesitated. "Leona? Do I need worry about you? You know, the hair of the dog and all?"

Leona's first reaction was irritation. "Of course not. I'll be fine."

Her second reaction was doubt. "I think I'll be fine."

Her third reaction was self-pity. "How would I know if I'll be fine?"

Her final reaction was the desire to see her friend smile. "Could you handcuff me to this bed? I assume you have the necessary manacles here somewhere."

Four hours later when she awoke, Leona was nearly herself again. No spinning, no upset. She went through what was left of her possessions to find a blouse and skirt that were reasonably clean. She smiled when she pushed aside the heavy pants that Ivy had made her bring. If she'd had them on that night, maybe getting out of them would have been just too much effort.

By the time Danielle arrived, Leona was ready. "I must go to the hospital to see the doctor. Then I could meet you at the Tongass Tearoom for a meal."

Danielle frowned. "No. I've patiently awaited the story, and I want it now. Before you fall back into the medical man's web. You talk, and I'll cook."

Leona told the whole story of the growing itch between Dr. Reardon and his nurse. She pulled no punches about their night together. It was booze that set her free of any reserves and unlocked her legs. "Alcohol makes me the life of the party. I feel so much happier and attractive when it runs through my body. But it kills me the next day. I have tried all my adult life to break that connection. And the stakes are so much higher now that Mikhail is counting on me. If he *is* still counting on me."

Danielle paused in her stirring, chopping, and frying to stare with a scowl. "Why do you need to see the doctor just now?"

"I must explain to him, of course. No matter how much it humiliates me."

"But why?"

"Well ... I ... we left it in a rather awkward place. I must tell him I will not be such an embarrassment again. That he owes me nothing. That we should go back to nothing more than doctor and nurse."

"Leona, take this from a woman who uses sex to make a living. I know more about men than you ever will. That doctor is not awaiting an apology. He is delighted that he had a terrific night with a beautiful woman whom he enjoys."

"But it can't go on. He must know …"

"Nothing. For him it is likely over and done with. If it weren't, you'd have heard from him. You owe him no explanations. Besides, if you want to keep your job, the less said the better. Discretion and all that."

It sounded wrong to Leona. But maybe Danielle was right. Ivy might disagree, but then, Leona might not tell Ivy just everything. She only had today because they were going back to Hoonah tomorrow. Ivy wasn't here to advise. *What should I do? What if the crewman or Captain Aleck or Mikhail sees me entering that hospital? What will they assume?*

When Danielle served a lovely salmon filet with spiced corn, Leona made her decision. She would leave in the morning and save what she could of her commitment to Mikhail. The doctor had gotten what he wanted. She needed to win Mikhail back. She would walk the line. No more drinks, no misplaced affection, no exceptions.

And yet, and yet. She did not open her bag and remove the bottle that was buried so deep that Charlie didn't see it when he stuffed it full of her garb. It was only one bottle. It wasn't for her, of course. It was for a patient emergency. It was wise to have it on hand.

Of course.

December 4, 1921
Leona Herkimer

Put a bag over your head if you must, but get off the booze and get on the boat. The village needs you. Hell, I need you.

Leona finished the last line of Ivy's note again as *Small Fry* chugged towards Hoonah through a day that was a study in grays. She'd read it four times, hearing the equal measures of dander and love that Ivy excelled at, either as a teacher or a friend.

Through the remnants of her hangover, she sighed. Ivy and Danielle. So different. Proof you needed more than one friend to see you through the rockiest times.

Mikhail had given her Ivy's note that morning when they met at the dock. "I wasn't sure you were ready for it yesterday. Ivy frequently has strong opinions." That's all he'd said, but he'd smiled before he turned away to help the captain and crewman load cargo into every available space.

Leona was ensnared in an emotional livetrap. She wanted to be home, but the shame of another drunken spree was unbearable. She wanted the last week to disappear, to be only a nurse around a man who was only a doctor. She wanted to explain to Mikhail, beg him to understand a craving she didn't understand herself.

Leona was trapped by more than emotion. She was literally confined to a tiny bit of bench on a boat, surrounded by crates and barrels. Maybe she wouldn't show her face again until they docked in Hoonah. She thought Mikhail had been right about Ivy's letter. *No, my love, I wasn't ready yesterday. I'm still not.*

Ivy was right, of course. Leona had proven herself undependable. She'd thought she was done with tears, but there was no end to the salt water that her eyes could manufacture. *How appropriate to be traveling miles of saltwater canals,* she thought as she gazed through icy fog at islands passing like ghosts. *Maybe I'll drown in my own puddle. Join Lot's wife as a pillar of salt to pay for my sins.*

The journey was more than half done when Mikhail weaved through the maze of supplies with the grace of a stag in deep forest. She scooted over as much as she could, and he wedged himself next to her, arranging a fur rug over them both. "The captain thought you might be cold." He put one arm around her shoulders and with the other hand, pointed at the note in her trembling fingers. "A tongue-lashing from afar?"

"Yes. Ivy wrote that my self-pity is not as important as the lives of my patients."

He winced. "Sounds like Ivy. But she loves you, Leona. She'd say whatever was necessary to get you home safe."

"Maybe. But when she finds out what I've done, she'll question her judgment for ever after."

"Maybe," he said again. "Why don't you practice by telling me?"

She'd thought about this. She didn't have to tell him about the doctor, of course. And yet, she did. Leona was a drunk, not a liar. Mikhail deserved no less than the truth.

She told him everything as they huddled between barrels of butter and crates of nails. She tried to express her joy at inoculating the soldiers with the help of young Charlie. At the hikes and sights around Chilkoot Lake. The pride of inoculating the tribes, saving lives. But then the battle with the translator. And finding the grisly decapitated body of a man who was only in the wilds alone because of her.

The next part burned. Leona told Mikhail about the calmative given to her by the doctor, which had activated her worst compulsion. "He had no idea how I would react to a serum comprised of alcohol. An opiate would have been better for me. A poison."

She tried to express how the demons in her system erased who she was. "It isn't about willpower. It wipes away all my inhibitions and my logic." She'd hoped to outrun it by leaving her homeland behind, but the need had followed her wherever she went.

Booze made the doctor her target. A willing one, to be sure, but he was not the aggressor. Leona was the one out of control. "I lay with Dr. Reardon. I'm no better than a wanton woman. So I ran away, from him, from you, from everything but liquor. Death appealed to me in those lost hours."

She felt Mikhail tense, but he didn't pull away. *How much more can he take?*

"In Hoonah, I have more control. I trust myself as a nurse and have Flower or Ivy to police me. I trust myself with you and the love I have for you. But it could happen again, next time the spirits literally move me." Her shame and despair were worse than nakedness. She gulped deep breaths like a diver who must soon survive without air. "I set you free, Mikhail. Of any commitment you've made to me."

He didn't leave.

"Please go," she said.

But he didn't leave.

They sat in silence, smushed together, until the little boat was near the dock in Hoonah. Finally, Mikhail spoke. "I love you, Leona. None of us is a perfect specimen. My first wife died in a fall that may have been a suicide. If I can live with that, I could live with your battle against drink. I could live with the doctor escapade." Here he sighed. "Although I must try hard not to picture it. I might kill him."

Leona felt tortured waiting for him to speak again. But he took his time. His voice was husky when he continued. "My issue is Wren. I can't be afraid to leave my child in the care of another woman who might be out of control herself. She adores you. But she's lost one mother, Leona. I do not know if she could face losing another."

He stood. "This will take some time for me to grapple with. I know what is best for me. But I need time to decide what is best for her."

So there it was. His truth was incompatible with hers. Leona felt the full weight of abandonment. "I can't deny that I'm not fit."

Mikhail pulled her up and kissed her with the passion that comes with things forbidden. "I'll go help the captain now. I see Wren and Ivy on shore, waiting for us. Whether or not we can count on each other, we can both count on them."

CHAPTER EIGHTEEN

December 2, 1946
Ivy Bolton

Ivy put down the letter from Wren. "Thunderation," she muttered to herself. The girl would be nearly thirty now. Ivy still pictured her as a nine-year-old.

A nine-year-old might be less trouble than this is going to be. But Ivy knew it was time to make some confessions. When Maki and Rome got back from Lake Crescent, she'd tell Rome what was what. Why put off till tomorrow and so forth. It was not Ivy's nature to shrink like a violet.

She knew Rome still felt sorrow over the death of his mother. How would he feel to know she wasn't his mother? And that his real mother was alive? And that he had a sister he'd never met? And that she, Ivy, had been keeping secrets?

Who knows what the boy might say? Will he ever forgive me? The boy. That's what Maki called Rome. Ivy grinned. Having Maki around might keep Rome and Ivy from battling to the death like wolverines. In the meantime, she'd make macaroons. They were Rome's favorites.

Maybe I'll add a dollop more butter to the potpie crusts.

Her legs bothered her, more so after this many wet days in a row. She sat a little longer at the kitchen table, rubbing her knees before standing to get about her chores. Glancing again at the letter from Wren before stuffing it into her apron pocket, she thought about Rome's place in her heart. And now his place in Maki's. The boy and the man had become thick as thieves in the six weeks since Maki appeared at her back door for the winter months. It pleased her to have Maki in a co-conspirator role, although she knew he wouldn't lie to the boy. If Rome had asked him about the past, Maki would have answered.

She and Maki had been together Outside for twenty-five years, ever since leaving Alaska. Imagine that! It hadn't taken them more than one winter to realize too much togetherness was too much togetherness. Maki moved to Forks the following spring to work from the Forest Service office, fifty miles of bad road away. Every autumn he came back to her, loyal as a migrating bird. They cuddled through the short days and long months of winter together before he flew away in the spring. The arrangement suited them well and gave the neighbors a juicy nugget to gossip about.

Maki liked Rome from that first night the boy stayed for dinner. In the following weeks, they put skid strips down on the front steps together. Maki took Rome into the woods to teach him how to throw a wicked knife, a great skill for a one-armed ex-soldier.

"The boy hurls like Claude Passeau winning the World Title for the Cubbies," Maki bragged to Ivy. He'd come home early the year before so he and Ivy could listen to that game on the radio she dearly loved.

Maki had long since retired from the Forest Service in Forks, but in the summer months, he lived near Lake Crescent just a few miles up the road. He guided pack trips for the tourists deep into the Olympic Peninsula forests or to Sol Duc hot springs or fishing spots he considered his own.

Ivy understood about hidden things. Maki's fishing spots were like her blackberry and chanterelle patches. Those are the important secrets in life.

Maki was teaching Rome how to ride a horse, hoping the boy might assist next summer, or whenever the bookmobile job stopped suiting him. "Gotta be dull, handing out books," Maki said to Ivy. He knew how to make her squawk.

The two men would burst through the door any minute, smelling of dirty clothes and wet horse. Ivy heard them laughing as they removed their boots in the garage. Maybe Rome was sharing a racy story from his days in the army, a story too off-color for Ivy's delicate ears. She didn't worry. She'd hear the story later in bed with Maki.

Rome was quick to spot the bottle of Italian Swiss Colony burgundy on the table. "The good stuff, huh?"

"An Italian wannabe from the Pacific Coast. Sort of like you." Ivy pecked both men on the cheek.

While they ate the flaky-crusted pot pies, Maki told Rome about the time Ivy joined him on the ranger boat to explore Glacier Bay and how the boom and crash of the glaciers calving scared her. "It was the first time she let me put my arm around her."

"I wasn't scared," Ivy observed.

"Yes, you were. That's how I learned loud noises can do a romance a world of good."

"I wasn't scared. I just finally gave in," she said.

Ivy was clearing the table when Rome said, "I see that platter of macaroons on the counter. You must have something to tell me."

Ivy put them on the table in front of him. "Oh, why's that?"

"Because you know I love them. You make them every time you want to rope me into doing something I might not like."

"Ha! If I'd only known it was that simple to understand her," Maki laughed. "All these years wasted."

"Am I really that shallow, Rome?" Ivy asked.

"Not shallow at all. But you are a schemer. Macaroons give you away."

She pulled her apron off its kitchen hook and took Wren's letter from the pocket. "I've heard from your sister. She's coming for a visit. Or wants you to go to her."

Rome's hand stopped momentarily as he reached for a second cookie. "My sister? Vienna or Geneva? Why would either write to you?"

"Not those sisters. Your Alaska half-sister."

"You heard from Wren?" Maki asked, sounding surprised. "Been a few years since she wrote, hasn't it?"

Rome set the macaroon down before he took the first bite. "Who is Wren?"

"To understand that, you have to know the truth about your mother."

"My mother? What truth? What does that mean?"

"Nancy Herkimer Coleridge was not your biological mother. Leona Herkimer has that honor."

Ivy watched him. Rome looked, well, nothing at all for a moment. Slowly his deadpan turned to knitted brows and a downturned mouth. Finally, he sputtered, "Aunt Leona? *Aunt Leona?* You only told me a while ago that an Aunt Leona even exists."

"Your Aunt Nancy wanted it that way."

"Oh, come on, Ivy. How do you know more about my mother than I do?"

"Guess I'll make us a pot of coffee," Maki said.

December 2, 1946
Rome Coleridge

Rome's brain scrambled to catch up with the conversation. Maybe he should be angry or tickled, but he was nothing but dumbfounded. A bite of the macaroon offered a bit of solace. Throughout he kept his eyes on this frustrating, aggravating old woman who owned a sizable piece of his heart. "Ivy, before I get the heebie-jeebies, you better explain."

"I worked with your mother twenty-five years ago when I taught in Hoonah, Alaska. Leona was a wonderful nurse, a good friend. I helped bring you into this world, and then I brought you to your Aunt Nancy at Leona's request."

Rome turned to Maki. "Do you know what she's talking about?" Maybe a man would make more sense. But when Maki answered, Rome thought Maki was crazy, too.

"Yes, I knew Leona. Wren and Mikhail, too. Better folk you'll never meet."

"Mikhail? Oh sure, *Mikhail*." Rome flapped his arm in the air. "Let's add a Russian to this fairy tale."

"Mmm, only half Russian. The other half was Tlingit," Maki clarified.

"Oh, then. Now I understand."

Ivy said, "Mikhail was your father. Although there's a slight chance the doctor might have been."

"Is this a joke? It's a joke, right?"

"This is going to take some time," Ivy said to Maki as he poured the coffee that Rome felt too astounded to touch.

Had a lot of people spent a lot of time lying to him? Rome breathed deep, the way Barbara taught him when he got upset. Was she in on this, too? Was the garage mechanic and the former bookmobile driver? The people out at Lake Crescent Lodge? A deep breath wasn't going to do it. "Well, start talking," he said. "I have all night."

Ivy began at the beginning.

CHAPTER NINETEEN

December 11, 1921
Wren Elim, age 8

Wren was scared. She had to find out what was wrong with Daddy and Leona. But Mrs. Bolton said she was far too busy to gossip, Mrs. Binder told her to mind her own ps and qs, and Cook made her roll out a ball of dough just for asking.

Wren also tried to get information from Flower who was the easiest of the batch. The rest might lie. "Why is Leona mad at Daddy?"

Flower acted like she knew nothing. "I don't know that Leona is mad at your Daddy."

"You're with her every day so you must know!"

"Well, you're with him every day so you must know."

Wren could usually bully Flower, but not this time. "Does Leona hate Daddy because he's half Indian? Does she hate me because I'm more Indian than he is?"

"Now you listen to me, Wren," Flower said, squatting down to be nose to nose. "Your father loves you to pieces. Leona's proud that he's half Tlingit, and that you have even more strong native blood than he does. You should never say something like that again."

Whoa! Wren had never seen Flower disturbed before!

She let another day pass, but Wren was getting very upset at Leona. She *had* to get answers. Wren sat on her school bench waiting Mrs. Binder to finish up about the animals on a farm. Wren wanted to squeal like a pig herself. "Hurry up!" she finally yelped, throwing her book on the floor in frustration.

"Why, Wren! That will be quite enough of that!" Judith said. Then she made her stay late to straighten up all the books.

Now Wren was very, very upset. She marched out of the schoolroom, through the lobby of the government building, and into the clinic. She ignored Flower at the exam table, administering Listerine to the scraped knuckles of a Dog Salmon elder. Wren zeroed in on Leona who was fitting sheets to empty patient beds. The child pushed the nurse with all her might, and Leona tumbled onto the bed.

"Wren! Whatever was that for?" Leona yelped, as she turned and sat up straight.

"I hate you!" Wren didn't want to cry, but tears burst through the log jam of fear and worry. Leona caught her fists and would not let go when Wren tried to pull away.

"I hate you!" she bellowed again, before collapsing against Leona's chest, then curling onto the nurse's lap. Leona rocked her gently while Wren wept for the ills that befall children. Finally, her sobs slowed to great gulpy hiccups.

Leona gave her a hanky and said, "Blow."

Wren blew like a windstorm.

"Now, let's talk. Ask me anything you want."

"Daddy says you're sick."

"... Yes, that's true."

"Are you dying?"

"No! I'm not dying!"

"I already lost one Mommy. Don't go." Wren drew out the word in a howl of misery.

"Wren! I love you. I always will no matter what. And I'm not going anywhere."

"Daddy's not happy. What's going to happen to me?" Wren was no fool. She could add two and two. Leona hadn't been to the cabin, and her Daddy was glum. Daddy said Leona was sick, and his eyes looked lost.

"Well, your Daddy and I aren't sure about us, but we're sure as eggs is eggs about you. He's still here, and so am I. Nothing bad will happen to you."

"Is it my fault?"

"Not even a little bit. Nothing is your fault. Big people have things to work out that little people don't understand. Your Daddy and I don't have all the answers yet."

"I don't really hate you," Wren whispered into Leona's ear.

"I know. And I love you," Leona whispered back.

"I love you, too."

"Would you like me to walk you home so we can keep talking?"

"Yes, please."

As they trekked along, Wren stomped her feet in the fluff of snow, making a slurry of cold mud. She wiped her drippy nose on her sleeve until Leona told her that was the kind of thing boys did. Then Leona explained her sickness.

"I have what is known as the alcoholism disease. I can't tolerate drinking spirits."

Wren pursed her lips liked she'd seen Judith do. She'd heard of drinking too much. "That means you're a drunk."

Wren heard Leona moan low in her chest. When the nurse finally spoke, she said, "Yes, I guess I am."

"Why don't you stop? If you loved us, you would."

"That's the mystery of it, Wren. It's like wanting to fly. No matter how hard you flap your arms, no matter how fast you run, you can't get off the ground."

Wren knew how that felt. She'd tried it a jillion times.

"But Wren, drinking isn't the bad part. It's what it makes me do or forget to do. What if I left the stove long enough to burn the cabin down? What if I forgot to feed you? What if you fell down a rabbit hole, and I couldn't go for help?"

Wren thought about it. She knew how to cool the stove. And she could miss a meal although it would be very hard. But worse things happened to some of the other children. "Will you hit me when you're drunk?"

"No, never."

"Will you hurt Daddy?"

"Again and again. But not physically."

"Some kids at school know to get out of the way when their Mommy or Daddy gets drunk. They go to a friend until they feel safe to go home."

She felt Leona staring at her so she looked up. Leona looked surprised. "Does that happen to many of the kids?"

"Yes. They know what to do. I could leave when it gets bad, like they do."

"Not acceptable. I'd be the one to leave." Leona grabbed Wren's hand.

"But Mrs. Bolton would take care of me. She said she would if the time ever came I needed another place to go."

"When did Ivy say that?"

"When Mommy died. I was little."

Mikhail wasn't at the cabin when they arrived.

"He's probably tending traps," Wren explained.

"Ask your Daddy to come see me, Wren. We'll work out more answers for you. I promise. Don't be afraid anymore."

December 14, 1921
Leona Herkimer

Leona had returned to Hoonah ten days ago. Her humiliation caused her to lose both weight and sleep. The hollows in her collar bones and the murky circles beneath her eyes were as noticeable as her baffling lack of enthusiasm. She worked, and she mourned. Only Ivy and Flower knew the full story of her trip, and she was pretty sure Ivy told everyone else to give her time and space. The real Leona would be back.

But who the hell is the real Leona? In fairy tales, the dragon was always defeated. Leona had believed she could outrun it with her escape to the north country, away from all she'd ever known. Now she realized how far Hoonah, Alaska was from a fairy tale. The dragon had singed her with its fiery breath twice. She lost all confidence in herself to stave off a next time.

The stress caused by her drinking made her want to drink. She told herself that it always would. "Just when I think I've made progress, I shoot myself in the foot," she said to Ivy.

"I know you're strong enough to defeat it if it is simply mind over matter. I don't pretend to understand this battle with drink. Is it an inheritance from your parents, or how they brought you up? Is it like one of those germ things that eats you alive? Will a cure be found, a new vaccine? Is it unstoppable, like the impulse to breathe?"

"Nobody can answer questions like yours," Leona responded. "Nor can any of my medical books. I suppose Reverend Binder would call it the sin of gluttony which, in my case, leads my heart to defile me with unchastity and folly. At least it isn't making me fat."

"Yes, there is always a bright side," Ivy said. "You're so thin now the next *willowaw* will topple you like a seedling."

Leona knew the word for coastal squalls and accepted the truth of what Ivy said. She continued healing others, if not herself. She needed needy patients to wean her away from self-pity over the unfairness of life. Nursing was the best medicine for her mood.

When Mikhail came looking for her, the vibrant smile animating his wide mouth lifted her defiled heart. He even took her hand as they left the government building to walk along the water's edge. "Wren tells me she had a talk with you. She even tapped her foot at me!"

The thought of Wren modeling a stern pose of Judith's tickled a grin out of Leona. Meanwhile, butterflies tickled her stomach.

Mikhail shook his head. "I made the mistake of underestimating my own daughter. It's harder on her *not* to know than to know."

"Mikhail, what have you told her?"

"I confirmed you have a disease that makes you do things you don't want to do. That drinking alcohol wasn't safe for you. I did not tell her about the doctor. She doesn't need to hear that." He squeezed her hand.

Leona ached. A child let down by her and her alone. A child who loved her, wanted her for a mother. A child she loved. Maybe alcohol was about death after all. She wasn't sure she could stand this. "She called me a drunk."

"Leona, I'm sorry. She doesn't know that's cruel."

"No. And it wasn't cruel, not really. It's true." The butterflies in Leona's stomach all dive bombed her at once. "I'm scared of damaging her more than I already have."

"I think she may be the toughest of the three of us. Nothing would hurt worse than if you backed out now. And I don't want to be without you, Leona. I say we keep trying. And I think that teaching Wren to go to Ivy if the need ever arises is a good idea."

He still wants me. Leona's defiled heart wanted to cheer. But that was the damn fairy tale seeking its happy ending. "Mikhail. Can you really accept me, knowing *you* might have to run off to a friend now and then?"

"I haven't got that kind of friend. When you need me, I want to be there. I'm asking permission to try again."

It was more than Leona could ask and more than she deserved. "You're both so deep in my heart you'll never climb out. But I'm convinced I'll fail."

He put his arms around her even though tribespeople were likely to see. "No. You'll drink again. But you are no failure. You keep fighting back. That's enough for me."

The next days were delicate. She dared to hope. Could it work?

But the fairy tale dragon wasn't done with her yet. By the short, dark days of Christmas, Leona knew she was pregnant. She'd missed her menses. What she didn't know was whether the baby was her love child with Mikhail or her bundle of shame with Dr. Reardon. Either way, she would love it. There was no question about that. But there were questions about damn near everything else.

It had been gut-wrenching enough before this new little fillip presented itself. It was time to talk with Mikhail again. To make their delicate footing even more unsure.

The morning was cold but there was little snow on the ground when she headed up the familiar trail toward his cabin, at a time of day when Wren was in school. As she went, she talked quietly to the baby within. "Are you awake in there, Squirt? You know what we're doing today? We're announcing your presence to the man I believe to be your daddy. Why don't I know whether he is? You're far too young for that story. But here's one I can tell." A clump of melting snow from a Sitka spruce splatted on her neck. As she tightened her scarf, she began.

"Once upon a time, there was a woodsman and a nurse who loved each other very much. They hoped to marry and live happily ever after. But the nurse had an illness she could not cure no matter how hard she tried. It was far worse than a big bad wolf. It forced her to do ugly things. She feared the woodsman couldn't count on her. It was all so sad. What were they to do?"

Leona stopped long enough to blow her nose. The wind always made it drip, a quirk she shared with Wren. She didn't hear him coming until Mikhail said, "Who are you talking to?"

She gasped and a foot slipped on the slick trail. Mikhail caught her arm. "Sorry I startled you. But I heard your voice. Who's with you?" He looked around to find where her companion hid.

"Mikhail. I've mucked things up worse than you know."

"I thought you'd stop blaming yourself by now."

"This time, it might be *you* doing the blaming. I'm with child. In the family way. There's a bun in the oven."

He seemed stunned but managed to ask, "Are you sure?"

"Mikhail!" she snapped. "I'm a nurse. I know I'll be wearing the bustle backwards in a very few months."

He said nothing. But she wasn't through. "And before you ask, I don't know if it's yours."

They walked on. Winter birds chirped, distant waves slapped the shore, wind danced in the firs, as though life as usual went on.

Finally, Mikhail said, "Have you told the doctor?"

"No. I don't intend to tell the doctor. Not if I can avoid it. It's no business of his." She knew this was not exactly true.

Their boots crunched in the snow. Leona thought about rubbing her nose on her sleeve a la Wren. What the hell did it matter anymore how ladylike she was? She'd proved herself far less than that.

"You present a man with many problems, Leona Herkimer."

"I don't mean to. But this problem is rather more mine than yours, wouldn't you agree?"

"I would like another child, Leona. I hoped we might have one."

She snorted, a bitter noise. "And that's exactly what's happened. You *might* be having one."

"I'm not looking for a way out, Leona. I'm telling you I want this baby."

She didn't deserve this good man. And it was a relief to know he would stand beside her. But her deepest truth, the one she hardly could tell herself? She wasn't sure she could raise a baby with or without him. What business did an out-of-control sot have doing something like that? If Wren might be in danger from her, what chance did this defenseless bundle have?

December 23, 1921
Ivy Bolton

The captain had delivered what was likely to be the last mail of the year. If the weather got worse soon, it could even be the last of the winter. The town people, seeing *Small Fry* chug into the inlet this close to Christmas, hurried to the government building. Ivy barely had time to sort their letters, catalogs, and packages. Mail days were always busy in the lobby, a time that included no small amount of socializing and gossip.

When everyone was finally gone, Ivy sorted through the mail she'd set aside for the school and the clinic. The fourth letter down had an official aura to it. Looking at the vellum's upper left corner, she saw it was from Dr. Edward Reardon. And it was addressed to Leona. He might have written it two weeks ago, maybe three. But it had taken this long to arrive.

Ivy held it like it was a bug. She contemplated ripping it to shreds and burning it bit by bit. Burying the ashes under a quarter moon. Things were in a tenuous lull for Leona at the moment. She didn't need whatever drama the letter had to offer. Or maybe it wasn't a pledge of troth or a request for further fadoodling. Maybe it had to do with work. Maybe the doctor was sending a perfectly acceptable request to a nursing colleague.

Maybe.

Ivy fought a battle with herself. Finally, the side of the angels won. But the scoundrel better not hurt Leona. Ivy would see to repercussions about that. She left the letter on top of the rest of the pile for the clinic. And then she fretted.

By dinner with Flower and Leona that evening, Ivy couldn't stand it any longer. She knew Leona had shared her story with Flower, or Ivy would have stayed mum about it. But mum wasn't one of her virtues. "I see you received a letter from Dr. Reardon today."

"Yes," Leona replied, helping herself to a piece of Swiss steak made with moose.

"I wasn't snooping. I saw it when I sorted the mail," Ivy said.

"Uh-huh." Leona said, putting butter in a steaming baked potato.

Ivy tapped her fingers on the table. "Yes? *Uh-huh?* That's all you have to say?"

Leona smiled sweetly as she added canned green beans to her plate.

If it took being teased to get a smile out of the girl, Ivy was willing to be the goat, as long as it didn't happen too often or go on too long. "Well, are you going to tell me or sit there grinning like a Cheshire cat?"

Leona wriggled her nose. "He wants me to go back to Haines in March to continue inoculations."

"Aaaiii. With him?" Flower sounded shocked by the very idea. "What will Mikhail think? How could you stand being alone with the doctor that long?"

Leona nodded. "Good observations. But apart from anything else, I am the traveling nurse. It is my job."

"Yes, but what was said about something, oh I don't know, *of a more personal nature*?" Ivy drilled the words into Leona like a sergeant.

Leona sighed. "You know, Ivy, sometimes things are personal."

"Not around me, they're not." Ivy surprised herself with such an absurd observation of her own ability to burrow beneath the skin of anyone around her.

Leona laughed at her. "No, Ivy. You are refreshingly open with your requests. The good doctor writes that he enjoyed our last outing, finding me quite charming company as well as a diligent assistant. But I wasn't to take any deeper meaning from his natural interest. Although he'd like to express that interest again when we meet."

"What the hell?" snapped Ivy.

"What does that mean?" asked Flower. The green bean on her fork froze on its way to her mouth.

"As his plan is to return to San Francisco in the near future, he hopes I understand that our relationship is one of fondness and affection. No more than that. I believe, ladies, I am to recognize that a woman as easy as me should not think of myself as marriage material."

"The brute!" Flower's bean fell off her fork so she slapped the utensil back down.

"But he's my superior, nonetheless. I can hardly be the traveling nurse stationed in Hoonah if I refuse to go."

"You'll be, what, nearly five months pregnant by then?" Ivy was always good at math.

"Yes. And of course, I may lose my job for that reason alone."

"Well … well … shitsy-whitsy," Flower muttered.

A Tlingit phrase? Probably not, but right for the occasion. Ivy nodded. "You always say the right thing, Flower."

December 23, 1921
Wren Elim, age 8

Daddy and Leona were both paying more attention to Wren now. Even though Leona didn't visit as often, Wren felt secure again, and that's what mattered most. She allowed Christmas to wipe away her worries, replacing them with visions of the gifts she'd soon receive.

There'd be presents from the party at the church, of course, and a chance to play with all the other village kids. Daddy would make another stuffed animal for her from the softest fur he had; that was a Christmas tradition. Besides that, she needed new boots, but Wren really hoped for a canister of the Tinkertoys she'd seen in a Sears Roebuck catalog. She'd tumbled to the truth about Santa this year, so her last hope was Leona. She'd dropped a few hints, hoping the nurse was astute enough to pick up on them. But adults could be such dullards.

At the moment, she was working on gifts of her own to give. At school, Judith provided her a thin sheet of paper, and Wren traced flowers she found in a botany book. Their seasons and regions were of no consequence. If she liked them, violets went next to anthuriums next to ox-eye daisies. Among the flowers, she freehand drew a lady she labeled Leona with a little bird on her finger labeled Wren. She colored everything with Crayolas, rolled the paper, and tied it with a short piece of ribbon that she'd kept in her secret box of treasures, the one she hid under her bed. She hoped Leona would love the masterpiece.

Earlier in the day, Leona had helped her bake oatmeal cookies with bits of dried apple. They were for Daddy, although Wren battled not to eat them herself. Well, maybe she'd take just one. She was eager for the New Year. She'd soon be nine. Nine! Surely that was old enough to be a big kid. What a time it would be.

CHAPTER TWENTY

February 2, 1922
Leona Herkimer

Christmas passed. All that excitement and anticipation settled into a deep winter routine of school at one end of the government building and broken bones, frostbite, and births at the other. Daylight hours were getting longer, but they still used lanterns most of the time. On late afternoons after school, Leona and Flower held classes in the clinic on nutrition, cleanliness, and midwifery.

Now, when a Tlingit came to the clinic, there was a good chance Leona had already met her or a member of her family. She'd been in Hoonah long enough to earn a reputation for kindness and care. Her clientele trusted her. If any suspected she battled with the bottle, it seemed not to matter. She took care of them whether she took care of herself or not.

Besides, as Mikhail explained on one of the few nights they spent together, "Leona, most of us have family who drink too much. It's an Alaskan blight. It probably makes them accept you all the more."

Leona imposed some distance from Mikhail, not allowing discussions of marriage. The tribe may be trusting, but she was still unable to trust herself. She occasionally flew into a snit that Mikhail must forget about her. He willingly waited her out.

She said to him, "You're a man that any woman would want. Find someone worthy."

"I'm sorry my magnificence offends you," he replied. "I suggest you learn to live with it."

"You are such a frustrating man." If he would only provoke her, maybe she could lay some of the blame for their situation on his shoulders. But no. The guilt was all hers.

Tarnation.

Weary of her challenges, she forced herself to sit down and write a letter to the doctor. He was expecting her in Juneau next month. She was finally past morning sickness, so she *could* go to Haines to continue diphtheria inoculations. But she hated the idea. It was Flower who hatched a plan.

Leona started to write. *Dear* … she stopped. Dear Edward? Dear Doctor? Dear Lover Boy? She settled for no *Dear* at all.

Dr. Reardon: I must send my regrets as I will be unable to meet you for an inoculation journey to Haines in March due to …

Due to what? The fact she might be carrying his bastard? The fact that he represented her very worst side? The fact that she'd suffered enough humiliation regarding him for a lifetime? Leona decided no explanation whatsoever was the best solution, so she began again.

> *Dr. Reardon: I must send my regrets as I will be unable to meet you for an inoculation journey to Haines in March. Instead, I propose to have my assistant Flower accompany you. She is experienced in the skill of inoculation and, of course, offers the added benefit of speaking the Tlingit language. You will need no other translator as replacing Coy may be difficult for you. When you have made plans for the trip, contact the clinic, and Flower will arrange to be in Juneau on your schedule.*
>
> *Nurse Leona Herkimer*

There. It was written, sealed, stamped, and placed in the mail for the next trip anyone made to Juneau. Leona literally washed her hands of it and went back to work. Nonetheless, she was aware that, sooner or later, another shoe would drop.

It took little more than a week. One afternoon, Leona looked up from wrapping a boy's sprained wrist and there was the doctor, staring at her from the doorway to the lobby. He doffed his hat and smiled.

"Dr. Reardon!" she gasped.

"Nurse Leona. You're looking well."

So was he.

"Thank you. I am well." Later she would praise herself for her splendid conversational skills. But now, she finished the wrap, staring at it overlong to buy herself time to think clearly. Finally, she sent the boy on his way.

"Why are you here, Doctor?" she asked although she knew the answer.

"You know why."

"Well, um, yes. Would you like tea while we chat? Flower, could you handle Milly? She'll be here for more of the liver pills. Oh, Doctor, you know Flower, correct? And Flower, you know Dr. Reardon. Of course, you do. How silly of me. Come through to the kitchen with me, Doctor." She dithered until he put a hand on her shoulder.

"Am I making you nervous, Leona?" He asked, near enough the truth to make her shiver. She stared up at him and saw the gremlin laughing through his eyes. He was making fun of her. That was enough of that.

She huffed. "As the last time I saw you, you were asleep in a patient bed, naked rear end in the air, I should think you'd be the least bit nervous, as well."

He laughed. It was a rich, rolling sound, very freely given. "Ah. You are such a delight, Leona. It was a night of folly best forgotten. Not that I have been able to get it out of my mind. You have a certain, shall we say staying power in my imagination." His smiled disappeared. "But that's not why I'm here, my dear."

"It's nurse, not dear. You are here to demand I go to Haines next month."

"Exactly that."

They sat at the kitchen table, and she poured him a cup of tea. She would rather have the privacy of the outdoors, but it was so cold that would be ridiculous. Besides, she had little left too personal to say where the women of this building were concerned.

"Flower will do you an excellent job, Dr. Reardon. She is quick, pleasant, bi-lingual. You should be quite pleased."

"Leona, I know she is fine. But that's not the point. I don't understand why you feel you can disregard the request of the closest doctor to the clinic, and the only one who comes to Hoonah. I feel that it is a mistake to allow our little dalliance to endanger your career. I assure you I carry great weight with the medical boards that oversee this territory."

A threat! Leona wanted to slap his oh so handsome face hard enough for a bruise to grow. But she bit back her anger. It was true that he could create serious trouble for her if he chose. And for the tribe if he refused to come back at all. The threat was very real, very dangerous.

She pleaded. "Don't ask for an explanation. Just take it as truth that I cannot go."

"I'm sorry, but that doesn't solve it for me. I need an answer so I can understand. I don't mean you harm, you know."

She'd never wanted him to know, but of course he would sooner or later. When she showed enough that it was obvious she was pregnant, he would be more than capable of counting the months. Realistically, the matter could no longer be ignored.

But she felt such shame. "Our little dalliance, you call it. Well, it appears our little dalliance will soon need a name. I am in a condition that makes it unwise for me to travel around in the wilderness."

He froze, staring at her with all the disapproval of the family patriarch in old time photos. "But … but you are a nurse."

The blush across her body made her far too warm for a cold day. "Nurses have babies, too, you know. This is no exact science."

"No, indeed." He continued to stare at her as though she were the only one who misbehaved.

Anger stiffened her spine. "You had been drinking. So had I. Otherwise it never would have happened. I admit I drank so much I have little memory of our, ah, activities. But it happened."

"There is no doubt? This is my child?" His lips moved but otherwise, he was still glacial as ice.

"I don't believe it to be yours. But it could be." Leona hated the admission and hated even more that he immediately pursued the loophole.

"You have another man as the candidate? You were drinking then, too?"

She responded, "No, Dr. Reardon. I am sober when I am with him. Alcohol was my mistake with you."

"More than one man comes calling? How many do you allow in? Is alcohol often a problem for you?" He moved to another position and held it again.

Like a lizard, she thought. "No. It isn't. Alcohol is under control … nearly always."

"Do you expect me to marry you?"

She could not keep the sneer out of her voice. "No, of course not. I have no interest in such a proposal. You go on to San Francisco to find a suitable lady."

"But leave an endangered baby behind, one that could be mine?"

"Endangered! How dare you?" *Go away. Forever.*

Her anger apparently thawed him. He shrugged his shoulders and waved his arms. "For heaven's sake! A doctor can hardly leave a baby with a woman who becomes so delirious with drink that she loses her control, her ethics. Don't you see an issue with that, Nurse?" He hissed out that last word as though it tainted his mouth.

"The baby will have me, the other women who work here, and the man who is most likely its father."

"That is not acceptable, nurse. No baby should be at the mercy of an alcohol-addled parent. You know that. How often have you seen it lead to tragedy? Liquor is a cause for abuse of so many children in Alaska. Surely you see I can't allow that."

It was as if an icicle pierced her spine. Leona's muscles bunched as she growled, "You mean you will try to take this baby for yourself?"

"Of course not. Don't be absurd. I don't want the child. But I will propose it be given to a trustworthy couple at birth." He stood, pointing a finger at her. "You are unfit for motherhood at this point in your life."

She could take no more of his superiority. His taunt reverberated within her like an echo, rekindling the similar thoughts she had about herself. *Unfit mother.*

Leona arose directly in front of him, drew back a right, and slapped his face as hard as she could. She'd never struck anyone before. She was surprised how it stung her hand. But she experienced unnursely delight feeling his soft tissue squash against his cheek and jaw bones, his head lurch to the side, and his eyes water after her blow.

"Show yourself out," Leona hissed. She left the kitchen, shoulders squared, for the privacy of her room.

February 2, 1922
Ivy Bolton

Ivy was in her classroom where a gawky boy, voice breaking on every sixth word, was trying to read Hamlet's soliloquy to the rest of the class. Ivy sensed motion at the doorway. She looked over to see Flower motioning her to come. She already knew something was afoot because she'd heard raised voices, hurried footsteps on the staircase, a door slam upstairs, and then a mightier slam of the building's front door. She'd peeked out one of the high windows in the schoolroom to see Dr. Reardon heading toward the boat at the dock, still working an arm into his coat. He was moving fast.

Flower whispered to her at the classroom door, then went back to the clinic. Ivy assigned her students to write down what Hamlet meant. She asked Judith to keep an eye on her kids over Harold's Wall while Judith's own little scholars, in two separate groups, practiced penmanship or colored countries on maps.

Ivy galloped up the stairs, knocked on Leona's door, and entered without awaiting an invitation. The nurse was not boozing from a bottle as Flower and Ivy feared. Instead, she was pacing the short distance from bed to wardrobe, fuming with each step.

"If you were a cartoon, steam would be rising from your head," Ivy ventured.

"Steam *is* rising from my head. I want to drink till a bottle is empty, then break it over that faultfinding sourpuss of a doctor's head."

"He frequently brings out the best in you."

"He is a contemptible, despicable … poop!"

"Dare I hug you or would I be burned to a crisp by such a violent outburst?"

"Get over here. No don't. Go back to your class. Tell the troops to stand down. I won't drink. No wait. Give me a hug before you go."

Ivy complied. She felt how thin the nurse had become. She wondered if Flower knew how to force feed a patient.

"Oh, Ivy. Dr. Reardon said I was unfit to be a mother."

"Well, he is unfit to be a human. Did you tell him we have it worked out? That we're all ready to help?"

"He said that wasn't good enough. He implied any nurse should know that and agree with him."

Ivy thought it through. She felt the frown lines tighten her forehead. Suddenly, she knew the worst. "Leona, does he intend to take the baby?"

"Yes. To give it to a dependable couple." Any effort she'd been making to hold back tears gave up the ghost.

"He'll do no such thing."

"And he's right, you know. I get scared or angry, and all I want to do it drink the hurt away."

"You will do no such thing, either. Not this time. You'll come downstairs now. Flower says she's holding the fort, but the natives are about to break in."

The absurdity of that statement brought a touch of humor to Leona's lips. "I can see her now, barricading the door as Old Woman Sheet'ká tries to burst through to steal all our diuretics."

"You best get down there to help her. Work on a smile, and I'll tell her the cavalry is on its way."

Ivy went through the clinic to nod at Flower, cut into the kitchen to ask Cook to make more tea for Leona, and whisked back into her classroom with a brief smile at Judith. Their team had worked. Leona had no time or privacy to drink even if she'd wanted to.

"Now then, who can tell me what Hamlet meant? Raise your hands."

CHAPTER TWENTY-ONE

December 2, 1946
Ivy Bolton

Ivy was cold. She put on a flannel nightgown, one she'd bought in Juneau decades before. It had been robin's egg blue but was now granite gray.

"I love you, Ivy, but I hate that old rag. Looks like Omar the Tentmaker designed it."

"It's comfy. And I'm cold." She slipped into bed and touched her feet against his.

"Judas Priest, woman!" he yelped, but he put his arms around her anyway and let her tuck her feet behind his legs.

They lay still for a moment, breathing each other in. Nobody had ever smelled the way Maki did to Ivy. Even after a long bath, it was as if he brought the spirit of the forest to bed with him. He had a wonderful musk of cedar, meadow, and wildness. It was true when he was young, and it was true in his twilight years. It managed to make her heart still dance, the rawboned body of this old man so close to her.

Maki said, "I think the boy took it pretty well, considering his family is a whole different cast of characters than he thought this morning."

"I think we stunned him. He'll have lots of questions before he decides to go along with Wren or not."

"You mean to meet Leona?"

"This spring. When weather allows. Wren wants him to come home." Maki's warmth became hers, and her feet thawed. "You know, Maki, I'd kinda like to go along myself."

"Because you're a busybody?"

"Mmmm, yes. And because it's my story, too. Wouldn't you like to see Alaska again?"

Maki humphed in interest. "Never thought about it. Wonder how the boy would feel about that. Showing up as part of a herd."

"He's perturbed with me for holding back so much, but he'll get over it. If anyone knows how he truly feels at this moment, it'll be Barbara. I imagine he's in her arms about now."

"Nice he's not alone, Ivy. But you know, I thought she, uh, hiked the other side of the trail."

"She does, mostly. But men are okay, too, I guess." Ivy chuckled softly. "She told him she prefers halibut, but enjoys a good salmon. Beef is better, but she doesn't turn down chicken."

Maki laughed. "I'll be. Guess we're all Outsiders in our own way." He pulled Ivy close. "Are you warm yet?"

"Yep."

"Enough to warm me?"

"Lucky for you I prefer the old vintages."

December 2, 1946
Rome Coleridge

Cold blue light from the moon pierced the darkness of his loft above the garage. Tucked beside him, Barbara snored, not loudly but with the regular rhythm of a practiced log sawyer. Rome hadn't known that women snored. It was another thing on the lengthening list of stuff he hadn't known. He looked at her, the comfortable warm lump she made in the bed. Marshmallow breasts to cuddle between. A handful of hip. Rome decided it would be a lucky woman who won this woman.

He had talked late into the night with Barbara. She'd known him before the war, when his parents were still his parents. Now that truth had changed.

He would pepper Ivy and Maki in the days to come with questions about everything else, but neither of them knew Nancy and Cecil Coleridge, at least not well. Nancy, biological mother or not, treated all her kids the same. But that had never been true of her husband, Cecil.

"Frankly, a different father would have been all to the good," Barbara had said as she unsnapped her garters and slipped off her nylons, an act Rome loved to watch. "Cecil was a real pillock, if you want my opinion which you must, or I'd be sleeping in my own bed."

"I guess I finally have a reason why Cecil never treated me like his other kids. I *wasn't* one of his kids." Rome figured Cecil had seen him as no more than another mouth to feed. He wished he'd understood when he was younger. It would have saved a lot of hurt, maybe for both of them.

"What does she want, this Wren?" Barbara asked, shimmying out of the girdle.

"To come for a visit. Or for me to go there."

Barbara, naked, scooched in beside him, and placed her hand on his already expectant penis. "All these dangly bits are gross," she teased. "On a woman, this sex stuff is tucked up inside. Much tidier."

He reached for her. "Hmmm, I see what you mean."

"Let's forget about mom, dad, and sis for a while, whoever they are."

After a long, athletic lapse in the parental conversation, Rome's thoughts turned back to Leona and Mikhail. Or the doctor. *Doesn't the doctor have a name, for shit's sake?*

Rome didn't instantly cut Nancy and Cecil from his withering family tree. He munched on it, rolled it over in his head. Maybe this was how adopted children took the news. Shocked, sort of. He wasn't sad, not really, although maybe that was callous. Mostly, he was curious. And kind of irked at Ivy. She'd kept secrets for so long. Why had his mother given him to her sister? How did her baby get to Nancy? Did Ivy have answers?

Ivy would get shirty if she felt badgered. Rome knew that, so he needed to keep his curiosity under control. Besides, sometimes a fella just wanted to talk with another fella. In the past few weeks, Rome had come to treasure the days he spent with Maki almost as much as those with Ivy. With his brother dead, Rome soon accepted Maki as his closest male friend.

Through the autumn, Maki had helped him grow stronger. One of the many things Rome hadn't anticipated about losing an arm was how it affected the way he walked and moved. In addition to phantom pains that tortured a missing hand and arm, Rome suffered unsure balance. The mechanics of moving had to be adjusted to his altered state. Maki made him work at it. Many days, the two walked the unsteady shifting pebbles or loose sand on the beaches of the Peninsula. Or they turned inland, climbing through forest toward the Olympic peaks. Crossing streams and circling rocks were making Rome sure-footed once again.

Maki was hard on him, even joking when Rome stumbled or ended ass deep in a creek bed. He might say, "There's a fishing technique new to me ... sitting on the trout."

This day dawned dry and clear. After seeing Barbara home, Rome met Maki on the trail they were cleaning to accommodate Maki's horseback tours come spring. "Did you know my real father?" Rome asked, comfortable that Maki would be an honest source of information.

"I did. He was a fine man."

"What's your guess: was he the Russian or the doctor?"

Maki didn't hesitate. "Mikhail was half Russian, half Tlingit. I see his nose on your face every time I look at you. That's how I know that doctor was no blood of yours."

"You liked Mikhail?'

"You would too if you'd known him." Maki slashed back a clump of ferns determined to cross the trail. "Mikhail ran a trapline. He had lines others wanted, but he could fight to keep them since he was half white. Otherwise, whites elbowed territory away from the natives. It's what a lot of sourdoughs did in the winter when they couldn't pan for gold." Maki grabbed a broken limb, and Rome cut it away from the spruce; his knife skills now included a machete.

Maki carried on as they worked. "When I was a ranger in the Tongass, I'd stop at his cabin, check it out. He stayed within his territory, ran as clean an operation as a fur trapper can run. He was talented past the trapping, too. Made fine goods from the skins and pelts. He learned that from his Tlingit mother."

"When did he die?"

Maki picked up a stone and examined it with considerable interest. "Long time ago, Rome. Before you were born. I'm the one found the body. Not a pretty story."

"Tell me anyway," Rome said.

"You're as pushy as Ivy, for cripes sake."

"Yes, she's taught me many social skills."

"You still have some of that coffee?"

They stopped, and Maki hunkered on an enormous log that crossed a small creek beside the trail. The sound of its galloping water accompanied the older man's voice. "It was winter, 1922. I remember because that's the same year Ivy and I left Alaska for Outside. Year you were born."

He stopped and ran a hand down the sleeve of the old fur jacket he wore. "Year I got this coat. It was Mikhail's. He trapped the pine marten and cured the hides."

Rome opened his Thermos, poured two cups, and closed the bottle. All one-handed. Easy chore now.

Maki took a sip, grunted, and threw the rest away. "I'd been walking the forest outside Hoonah. A couple logging operations on Chichagof Island were on my check list. The Forest Service always had to keep them on the straight and narrow, 'cause they'd cut first and ask forgiveness after. Even truer decades ago than now."

Rome sat on the log and watched Maki watch the creek. The old man was wiry and seemed impervious to weather. After so much time in Alaska, he always claimed the Olympic Mountains were damn near tropical. He was still flexible enough to squat there bunched up and balanced, looking like a blue heron ready to strike.

Maki spoke dreamily of the distant past, like a storyteller at a campfire. Rome felt the chill of a boy listening to a ghost story. "The day was cold, but decent, so I thought I'd cut over to howdy Mikhail if he was out. He'd go out for days sometimes now that Wren could stay with the womenfolk at the government building. Some of his traplines weren't far from one of the log camps. Time might have come when there'd be a conflict of wills about that, but so far, nobody'd complained to me. I knew Mikhail's secret hunting ground for most of the wolverines he caught. He always had more luck with those mad buggers than anyone else."

Maki stretched out his legs and sat down on the log, dug into his backpack, and gave Rome one of Ivy's brownies, wrapped in Cut-Rite wax paper. "There wasn't a lot of snow but enough for me to pick up a hint of footprints and the tracks of a sled. Not real fresh, but still maybe Mikhail was in the area.

I came to the top of a ridge. I saw his body down below. If he wasn't dead, he sure as hell was broken. I called his name. No answer."

Maki sighed. "I lowered myself, hanging on to scrub in the rocks. There was no going for help, you understand. I didn't need Nurse Leona to tell me he was dead. I was the closest thing to the law on the island, so I investigated as much as I could. The thought went through me that someone might have pushed Mikhail and the sled off that ridge. One of the loggers maybe or a fur buyer. I guess I was in shock, not thinking clear. Such a loss. Such a fucking loss."

To Rome, Maki sounded angry enough to shake a fist at the sky, but he sat there hunched, contained. "Anyhow, the body didn't reveal those kind of clues. Not human clues. There was a dead lynx near it, a big cat. It looked like it might have died of a knife wound. The knife was still there, although a lot of the carcass was eaten. Maybe Mikhail and that cat went over the ridge together. I couldn't tell if Mikhail's broken bones were due to a big animal or the fall. They'd all been gnawed on by little critters by the time I got there."

Rome was lost in Maki's story, but it didn't feel real. His father, killed in a knife fight with a cat, careening over a cliff, and both eaten by scavengers? Is that how people died back in the day in Alaska? Or was it fiction from Jack London?

Maki continued. "I saw no bullet holes in his clothes. But the biggest clue? He had pelts with him on the sled. A human enemy would have taken them away. Far too valuable to leave out there. Whatever got Mikhail had four legs, not two. And cats are sneaky bastards."

Rome found his voice if not his good sense. "He was experienced out in the forest, wasn't he? I mean, he knew what he was doing?"

Maki looked peeved. "Ain't you been listening? Mikhail was a woodsman through and through. He knew if you lived out there in the Alaska woods, you'd find some way to die eventually. All I can hope is it happened fast."

"What the hell did you do, Maki?"

"I had little choice what to do. I didn't have a pack animal to haul him out, and something would have dug him up faster than I could bury him in that cold ground. Besides, Tlingit custom is to cremate. They think corpses are contaminated. I agree. And I tell you, Wren and Leona didn't need to see the last of Mikhail.

"I built a big fire. Just that took hours what with most of the available wood damn wet. I did away with Mikhail's remains right there. Took a long time. Finally, ravens began to circle and caw. So I spent that night with Mikhail, keeping watch."

"No sign at all of foul play?"

"Not by humans, anyhow."

Rome watched tears gutter their way down Maki's leathery face. The old man ended his story. "Worst thing I ever had to do, tell a pregnant woman her man was dead."

Rome let his friend mourn the decades-old loss, and he mourned the man he'd never met. There was nothing more to be said. They each looked at the wax-wrapped brownies in their hands as if they'd appeared there by miracle. Quietly they unwrapped the comfort food and took bites while the creek water made its noisy way through the ice channel it created.

CHAPTER TWENTY-TWO

March 4, 1922
Ivy Bolton

"Maki is in kitchen. You come now," Cook ordered Ivy.

What on earth? It was only mid-morning, and he rarely appeared before dark. Ivy turned her class over to Judith and walked to the kitchen where Maki was still in front of the kitchen door, stamping muddy snow from his boots.

When he saw Ivy, he said to Cook, "Now get Leona." Cook might not have taken orders from a different man, but she liked Maki, as far as anyone could tell.

"Maki!" Ivy noticed a pallor on her lover's face, one that she'd never seen before. "You look like you've seen a ghost. What's wrong? Why are you here?"

"Sit, Ivy, my girl. I'll make some tea."

"Maki, what are you talking about? Why on earth would you make tea?"

His wide shoulders slumped, and his eyes welled. "Because women always want tea in bad times, and I don't know what else to do."

Ivy crossed the room, grabbed him, and hugged. He was scaring her. "What, dear one? Tell me."

"Oh Ivy. Mikhail. He's dead," Maki lamented in her ear. And then he held her, their strong arms supporting each other as she gasped for breath. Ivy thought she might collapse otherwise. *What is he saying? I don't understand.*

Leona entered the kitchen, drying her hands. "Hey, you lovebirds. What do you want? I'm too busy to watch you woo."

Ivy turned and crumpled onto a chair. "Sit here, Leona. With me."

"But why?" Leona sat, as requested. Her white apron stretched over her growing belly. "What's wrong, Ivy?" She looked at Maki. "What's happened? Should I get my medical bag?"

"No, Leona. You won't need it," Maki said.

"Maki, tell us." Ivy thought she might faint from lack of information.

"Leona, honey," Maki said. "It's Mikhail. He's dead."

Cook, overhearing, silently took over the duty of making tea.

Maki pulled a chair between Leona and Ivy, taking Leona's hand.

The nurse looked dumbfounded and tried to laugh. "Oh, Maki, you're such a joker. You are joking?"

"No. It's true. I found his body in the forest. At the bottom of a ridge near one of his traplines."

Leona tried to stand, but Maki grasped her hand tightly.

"Let me go! I have to get to him. Save him," Leona snapped at Maki. "That's what nurses do."

Maki held his ground. "Leona. You can't save him. He is dead. I took care of him in the Tlingit way. Mikhail is gone."

She didn't so much sit as fall back into the chair. "You mean ... you mean there's no ... remains?"

"No. Nothing for you to attend to. It is done."

The air whooshed out of Leona loud enough for Ivy to hear. The nurse crumpled forward, her chin nearly resting on the baby within. Ivy leaned into her. "Breathe, Leona. Deep breaths, now. Breathe. Your baby needs you to keep breathing."

Leona threw her head back. "Mikhail..." she wailed.

Maki looked to Ivy. "What do I do now?"

Ivy pushed her agony aside for now. She was Ivy again. She could act. "Wren is here. Go to the cabin, grab her clothes. A doll if you see one. Her Tinkertoys. The box of treasures under her bed. She'll not be going back there again."

"Wren! What about Wren? Oh Wren!" Leona gasped.

Ivy sounded as calm as she could. "Judith won't release Wren from class until later today. We can talk with her then, after Maki's back with her things. She'll stay here. She'll be loved. So will you."

"No, I should tell her now. Before she hears it from anyone else. I'll get her..."

Ivy considered it. Leona was right. Wren was not the type of child who would thank anyone for withholding information. "I'll go," she said. "You stay here." Then she turned to Cook. "Tell Flower to come at once."

Cook must have told Flower what had happened, because when the nursing assistant arrived, tears were already wetting her round cheeks.

Ivy said, "Flower, we need you. Stay with Leona. I'll send anyone waiting for the clinic away for the day. And I'll be back with Wren."

March 4, 1922
Wren Elim, Age 9

Wren felt a mystery brewing. First, Mrs. Bolten had asked Mrs. Binder to watch her class, then she had left the schoolroom. What could that mean? Maybe there'd be a surprise party! Cupcakes from someone's mom. *Whose birthday?*

But then Mrs. Bolton came back, and asked, "Wren, could you come with me?" The teacher didn't look happy.

The whole class stared as Wren stood. "You're gonna get it now," whispered Sammy, the pug-nosed boy on the bench next to her.

Wren felt the first pangs of panic. Maybe not a party. Maybe they'd discovered she'd taken home one of the big kids' books. One that was 'over her head' whatever that meant since it had been on a shelf nowhere near her head.

"I'll bring it back, Teacher," she said, in case anyone was about to be spanked if they were not sorry for their theft.

But Mrs. Bolton didn't seem to hear. Instead, she took Wren's hand, and they walked toward the kitchen together. So nothing too bad was happening. Wren decided to say no more about the missing book. What the big people didn't know wouldn't hurt them.

When they entered the kitchen, Wren saw Leona and Flower at the table. They were crying. That's when Wren's panic burst free. Big people didn't cry unless something awful happened. In her nine-year-old view of the world, Wren's first thought was, *What's going to become of me?*

Wren had seen that look before, the one now on Leona's face. It was the look on her Daddy's face when he'd told her that Mommy wouldn't be home anymore. A look of pity for her, mixed with grief for them both.

"No!" Wren shrieked. "Don't tell me!" If she didn't know it wouldn't be true. Nothing would change. But that wasn't the case, and she knew it. She wasn't a baby. Through a flood of tears, she gasped, "Is Daddy dead?"

"Yes, Wren," Leona said, putting her trembling hands onto Wren's thin shoulders. "It's the two of us, now. You will live here with me because I love you and want you. Flower will be here, too, along with Ivy and Judith and Cook. We'll be a family. You'll be safe. And you'll be happy again, I promise."

They clung together, vulnerable and lost. Wren wasn't convinced. She didn't believe the stories that big people told anymore. Mommy was gone. Daddy was gone. Leona would just as likely be gone, too.

March 4, 1922
Leona Herkimer

Leona finally got Wren to nap in one of the patient beds. The child had exhausted herself with misery and fury at a quicksilver world.

Wren's outburst had terrified Leona, who would have done almost anything to stop the torture for the little girl. But Leona knew she'd made a promise that might not be hers to make. Could she actually keep Wren? Would there be other claims, maybe from her real mother's relatives, maybe from Judith and Harold at the orphanage where adoption was a far more official affair? Would Wren be better off with others?

Enough! Leona could not deal with it now. She first must bring her own emotions into some semblance of control. And she only knew one way to do that. She wearily stood up from the bedside, squared her shoulders, and left Wren under the care of Flower, who was working out her own sorrow by scrubbing the clinic with quiet ferocity. Leona went to her room and packed a small bag. She came back to the kitchen for a few food items, although she could not imagine how she'd ever eat again. Or smile or hope or plan. Nothing normal that the living did freely, every day.

What she needed most was alcohol and the blindness it would provide. Long term, it might be her enemy, but in the short run, it soothed the hurt. She must obliterate the shock of it, slow it down, until she could take it in.

Leona was aware how much the clinic relied on her on these winter days of frostbite, pneumonia, croup, and strep. But she believed a healer must heal herself first. It was a tenet of basic nurse training. If it took a descent into dipsomania to diminish the grief, she would do it.

She sat in the kitchen waiting for Ivy to finish with her school day, then she called Flower in, too. When they appeared, Leona saw Ivy look at her bag, and at the anorak that Leona wore.

"You're going." Ivy said it gently and so sadly.

"For two nights. To the cabin."

"You need to do this?"

"I do. For me, for now, alcohol is more help than hindrance. I don't think I can live through this without it."

"And you can't do it here where we can keep an eye on you?"

"No. I can't do it here, not in front of Wren. Not in front of anybody."

Ivy nodded and left. Flower fought the idea that Ivy had accepted so quickly. "I don't want you to do this. You could get hurt. You could hurt yourself."

"I'll be fine, dear Flower. In fact, this is the only way I may ever be fine again." Leona put her arms around her belly. "This baby needs me to calm down."

Flower finally nodded. "Then you take care of yourself, and we'll care for Wren until you return."

Ivy came back into the kitchen with a bottle of whiskey. "Take this. Maki and I share it sometimes."

Leona smiled, her mouth trembling with the effort. "I have a bottle."

"Take it in case. I'll come for you after two nights. If anything's left, we'll finish it together."

Leona's gratitude to these women was as boundless as her grief for Mikhail. Neither lectured. Both offered love. There was one more request Leona made of them. "Please. Tell Wren I am off to visit the tribe in Angoon. Tell her it's a flu outbreak if she asks. I hate to lie to her, but I don't want her to think I've abandoned her. She must believe I'll be back." After a bitter snort, Leona added, "I don't think she needs to hear that her new mother is out on a bender."

"Do you want Maki to take you to the cabin?" Ivy asked.

"No. Mikhail will walk with me."

Leona avoided the village by circling it on a path between the buildings and the ridge behind them. It intersected the trail that went toward Mikhail's cabin. She knew this route well, from all the times she'd walked it with him, with Wren, on her own.

"It won't be the last time I come this way, Mikhail," she said. "Wren will want to see the cabin again, and I'll bring her. As long as she needs to visit it, we'll come." The trail leveled at a rock outcropping before it climbed upward again. Leona stood looking back down on Hoonah, busy with its everyday commerce as if the world hadn't stopped for her. The nurse in her battled against the role of victim.

I can't think that way. These very people are in my care. I'll come back to them, ready for their aches and pains.

Leona walked on toward the cabin. "I'll be the nurse I'm meant to be, Mikhail. But you know I need to do this to gather the strength to go on. And I promise you I'll raise Wren the best I know how. You will never be forgotten by either of us. We'll talk about you. You have no worries to trouble your spirit. We'll be fine because you showed us what goodness we should demand from life."

For two nights, Leona slept alone in Mikhail's bed. She told him about the baby, how it kicked, how it must be his son to be so strong. Meanwhile, she drank. She cleaned the cabin the first afternoon before collapsing. Leona sobbed through the first night, clutching to her chest the copy of *The Call of the Wild* she'd given Mikhail for Christmas. He'd loved it.

The next day she scoured the outhouse and packed up the perishables to take back to the clinic. She wanted to finish that before she wallowed in booze again. Maki stopped by in the late morning, on his way back into the deep forest to resume the work of keeping lumbermen in their places. "Not here to spy," he said. "Here to say goodbye for a while."

Leona asked him to check Mikhail's traplines, release the jaws and snares, and to dispatch any caught animal that might still be alive. She also gave him the marten jacket that Mikhail had made and worn himself. "He'd want you to have it, Maki. Don't give me any guff about taking it." When he put it on, she buried her face in the fur, and sobbed. As she geared down to a sniffle, she patted him and said, "Now go away." The brandy and whiskey called to her.

By the following morning, Leona had made decisions. She talked with Mikhail, and in the end, she knew she could live without him. She could become a good mother to Wren, given the time to return to the routine at her beloved clinic.

But she could not be a good mother to her baby. A baby should not have to depend on a booze-crazed mother. She might forget the baby, neglect it, even hurt it. All the feedings, all the changes, all the everything. She simply could not risk its life. Even though she wanted it for her own, it wasn't the right thing. Wren was big enough to weather episodes that Leona was likely to have. But a baby was defenseless. That was the heartbreaking truth.

And yet.

Everything in her recoiled at giving her baby to Dr. Reardon or anybody that he chose. Her baby would never be his, never be within his reach, never be raised to be as heartless as he was. The good doctor would always look at this baby as baggage from a sordid mistake. Leona wanted it raised with love and with a chance to become anyone it wanted to be. Her only option was to hide the newborn where the doctor would never find it.

By the time Ivy came for her, Leona was not clear-eyed, but she was clear-headed. She was ready to pick up the traces once more.

March 6, 1922
Wren Elim

Wren tried to maintain a sulk while drawing at the kitchen table. She did not leap up to hug Leona on the nurse's return. Instead, she accused. "The people in Angoon mean more to you than I do."

"No. They had no one else to look after them. You had Ivy and Flower and Judith."

"You'll go again."

"Yes, when people need me. That's my job. Like your father left the cabin to tend to his trapline. Like Captain Aleck goes to Juneau, and Maki heads off into the woods. Adults have rules they must follow, just like children do."

Wren seemed to roll that around in her mind. "Well, okay. As long as you are my mom when you are here. And then I don't have to take orders from anyone but you."

Leona laughed and it felt wonderful. "Well, my little attorney, we'll negotiate the terms as we go along."

At last Wren came to her for a cuddle. "I think I'll give you another chance."

Leona was very glad that Wren did not seem to know she was pregnant. That would be a discussion for another day.

The village had begun the traditional four-night memorial for a lost tribesman. Flower escorted Leona and Wren to the third night of mourning. Mikhail was honored with ceremonial singing, dancing, and feasting. His spirit, everyone agreed, would reside in *Kiwa-wa*, the Tlingit version of heaven, until he was reincarnated back into his family one day. In a couple of years, a memorial potlatch would be held in his honor.

The following day, Leona, Wren, and Ivy attended Harold's Presbyterian service for the white part of Mikhail, a far more dour affair with somber music and no dancing. There was a meal at the clinic, prepared by Cook.

Flower moved out of Leona's room so Wren could have her bed. Hence, Flower inherited the relative luxury of the guest room, where the pitcher and the wash basin were an actual match. She promised to be ready to vacate to a patient bed when the room was needed for a visitor.

"No mere visitor will ever be as important as you," Ivy had said to her.

Routine in the government building began again. The age-old curative of time took effect as Leona and Wren began to establish a pattern together. Leona pinned to the wall her Christmas present, the crayon drawing of Wren as a bird on her finger as she strode through a wild field of blossoms.

Late in March, Flower went off to vaccinate Tlingits in the Haines area, under the tutelage of Dr. Reardon. "Don't let him bully you. He will appreciate the quality of your work, and the doctor at the fort will, too," Leona said the morning the nervous young woman left on *Small Fry*. She could only hope the white soldiers and residents would accept a native as nurse. "Don't give the doctor information about me or the baby if you can help it."

"Leona who? What baby?"

By April, Leona began to sleep again, even though the baby demanded she lie on her side. Wren was quieter too, her nightmares diminished and her fits of anger less startling. Judith said she was not misbehaving so often in the schoolroom and that the crayons were much safer from breakage.

As much as Leona could figure, the child was responding to the benefits of living close to so many caring people. Ivy taught her to knit so the two often sat together after school, chatting as they made mittens and scarves. Leona helped her have a tea party for the other girls in her class. Captain Aleck took her to Juneau on *Small Fry* for a day. The other kids taught her dirty words in the Tlingit language, and they chose her in games because Wren could run like a deer.

It was spring and life was in bloom again. It was time for Leona to share the decisions she'd made during the long dark weeks before.

"Ivy, I need to speak with you," she said one mild afternoon. Ivy was in the schoolroom, cleaning after the kids were gone for the day.

"Okay, I'll be done here soon. We could take a walk."

"I'll help." Leona picked up a broom to sweep the floor while Ivy erased equations from the blackboard then wiped dust off the small windows. Sun tumbled in.

"Ah, I love these long days. What a wonderful time of year," Ivy said.

They didn't need heavy coats. Leona slipped on her anorak which stretched to circle her belly, and Ivy donned a thick knitted shawl, saying, "Let's walk the beach."

Pebbles crunched under their heels. The inlet was so still that the water barely hummed below the raucous sea birds. Leona heard engine noise from the fishing boats at the cannery far across the way. Briefly she wondered if they would ever desalinate the way they did in Tenachee.

"I love it here," Ivy said. "I'll miss it."

Leona's mind came back to the reason she needed to speak with Ivy. "Have you set a departure date yet?"

"No, not really. There's no rush, although I want to get to Sequim well ahead of the school year. Lots of prep for new classes. End of June, I should think, to settle into a new routine."

Much to Leona's surprise, she needed to take Ivy's hand. Ivy seemed startled, too. "Leona? What is it?"

"I … I miss you already."

"Dear one, if I'd have known what would happen to Mikhail, I would have held off for another year. I could …"

"No, Ivy. I'm not asking you to wait until next year. Just stay a little bit longer if you can. My baby is due in July."

Ivy smiled. "I'd like to see your baby. What a little troublemaker it's been so far."

Leona said, "I know I can't raise it. Not while I battle a demon I can't conquer. What if I hurt it when I am drunk? Neglect it? Wren is worry enough for me. She can get help if I fall again. When I fall again. She understands. Wren is a survivor."

"Losing both parents? I should say she's a survivor. The girl is tough as a weed. She's been through too much for a child just turned nine."

"True. We'll make it together. But Ivy, I am terrified the doctor will come as soon as he hears I have delivered.

I can't keep the baby, but I won't let Reardon take it. He said he would. And he will."

"Spiteful bastard."

"Can you wait for the birth?"

"Yes, of course."

"Oh Ivy, thank you." Leona let out a deep breath.

"It's nothing, my girl. It will be fun to greet it."

Leona came to the hardest part. "As soon as it is born, I want you to take the baby to Washington with you. We'll tell no one we don't trust. You and Flower will help me deliver in the clinic, then you'll take the baby to my sister and her husband in Port Angeles, not far from your destination. Nancy will raise the child as her own. I can be sure it is safe."

"But ... but it's your baby!" Ivy's composure appeared threatened as she stopped to stare at Leona, her eyes wide open as an owl's.

"And it grieves me. But the little one will be safer away from me and from Alaska. I want it to have the best start possible. And maybe someday, if I cure myself of my sickness, well ... maybe we could meet. Oh, Ivy, do you understand? You've done so much for me already, and this is such a huge thing to ask."

Ivy blanched in the watery sunlight. She turned to continue walking.

Leona followed. "My sister has agreed. Don't say no." She squeezed the older woman's hand tighter and felt the return pressure.

Ivy smiled. "I was just thinking how strange an aging lady will look with a newborn baby. Oh, the scandalous talk on the ferry. Such a mystery woman I'll get to be."

CHAPTER TWENTY-THREE

June 14, 1922
Ivy Bolton

Leona swayed into the kitchen, her belly entering the room before the rest of her. Ivy looked up from her list, and even through the scrim of her own sour mood, she smiled at the obvious weight gain.

"Ivy, could you do this cuff for me? I hate these tiny buttons." Leona held out her wrist to Ivy, who set down her pen.

"I am far too busy to help you dress," said Ivy. Nonetheless, she began buttoning the finicky closures. When finished, she smiled at Leona and patted her hand. "Now please leave."

"What's got you all churned up this morning?" Leona asked, pouring a jolt of Cook's vicious coffee.

Ivy stretched her back. "Well, final exams to grade, preparations to depart after twenty years in this place, and a desperate effort to figure what you need to travel with a baby. So my state is at least half your fault."

Leona laughed, kissed the top of Ivy's head, and left the room for the clinic. "Hope my patients are happier this morning than my friend."

Ivy watched her waddle off, hips and back doing their damnedest to maintain some sort of alignment. Then she resumed writing a list of things to do before she left for Outside.

Her letters had been flying out of the government building as fast as mail boats could reach distant shores. Ivy said aloud to the empty kitchen, "Anyone who knows her onions can see the day is coming when mail really does fly."

Her biggest concerns were about a newborn. It had been many years since her own child was born. The idea that Poppy was now in her early thirties was astounding. "When did that happen? How did she get so old?" she wondered. Ivy, who was not prone to such silliness, came close to her first age crisis. She didn't like it one bit.

June 6, 1922
Nordstrom Store
Seattle, Washington

Dear Sirs: I am in possession of the Nordstrom advertisement from The Seattle Star, an issue from last winter, for the collapsible Pullman pram for infants. Specifics include: twelve-inch wheels with rubber tires, mud guards, ball and socket direct bracing, padded seat and bed. The pram is a foldable model, and the interior is corduroy with gold striping. It claims to have a new auto-style hood with nickel plated, tubular fixtures (although I do not actually know what this means). The advertisement stipulates that 'features are many and of a nature to secure' my entire approval. The price is $14.95.

In hopes you still have this or a similar item in stock, I have enclosed a postal money order for that amount. You must ship to me, General Delivery in Juneau, Alaska with guaranteed arrival by early July (as the infant is soon to arrive, you have little time to lollygag). I will pay shipping when the conveyance arrives in Juneau or sooner if you can quote me the full cost.

Cordially, Mrs. Ivy Bolton

Ivy had already secured a teaching post in Sequim, a town quite close to Port Angeles. That was, of course, part of Leona's reasoning regarding Ivy. It would not be an impossible effort for Ivy to get the baby to one place and herself to another. There was even a road between the two communities. Since Ivy lived in a territory with virtually none, the idea of easy transport astounded her nearly as much as Poppy's age.

June 6, 1922
Miss Luella Brumble
Sequim School District

Dear Miss Brumble:

I consider it a great honor to have been selected by the Sequim School District as one of the first teachers in your new school on Sequim Avenue. It is a pleasure to imagine an actual brick structure with multiple classrooms. My own teaching experience has been primarily within the confines of wooden structures with at most two rooms for students.

I am writing to you, Miss Brumble, as the district's office manager and a woman of business yourself. I intend to purchase a home in the area, but at first will settle in a rooming house, hopefully near enough the school to walk. Can you provide me with the name of such a facility, appropriate to a widowed woman? I will need the accommodation by early August.

Sincerest gratitude from your new colleague,
Mrs. Ivy Bolton

With some help from Maki, Ivy had decided that arriving by ferry in Port Townsend would be the most convenient location. Besides, she was curious about that town since it was where she had lived over twenty years ago. A world war had been fought since then, a Carnegie library built, women could vote, and the bastard who'd burned her body was dead.

June 6, 1922

Dearest Poppy,

In little more than a month, I will catch a ferry south to take up life in Sequim, Washington. I am seriously appreciative of your offer to meet me at the ferry when it arrives in Port Townsend. I certainly can use your help setting up a new household.

However, I must alert you to a change in my schedule. I will transfer to another ferry in Port Townsend and set a course for Port Angeles. I will explain why when I see you, but I am hesitant to write the story of a friend when it is highly secret and truly not mine to tell.

Oh, bother. I think you should know at least the barest of bones … I will be travelling south with an infant in tow! Yes, I escaped to Alaska twenty-four years ago with you in secret, and now I'm coming back with another child in secret. What a sneaky woman I am!

Could you meet me in Port Angeles instead of Port Townsend? I can deliver this little package to its family, then we will be off to Sequim. I am not sure of my arrival date at present, as it depends on the arrival date of this bundle of joy. Certainly, I intend to be in my new hometown by August, ready to plan a new school year.

Your help in getting established will be received with great joy. I admit that even Sequim seems to be a big city to me now after so many years in Alaska. I understand they even have five traffic lights although it is still a local farmer who grades the dirt roads, so maybe they're not all that much ahead of Hoonah!

Your Loving Mother, the Smuggler

Leona had been communicating with her sister, of course, and much to her irritation, Ivy had not been offered the chance to see the letters between the two. She was possibly a bit over-curious about Nancy Coleridge; Maki had dared to say nosey!

But so be it, nosey then. The woman was about to receive a very personal delivery from a total stranger. How would it affect the Coleridge household? Her other children? Was she a lot like Leona? Would she treat the baby as an equal to her natural-born infants? What about her husband's point of view? Ivy had many inappropriate questions to ask. Maybe, if Nancy and she stayed in touch, the day would come when she would have her answers.

June 7, 1922
Mrs. Cecil Coleridge
Port Angeles, WA

Dear Mrs. Coleridge,

I am aware that Nurse Leona Herkimer has introduced me via her letter of April 28 to you. I have worked with Nurse Herkimer at the government station in Hoonah, Alaska, and have come to respect her very much. I can only believe her decisions on the raising of her child are for the best, and that you are an excellent choice.

I am not sure of my exact arrival date in Port Angeles. I will alert you at the earliest moment and hope you forgive being kept in the dark until then. My daughter Poppy will come from Oregon to meet me at the dock. If our arrival is late in the day, we will book a room for the night at the Lee Hotel. If it is early, we will come to your home in the morning to leave our delivery with you before we go on to Sequim, where I will be a teacher in the new school. Perhaps you will recommend whether a driver with car or carriage will be available to take us that distance.

Please feel free to contact me with any suggestions that will make this transition easier for you.

Mrs. Ivy Bolton

In the middle of her letter flourish, Ivy received one herself. She opened it as Captain Aleck unloaded other cargo for the government station. The contents of the letter infuriated her. "Confound it!" she cursed. "Damnation."

Captain Aleck listened in silence to a diatribe about the dependability of men in general. "Ivy," he finally said. "I wish Maki was around to take the brunt of this. I'm not virile enough to answer for fellas everywhere."

It broke her mood, and she snorted. "He's no doubt heard I'm mad as hops as far away as wherever he's taken himself. We won't see that sly old fox around here any time soon. Sorry to be such a sourball, Captain."

The letter that had ignited her anger had come from the doctor.

June 10, 1922

My Dear Mrs. Bolton:

I feel you are a woman of lofty intelligence and reputation. As such, I am confident you recognize and share with me an issue of concern within the confines of the government service operation. I am referring, of course, to the upcoming delivery by Nurse Herkimer, a woman who is both single and controlled by the worst properties of alcohol. I trust you agree that a superior situation should be found for the ongoing health of Nurse Herkimer's baby.

I will count on you, Mrs. Bolton, to inform me of the child's delivery. I will arrive as soon as the following day to remove it from the government building and place it with a qualifying family. In my experience the sooner these ties are cut, the better for all parties.

I have reason to believe that the nurse is resistant to this solution. I thank you in advance for sharing your wisdom with her and for your assistance in this sad situation.

Dr. Edward Reardon

That evening, over tea and crumb cake, Ivy shared the letter with Leona. Much to Ivy's surprise, Leona had a good laugh. "Such a floozie I am! Clearly a woman destined to scrape the very bottom of existence."

Ivy's smile was more reluctant. Her fury with the doctor had not yet burned itself out. "Considering I am about to be a thief in the night, the good doctor will soon discover no woman can be trusted."

"He will curse you as a kidnapper and all-around evil doer. I have sullied your reputation along with my own," Leona snickered. "I should be ashamed."

"Proud to help." They clinked teacups.

Leona said, "I have a similar letter from him, admonishing me to prepare for the removal of the infant post-delivery. He even mentions how a white child must be given a better situation for an improved future than an Indian village can provide."

"Especially if it is his white child."

"He would not put that in writing. Nor am I convinced there is a couple that would pass muster for this child. I believe he intends to take it with him to San Francisco. Of course, only if he can see it is his in its newborn face. This cannot happen. No child of mine will ever be his."

"Such a prig the man can be." Ivy breathed deep and added, "And speaking of men, you are aware there is one more judgmental male in the picture, aren't you?"

"There is?"

"There is. The honorable Reverend Harold."

Leona rolled her eyes. "Ah, yes. I suppose I must speak with him. If I wait until he speaks of it first, I fear I might call him a troublesome devil-dodger meddling where he doesn't belong. But I adore Judith, and we all must continue as colleagues in the future." She shrugged and appeared to consider backing out of it. "On the other hand, maybe he's too busy with spiritual matters to notice my new figure."

Ivy eyed the rising hill under the nurse's straining apron strings. "I doubt that will work."

"No." Leona patted the mound. "That's exactly why you are going with me after services tomorrow to explain the situation to them both."

June 13, 1922
Leona Herkimer

Leona and Ivy stayed after church while the orphans organized the hymnals and swept the floor. The two women went to the reverend's office, requesting that Judith join them.

"Usually, members of my flock choose to meet with me in confidence," Reverend Binder proclaimed, giving a lift to one eyebrow as proof that Leona was requesting the unprecedented.

"I realize that," said Leona. She placed a hand gently on top of her growing belly. "But my issue will not remain confidential for much longer."

"Please have the chair," he said, gesturing to the only guest chair in his office. "Ivy and Judith will both have to stand."

"Ivy knows my situation, and Judith has no doubt guessed a great part of the story."

Peering at Judith, the reverend said, "My wife has said naught to me about it."

Good for Judith. Leona risked a smile at the tiny teacher. "Well, I have said naught to her. And she would never spread unfounded rumors."

"Indeed. It would appear you, a single woman of my parish, are with child."

What an observer! "Yes, Harold, that is true."

"And who is the child's father?"

"I'm afraid that stays under the heading of confidential, as the man is not here to defend himself."

The reverend's brows wriggled until they settled into a channel of deep concern. "We were all aware of your connection to the late Mikhail Elim. Possibly he was an even greater loss to you, Nurse Herkimer, than to the rest of us."

"That is possible."

"While I cannot condone the choices a single woman makes to lie with a man, I must also be cognizant of the pain of your loss. I grieve for you and offer prayers on your behalf."

Leona bit her lip. She had not expected kindness along with censor. Probably she should lighten up on this man who saw the world in black and white with very little gray.

"Mikhail was a fine man, and Wren needs a woman to help mentor her. I hoped that might be you. But then I received a most disconcerting letter from Dr. Reardon. He seems to display unusual interest in the situation."

Leona felt the baby give a good solid kick as the reverend handed her the letter. She seethed but chose to read the poisonous words aloud for the benefit of Judith and Ivy.

The Reverend Harold Binder
Hoonah, Alaska

Dear Reverend:

It has been my great pleasure to meet you on rare occasion as a guest at the government building in Hoonah.

I wish to bring to your attention the condition of the unfortunate young woman who is the government's chosen nurse to your town, Miss Leona Herkimer. Through ignorance or depravity, she finds herself in the family way. Also, she has an unfortunate dependence on alcohol. I would not reveal this to you if she were a patient of mine, but she is not.

I have told her I will find a situation for the baby that will be altogether safer for the child. I've tried to assure her that, given time to overcome her addiction and change her ethical path, she may yet take on a motherhood role sometime in the future.

While I have discussed this with her, I fear she will not listen to reason. I worry that she may bring the baby to your orphanage, thinking it is a way she can continue her relationship with it. But Reverend Binder, this child will be at least half Caucasian, and I doubt it belongs in an orphanage for Indian children. You see, I am sure, the issues with this.

I respectfully request your compliance with the removal of the baby from the scene altogether for the betterment of its future. I hope you see your way to rejecting the infant should the nurse come to you.

Cordially, Dr. Edward Reardon

Leona cast her eyes downward. She didn't have words to express how trapped she felt by this odious man whose lust for her had turned to such hate. She looked up toward Ivy, seeing the pallor on her friend's face.

Ivy said, "Judith. Harold. We are not here to burden you with a child that the doctor ..."

Harold raised his hand, and Ivy stopped. He pronounced, "I would be delighted to have the little one here."

"Me, too," said Judith in a far less resonant tone. "I would love the baby, Leona. You know that."

Harold cut her off. "I am greatly offended by the doctor's slight toward the native children here, many of them orphaned through sickness and war that white men delivered to this area. It is hard to fathom how a doctor who is here to cure this population could have such a low opinion of it."

Leona felt dumbstruck. The doctor had managed to poison his own well with the only church in Hoonah.

"I feel moved to report him to the state medical authorities, however, I must admit to some trepidation. I am willing to raise the child here. But I fear that the doctor may have the power to intervene, even take the baby. And we are as dependent on him to care for our flock as we are angered by his desire to pick and choose."

"Oh, Harold, I worry, too," said Leona. "I am so relieved you see the flaws in his proposal. So here is what I'm going to do." She explained her plan to raise Wren with Judith to support them, her plan to send the baby to her sister with Ivy, her plan to continue as the nurse for Hoonah with Flower's help, and her plan to battle alcohol as best she could. It helped to say it out loud, made it seem without flaws.

The reverend smiled. "I will not lecture about your single status, Leona, as Mikhail is no longer here to change that situation. But I will warn you of something you may not see coming at you."

Judith said, "When you run an orphanage, you know what it can cost a mother to give up a baby."

Harold took control again. "That is correct. The sorrow of mothers who give up their children can last and last. Depression, anxiety, insomnia. We don't mean to scare you, but to prepare you that the road ahead may be rockier than you expect."

Just as the man had raised Leona's spirits with his understanding, he slapped them back down with his dose of reality. She'd read about baby blues. And worse. She'd nursed women through it. She'd seen grandmothers take up the reins when granddaughters were too young to mother. She'd heard natives cry in Flower's arms as she herself wrapped tiny stillborn bodies. Baby blues. She knew what might lie ahead.

June 13, 1922
Wren Elim

Wren missed her father. Nobody matched his bear hugs or silly jokes. Still, she had been lonely in the cabin, after her mom died and when her daddy was off running his lines. Wren liked this new life. Leona was eager to see her after school, Judith seemed a kinder teacher than before, Ivy asked her opinions on what to pack and what to leave behind. Flower groaned when Wren told those silly jokes of Mikhail's, but she tolerated them again and again. The child was the center of adult attention. Wren felt sorrow, of course, but she also felt safe. And the food was a lot better than at the cabin.

At first, she thought Leona was getting fat from sleeping so much. But the other kids set her straight soon enough. They tittered and one girl whispered that Leona was pregnant. The very idea threatened Wren's lofty position in the household. A baby could mess up everything.

Wren got her answer the way she got all her answers. She asked whether appropriate or not. "Are you pregnant?"

Leona seemed flustered and stopped whatever she was doing with a vial and an eyedropper. She sat on an empty patient bed and took Wren's hands.

"Well, yes, actually, I am." Her face got red. "But that isn't a word used in polite conversation. 'In the family way' or 'with child' are considered more acceptable."

"Why?"

"Well … well … I don't know."

"That's dumb."

"You're right. It is. You can say pregnant if you want. Do you want to talk about it?"

"Yes. Will you love that baby more than you love me?"

"Of course not. Love is a miracle because it just keeps expanding."

"Like your belly? How did the baby get in there? Wren pointed at the offending mound, putting Leona in the very uncomfortable situation of explaining the whole process.

"Well that just sounds crazy to me," Wren huffed when the facts were clear. Clear-ish. "Why would a man put it in there if it was just going to come out again? Leona was pretty smart and mostly truthful and looked like she meant it as she explained again. Wren finally shrugged. "Well, if you say so. Is this a secret? Do only nurses and doctors know about this?"

Leona laughed. "Most adults know."

"There's sure a lot you people don't tell us kids."

"I can see how you feel that way."

"Hey! If a man is involved, was it my daddy?"

"Maybe. And maybe not. It's possible for a woman to have more than one man."

Wren wrinkled her nose. "Sounds creepy. Babies seem like troublemakers to me."

Leona smiled at her. "Someday, you may feel differently. But for now, it means you get two cookies instead of one."

Everything was working out just ducky. Wren felt reassured. Maybe the time was nearly right to ask for that puppy she'd been wanting.

CHAPTER TWENTY-FOUR

June 17, 1922
Leona Herkimer

Lancing a boil was unpleasant. So was treating a man's tallywacker when it was weeping with disease. But more than anything else a frontier nurse was called on to do, Leona hated pulling teeth. The rot smelled dreadful. Usually, the tooth pulsing with pain was surrounded by a ridge of others in nearly as blighted a condition. Leona's physical strength was mightily tested, even with Flower behind the chair, holding the patient's head as still as she could. And patients often showed up well-oiled for the operation. Leona really didn't need alcohol anywhere near her.

Oral health was a dreadful issue for a tribe whose most common dentifrice involved a frayed stick to chew. Gum diseases had never been explained to the generations of natives. Leona believed that the children should be educated about mouth care from a young age in the schoolroom.

She talked Colgate into sending free samples of their ribbon dental cream. Squeezing a tube onto a brush looked fun for the kids, and the company promised superiority over "gritty, soapless toothpastes." They also provided hog bristle brushes each year. Flower and Leona demonstrated the tools to Judith's small fry and Ivy's teens once each term. They hammed it up, pretending the agony of dental patients. Flower writhed in mock pain as Leona pulled an outsized model tooth from her mouth. The moral of their story: only paste and a brush were weaponry against this awful fate.

The kids laughed, and they learned. Judith had them repeat the performance for all the orphans. Hoonah children were changing the frayed stick tradition. "There is no other place in Alaska where smiles sparkle so," Ivy observed to Leona's delight.

Now that school was in recess, Flower and Leona tried to conduct a workshop with Hoonah mothers. But the women were far more interested in Leona's condition. The group tried to use English amidst their chatter, and Flower translated for the ones who couldn't manage it.

"White babies born like normal babies?" asked Arrluk, a venerated tribal elder as wrinkled as tree bark. Time had shrunken her into herself so she barely peeked out of her blanket like an owl from its hidey hole. Leona was one of the few whites these Tlingits were comfortable with at all, much less enough to ask such personal questions.

"This one will be, Grandmother," Leona said, smiling at the old crone and her own belly. To show how some silly white doctors believed women should deliver, she clambered up on the exam table on her back, knees bent. "This is how some new doctors think women should be positioned for a birth."

She stood back up as the women began to squawk with each other.

"But …"

"Baby come down not up …"

"This doctor never have baby!" Arrluk said with a derisive humph.

Leona said, "Some white women go to the hospital and receive medicine for pain so they feel very little. But too much chloroform or morphine is bad for them."

"How you know you have baby if baby don't hurt?" asked a woman, holding her own infant to her breast while she looked quizzically around the group.

"You take big risk. Babies hurt. And babies die," a young one said with sorrow.

"That is true, Miska," Leona replied to the plump girl whose baby was stillborn not long ago. "It's very hard, the bringing of new life. It's always a bit of a mystery. I will be careful of bacteria, and I will squat like I've seen you ladies do. You have taught me much."

This clearly pleased them. Several demonstrated the squat technique to the laughter of the others, then they shuffled out the door, each with a new toothbrush.

"Did any of them understand a thing about cleaning their teeth?" Leona asked.

Flower replied, "Probably not. But maybe their kids will show them how. And Leona? These women love you. This is a rare thing, a thing to cherish. I am proud to be with you. Never leave here."

Leona nearly purred for that moment of respect. She never felt the mythical "rosy glow." She felt heavy and awkward and always in need of a nap. But what Flower said and the friendship of these women? They moved her to a long-overdue, full-blown gloat. What a joy to have the tribe appreciate her when everything else had fallen to pieces.

Yes, she drank. That was a fact. Maybe she couldn't help herself, but she could help others. *That's not a bad way to be,* she thought. For the first time in months Leona felt, if not good, at least not bad about herself. *Go to hell in a runaway handbasket, Dr. Reardon.*

After the meeting with the women, Leona surprised Wren, who was on the beach, cutting paper doll clothes from a *McCall's* magazine. Leona knew better than to sit on the blanket next to her since no one was around to help her back up. Wren was sturdy but not tall enough. Leona leaned over, kissed the little girl on the head, and said, "Tell me. Am I an unfit mother to you?"

"Yes. You said no to a puppy." Wren carefully cut around the tabs of a blue and cream high-waisted skirt and blouse.

"I've changed my mind."

"Really?" The scissors were dropped.

"Really. You are big enough to take care of a puppy yourself."

"You are a wonderful mommy." Wren leapt up squealing, paper doll clothes fluttering away in the onshore breeze. "Where is this puppy?"

"We will get it this weekend. It's waiting for you." Leona had already planned the trip for Saturday, via messages back and forth via Hambone to Danielle.

Amidst excitement so great it was positively giggly, Ivy, Leona, and Wren boarded *Small Fry* to Juneau. Wren was now an old salt according to Captain Aleck, since she had ridden the seas with him once before. But this child was not the sad little person of a few weeks back. This child was as high as an army blimp on coastal patrol.

"Wren! Sit!" Leona called over the sound of the steam engine to the child who was skipping around the steamer's interior perimeter.

"But my legs won't let me," Wren replied.

Ivy said, "In Juneau, we are going to be so busy there won't be time to sit, so you better save it up now."

The captain, after looking at Leona who was definitely sitting, her baby big as a basketball under her anorak, called out, "All passengers sit, including you, Miss Wren."

She stopped and stared at him as he emerged from below deck via the trap door, rubbing his hands on a dirty rag. Placing her own hands on hips - in sheer mockery of Cook's most common stance - Wren sassed. "You didn't say I was a passenger. You said I was an old salt."

"That's right. But old salts are passengers, too. And they never skip. They haul ropes and stow freight and sing bad songs. But they never skip. Rocks the boat. Upsets the whales."

Wren complied, landing on the wooden seat next to Leona and announcing to the captain, "We're staying a night with Leona's friend Danielle."

"I wouldn't mind staying a night with Danielle."

"Captain Aleck!" Leona huffed, hoping to sound scandalized.

"Captain Aleck," Ivy laughed, not sounding scandalized at all.

He grinned at the women, exposing the hole in his head where Leona had recently relieved him of a tooth.

Wren continued to chatter. "Danielle! What a fancy name. She lives right in the city. Can you imagine? She's taking us shopping. That's what you do in places called milliners and salons. Leona promised to buy me a dress, my very first brand new one ever. Ivy says I'll be too ritzy for Hoonah, whatever that means. And if there is time, we're taking Danielle to a rest … rest…" Wren stared at Leona.

"… aurant." Leona said.

"Restaurant. That's where you ask for what you want from a piece of paper, and they bring it to you. Isn't that amazing, Captain Aleck?"

"News to an old sea dog like me!"

"Dog? But that's the best part!" With a squint of suspicion, Wren turned to Leona. "Did you tell him already?"

Leona shook her head and locked her lips with an imaginary key.

"Tell me what?"

"I'm bringing home a puppy!"

Leona said to the captain, "Danielle has found what she considers a proper litter of pups. Wren can take her pick."

Wren leapt up. "I need to skip even if old salts don't." Off she went circling the interior of the little craft once again.

Captain Aleck went to the pilothouse, yelling to Leona over his shoulder, "That little girl's not had much joy. Nice to see her share a cup of it with you."

"Works two ways," Leona called back to him. Her heart ached for Mikhail. The doctor terrified her. Staying sober was an everyday battle. But Wren! That bright spot supported her, held her together as if Wren were a lifeline.

And what about her baby? It wasn't very real to her, and she tried to keep it that way. It was actively growing, of course, but she knew it couldn't be hers for long. She tried keeping it out of her everyday thoughts. She called it "it" instead of cooing tender phrases. She never thought about names like she'd heard other pregnant women do. She had no nursery to set up, no baby furniture to paint. But Wren was hers, here and now. If there were never any more babies, she had this bossy, scheming, funny chip off Mikhail to love from this day forward. That must be joy enough.

June 20, 1922
Ivy Bolton

Ivy sat on a *Small Fry* bench, watching Leona stare into a different space, far away from the little steamer. The nurse was doing okay, as far as the teacher could tell. Grief takes the time it takes.

Ivy drew her cardigan closer although the maroon wool was scratchy against her neck. It was always cold on the way to Juneau, no matter the sun shining on land. She'd been tickled when Leona suggested this overnight trip. Ivy was curious about Danielle, the dashing damsel of Leona's stories. Even more than that, Ivy desired several things before her journey Outside. She was a good enough seamstress to follow a Butterick pattern, and that was plenty good for the new school in Sequim. She'd purchase dress material.

But Ivy had a yen for a traveling suit. A real traveling suit from a soft wool or heavy silk. Could such a thing be found in Juneau? That would be really something. She'd be the only granny on the ferry who looked like a fashion plate.

Ah, the ferry. Would it be the same as a quarter century ago? She'd been so sick then that anything would feel different now. The route was the same, only in reverse. When Ivy left Alaska, she would take a small steamer from Juneau to Ketchikan, then a larger ferry to Port Townsend, Washington. After that, she and the baby would transfer to another small steamer to Port Angeles.

She might get a trunk, but she didn't really own enough to fill one, even with the pile of baby clothes she'd crocheted in the evenings and the doll Flower had made from sinew thread, felt, and bits of fur. Ivy came to Alaska with nothing but a carpetbag. It was there at her feet now, not much worse for wear, carrying overnight things for all three of them. Ivy had read about new luggage called suit-cases that were flat-sided with a handle on top. Maybe one of those could be found in Juneau.

Maybe two. She'd get one for Maki. He would be leaving for Outside in the fall, and since he was moving because she was moving, she figured she at least owed him something to hold his shirts and trousers. She smiled at the thought of him. Regardless of the weather, he'd be wearing Mikhail's pine marten jacket. Even though it was at least one fur too big, it was his most prized possession these days.

When they arrived, the three females climbed up the docks and walked to the main streets of Juneau. Ivy found the town exhilarating so she couldn't imagine how Wren was containing her excitement. A bit of skipping might do them all good.

They found the alley and staircase up to Danielle's apartment.

Leona knocked.

There was no answer.

"Maybe she's working," said Ivy.

Leona shrugged. "It's 10 am, and she is a saloon dancing girl."

"In that case, she's still asleep."

Wren solved the problem. "Let's go do our shopping while she rests."

The trio backtracked to the main streets and began their expedition through the delectables of Juneau. Everyone had heard of Nugget's with its totem poles out front to catch the attention of travelers. Leona and Ivy agreed the native curios and crafts paled compared to those they had in Hoonah at far less expense. Wren was fascinated by large jars of colorful paper-wrapped candies.

"Is it really made of salt water?"

"Rumor has it a taffy shop on the Atlantic Ocean was once flooded, so that's what they called it ever since."

At a leather goods shop, Ivy lost her heart to a spendy $3.59 pair of black two-strap kid pumps. They sported what was described as a Spanish heel. "For those evenings Maki and I cut a rug with a tango," Ivy joked to Leona. She also purchased two suit-cases, each not much more than the shoes. The storekeeper promised to deliver them to Danielle's address before the end of the business day.

Cecilia at Shoppe Moderne was delighted to help the ladies with wardrobe issues. She was done up with a flapper-ish drop-waisted dress, patent black hair bob, and a beauty mark on her cheek, not unlike Clara Bow. Ivy thought she was a bit too broad in the beam to totally conquer the new elongated look.

"Nothing for me, thanks," said Leona, "unless you feature oversized flour sacks. On second thought, I could use a chair while they look."

"And I prefer to look on my own for a while," Ivy said to Cecilia whose lip crumpled at the suggestion she was not wanted.

"I'd like your help," said Wren. "I want to see everything."

The storekeeper readily accepted the child who was three-quarters Tlingit. If she'd seemed put off by the native blood, Leona and Ivy would have left in a huff. But Cecilia rose to the challenge and off she went with Wren to the other side of the shop.

Using the tracking talent of a hound, Ivy zeroed in on a travel suit so gorgeous it nearly made her gasp. The soft wool was a lavender herringbone. The waist of the jacket nipped in with a dark purple suede belt, and the full skirt fell in luxurious pleats. "Imagine such an outfit ready-made with no sewing on my part. What a brilliant concept," she cooed to Leona. When she tried it on, it was clear the suit had been made for a woman with an hourglass figure just like hers. Ivy was sold.

Ivy could tell that Leona, ensconced on a Queen Anne chair, was too wrapped up in Wren to properly appreciate the travel suit. The child was trying on all the girl-sized dresses, preening in front of the first mirror she'd experienced that was large enough to see the whole of herself. Cecilia pointed out highs and lows of each look. Eventually, Wren settled on a simple sky blue high-waisted frock with decorative buttons on the bodice that repeated themselves lower on the hem. A touch of lace at each elbow matched the lace collar. The dress was spacious enough for Wren to grow, but its hem already skimmed the knee. A few inches of bare shin were revealed between the hem and the reach of light blue socks.

"This is my first dress not cut down from anyone else's," Wren said to the hovering Cecilia.

"I'll just wrap it for you, shall I? You are a vision!"

"I think I'll wear it. Is that okay, Leona?" Wren did one more twirl in front of a mirror. "Maybe I'll wear it forever."

Several packages of underwear, cotton fabric, colorful candy, and baby bottles later, they returned to Danielle's apartment. She apparently heard them clatter up the stairs and threw open her door. "I hear laughter! Come in, my darlings, come in. Your empty suit-cases arrived so I knew you would not be far behind. I see you have packages enough to fill them up." Danielle hugged Leona, gave Ivy a friendly handshake, and beamed at Wren. "Oh, what a lovely girl you are. And such a beautiful dress."

Ivy was thinking the same thing about Danielle, although the dancer's attire at the moment was more of a silken bath robe than a dress.

The rented rooms were a grand bazaar in a compact space. Fading wallpaper, tiny windows, and dull overstuffed furniture were enlivened with colorful paintings, throws, and Oriental rugs everywhere. Danielle had hung her risqué gowns along one wall for a parade of feathers, sequins, lace, and silk. The main room opened onto a small kitchen through one door and a bedroom through an alcove. Hints of the bed and a chaise lounge were visible behind a folding Japanese screen. Nothing matched, but everything was wonderful. Ivy was delighted.

Wren's curiosity bubbled over. "Are the puppies here? Can I see them?"

"No, my moppet," said Danielle. "But we can see them in the morning. They are not far from here. I work tonight, and then I will take you there."

Wren drew in a great breath. "You smell like flowers."

A lot of flowers, thought Ivy feeling overcome by the aroma.

"A whole meadow," Wren added with another big whiff.

Danielle merely laughed and said, "You'll understand a woman's perfume one day."

She had made a fish stew for them. Wren objected. "But we were going to a rest … rest …"

"Restaurant," Leona said. We will leave that for our next visit."

"I'm sure the fish stew is marvelous," added Ivy.

"And I really don't have time for a restaurant tonight, little one."

Wren appeared startled by so many explanations. She held up her hands as if warding off bees. "That's all right everyone. A new dress and a new dog is quite enough for one trip."

"Such a sensible girl." Danielle beamed before turning to Ivy. "I hope you don't mind, Ivy, but I really must leave for work sooner than I wish. So let's dine now."

They ate the hearty meal and chattered.

When Wren's eyes began to sag, Danielle pointed out the chaise in her tiny bedroom. Leona took Wren by the hand to the bathroom with toilet off the hall, one shared with other renters on the floor. When they returned, Wren curled onto the lounge and settled right away. It had been a long day for an enthusiastic child.

For another hour, the three women sat at the table to laugh, mourn, and share secrets. "I so looked forward to meeting the smuggler before she arrives with the newborn," Danielle said.

"Leona has already explained? That I'll arrive with the baby as soon as it can travel?" Ivy stopped herself. Of course, Leona would have told her. *I must not appear to worry. Leona is in charge.*

But Ivy was worried. She had so many things on her mind including her move Outside which was just around the corner, and she already missed the people she loved. Besides, what would she do if the baby got sick, or Leona's sister seemed all wrong, or …

Danielle said, "Yes. Such excitement, this escape from the evil physician. I have a key to give you so you can get in if I am not here when you arrive. You'll find food, and I'll have cans of evaporated milk for the baby."

"A bit of corn syrup would be good, too. Mix a small amount with the milk and water. Not breast milk, but healthy," said Leona.

"I may have to stay two or three days, Danielle. We'll be in your way, I'm afraid." Ivy said.

"Not at all. It will be fun. And you will be safe from the doctor."

Ivy laughed. "Yes. I doubt Dr. Reardon would look for me here."

"But now, I must dress for work," Danielle finally said. She stood, shed her robe revealing breathtaking underwear, then shimmied into one of the dresses that had moments before been a wall decoration. "You two share the bed, and I'll take the divan when I come in. It will be very late, but I will not wake you. Just leave the lamp on low, here on this table."

After Danielle's departure, Ivy cleaned the dishes in the tiniest sink she had ever seen. Then she made her own trip to the bathroom in the hall. "So much nicer than a run to The Bog," she remarked to Leona when she returned.

"Especially when one needs to run there every other hour," Leona answered, rising to make her fourth trip since their arrival to Danielle's little hideaway. "I can now understand the many complaints of my pregnant patients. I believe I share them all."

June 21, 1922
Wren Elim

"Absolutely not," Leona whispered to Wren the following morning over a breakfast of Quaker Puffed Rice. They were trying not to awaken Danielle.

Wren wanted to wear her new dress, but Leona wouldn't allow it since they were going to choose a puppy.

"But why?" Wren hissed.

"Dogs are big dirt magnets. Puppies are little dirt magnets."

After giving it a moment's thought, Wren decided on the wisdom of going with the flow. "You're right, Leona. I should keep my dress for nice." There was a chance Leona actually was right. More important, Wren didn't want to risk a possible change to Leona's mind. This taking on a new mother stuff was a twisty road for them both to negotiate.

"Good thinking, kid," mumbled Danielle from the divan. She sat up, stretched, and donned the first pink velvet and lace peignoir that Wren had ever seen.

"That's beeee-u-tiful," Wren crooned. "I would love one of those."

"Clearly our flannel has left something to be desired," Ivy said to Leona as Danielle glided to the table and poured herself coffee.

Danielle finished a yawn then said to Ivy, "Don't be silly. If either of you wants a job at the dancehall, they'd hire you in a flash. You're a couple of lookers."

Ivy laughed. "But all I can do is the tango."

Wren lost track of the adult conversation, and she forced more cereal into her mouth. If everyone chewed faster, they could leave sooner. Meanwhile, she settled an issue of immediate importance. Her father had read parts of *The Call of the Wild* aloud to her. They both loved it. So she would name her puppy Buck.

Captain Aleck was to pick them up at noon. It was nine now. That only left three hours to choose the dog of her dreams and get all their new things down to the dock. Wren wanted to shriek, "WILL YOU HURRY UP?" but thought better of it. She settled for, "We don't want to be late for the captain. And it might take me a while to pick the right dog. I can be very picky."

Leona put Wren out of her misery. "You'd like us to hurry along, and so we shall. First dibs on the bathroom."

"You've called dibs twice already this morning," Ivy said.

"May you be cursed with a pregnancy once more," Leona answered.

"I'd have to be cursed with the curse again for that to happen. And that's highly unlikely."

"What's a curse?" asked Wren.

June 21, 1922
Leona Herkimer

Leona did not want a dog. Especially a dog that was allowed indoors. Muddy prints on the clinic floor … hair everywhere … a person might as well bring a barnyard animal inside. She'd only agreed to a pup after Wren had promised to keep it outdoors. Then Ivy the Realist had reminded Leona of the Hoonah eagles and bears and wolverines, any of which would find a fat tender puppy quite delectable.

"Well, then, fine. But where will we keep it?"

"*We?*" Ivy had answered, eyebrow cocked.

Leona cocked an eyebrow back at her friend. "I suppose the storeroom now that you and Maki won't be visiting it for old time's sake."

So the puppy's safe quarters had been assured. Now, looking at the wriggling ball of multi-colored ears, paws, and tails, Leona was having doubts once again. "How many are there?" she asked the rawboned woman who had them contained in a pre-Prohibition wooden wine shipper in the backroom of her grocery store.

Wren gushed, "Soooo cute. What are their names?"

The woman said, "I call them all Potato." As she lifted them from the box to the floor she recited, "One Potato, Two Potato, Three Potato, Four. I'm sure you can do better, little miss."

Leona's doubts escalated when she saw the floor was already filthy with paw prints. The pups charged the strangers, and soon Ivy and Danielle were cuddling mutts as Leona tried to get a third to remove its paws from her skirt. In protest, it nibbled her ankle causing a sock to ladder. *Great. This is fun.* But the joyous look on her daughter's face brightened Leona's soul.

The fourth pup eyed the three women but did not choose them. Instead, he selected the smaller creature, a miniature of the pink things that walked on two legs. His dark eyes met hers. She made a lovely soft sound and lowered herself onto the floor. He nuzzled up to her throat to detect where that "ohhh" was coming from. He licked the very spot, just below her chin. The sound became that of a giggle. This pink thing smelled good, sounded good, radiated warmth. For Potato Four, the deal was done.

"This one," said Wren. "This one is my dog. Good boy, Buck."

Leona sighed. Potato Four was now a big-footed, thick furred, brown and white Buck. *This is your fault, Mikhail.* She took the woman aside to put a coin into the eager boney hand.

Clutching it tight, the woman asked, "Sure you don't need two potatoes?"

Leona hissed, "I'll give you another coin not to say that again so loud."

CHAPTER TWENTY-FIVE

December 25, 1946
Rome Coleridge

"Our first beef roast since Truman set price controls," Ivy said, setting down a platter of enormous pink slabs, spilling not one drop of au jus on her linen tablecloth.

Rome's nose rejoiced at the aroma of good meat. Ivy's was the best cooking he got, considering Barbara's culinary skills. She baked fair to middling, but she was no head chef.

Ivy stood back with a smile. "Merry Christmas everyone."

Rome loved the flush in her old cheeks, probably from the heat of the kitchen, or it could be from the pleasure of being together on this day. Or maybe that was a new dress Ivy was wearing. He hadn't noticed it before she removed her apron. Rome was good at recognizing military uniforms but not so good with frocks. Whatever, he was once again bemused at the beauty still residing in that beloved woman.

She must have been a looker in her day, Rome thought. He smiled to himself. Hell, she'd hate that. She'd point out she still is. She'd also point out where I could go with my opinions.

The four friends usually ate in the kitchen, but today they were in a dining room festive with candles, ribboned bundles of mistletoe, spruce sprigs, and cinnamon sticks. Tinsel and baubles reflected the light of candles on a small cedar tree, visible through the archway to the living room.

"They say hospitals back East are still having to serve horsemeat," Maki said, forking a thick slice of beef from the platter as soon as Ivy took her seat and unfolded her napkin.

Barbara wrinkled her nose. "That would be worse than whatever made you sick to begin with." She placed a large dollop of mashed potatoes on her plate and passed the bowl along. "At least we had game most of the war. A wild goose once in a while. A deer to share with all the neighbors." Honeyed sweet potatoes, creamed onions, cranberry relish, and yeasty rolls followed the potatoes around the table.

Rome had left his loft that morning and driven the Studebaker to pick up Barbara. They'd exchanged gifts. His to her was a single pearl with two diamond chips on a gold chain. He figured it was beautiful, sure, but a gift from an admirer not a suitor. Barbara gave him a single fur-lined deerskin glove which made him laugh at himself, something he couldn't have done a Christmas before. Because she wasn't totally heartless, she also gave him a hat. "It has flaps for two ears."

For Christmas dinner with Ivy and Maki, Barbara made pies with real sugar. Rome knew she'd amassed enough sugar by trading ration stamps with other waitresses at the restaurant.

"They say sugar rationing will end soon," Ivy observed. "But for now, these are a real gift."

Over a slab of warm apple pie, served with cheddar or drizzled with thick cream, Rome said to Ivy, "I might write to Wren. Can you give me her address?"

She set a coffee cup into its saucer and patted her lips with her napkin. "Of course, Rome. But if you write directly to each other, how will I know what's going on?"

Rome believed she actually batted her lashes at him just the once.

Maki chuckled. "Careful, boy. You don't want to get between Ivy and information."

"Maki! Are you suggesting I'm a gossip?" When she lifted her brows, the wrinkles around her eyes nearly vanished.

"Of course not, my love."

"All right, then," she said. "I must have misunderstood."

"A chatterbox, maybe?" Rome offered. Barbara put her napkin in front of her mouth, as if hiding a laugh in the making.

Ivy shot Rome a similar look. "You stay out of this, Mr. Know-it-all."

Rome couldn't help himself. "Babble merchant? Pratpie? Oh, the many words you learn working for the library."

Maki's laugh pushed his taut cheek muscles back into ripples. "No, no, no. I meant information, not gossip. More like a journalist providing us the news."

"Newsmonger? Newshound?"

"Ivy tells us what we want to know," Barbara rallied to Ivy's defense. "She tells us what we need to know. You two jokers can go fish!"

Rome was not always aware of the dynamics around him, but he did notice that Barbara abandoned him to side with Ivy. *What's this? Women getting chummy?* He really didn't want the two of them clucking about him together. He'd need to watch that.

Rome had not received an answer to his request, so he asked it again. "Okay, okay. But I still would like Wren's address. Since she reached out, and Leona didn't." Such a mystery, this stranger who was his mother. He grew to manhood without her, so why did she occupy so much of his brain now? Did he hate her or love her? Did he not care one way or the other? He waffled with the time of day, the emotion of the moment, the difficulty of redefining his own future. He shook his head to clear the conundrum away for now.

Then he offered to help clear, but Ivy kicked him out of the kitchen. "Some habits are hard to break, even for independent women like Barbara and me. We'll clean up. You and Maki would make a hash of it. Go attend the fire in the living room."

So much for keeping them apart.

When the women finally joined the men in the main room of the house, Ivy asked, "Have you smoked all the cigars? Drunk all the port? Told all the lewd jokes? Ready or not, here we come." She handed Rome a piece of notepaper with an address, then plopped down on the love seat next to Maki, leaving the overstuffed armchair for Barbara.

Barbara aimed the conversation into the past after the foursome was comfortable. "Ivy, you left Alaska with Rome in a pram over twenty years ago. Nobody to help. What was that like? Such an adventure."

Rome knew how eager Barbara was to travel. She was looking at Ivy with what could easily be envy. Here was an old woman who'd seen more and done more than Barbara might ever manage, stuck out on the Olympic Peninsula. Rome felt a new burst of understanding for her plight in life. He loved her and hoped the day would come when she would find the woman who matched her desire to see the sights. He hoped for himself he'd find the woman whose heart would be filled a little closer to home. He wished it could be Barbara, but that was not to be.

Ivy picked up her knitting before answering Barbara's question. "To tell you the truth, it was scary. And difficult. I don't like to admit feeling vulnerable, but I did. And I thought I might never see Maki again. It might be hard for you to believe, but I loved this man many years before he turned into an old poop."

"I told you I'd come," Maki said.

"Yes, you did. But I knew too much togetherness wasn't right for either of us. You might have made the decision to stay behind once I was gone from Hoonah. Nobody left to remind you what you were missing."

Rome watched the two smile at each other. *Yin and yang,* he thought, having recently finished a tome on centuries of Chinese culture. Nobody else had ever checked it out of the library.

Ivy, hands continuing to knit automatically, turned back to Barbara. "The most immediate problem, of course, was being seriously out of practice with babies. This newborn was nothing like Poppy. He was opinionated and highly unimpressed with condensed milk. He knew he was missing something much better. He let the whole ferry know he was angry about the lack of mother's milk."

Still like a good breast, Rome thought, sneaking a look at Barbara. Listening to Ivy talk about the baby in the third person, he wondered if she thought of the newborn as a separate life from the adult here in her living room.

"He was at his happiest when the passage was roughest. The closer to seasick I got, the more likely he was to sleep happily rocking with the ship."

"I still don't get seasick. Learned that on a troop carrier."

"Yes, you were fine on the trip. But as for me, well, I was tense the whole time. You have to remember communication was not as good in the twenties as it is in the forties. I had no way of knowing what was going on back in Hoonah. I wanted news of Leona. Was she well? Had the doctor confronted her? Would he be on my heels? I guess Maki's right. I hate not having information."

Her eyes glistened, perhaps from the fireplace smoke. "I took you from your mother on your birthday, hustling you away. We were both ripped apart from Leona that day. And she from us. Poppy met me as planned in Port Angeles. She was the fourth person to hold you. Flower to me to a woman named Danielle to my daughter."

Ivy stopped speaking for a bit as her needles danced across another row. In the silence, Rome observed, "No wonder I admire women. A pack of she-wolves to the rescue."

"Poppy and I delivered you to Nancy the next day. Turning you over …leaving you behind … that was hard, Rome. Very hard. I sure didn't feel like a mere delivery service. I missed you always."

Rome didn't want to hurt her. But he had to ask a question that bothered him since he first heard about his infancy. "Then why did you keep away? Why didn't you stay in my life? I could have used you then, Ivy. Just like now."

Her voiced tightened. "Because Nancy asked me to stay out of your life, that's why. Oh, she did it politely enough. But she confirmed that Cecil wasn't crazy about taking in the bastard of a fallen woman, whether she was his wife's sister or not. Cecil was not a kind man."

"On that, I can agree."

"He made Nancy keep it quiet, just another kid in the group. Maybe claimed you were a visiting cousin if anyone asked. I don't know. But it wasn't only Cecil and Nancy." She flinched at a loud snap from the fireplace logs. "In the early days, I thought it was for the best, in case the doctor ever came looking for me. I doubted he would, but I really didn't know."

She looked up from her yarn. "I hope you can forgive me. And Leona. If we made mistakes, it was in the name of love."

Could he forgive? Rome was angry he'd lived a lie without any choice in the matter. He needed to know his own story. Didn't everyone? Or maybe he was being petty in the face of this old woman who'd saved him as a baby long before she did it again in his adult years.

Was Nancy so happy to be his mother that she didn't want him to know the truth? She'd always been enough for him until now, although he'd never understood why she put up with Cecil. He figured it was a woman's way not to leave. Now he felt upset with her.

Mostly, he had a very large bone to pick with the woman who was his actual mother. Leona. But not with Ivy. He could see it had been a hard call for her to keep his past to herself. She owed him no apologies, that was for damn sure.

Ivy interrupted his meditation. "Rome, do you have a birthmark on your shoulder?"

Barbara lit up. "Why yes, he does! I mean … well, I've seen it …when his shirt's off ... I mean …" Barbara's confession petered out, but the damage was done.

"That blush on your cheeks must be about the same color as a strawberry birthmark," Maki observed.

"I guess you know we spend time together," Rome muttered, reaching over to pat Barbara's hand.

Ivy seemed delighted. "That confirms it. Mikhail had one on his shoulder, too. We didn't see it at your birth because they often take a few weeks to appear. I've always wondered."

"His nose confirmed it to some of us," Maki muttered.

"Well, I'm very pleased. We all loved Mikhail. Something for you to research now, the Tlingit and Russian blood in your veins."

"Anyway, Rome, you were not exactly out of Ivy's life. Not really. She watched you grow from afar all these years," Maki said. "We drove slow past your house often enough just so she could get a look at you."

She nodded. "I taught in the Sequim school at first, so I was out of town. Nancy and I didn't cross paths. Maki didn't get Outside here until the following spring."

Maki explained. "The youngster they hired to replace me in the Tongass was a rookie. Now there's a story for you. He was the first fullblood Tlingit hired by the forest service. Your ma, I mean your real ma, saved his life when he was living in Angoon. Would have died of TB without her. Edensaw. He worshipped her and Flower."

"Flower?"

"Leona's assistant. Anyhoo, Edensaw was so new, it took me some time to teach him a thing or two. Then the winter weather trapped me."

Ivy said, "A couple years later I found work in the Port Angeles school. That's when I bought this house."

"Easier location for us both. Forest service jobs center in Port Angeles and Forks, not Sequim."

"We worked, we stayed together in the winters, parted in the summers. We even went through another world war."

"With any kind of luck, our last," Maki said.

"I knew Nancy and Cecil had died in that fire. When I heard you were back from the war, I made myself available to befriend the new bookmobile driver, a boy I had loved for years and never told."

"In all that time, did my mother ever ask about me?" It sounded pathetic, even to himself.

"No, Rome, she didn't." Ivy could be brutally honest.

"But why? Had she never wanted me?"

"Rome. Yes, she wanted you. She loved you. She lost your father and was at war with the doctor, but she would have battled through it, even run with you into the wilderness. She loved Hoonah, but the fort at Haines would have taken her anytime. The doctor there had told her as much. She could have stayed away from Dr. Reardon."

"Then why didn't she keep me?" *For the love of all that's holy, don't let me cry.*

"Because she was not capable of taking care of a baby. Wren, yes, because Wren was older. But not you. She drank, Rome. She drank herself unconscious time and again. We didn't know the word alcoholic back then, but we did realize it was a disease. She knew she couldn't control her binges and that no baby is safe in a situation like that. Her lack of control was a humiliation for her and the cause of her greatest loss. Namely you. She knew you'd be better off with Nancy, and she had the courage to make it happen whether or not it broke her heart."

The fire crackled, the tree sparkled, and they all settled into a quietude of reverie. Images like those on a View Master clicked through Rome's brain, images of all the times he'd hidden from Cecil or loved it when Nancy laughed or played with the kids he'd taken as brothers and sisters.

By evening, they'd rallied. Rome and Barbara each wore a new cable knit sweater from Ivy. Rome gave Maki a red soldier knife of the type presented to Swiss military. For Ivy he gifted a new journal. On the opening page he'd written, *For my friend who is stubborn, funny, bossy, loving nature has brought me back from the brink. But please! No more secrets. Rome*

CHAPTER TWENTY-SIX

July 22, 1922
Wren Elim

"Shhhh."

Neither of them was supposed to be in the clinic when the time came. Wren had been warned well in advance. Leona was very clear about that. "When the time comes, I want you to stay out of the clinic."

"But why?" Wren had countered.

"Because women having babies is a very private matter."

"But don't you and I share our secrets?"

"And women having babies use the kind of language you should not hear."

"Why can't I hear it?"

"Because you would use it."

Wren was more than capable of breaking the rules. The nine-year-old sat legs akimbo on an empty patient bed behind a curtain. Her great hulk of a pup, Buck, curled up beside her. In the month she'd had him, he'd grown nearly as tall as a small pony.

"Shhhh," Wren warned him again. "We're not here." Buck was never allowed inside the clinic, especially after what he had done to their rag rugs. And never ever on a bed. He gave her his goofy smile, appropriate to the Newfoundland who factored somewhere in his heritage. There was sled dog and shepherd in the mix, too, according to the woman who'd sold Buck to Leona. Leona didn't care what he was, but Wren had looked up each breed so she'd know all she could about Buck. "It turns out, we're both mutts," she'd told him when her research was done. "And that makes us really smart."

It was so early that morning light was just working its way into the clinic. Wren stealthily peeked between the curtain and its metal frame. She couldn't see everything. But women were hustling this way and that: Cook with water, Flower with towels, Judith with tea. Ivy was holding Leona's hand, but Wren couldn't hear what she was saying. Leona, perched on the side of the examination table, smiled briefly at Ivy. Then she groaned.

The groan crescendoed. "Oh! Oh! Ye gods and little fishes!" Leona yelped.

Wren thought that language wasn't so bad. It was funny, and Leona was right: she would use it. But then Leona spat out, "From now on all men can haul their own ashes!"

"What you suppose that means?" Wren whispered in Buck's ear, the one that stood upright instead of flopping over. He grinned.

Her knowledge of the birth process was piecemeal at best. She knew there would be some crying, followed by some strangeness about a baby popping out of a lady's stomach from between her legs. But that couldn't possibly be right. Wren needed to see the process for herself.

She was not prepared for Leona's first yelp of intense pain.

Buck whimpered when he heard Leona's cry. Wren gasped in fear, and they both trembled.

At first, nobody overheard or paid attention to Wren's plight. That was the problem with hiding behind a curtain. Leona continued to moan as she tried to squat beside the table, and Flower was squatting in front of her, ordering, "Push!" Cook was wiping some kind of liquid off the floor. Ivy was telling Leona she was doing well, but Wren didn't believe it. Leona must be dying! When Wren began to cry, Buck howled.

It was Judith who finally took notice of Wren and came to comfort her. Buck licked the teacher right across the face, beside himself with joy over the appearance of a savior. Wren would have found it funny if she wasn't so terrified. Judith flinched, pushing Buck away to draw the child near. "Neither you nor this hound should be here, Wren. You both know that."

Leona cried again, an inhuman wail part sob and part howl.

Wren's tummy clutched and her tears flowed. "Is she okay? Is it hurting her? Are you seeing this, Mrs. Binder?"

"Yes, I am seeing this. But you should not be here. Leona would worry about you when she should be worrying about herself. She would not like you to be upset."

"I'm scared."

"No need for fear, child. It's God's miracle."

"But God's miracle is killing my new mommy!"

"She'll be fine, Wren." Judith cuddled her. "This is woman's work. It's what we do." In a softer voice, she added, "I so wish I'd had babies of my own."

"I never, ever, ever want a baby!"

Judith grinned. "Oh, you will surely change your mind."

"No, I won't."

Suddenly the room went still. A second passed. A minute. More. Rustling, scurrying sounds came from the women.

"It's a boy," Flower said. Then a tiny, furious cry announced itself to the world.

"There. It's over, Wren. Out we go now." Judith took Wren by the shoulders and marched her from behind the curtain toward the door. "You, too, Buck."

As Wren was ushered away, she cast a glance back over her shoulder. She saw Flower offer Ivy a tiny bundle of redness wrapped in a blanket. Ivy took it in her arms and turned away from the rest of the women.

Later Wren wasn't sure if the whimper she heard as she left the clinic was from Buck or Leona.

July 22, 1922
Ivy Bolton

Ivy was ready. In case the babe came early, she was packed, and her plans were made. Still, the ache of leaving Hoonah was like a punch to her gut. She steamed away late that afternoon, leaving twenty-some years of her history behind. People she loved. Places more familiar to her than any Outside.

That afternoon, Captain Aleck was nowhere near Hoonah, but Hambone found a fishing boat heading toward Juneau. It stopped for Ivy.

Her spirit was somewhat lifted by the lovely weather. The days were so long that no part of the journey was in the dark. And it was warm by Alaska standards. She sat on a crab pot on the deck. When she wasn't cradling the baby, she put him in the fluffy warm nest she'd made in the stroller.

Ivy hadn't had much time for mulling since the baby entered the world. Now in the relative solitude around her, her brain turned to Leona. Poor, lovely, haunted Leona whom she would likely never meet again. Leona had not seen her baby. She had not held him or fed him. She wanted no linkage between the two. Ivy couldn't imagine the strength it took to admit another woman might do a better job of raising your child. She was not as worried about her own journey as she was about Leona's in the days to come.

"Babies do fine without their mothers. Of course, they are more likely to get infections from hand feeding than at the breast, but I know you will do the job brilliantly." That's what Leona had said. She'd smiled weakly after she said it.

Babies do fine without their mothers. But how did mothers do without their babies? With nobody watching, Ivy wept.

Hambone sent a message to Danielle that Ivy was on her way with the 'package,' but he had not been able to connect with Maki by the time Ivy left. No goodbye kiss, no you-can-do-this, no I love you. Ivy was not a crier by nature, but now she wept again. Would Maki, too, fade into a memory of the past? Once she was gone, would he forget the woman whose scarred body he claimed to cherish?

A tiny answering mewl made her stop her nonsense. She lifted the corner of a blanket she had knitted and stared at the wrinkled red face, the cause of all this bother. *Mikhail or Reardon?* She couldn't tell. She picked the infant up, rummaged into her own clothing to extract a baby bottle, and inserted its nipple into his mouth. The bottle was warm because she'd been carrying it against her stomach. On this, the third feeding of the first day of his life, the baby had no problem understanding the sweetened condensed milk was for him. Ivy smiled as he sucked, remembering that Flower said if she couldn't find bottles on her journey, make a leather spout on a gourd. As if that would be easier to come by than a baby bottle on a ferry.

She wished this aging craft, with its stink of the sea, was *Small Fry*. Captain Aleck would never mention where he took the schoolteacher and the baby. Ivy wasn't so sure of this three-man crew. Gossip was a staple in the diet of Juneau residents.

The baby suddenly smelled far worse than the hold of the fishing boat. Ivy changed his diaper, glad the little one's systems seemed to be functioning loud and clear. She picked him up into her arms again, and they rocked together to the motion of the Gastineau Channel.

At the dock, the crew unloaded her suit-case, carpetbag, and stroller. It was silly, but she took a stealthy look around, lest the doctor was lurking on the waterfront.

The thought of him prowling behinds piles of fishing net managed to make her smile.

Ivy flagged down a dray pulled by two muscular mules. The drayman lifted her possessions aboard, then helped her up to the seat next to him, as she clutched the newborn. The team plodded slowly to the alley, dropping the dray's passengers at the foot of the staircase that led to Danielle's door. Ivy knew Leona's friend would be working, but she had the key to the apartment. It's what the three of them had planned. She let herself in, placed the swaddled baby on the floor, then scurried back down for her luggage.

The first leg of her journey was done.

July 23, 1922
Leona Herkimer

What have I done? What have I done? Deep in the night, Leona sobbed into a pillow trying to drown the noise of her sorrow from Wren's ears.

Where is Ivy now? Where is my baby? Is he alive?

Her brain and her body raced in a derby of pain to establish which had been more abused in the past few hours.

Leona stilled herself to listen. Wren's soft even breath proved she slept through Leona's storm. But when the swollen slits of Leona's eyes opened enough to look toward the child in the other bed, Buck's enormous face was mere inches from hers. He placed his soft snout on the pillow next to her. Leona stared at him. *Are you judging whether Wren is safe with me?*

She placed a hand on the top of his head and whispered, "That's your job, Buck. Keep Wren safe. If you do that, I won't complain anymore about the size of your poops."

Seeming to be content with the promise, Buck licked her cheek and returned to the foot of Wren's bed to curl onto his nest of rags. Leona arose and padded over to the water pitcher. She dipped a cloth then wiped away her tears and the dog spit. *That's quite enough of both. There's work to do in the morning.*

Leona managed a little sleep after that. But she was up early, dressed in her nurse's apron and ready to work. Her breasts ached already, but Leona knew that would get worse as her milk wanted to come in, and there was no suckling to help. She found the message from Hambone that Flower must have taken during the night. It was placed next to her coffee cup where Leona was sure to see it. It read: *Both safe.*

It didn't say who it was from. It didn't have to. Leona breathed a sigh of relief. A sigh of finality. A sigh of life going on.

July 25, 1922
Ivy Bolton

Ivy opened Danielle's door, and there stood Maki. It was late morning, Danielle was eating breakfast, and the baby was asleep following another feeding.

Ivy fell to pieces on the doorstep. She cried as she thought she'd never cry again in front of any man.

Maki may have been startled by her implosion, but some vestigial knowledge of the female took over. He reached his arms around her, making no quips about how she must have missed him or any other stupid thing. He merely held tight while Ivy's dam burst.

When her reservoir drained, she started several conversations at once. "You came! We're okay. No doctor sightings. You made it before I have to go. The baby eats like a piglet. The ferry is tomorrow. Danielle, this is Maki. Oh, Maki."

He waited for her to run down then said, "Leona got word to me. Of course, I came. How could I see you off if I wasn't here when the ferry leaves?"

"I thought I might never see you again. That you'd forget me. That you'd never move Outside."

He frowned at her. "Ivy, did I say I would follow you?"

She didn't answer.

"Did I tell the forest service I'm going?"

She didn't answer.

"Did I start training Edensaw?"

She gave in and squeaked, "Yes, you said all that."

"Well, then."

Danielle said, "Nice to meet you, Maki. Please close the door. Both of you come sit. Have coffee. Want some breakfast?"

"Pleasure's mine, miss. While Ivy is acting the ninnyhammer, care to tell me what's what?"

"We've been good girls, staying in with the baby. No shopping, no eating out. Only I leave to work. Nobody knows Ivy is here. Well, nobody but you." Danielle explained that she had purchased the ticket on tomorrow's ferry to Ketchikan then transfers on to Port Angeles.

"I thought so, after the message Hambone left that you had made it. I figured you'd be gone on the first ship out."

"Tell me of Leona? Is she well?" Ivy asked.

"Ivy, you know how she is. Flower says she went back to work immediately. Refuses to talk of the baby. Acts like it never happened."

"Is she taking spirits?" This was the biggest worry to Ivy. Would the loss of the child push Leona into an uncontrolled battle with her demons? Ivy was not so naïve as to believe Leona couldn't get to alcohol if she chose to. The problem wasn't controlled by logic.

"Not to my way of thinking. Seemed in control to me. She gave me this note for you in case our paths did cross."

Ivy's hand trembled when she took the note. She left the table to go to Danielle's bedroom just in case she sprouted another leak. She sat on the edge of the bed and opened the fragile envelope.

My greatest friend Ivy,

If you are reading this then Maki connected with you. My heart leaps at the thought. What a thing you are doing for me! I don't deserve you; it seems you have only seen the worst of me. It is appropriate you have now seen the last of me.

I am sure the good doctor will raise Cain with me when he arrives, just as we predicted he would. He will not find the baby, of course. I will tell him it died at birth. The women here don't even ask. They are so used to losing infants in childbirth, I am sure that is what the tribe must believe has happened. And we non-natives are so odd to them; they probably believe we have our own private ceremony of grieving where theirs is far more social.

The doctor won't likely believe the baby died, and as you and I have discussed, he will search the village. He'll surely see that I lose my position at the clinic. This job and Wren are all I have left, and he will want to hurt me before he leaves for San Francisco. If that happens, I will go to the fort in Haines for work. Or, Flower believes, I should set up practice for Hoonah but not with the clinic. Maybe in Mikhail's old cabin. She says the people would come to me. And Wren would like that.

Goodbye, my heart. Please drop me a line now and then. Let me know of you and Maki and of the treasure I have sent with you. Or, on second thought, maybe it is best if you don't.

Leona

Ivy's tears began again. She did not wish to dampen Danielle's pillow, so she cried into her own hanky held up to her nose and eyes. A few moments later she felt the bed sag as another weight was added to it.

Maki was there. "C'mon, Ivy. Both of your men need you now." Danielle came in and handed Ivy the infant to cuddle. Then Maki's arms encircled them both.

That evening, when Danielle left for work, she assigned the bed to the two of them. "I'll take the sofa when I come in. It will be late." So Maki was on hand to help Ivy with her luggage the next morning. The ferry to Ketchikan was small, not much larger than the one that had brought Ivy to Juneau all those years ago. Maki was allowed on board to see her settled in the small passenger lounge, the baby asleep in his stroller. Their goodbye was not hard. Ivy knew she would see Maki again. Besides, she figured she'd used up the next decade's worth of tears just in the past three days.

She watched him debark and walk along the pier where Captain Aleck greeted him. Maki had told her *Small Fry* was taking him back to Hoonah since a ranger boat was not in the area. Then Ivy noticed another passenger already aboard. A tall dark-haired man in a smart black coat and hat stood at the rail looking out at the town. Ivy turned away lest he see her face through the glass of the ferry window.

The man was apparently on his way to Hoonah as well. It was Dr. Edward Reardon.

July 26, 1922
Leona Herkimer

Leona held the days together by grit. A bout of summer diarrhea among the village children gave her something to focus on other than her own misery. She'd faced this illness before so the clinic responded with speed. Experts disagreed on the causes of the seasonal complaint. "We'll fight them all," she said deploying her troops.

Flower made sure the tribe was boiling water, warned mothers not to let babies crawl on the ground especially where there was animal feces, and she gave older children whippy screens on sticks to kill flies.

Wren organized the orphans into small teams going building to building. "Quit swatting each other!" the little corporal commanded. The kids who blasted the most house flies received bits of horehound. A serious outbreak of summer diarrhea was avoided due to the medical team's immediate vigilance.

It was Saturday, and Leona was alone in the government building, feeling glum. A new teacher would soon arrive to replace Ivy, she supposed. She would greet that teacher with arms as wide as Ivy had greeted her. Judith, now on summer break between school years, was rarely in the government building; instead she mostly worked up at the orphanage. But together they would hold a community luncheon for the new teacher.

Leona was sterilizing clinic equipment, getting ahead of the task. Belly cramps still plagued her, but it was only four days after the birth, so she knew it was normal. Her swollen breasts nearly burst with their unwanted load of milk. Her body and her mood were both grouchy. That's when Dr. Reardon entered the clinic. Leona's first thought was that a new form of the summer pestilence had just strolled in.

"You look well, Nurse Herkimer. I see the baby has been born."

"An astute observer you are," she returned. "Please look away from my body." If she was going to be fired, she saw no reason to temper her tongue. She was not in a mood to be compliant in order to save herself.

"You'd do well to remember that I *am* astute. And the next thing I observe is that the baby is not here. Nor a pram, nor a crib." He made a broad parody of looking around.

She was about to answer when Wren burst through the door, twirling a fly swatter. "Melody's baby is much better, and the ..." The child's feet and tongue came to a halt.

"Ah," said the doctor. "I recognize this as the urchin I saved from your attempt at surgery. You have tried my patience often, Nurse."

"Wren, go do that errand. The one we talked about."

"But I ..."

"Do it now, please."

The child scowled, but she turned to leave the way she came in. Leona could hear her outdoors yelling, "Buck! Let's go!"

"This Melody's baby that the child mentioned. Might that be yours? Seeking a place to hide in the village?"

"No, it isn't. Mine is gone. Stillborn. Your journey here to steal a child has been for naught."

He exhaled forcefully. "Oh, Leona. Stillborn? You know I will look for it. Please don't mistake me for a naïve fool."

"Naïve? Fool? No, those are not words that I would apply to you." Suddenly, Leona felt exhausted. "Dr. Reardon, Edward, why are you so insistent on separating a child from a mother? I know you have little respect for me, but what upsets you so?"

"We've discussed that. Alcohol makes you unfit. You are a danger to a babe."

"It's more than that," Leona said, stepping nearer to him and cocking her head. He stepped back, and she advanced. She would have an answer. "Something more than that. Something more about me than drinking makes you livid."

He stood his ground. Emotions distorted his handsome features. The words, when they came, burst like birdshot. "I thought you were special. I could talk with you. Then I find you leap from one man's bed to another. You trampled on my affection. You will not prosper from our alliance in any manner. Not with job, not with child."

Leona was flabbergasted, and for the first time felt in physical danger of this man. She'd no idea his affections burrowed so deep, or that his anger now dug deeper. He could destroy her. Or her child.

"I would have taken you as my wife," he hissed. "To San Francisco. To a society far above the ignoramus population in this territory. Now I am ashamed of you. But no more so than of myself for falling under your spell."

"I never lied to you. I never made promises. I don't cast spells. Your mistakes are your own."

He grabbed her wrist, and she winced. He leaned close. "I will find that baby. I will tear this village apart until I locate the little bastard. If it is not here, I will bring the law down on you. And not that ridiculous forest ranger, but a lawman from Outside if necessary."

"You are hurting me." She felt her lips pull back as she growled.

"You will lose this job and not get another as a nurse. Not anywhere."

The door snapped open. As the Reverend Harold Binder hustled in, Leona pulled free. "Dr. Reardon!" Harold scolded. "I believe you forget yourself, sir."

With the reverend was Judith and two tribesmen, each carrying a workman's tool.

"Ah, if it isn't the religious leader," spit the doctor, apparently too angry to recover his poise. "Any chance there is a new baby in that orphanage of yours?"

"Dr. Reardon." As Leona watched him, the round little reverend nearly raised to tiptoes in order to meet the doctor eye to eye. "You have cared for my village in days past. This nurse represents you, caring for us now. And we for her. If she loses employment for any reason whatsoever that I can attribute to you, the Presbyterian Church will soon hear of it. We shall see an interesting collision between Church and State, sir."

"You can't threaten me, you bible thumper. I am a doctor, and there are too few as it is."

"You will find that the shortage of men to cure illness is rivaled by the shortage of men to cure spirits." Harold's jowls wobbled with anger. And maybe a little fear. "I suggest we not test each other. You be on your way to your side of the strait. And I will stay on mine unless I find reason to seek out your betters regarding your comportment."

The doctor stared at Harold, both trembling and ashen. It was Reardon who recovered himself first. He turned to Leona. If his dark eyes could burn, she was sure she'd been issued a ticket on the ferry boat to hell.

Without another word, he withdrew and was gone.

There was a long pause and then …

"I believe it worked, Harold!" burst Leona.

"You were magnificent, my dear," raved Judith.

"Ivy told us it would work. Bless her soul," said Harold. "So glad she made me rehearse."

CHAPTER TWENTY-SEVEN

December 26, 1946
Ivy Bolton

Ivy pulled a tray of biscuits from the oven. Maki left before sunrise, and she thought she'd have time alone to take down the Christmas decorations. It was a depressing chore, storing away all the tinsel and glittery bits. Winters were so gray before color returned.

She was humming a very flat "Silent Night" when she heard the crunch of a car pulling over a thin sheet of black ice. She looked through the back door and saw Rome parking the Studebaker in front of the garage on the alley. Ivy smiled to herself. She wasn't surprised he was there. She knew he'd be eager to talk about the bundle of Wren's letters she had given him.

He brought the letters with him. "Read them last night," he said. His face revealed nothing as he poured coffee from Ivy's new Pyrex Flameware perculator, a holiday gift from Poppy.

He must feel something, Ivy thought. Who does he think he's kidding?

Ivy sat at the table and read the oldest letter in the stack while Rome buttered a biscuit for each of them.

"Put a dollop of those cherry preserves on them."

He did as instructed, even adding a second dollop. "Boy's gotta eat," he said. "Best biscuits in town."

"Are you buttering me up along with that biscuit?"

"Yes. I want information so I'm willing to pay the price."

Ivy reveled in his comfort with the kitchen these days. Rome had developed a method of almost anything for a one-armed man. Nobody could call him a cripple anymore.

Watching him refill their coffee cups, she said, "Wren was little when she wrote the first one. Nine." She lifted it off the stack. "Must have written it just after I left, but it took six months to make it all the way to me in Sequim. I hadn't really thought about being the only person she had to confide in. Then I was gone." Ivy felt a pang of guilt.

"Wren sounds older than nine," Rome said, eyebrows furrowed. "At that age I only gave a damn about hurling the fastest ball in school."

"Yes, she was old for her age. Of course, Wren had to grow up pretty fast. She'd lost both parents, and her new mother was flawed at best. Other than Buck, she was short on secret sharers."

Dear Mrs. Bolton,

This is Wren and Buck. We miss you. Do you still have that baby? Is his daddy my daddy? I am glad you took him with you. I use up all Momma's spare time. Not much need for a baby around here.

My teacher Mrs. Binder told me you went Outside. I looked and looked for you out there. Even Buck couldn't find you.

Captain Aleck said our outside isn't your Outside. Yours has a big letter O. It's a long way away. Is it like Wonderland? Buck wonders if you have seen that Cheshire cat. He says you should kill it if you do.

I know Momma is sick from alcohol. She explained and you explained and Flower explained. But I don't understand. Momma says I am to go to Mrs. Binder if she starts acting goofy. I know she loves me. So why doesn't she quit? She says she can't. But if she loved me enough, she would, wouldn't she?

She hasn't acted goofy since you left. Just sad. I hope she gets happy again. She's more fun.

Goodbye,

Wren and Buck

Tears threatened as Ivy pushed the letter back into its envelope.

"The kid had a point, you know," Rome said. "Leona did choose the sauce over Wren or Baby Me."

"Oh, Rome, don't be judgmental. We knew almost nothing about alcoholism in those days. Didn't even use the word outside medical books. We thought it was a dirty habit, like nail biting or nose picking. Most people believed you could stop if you wanted."

"Well, can't you?"

"That's still a mystery, far as I can tell. Some do, some don't. I think it's more than a matter of will power. Mostly, some people learn to manage it. Leona did. She had spells of it, but in between, she worked and lived in a normal fashion."

"I knew men who went into battle drunk."

"Maybe it was the only way they could get there."

Rome nodded and stretched his shoulders. "Okay. My mother gave me up because she worried she'd harm me. I guess that's kind of noble. It hurt her more than it did me. I shouldn't judge her. Another biscuit would help."

Ivy smiled then looked at the second letter from Wren. "Oh dear. Three years later, January '25. Female troubles have begun."

... We've been learning letter writing in school. Of course, I learned long ago so I have to sit quietly while the other kids thrash and whine about what to write. Mrs. Binder says letters carry your news, so here is mine.

We have a new toaster. Toast pops right up out of it when it is ready! How does that happen? I think that is a miracle, but Momma is more excited about a medicine called insulin. She says it is even better than hot toast.

Flower and Momma are busy with diphtheria inoculations. A bunch of mushers are taking vaccine to Nome. Momma and Flower say it is an epidemic. The paper says it'll take 150 dogs to move those sleds all those miles. Buck is plenty glad to be warm near the stove.

Do you remember Flower? She has a boyfriend. His name is Edensaw. He is a forest ranger.

I thought I was sick when I started to bleed from my you-know. Momma had told me about the monthly, but it was still a surprise the first time. I hate it. She says it is natural, although people don't talk about it much. If it's natural, why don't people talk about it especially when it pesters you once a month? Momma calls it hormones. Do boys have hormones, too? If they did some bloodletting once a month, it might clear their heads.

Momma says hormones are why I am moody, but I think she's the moody one. Cook died of a heart attack last month, and Momma couldn't save her, and that made her have a drinking fit again. She went to the cabin but made me stay here with Mrs. Binder and Mrs. Ferrell. You probably don't know Mrs. Ferrell. She came to teach after you left. I once heard Momma call her a bellyacher. Maybe that's why she's such a sourpuss if her tummy hurts all the time. I'm not supposed to say this because it is mean, but I don't like her. If you write to my mother, please don't tell her I said so.

I don't think Cook would have liked the new toaster, but I miss her. Not as much as Momma does. I mean, it doesn't make me want hooch. Momma's okay again, I guess, but I know she is sad. I never heard Cook say very much, but she knew how to make Momma happier. I wish I did. Do you know?

Also, Mrs. Bolton, if you write to her, could you tell her I AM TOO grown up enough for lipstick. And I would like my hair cropped. I am tired of braids, and I saw a magazine where nobody had them. I wonder if Flower could learn to make those spit curls. Are they really spit, do you suppose? Buck could make a lot of them with all his drool. Anyway, if you could tell Momma, I would be very grateful.

Rome laughed. "Did you come to her rescue?"

"I don't know. Maybe nobody really came to her rescue. I wrote to Leona, but she didn't write back. Not then anyway."

"Do you remember Wren very well? Do I look like her?"

Ivy shook her head. "She was a sweet-faced child, as I remember her. Better nutrition than some of the kids in the tribe so she looked healthy. Eyes black as ebony that bored holes into you when she stared at you. Of course, she's three-quarters Tlingit so she was not a tall child, probably isn't a tall adult. If she got anything from the Russian in Mikhail, it was fuller lips and hair with a tiny bit of curl. Fortunately, she did not inherit Mikhail's nose."

Rome rolled his eyes. "You and Maki have a mean streak about my nose."

"He might. I love your nose. I have a suggestion. While we talk, you could take down those decorations, and put them in these boxes. Careful the tinsel doesn't tangle."

"Gosh, Ivy, I was enjoying my coffee."

"Okay. I'll make you another pot while you work."

Rome went into the dining room to pull thumbtacks from the overhead garland. "Something I wonder about, Ivy." He raised his voice so she could hear from the kitchen. "Wren doesn't mention the doctor in her letters, not until that news clipping. Why not? Do you suppose he was gone for good?"

"Don't know, but I always figured she didn't understand very much about that. She knew he was a wrong 'un because Leona sent her to get Reverend Binder when the doctor arrived. Wren would certainly remember that. But Maki never heard anything more about him in the months before he headed here."

"The doc couldn't have Leona, and he didn't want me even if I'd been there. It doesn't seem he had much to gain by hanging around."

Ivy came into the dining room with the letters and a tray of coffee with fixings. She started putting ornaments into their boxes as Rome handed them down from the archway. In time, he moved on to the tree. "It's what I've always thought," she said. "I figured he went to San Francisco, joined society, got an acceptable wife, and forgot about Alaska."

"It appears to me nobody ever forgets Alaska."

Ivy smiled. "Well, you know what I mean. But you're right, it's a hard place to forget. Love it or hate it. Either way, you remember it."

While Rome took the first loaded box to the garage, tucked under his one arm, Ivy picked the next letter from the stack. It was from Wren but included a rare note from Leona.

Dear Mrs. Bolton:

I'm in such a pickle. I don't remember you very clearly, but I do remember you are a problem solver. I'm fifteen, and I want to marry a wonderful boy. Momma wants me to go to school Outside. I know she values education above almost anything else. But I feel there is time for that. Dmitri is here and now and such a wonderful boy I am afraid I will lose him if I leave.

Do you remember him? He and I were both kids when you left, but he was in Mrs. Binder's class along with me. We sometimes shared a bench seat. He has grown up handsome and kind. He has a good job at the cannery. He does not yell at his siblings so I don't think he will at me. Oh, Mrs. Bolton, I love him so!

What should I do? Disappoint Momma? She might suffer her sickness for good if I disobey and stay here. But I'm afraid she will suffer it even more if I go. Or maybe that's just the excuse I use to stay here. Mrs. Bolton, what do you think?

With gratitude, Wren

On a second sheet of paper, Ivy found the few words from Leona. They were the first she'd received from the nurse.

Darling Ivy,

Wren has asked you to be Solomon. You always were the wisest of us all. I have not seen you in six years, and yet I remember you with a clarity I rarely have for anything anymore.

Thank you for your notes to me when you have written to Wren. I have left the clinic per se; I am living and working in Mikhail's old cabin. Wren's beloved Dmitri runs a couple of Mikhail's old traplines for me, and we split the income from the fur. I suppose I am responsible for the closeness that exists now between the two of them.

Ivy, do you see my boy? He'll be six this summer. Tell me very little, just if he seems well. I don't want to add more weight to my heart by getting to know him.

I left the clinic due to bad memories … the good one steamed away six years ago. I never liked the teacher who replaced you, and Cook died, and I tired of all the government paper and balderdash. I am now Hoonah's medicine woman. The nurse who is at the clinic gladly supplies me, as I take in the patients who don't trust other Caucasians for anything. After that last war and the one that seems to be brewing, I guess I agree with them that caution is a wise course.

Yes, I drink. The tribe gets it to me somehow; I don't question. It is seldom, but it happens. The people I love are all best off without me. My boy, you … and now, please convince Wren she must go, too.

Your devoted Leona

Ivy folded the letter into its fragile envelope. While Rome hummed another Christmas carol she was thoroughly sick of, Ivy said, "You read Leona's note when you went through these, of course."

"Yes, of course."

"Then do you still doubt her love for you?"

December 26, 1946
Rome Coleridge

The Christmas tree was denuded of baubles and lights. Rome used a towel to soak the last of the water from its stand, then gently tipped it to its side. The stand's metal screws were tight for a one-armed man to gain purchase, so he straddled the trunk to hold it still as he worked the screws loose. Finally, he picked up the tree and carried it out of the house.

Rome chopped the tree for firewood, plucking the last few escapee icicles from it as he went. He went to the garage for turpentine to remove the tree sap from his hand before going back to the kitchen.

"I assume you heard my question and didn't merely ignore it," Ivy said when he returned.

"I heard it. I'm thinking about it." They left the mess of boxes and needles to take seats near the fire. "First off, Ivy, the whole story feels like a fiction book to me. Accepting a new family is one thing. Accepting that your old one was never really yours, well, that is something else. I thought my sisters were my sisters, but they are my cousins. A total stranger is my half-sister. I was going to ask Vienna and Geneva about it. But now I think they might be happier not knowing their only living brother is not their brother. I think Genny especially might be distressed. She already feels the death of our, I mean her, parents as leaving her with very little family."

Ivy said, "I hadn't thought of it that way, Rome. I've only been seeing it from Leona's point of view. Selfish of me."

"Well, yes. Your love of Leona might be blinding you a little." He knew it was dangerous to criticize Ivy. She had none of the restraints shared by other old ladies of his acquaintance.

"I see how Wren's presence could be an issue for Vienna and Genny. I've been if not blind, insensitive. Thank you for pointing it out. I will correct such behavior in the new year."

He laughed. "Please. Never resolve to be anything but what you are, Ivy." Sobering, he continued. "I feel no loss over Cecil. Even dead, Mikhail has been a better father. You know, after I got stronger in the war, I wanted to come home to beat the crap out of Cecil for the things he did. But then Cecil died in a fire while I was gone. And I lost an arm. Right up till the end, he could have still beaten up on me. Life is a helluva jokester."

Ivy picked up her knitting, continuing to create another something. Rome gave a brief thought to how she had wrapped them all with warmth. Watching her swift hands at work, he said, "To answer your question, no, I don't doubt Leona's love for me. What I doubt is my love for her. Nancy was good to me … tried to keep Cecil away … did her best. In the ways that matter, she was my mother and a good one. I may never see Leona as anything but an aunt with a story. Do you understand?"

"I do. But Wren –

"– but Wren *is* my sister. Her letters introduced me to a willful, braided little tomboy, one easy to love."

"You realize she is now in her thirties, right?"

"Yes, I realize the braids and Buck are long gone, but I want to know her. Yet she cannot replace Vi and Genny. Maybe augment them? Maybe they could all meet some day."

He picked up the next letter on the top of the pile. The postmark was 1934.

Dear Mrs. Bolton,

You were right those five years ago! I could have both a husband and a calling. We all merely compromised a little. Dmitri and I waited to marry for two years, when I was seventeen. In the meantime, Momma "apprenticed" me to Flower to learn the hands-on nursing needed by the tribe.

I assume you remember Flower. She was so sweet to me when I was a child, almost like an older sister. But as a teacher, let me tell you she was a hellion. She stayed at the clinic when Momma left, to help the incoming nurse. Flower's love Edensaw died in the war. So many Tlingit men went off with their white brothers to the other side of the Pacific.

Flower moved to the cabin after that. Momma and Flower have never parted. They live there still, taking care of half the tribe and each other. Flower sees Momma through her binges, and now Momma sees Flower through bouts with emphysema.

When we married, Dmitri and I moved to Juneau. I took a year nursing course offered by St. Ann's Hospital. Halfway through the year, it was obvious I knew more about local medicine than any of the other girls. I became a teaching assistant to the nurses and received my nursing certificate in less than the full year. Dmitri was not happy in the big city, preferring Momma's traplines and his fishing boat. We were trying to decide what to do, when the nurse at the Hoonah clinic quit to go back Outside. They offered the job to a local girl this time, thinking she might stay… me! Native blood and all!

I am now running the clinic that Momma ran so many years ago. When she, Flower, and I get together, we talk medicine. And you, Mrs. Bolton. We often tell tales of you. Do you remember your lavender travel suit? That shopping trip to Juneau is one of my best memories. Sad days for you and Momma I realize now, but for me? A puppy, a dress, and Danielle. What gifts!

I have enclosed the following clipping from a July edition of Juneau's Daily Alaska Empire. Momma said it might interest you although I am not sure why.

JUNEAU DOCTOR MURDERED
IN BLOODY THURSDAY BATTLE

More blood is claimed by the stevedore strike. The long clash between the San Francisco Industrial Association and the unions blew out of control on July 5. Fists, bricks, and tear gas bombs flew amidst the rioters near the docks. Medical personnel from Harbor Emergency Hospital deployed to help the wounded in the street. One physician, Dr. Edward Reardon, was killed when flying glass from an exploded window lacerated his neck. The doctor was a onetime physician here in Juneau at the St. Ann's Hospital. He leaves a wife and two children …

"I suppose it was gratifying to Leona to learn she outlived the old bastard," Rome commented with a snort.

"It was gratifying to me. But I doubt Leona ever hoped for anybody's death," Ivy said. "It's no exaggeration to say she and Flower have saved thousands of lives, many of which might not have been worth the effort."

The letter at the bottom of the stack was the one Ivy received from Wren most recently. It is the reason that the whole story had slowly been revealed to Rome.

... So much time has passed since I last wrote to you. Time and events both. A short update on me: I am now a thirty-three-year-old nurse. If any girlishness is left in me, it is due to our ten-year-old twins that keep Dmitri and me from becoming too terribly stodgy. As they age, they want to know more about their family, and I suppose that is why I have become determined to meet my brother.

Momma doesn't talk about him, but when her sister died, the one who raised him, she told me if I wanted to contact him, I could try it through you. She doesn't know anything about him. She says you have her approval to reveal to me anything you know.

I remember the day he was born, well at least I think I do. Mostly, I was just glad he disappeared. Leona had only just become my Momma. And I wanted to be the only apple of her eye. I was afraid the day would come when she turned her back on me. That baby would have been competition I didn't need, I guess. I have a vague recollection about writing this to you a couple of decades ago!

That feeling has changed. I began to think about the baby when I came to understand he is my only living blood relative other than my own children. Curiosity has grown in me. I want to think of him as someone other than "the baby." I hope to like him better now than I did when he was a baby!

It was all too complex for me back then. I get it, now that I have children. Anyway, I decided to name him. I thought his name could be Mikhail, but I didn't want it to be the same as our father. Maybe I could call him Aleck because Momma and I both loved that old seaman until the day he died (his Small Fry sank somewhere around Admiralty Island. Flotsam washed up, but no Captain Aleck. He'd once told me if you live on the sea long enough, you'll die on it, a prophesy fulfilled).

I decided I didn't want to name my brother after a dead man, even one I dearly loved; it didn't seem so much an honor as a needless sadness. So I chose Outsider. It fit a boy who had gone away forever.

The more I've thought of Outsider in recent years, the more I realize I would like to meet him. And this appears to be a good time for it, Mrs. Bolton. Momma is showing signs of ill health, and I fear early stages of liver failure. If Outsider has any wish to meet his mother, I think he should consider a trip to the north country. If that is not to be, then I believe it is time for me to work my way down to him.

Would you share my address with him, Mrs. Bolton? Let him know I am trying to extend a hand. I can only hope he will clasp it.

With deepest regards,

Wren

Ivy replaced the letter in the stack. "I wrote her about you, told her your name, but didn't send your address. That's up to you." She cocked her head and frowned. "I don't favor Outsider much."

Rome snorted. "No. Rome was bad enough to grow up with. Outsider would have led to fights every recess."

"Now that we've been through this whole stack, what will you do about Wren? Will you write to her?"

"I already have. Last night."

"You mean we went through all of this, and you'd already made up your mind?"

"Ivy, on this one issue, I needed to decide my future without your valuable help."

There was a pause as Ivy removed her glasses and wiped them on her sweater. She replaced them and said, "All right this once. But don't let it happen again."

CHAPTER TWENTY-EIGHT

May 4, 1947
Ivy Bolton

Ivy came into the lounge from the deck. She liked to stand near the railing, watching for orcas and whales. But the morning wind in the channel was blustery, and the drizzle was creating an icy sheen underfoot. Her lavender traveling suit still fit beautifully although it was a quarter-century old. Now beads of water flew from it as she shook.

Ah, Alaska, she thought. *You're a welcome sight even in such a foul mood.* She took a seat next to Maki and across from Rome, removed her scarf, and shook out the moisture. "We should be there within the hour. I simply can't sit still."

"Your cheeks are red as cherries," Maki said.

"This is my third trip between the Outside and Alaska. The ferries have improved, but the weather hasn't."

Maki cupped her frigid cheek. "You're prepared for this Cold War I've been reading about. What a thing. Cold War." He nodded at the newspaper on his lap.

Rome looked up from his copy of *For Whom the Bell Tolls.* "Yep. Apparently, my American blood and Russian blood will soon have to choose sides."

They were packed and ready to disembark in Juneau. As their stay was not to be a long one, they did not have trunks in storage. Their luggage was stacked beside them. "Gratefully, I am not pushing a stroller this time," Ivy said surveying the pile then smiling at Rome.

An hour passed, and the weather cleared as they turned away from Admiralty Island, into the Gastineau Channel toward Juneau. A gift of sunrays brushed over the channel, stunning them with how achingly beautiful it was. They were cruising in an icy blue green bowl.

Ivy recalled a trip long ago when little Wren needed to skip around *Small Fry* in excitement. Ivy felt about the same now. Unable to stay put, she bounced up. I'm going back out."

Rome stood. "I'll come with you."

As they walked toward the door, Ivy said, "You're as excited as I am, aren't you, Rome?"

He nodded. "Yes. So much to take in. The place itself, my family. Will Wren like me? Will I take to her?"

"You will love this half-sister of yours, Rome. Wren is obviously a spirited woman with a will of her own. Just imagine the skill it would take a native girl to run the clinic all these years. She is the best of us, I think. She's what Leona wanted to be. A fine nurse who has overcome the livetraps of her youth."

"I wonder if my mother will be on the dock with her."

Ivy stiffened. "No, Rome, she won't. You'll meet her in Hoonah."

Rome turned to her and stared. "You've heard from her, haven't you?"

"Yes. I have heard from Leona. She is too thoughtful of your feelings to meet you at the Juneau dock. She wants that encounter to be about you and Wren. She chooses not to be there. Not merely due to her ill heath, but to your history with her. In other words, Rome, she's giving you the option to avoid meeting her at all." Ivy looked away from the channel carrying them to the city and up into Rome's eyes. "Leona is flawed, yes. But nobody ever questioned her backbone when it comes to impossible decisions."

"You're sure it isn't that she doesn't want to meet me?"

"I am positive that isn't true, and if you say such a stupid thing ever again, I will call you Outsider from now on. Knowing you were growing up well and strong? That is the reason she never gave in to the deepest pit of alcoholism, always did her damnedest to be worthy of her child should his path ever cross hers."

"Then I would be a worthless dolt to refuse to go to her. Refusing her never crossed my mind."

May 4, 1947
Wren Elim

The dock was full of greeters although only a dozen or so passengers came down the gangway. Ivy, Rome, and Maki were mid-stream, each carrying luggage. Wren squinted to see them as soon as they touched ground.

"There," said Danielle who was standing next to her. She pointed. "Oh, my! Ivy is gorgeous as ever!"

Maki appeared to see them first, recognizing Danielle. His craggy old face burst into a smile. "There they are," he yelled loud enough for Wren to hear him.

But her attention was elsewhere. She was staring at the young man in a wide-shouldered trench coat. One sleeve was folded and pinned so the lack of an arm was obvious; he carried two bags in his other hand. Wren could see he was tall, but his hat covered the color of his hair. Then, with a quick intake of breath, she noticed his nose. It was her father's nose. Above her father's smile. Wren would have known Rome anywhere.

As Danielle grabbed Ivy in a bear hug, Wren approached Rome. He beamed at her, and she saw her smile replicated on his face.

"Wren," he said.

"Rome," she answered.

"Now isn't that a ridiculous pair of names," he said.

"Parents really can't be trusted," she answered. Then Wren reached up and hugged him like her life depended on it.

In time, she noticed the luggage was disappearing with a porter and the driver of Danielle's car. "Come along, children," Danielle called. "The Tongass Tearoom is serving us lunch. Yes, Ivy, it is still there. A hangout of Leona's and mine. It's two hours until your boat leaves for Hoonah so we have time to chat."

The car was a 1945 Chrysler Town & Country, capacious enough for them all, along with their bags. Maki whistled at the gleaming machine and said, "Well then, Danielle. Business must be good."

Ivy hissed, but Danielle laughed. "My dancing shoes are in permanent retirement, Maki. But I own the joint. The gents now dance to my tune."

Wren, next to Rome, said, "Welcome to Juneau. Polite society is not yet a concept here."

"Are there roads into Juneau yet?" Ivy asked.

"No. But one can't be seen walking, you know," Danielle answered with a husky laugh.

During lunch, chatter between the six made it hard for everyone to hear everything. Wren and Rome exchanged stories about his siblings and her children.

Danielle told Ivy that Harold and Judith Binder had retired years ago, returning to the Outside with four Tlingit children they adopted. Wren assured Ivy she would like all three of the teachers they had now, as well as the new school. She told Maki and Rome that Dmitri was excited to take them fishing and that the current forest ranger was eager to meet Maki to hear about the old days. The missing presence in the room was Leona. Wren decided that nobody dared share stories of her in front of Rome, not until she was there to share them herself.

Soon enough, Danielle delivered them back to the dock. It was a nice cabin cruiser, bigger than *Small Fry*, with enough seating capacity for all four, and no one had to squeeze between barrels and boxes of cargo. A flotilla of gulls saw them off, the proceedings observed by eagles on boat riggings around the harbor.

Wren beamed at Ivy and Maki. "You'll find Hoonah looks much the same as it always has." The old couple went silent as the journey progressed. Wren was aware they were far away, in a time all their own.

Maki reached for Ivy's hand. "So much beauty all around," he said, squinting a long stare.

"I feel years slipping away," she answered as they turned into Icy Strait. The little village was soon visible at the base of soaring hills.

Watching Ivy and Maki, Wren whispered to Rome, "They say you never really leave Alaska. I guess it might be true."

Rome replied, "I can understand that. It is stunning here. You'd lose a lot by leaving. But I'll be showing you Outside in the future. At least that's my hope."

"The twins are already clamoring for that. Dmitri might take a bit more convincing."

"Wren," Rome lowered his voice. "Something I've been wrestling with. What do I call her when I meet her? Leona? Mother? I'm suddenly feeling very nervous of facing my past."

Wren smiled at him. "She's been nervous about meeting you for years and years. For her, this is not facing the past. For her, you are coming home. I don't know what you'll call her. But I know she'll call you son."

THE END

AUTHOR'S NOTES

My warmest regards to you who read ***Starting Over Far Away.*** I hope the story pleased you; it certainly pleased me to write it.

People who write historical fiction tend to be odd ducks. We follow facts and arcane nuggets deeper into rabbit holes than most well-adjusted people could care to share. Consequently, I'm pretty sure of my facts. But there is one I feel a need to clarify because it may be worrying you: in 1921, the problems potentially caused for a fetus by a mother's drinking were unknown. Fetal Alcohol Syndrome was not a diagnostic term broadly used until fifty years later. Even though she is a nurse, this is not knowledge that Leona would have had.

If you are a writer yourself, you likely know how important a critique group can be. It is a time-consuming job for group members who do it well; it can be very difficult to suggest tactfully to an overwrought writer that she could do a piece better; it is a sure way to feel like crap yourself when you know a group member is struggling, but you must stay honest anyway. If you find partners who can do all this well, you have a treasure. My treasures for this book are writers Heidi Hansen, Melee McGuire, Jill Sikes, and Jon Eekhoff.

Most authors ask beta readers to read the manuscript before publication. Donna Plumley Brubach, Dr. Joan Enoch, and Jill Sikes all did me proud … and Jill is a particular marvel at digging out typos that spring up like mushrooms in the dark when your back is turned. I was extraordinarily lucky to have Lauralee DeLuca as a beta reader. She lived in Alaska for over three decades and spent a fair amount of that time as a trapper. Since I haven't battled a bear or skinned anything larger than a peach, Lauralee was able to educate me when I made Outsider mistakes.

My sister and I took our first journey to Alaska before it was a state. We have traveled back to the Panhandle many times since. I owe her big time for shared memories that have appeared one way or another in the pages of this book.

Heidi Hansen is my co-founder in an endeavor we call Olympic Peninsula Authors. In working to promote the writers who live in this beautiful patch of the world, we promote each other. She is a joy.

Lastly, I don't think it is possible to write about Alaska without being overwhelmed by the land itself. It is a place where imaginations can soar. Its majesty is breathtaking. And, of course, the problems it faces are legendary. We must take special care so it will always be there.

ABOUT THE AUTHOR

Linda B. Myers won her first creative contest in the sixth grade. After a Chicago marketing career, she traded in snow boots for rain boots and moved to the Pacific Northwest with her Maltese, Dotty. She now lives in Port Angeles, WA, a town that figures heavily into *Starting Over Far Away.*

CHECK OUT LINDA'S OTHER NOVELS

PI Bear Jacobs Books:

Fun House Chronicles (prequel)
Bear in Mind
Hard to Bear
Bear Claus: A Novella
Bear at Sea
Three Bears: Short Mysteries from PI Bear Jacobs

Stand Alone Mysteries:

Creation of Madness
Secrets of the Big Island
The Slightly Altered History of Cascadia

Pacific Northwest Historical Fiction:

Fog Coast Runaway
Dr. Emma's Improbable Happenings

Please leave a review of ***Starting Over Far Away*** or Linda's other books on www.amazon.com

Follow **Author Linda B. Myers** on Facebook or email her at myerslindab@gmail.com

Made in USA - Crawfordsville, IN
66082_9781735247717
08.11.2022 1003